UNBROKEN

RILEY EDWARDS

Unbroken

RILEY EDWARDS

Written by: Riley Edwards

Published by: Rebels Romance

Editor: Jay C. Layne Monograph Editing

Proofreader: Janice Owen

Unbroken

ISBN-13: 978-1-7339667-4-0

Second edition – April 2019

This book is dedicated to our first responders. Those brave men and women who put their lives on the line each and every day. And to the families who stand behind these heroes and support them. Thank you! We are forever in your debt.

"There is a sacredness in tears. They are not the mark of weakness, but of power. They speak more eloquently than ten thousand tongues. They are the messengers of overwhelming grief, of deep contrition, and of unspeakable love."
~Washington Irving

End of Watch

I had news!

Big news that I couldn't wait to share. I checked my watch for what felt like the hundredth time in the last hour. I was like a kid on Christmas morning, giddy with excitement. I'd been on pins and needles keeping this secret for the last three weeks. But with Jacob's birthday so close to me finding out we were pregnant, I thought I would give him a birthday surprise he'd never forget. He was going to be over the moon with excitement, and JJ would be thrilled to have a new baby brother or sister.

Today was the day!

"JJ, come here, it's time to put the frosting on Daddy's cake," I yelled for my son. I heard the toy he was playing with hit the floor and his little feet scampering down the stairs. "Slow down, little man. A trip to the ER is not on tonight's agenda."

Jacob Junior came sliding into the kitchen with a smile so full of five-year-old enthusiasm I couldn't help but pick him up and pepper his cute little face full of kisses.

Today was the best day.

"You ready to decorate Daddy's cake? We have..." I checked my watch again. "...thirty minutes until Daddy gets home. Do you think we can fit all thirty-two candles on his cake?"

JJ's nose scrunched up in concentration as he tried to puzzle out where thirty-two candles were going to go.

"We can make them fit, Mama. But we have to put on an extra one for the good luck."

"Silly Mommy, I forgot the good luck."

"Mama, can I put on the chocolate this time? I never get to use the spreader. Please? I'll be extra careful with the spreader," JJ pleaded.

"Sure, baby," I said, handing him the spatula.

With a kiss to JJ's forehead, I left him with the chocolate frosting and a cake to decorate. This was sure to be a mess of epic proportions.

I watched as my son made a mess of his father's birthday cake. When he finished, there were globs of frosting on the top, and the sides were completely bare. It was perfect.

Today was the best day ever.

"Mama, this is gonna be Daddy's favorite birthday cake ever. Is it time to put on the candles?" JJ beamed with pride as he licked the extra icing off the spatula.

"I think you're right. It's perfect. He'll love it." Pushing aside my need to smooth out the globs of icing, I grabbed the candles and handed them to JJ. "Here you go. Want to count them out?"

Before he had a chance to answer, the doorbell rang.

"Hold on, baby. Let me see who's at the door. Don't touch the cake until I get back."

I hurried to answer the door. I knew I only had minutes before JJ decided to add the candles himself.

"Who is it?" I called out from behind the closed door.

"Ava, it's Mac," Jacob's best friend from the station answered back.

I quickly unbolted the door and threw it open. "Mac! What a great surprise..." My words died in my throat.

The Chaplain.

I blinked my eyes rapidly and prayed to God they

were playing tricks on me. It was at this very moment my world tilted, shattered into a million pieces; jagged and sharp pieces that would forever cut me.

I squeezed my eyes shut, praying when I opened them *he* would be gone, but when my eyes slowly focused on the men on my front porch, the Chaplain was still standing there.

"No! No, Mac, you can't be here!" I whispered. "Please, Mac."

I tried to slam the door, but Mac's hand quickly shot out and caught the heavy piece of wood before it fully shut.

I knew. I knew what this was. There was only one reason a Chaplain came to a police officer's home in his dress uniform.

"Mrs. Kelley, please, may we come in?" the Chaplain asked.

"No!" I shook my head.

The tears swimming in my eyes made it impossible to see the two men as they walked into my house uninvited. They had to leave. They couldn't be here. This was my worst nightmare. This exact scenario had plagued my dreams when Jacob first joined the academy.

A hand was on my shoulder, and I fought the urge to scream, not to touch me. "Ava. Sweetheart. Let's sit down," Mac suggested.

"No! Please God, NO! Mac, you can't be here. Where's Jacob?"

"Ava, you have to sit down. Where's JJ?" Mac's voice was more demanding this time.

I shrugged his hand off, my ears were roaring, my head pounding, and my gut was in knots. This wasn't real. This wasn't happening! This could not happen. Jacob promised! He promised me he would always come home. That's what he said, 'Ava baby, you know I am always safe. I will never leave you and little Jacob.'

"Where's my husband?" I screamed, ignoring his suggestion to sit.

In hindsight, I should've sat down. I should have listened. Instead, I continued to stand. Screaming and stomping my foot, demanding answers I knew I didn't want to hear. Demanding he confirm my worst fears.

"There's been a shooting. I am so sorry Ava, but Jacob didn't…"

I heard nothing after that. My husband lied to me. He was a Goddamned liar. He wasn't coming home.

He left us.

My body was cold, and I was numb. I continued to stand even after I felt my knees shake and my body sway. I realized my mistake too late. I should've listened. I was falling, and there was no time. No time to protect my belly before I hit the corner of the coffee table on my way down.

"MAMA!" I heard JJ scream before my world went black.

Today was the worst day of my life.

FIVE DAYS LATER.

Miles and miles of flashing red and blue lights lined the streets. Officers and citizens stood shoulder to shoulder on the sidewalk as the funeral procession crept by. JJ sat next to me in his new suit, gripping my hand with a strength I didn't know a five-year-old could possess. His little face was pressed against the window of the limousine, watching all the people on the street.

I couldn't do this. I couldn't be strong for my son when I was so broken. I tried not to cry in front of him, to be the strong mother that Jacob would want me to be. But I couldn't. I couldn't hide my tears; they were never-ending.

I was hollow. My heart was shattered. I was literally empty, the baby I had been carrying ruthlessly stolen from me as well. A child I would never get to hold, never get to watch grow. He or she would never know my love. In an instant that was taken from me too.

Fire trucks, police cars, ambulances, and EMT vehicles had taken over the cemetery. I had barely made it through the church service. How was I going to watch my husband being lowered into the ground? JJ sat next to me, stoic yet blissfully unaware. Five. He was five-years-old and could not begin to fathom what forever meant. He would forever be without his father. He would forever have a mother who was half the woman she once was.

We were forever changed.

The limousine came to a stop at the graveside. The large mound of dirt next to my husband's gravesite was covered with fake green carpet. Why did they do that, hide the dirt; was I supposed to pretend that my husband would not be lying at the bottom of a hole with all that dirt on top of him?

Jacob's casket was already out of the hearse. Six pallbearers held the flag covered casket. All in full dress uniform, all staring straight ahead. Emotionless.

Mac made his way over to us. I had refused to allow him to ride to the cemetery in the limo with us. It was just JJ and I now. I had to learn to be on my own. I didn't have Jacob anymore.

I couldn't stop the tears when Mac knelt down in front of my son with a black leather badge holder in his hand. I knew what it was. I had seen it on the nightstand almost every night.

Wordlessly, he placed the chain over JJ's head. The badge fell over JJ's heart, and Mac put his hand over it.

"Always, JJ. Your daddy will always be right here, inside of you."

"Thank you, Uncle Mac." JJ wrapped his little hand around his father's badge and stood tall and proud. My brave boy.

Mac stood and wiped the tears from his face.

There were hundreds of people gathered around the gravesite. Some in uniforms, some were dressed in black. Some were softly talking. Others were crying. I wondered who all these people were. I didn't know but a handful of them.

"It's time, Ava," Mac whispered.

Afraid of my own voice, I nodded my head in acknowledgment.

This was it.

With my first step, the bagpipes started, and I closed my eyes, taking in the first chords of Amazing Grace. Every officer was standing at attention, saluting as we passed. I knew my husband's casket would be right behind us as we walked to the graveside. His fellow officers carrying him to his final resting place. My strong, brave husband was being carried. I was completely numb.

I cannot remember how I got to my seat, who spoke when, or what was said. It was all a blur. Through it all, JJ sat quietly between Mac and I, staring at the casket. JJ and I both jumped when the buglers started playing, breaking the silence as Jacob's flag was being folded.

I didn't want to be here. I didn't want to hear the kind words spoken about my husband, about his service and bravery. I didn't want any of these people to know these things about him. Not because he wasn't every bit of what they said, and more. Not because he didn't deserve to be honored. I just didn't want to *have* to honor him.

I wanted to be curled up in bed next to him. Breathing in his scent. I wanted to feel his strong arms around me and his lips on my neck. I didn't want to hear the bagpipes, I wanted to hear his laugh. What I wouldn't have given to have him call me, 'Ava baby,' one more time. He promised me I would never be here. He had sworn I would never have the folded flag.

"Mrs. Kelley?" An officer knelt in front of my chair.

I opened my mouth and tried to answer, but no words came out.

The officer took pity on me and continued. He leaned in, speaking only to JJ and me. "On behalf of the City of San Francisco, the State of California, and all of its citizens, I would like to thank you for your husband's exemplary service. It is with the greatest respect and deepest condolences that I present this flag to you. May God be with you and keep you." The officer turned to JJ. "Your father was a brave man, Jacob Junior. He is a hero and loved by all. Always remember, son, greater love hath no man than this, that he lay down his life for his friends."

"Thank you, sir," JJ managed to say through his tears.

The officer nodded at Mac and they both stood.

Mac pulled his radio out of his jacket pocket.

"Foxtrot 257 to dispatch," Mac spoke into his radio.

"Dispatch to 257, go," a voice crackled through the radios of every officer in attendance.

"Stand by for a special announcement, emergency traffic only." Mac waited and cleared his throat.

"Dispatch to 305, come in," Mac spoke loud and clear.

The call echoed through the crowd.

I silently prayed for the miracle of all miracles. That my husband would answer.

"Dispatch to Officer 305," Mac called out again.

The call remained unanswered.

JJ held onto his father's badge and crawled into my lap, the flag nestled between us. I snuggled my boy as close as I could. I wanted to absorb all of his pain, take this all away so he would never have to feel an ounce of this tragedy. I sobbed at the injustice of it all. In a matter of seconds, I had lost my husband and my unborn baby. Our lives forever changed.

"I love you, Mama," JJ whispered.

"To the moon and back, baby," I replied.

"Officer 305, Jacob Mitchell Kelley, we thank you for your dedication, loyalty, and service to the citizens of San Francisco and to the State of California. You've made the people you served proud. You have inspired many, including your fellow officers, with your compassion and unwavering dedication to law enforcement. The people you served with will always remember you." Mac's voice cracked as he spoke, he no longer tried to hide his tears as he finished. "Your sacrifice will never be forgotten. Godspeed, my friend. Officer 305, 10-7 forever. Officer Jacob Mitchell Kelley, End of Watch."

Mac's final words boomed through the crowd.

End of Watch.

1
———

THE WHISTLER

Ava

"Ava, the weird guy wants pie again," Laura called out as she frantically rushed into the kitchen, her arms stacked full of dirty plates.

The breakfast rush was still in full swing. We had at least another hour before we hit a lull and my caffeine high was slowly waning. I needed coffee stat if I was going to get through the morning without killing a customer. Or a waitress. The loud clatter of dishes being dropped into the dishwashing station made me cringe.

"The whistler?" I asked, ignoring my need to remind her that I had to buy new plates every time she chipped one.

"The one and only," Laura laughed, picking up a

new order off the cook's line. "You know, he's kinda hot. All mysterious with his fedora pulled down low and all those tats. Bad boy hot!"

"He's weird, Laura! Who eats pie at nine AM? And he never talks, just sits in the corner and whistles. You know, I don't even mind the whistling, but could he possibly pick a new tune? I am now having recurring dreams about *Ring Around the Rosy*." I handed Laura a plate of hash browns and stared at her in wonderment. It truly was amazing that she could balance five breakfast plates on one arm, but couldn't balance a tray full of glasses worth a shit. "And besides, last week, after that Dateline special, you told me you thought Erik Menendez was hot. The man killed his parents. You can't think someone is hot after they kill their parents."

"Oh, come on, that man was fine as hell when he was a teenager. Not so much now, prison did not agree with him." Laura added the hash brown plate to her stack and went for the door to the dining room. "The pie? Do we have any this morning?"

"Pumpkin?" I asked, already knowing the answer.

The whistler always ordered pumpkin. The man needed some variety in his life. Maybe I should introduce him to blueberry cobbler.

"You guessed it. And Reid and Mac are both out

there at the counter." Laura winked and rushed out with her order. I suspected she had a secret crush on Mac. Anytime he was around she doubled up on her sass.

"We have pumpkin," I yelled, hoping she heard me.

I really didn't have time for a stop and chat with Mac and Reid at the moment. Del Mar's was slammed, and I had to get the rest of my walk-in inventoried if I wanted to get out of here on time to pick up JJ. Thursdays were his spelling tests. If he got a B or above, we stopped at our favorite ice cream shop for a cone. I never missed a Thursday, but if I didn't get this food order in, the café would be out of just about everything.

I found both men sitting at their normal spots at the end of the counter. I don't know how it was possible that they always got the same two seats every morning they came in. I often wondered...if customers were sitting in those chairs when they walked in, did they tell them to move? That wouldn't surprise me at all.

"Good morning, gentlemen. Running a little late I see," I taunted Mac. He was a stickler for being punctual.

"No, smartass. We were going over a case," Mac told me.

"Ohhh..." I leaned over the counter towards the men so no other customers could hear me. "Anything good? What diabolical scheme is the dynamic duo, Batman and Robin, saving San Francisco from today?" I teased.

"A missing persons case was ruled a suicide by the coroner," Reid spoke up.

"Oh, nothing to joke about then. Sorry. Would either of you like more coffee?" I asked, feeling like a shit-heel for joking.

"Please," they said in unison.

"Jinx!" I threw over my shoulder at them on my way to the coffee station.

Jinx? What was I, twelve? The joys of having a ten-year-old boy as your closest friend. Not that I would ever have it any other way, but sometimes my brain forgets I am around adults and I embarrass myself.

Laura rushed past me with a huge slice of pumpkin pie with a mile-high dollop of whipped cream. The whistler. I glanced around my small café and, sure enough, there he was in his corner. He had his back to me so all I could see was the same damn fedora he wore every time he came in. Strange! The man was just downright strange.

I heard the loud rumbling of pipes before I actually saw the motorcycle pull to a stop in front of the café.

The large windows allowed me to watch as the bike parked. The shock of blue hair sticking out from under the driver's helmet told me my day was about to get interesting. Misty. And if Misty was here, I knew Reanna Rains wasn't far behind.

The last thing I had heard about Reanna and her band, Shadow & Flame, was from one of those rag magazines. She made the cover again. This time it was something about her beating the hell out of some paparazzi jerk that was trying to sneak a picture of her. I couldn't wait to hear about all of the trouble she'd gotten herself into during this last tour. Reanna was one of my favorite people. I wouldn't say we were close friends. We were more than acquaintances, less than BFF's, but she always had the best stories.

I went back to my task of filling coffee cups and clearing dishes. I was short a busboy this morning, leaving me to fill in. Yet another thing I didn't have time for. I cleared three spots at the counter, knowing if Misty and Reanna were here, chances were Reanna's guy, Royston, would be with them.

"Where's the fire, Ava?" Mac asked as I quickly reset the now clean spots next to them at the counter.

"Customers, Mac. Have you looked around? Gotta be quick around here. Reanna and Misty are here. Can you please make sure no one bothers them, or God forbid someone tries to take a picture of her? I like my new bar stools."

"Sweetheart, I think that was you that broke the last bar stool, not me," Reanna said as she approached, pulling me in for a hug.

"Well, no one likes their picture being taken while they're eating. That's just rude. I asked him to leave nicely like five times. I swear you throw one bar stool at a photog and you never live it down," I laughed and returned Reanna's hug. "And honey, if you want to go incognito around these parts, you might wanna tell Misty that blue hair stands out."

"The blue hair stays. How've you been, Ava?" Misty kissed my cheek as she sat at the counter. "Reid, Mac. Getting into trouble, I hope. Nice to see you two."

"Would you both like some coffee?" I asked as they sat at the counter. "Where's Royston?" I looked around the café, but didn't see him.

"Oh, he'll be here in a minute. Work call or some shit. I never know what he's doing," Reanna answered.

I hurried off to grab three cups of coffee and the guys' order. I really had to get my inventory finished. As much as I wanted to visit with everyone, I didn't have time.

Royston was seated and already engrossed in

conversation with Mac and Reid by the time I got back around to them.

"... I've been following the case closely. Let me know when you have time to sit down, to go over my notes. I think I found something of interest," Royston spoke softly to Reid. He turned his attention towards me. "Ava, dear. A pleasure to see you. You are looking radiant this morning. New moisturizer?"

By the time my laughter subsided, my cheeks hurt. "How nice of you to notice, Royston. Always the gentleman. And to answer your question, yes, I gave up on the expensive wrinkle cream and went back to good ole' fashioned Vaseline Intensive Care. I figured if it was good enough to smooth my elbows it should be good enough for my face."

The five of them laughed and carried on while I dropped off the coffee and Reid and Mac's food.

"Seriously, Ava, you know I am only joking with you. It is nice to see you." Royston flashed me his award-winning smile.

He was kinda hot in that nerdy-sexy way. Quite possibly one of the smartest people I have ever met. When he came in during a lull, I loved talking books with him. Him and Reanna both. She put on this badass rocker persona, but when she opened up and showed you the smallest sliver of the real her, you had to sit back and enjoy. She was wicked smart and extremely well read.

"Alright everyone, sorry to cut this short, but I have to get to my inventory."

"No, we just got here. Stay and play a minute," Misty suggested.

"While the invitation is tempting, I have to get out of here early today. I promised JJ ice cream if he did well on his spelling test." I leaned over the counter in front of Reanna and whispered, "But please come in again soon, I have to hear all about the photog you beat up. I bet it was great. Just tell me. It was great, wasn't it?"

"Oh-my-God-it was fucking hysterical. I promise I will call you this week to tell you all about it. The only thing that would've made it better is if I didn't break my guitar. But fuck it, sometimes you just have to roll with it." Reanna winked at me. "Go. Get your work done. Family first. Tell JJ we all said hello and I hope to see him soon."

"Sorry guys, I really wish I could stay and chat." And that was the truth, I really wanted to join them for coffee.

"...yea, text me when you're free and we'll meet up at Reid's office..." Mac was speaking to Royston.

"Sorry to interrupt, Royston, dynamic duo, I have

work in the back. Laura will be around to check on you. Laters."

"When the fuck did she start with the dynamic duo shit? And who's Batman in this equation? I'm not Robin, bro." Reid laughed and pointed to Mac. "You're Robin."

I waved as they shouted their goodbyes.

2

CRAZINESS AND CLOVES

Reid

I watched as Ava walked away. I might have let my eyes linger on her ass a tad longer than was appropriate. But Goddamn, the woman had a nice ass. It was days like this, when she was smiling and happy, that I had a hard time remembering why I hadn't made her mine yet.

In the beginning, after Jacob died, I watched her from a distance. She grieved in silence and refused to allow anyone to comfort her in any way. She even rejected Mac's help. The more she rebuffed Mac's offers, the harder it was on him. After all, Mac was Jacob's best friend as well as JJ's Godfather. Mac never complained, but I saw how much it crushed him not to be there for them the way he wanted to be. The way Jacob would've expected.

Recently something had changed in their relationship. Mac now pushed her buttons on purpose to get her to react to him. And Ava, well, she seemed to be overcritical of everything Mac did. It was like watching an old, disgruntled, married couple. I hated that for them. I didn't like the distance that was growing between my two best friends. The longer it went on, the more Ava seemed to resent Mac. I had to figure out a way to put a stop to it.

It had not escaped my notice that Ava didn't even ask Mac to get JJ from school anymore. When she was running late she called me. Not that I minded. I selfishly loved it. JJ was a good kid, and I enjoyed every minute I had with him. But I knew that Mac missed his time with JJ.

Ava had done well for herself. She single-handedly started a restaurant and had made it a success. I glanced around the café, impressed at the newly remodeled space. When Ava got an idea in her head there was no stopping her. Recently she decided the walls needed a fresh coat of paint. That meant new stools for the counter and new accessories for the walls.

A beautiful brunette caught my attention. I had to do a double-take before recognition set in. Sally Levenson. It was a rare occasion I saw the Medical Examiner out of her scrubs and with her hair down.

I nudged Mac, interrupting his conversation with

Royston. "Sally's here. You ever seen that man she's with?"

Mac glanced over his shoulder and Royston turned on his stool to get a better look as well. "I don't think so. He looks a little familiar, but damn, Sally looks hot with her hair down like that," Mac commented.

"I don't know what she normally looks like, but she certainly is eye-catching," Royston weighed in.

"Let's go say hello. I need to talk to her about an email she sent me anyway," Mac suggested.

Mac grabbed his coffee off the counter and followed behind me as we made our way through the cramped café.

"Hey, doc," I greeted. "Whatcha doing here?"

Sally was positively glowing. Maybe it was the relaxed setting, maybe it was because her hair was loose and not pulled up in the severe ponytail she normally wore while working. Either way, she looked beautiful.

I glanced at the man sitting across from Sally. He had a certain air about him. He screamed money and class. He was not a man to be fucked with. I liked that for Sally.

"Hey guys." Sally stood and kissed me on the cheek, then moved around me to reach Mac. "Fancy seeing you here. Did you get my messages?"

"We were just discussing that case," Mac said. He

held his phone out for her to see. It was a damn miracle he even knew how to check his mail on that thing. "I got your email."

"Yeah, I had to amend my initial report," Sally said.

"What made you change your mind?" I asked. I had never known Sally to change a report.

Her entire demeanor changed, she was now in work mode.

"Several things, actually. When I talked with you earlier, it looked like your typical OD. However, things weren't adding up. The victim has contusions around her throat suggesting strangulation, but that's not the cause of death. Then there are the puncture wounds from the needles."

Mac interrupted. "Wouldn't needle marks on a drug addict be normal? I mean, I'd expect she has track marks up and down her arms and legs. Hell, even her toes. Why would a few puncture wounds change your findings?"

I glanced around, making sure no one was paying attention to our conversation. The topic wasn't exactly, breakfast crowd friendly.

"Well, the track marks are normal, but the puncture wounds aren't self-inflicted. I'm thinking someone grabbed her, then stuck her with a needle several times. Either the same one, or several different ones. At least five marks that I can see. That's where the overdose came from."

I shook my head in disbelief. Even after all these years being an investigator, people still shocked the shit out of me. I had worked with the police on hundreds of murder cases, and I still got sick to my stomach at what people do to each other.

"How can you be so sure?" I asked. I was trying to figure out how Sally could possibly know if the needle marks weren't self-inflicted.

"Addicts are really good at finding usable veins, almost religious about it. Like Mac said, they'll use the veins between their toes if they have to. Thing is, they're experts and approach the vein at a forty-five-degree angle." She paused for a second. "But that's not even the weirdest thing."

"Go on," I prompted.

"She had cloves in her mouth. Aspirated a couple of the buds," Sally replied.

A sudden boom of laughter pulled us from our conversation. A man at the next table over had his phone out in front of him, obviously finding humor in whatever he was watching. He turned his head to see us all staring at him. Startled, he quickly pulled his fedora lower on his head and went back to eating his pie.

I turned back to Sally and continued. "Addicts are huffing cloves now?"

That was the first I had heard of addicts using cloves to get high.

"Not the spice."

"But you said cloves?" Now I was confused. I looked over at Mac to see if he was following or if he was as lost as I was.

Of course, the ever-prepared Mac, had his handy-dandy notepad out taking notes. No technological skills whatsoever. He still used pen and paper.

"You're thinking of the spice used in cooking. It's ground from the dried flower buds of the clove plant."

"What's your gut tell you? I've never known you to be wrong." Mac spoke up.

"I think someone tried to kill her in that alley. Maybe they fought over drugs? It could explain the marks on her neck. But if she was incapacitated, I don't understand why they'd inject her with a lethal dose of heroin rather than just run away. Either way, those puncture marks in muscle weren't self-administered."

"The cloves? What part do they play?" Mac looked up from his pad.

"For a junkie who's missed a fix, and in the early stages of withdrawal, maybe she thought it would make her nausea go away?" Sally explained.

I must've misunderstood what Sally had said. The café was loud and dishes were clattering all around me. And now the pie eater the next table over was driving me crazy with his fucking whistling. What was with that guy?

"By chewing cloves?" I questioned.

"Some people think clove buds have antiemetic properties. But I'm just guessing here. My job is to report the facts. Yours is to figure out what it all means. If I had the answers, you'd be in the unemployment line."

Next to me, Mac chuckled and shook his head in amusement. Sally had jokes today. There was something a little different about Sally this afternoon. She seemed to be... happy. Not that she ever looked unhappy. But today she was different.

Ava caught my attention, as she rushed passed us. She was hustling around the dining room clearing more tables. She leaned over a table to wipe it down and I almost swallowed my tongue. Her ass looked so hot in those jeans.

Sally cleared her throat and I realized I had been staring at Ava's ass a little too long.

"Hmm...thanks for the update," I tried to recover. "We appreciate it."

The man sitting at the table with Sally set his glass on the table, drawing my attention to him. He looked vaguely familiar.

"Oh, I'm sorry," Sally said. "This is my..."

Sally seemed at a loss for words. Ah, so this was a new relationship.

He stood and extended his hand. "Derek Lemark. Pleasure." Derek shook Mac's hand before he turned to me.

A handshake tells a lot about a man. Derek had a nice strong grip, not over the top or too rough. He was not trying to pull any tough guy, macho bullshit. Cool, calm, and confident.

"Nice to meet you. Do I know you?" I asked.

"It's possible," Derek said, but he didn't elaborate. I'd have to remember to ask Austin to run the good doctor's date through our database and check him out.

Mac rubbed the back of his head. "Doc, you really gave us an odd one this time."

That was an understatement.

"I should have another one for you later today... maybe tomorrow," she said.

"Really?" I chuckled. "You're going to have to work hard to top this last one."

"Just trying to keep you employed, Reid," she joked.

"Well," Mac said, "give me a call when you finish the new case."

Her voice cracked, and she cleared it. "I doubt I'll have it to you by tonight. I'll give you a call tomorrow."

If Sally's pretty blush was any indication, she would otherwise be tied up with her new man tonight. Work would be the last thing on Sally's mind.

"Catch ya' later, Doc." Mac nodded his head in the direction of Derek.

"Tell George to call me. I missed out on his last trip to the mountains. Been busy, but I want to see how big that mutt of his is getting," I said.

"Don't let George hear you calling Tank a mutt." Sally laughed.

George's pride in Tank's pedigree bordered on obsessive.

"Well, tell him I'm sorry I bailed on him last week, but I'm definitely ready for a trip to the mountains."

"I'll let him know." She glanced over at Derek and smiled.

The look of annoyance was clear on Derek's face. I couldn't blame the guy. He was trying to enjoy a nice breakfast with his woman and we hijacked his morning. "Nice to meet you, Derek." With a lift of my chin, I turned to leave, giving the whistling fool one last look.

By the time I made my way back to the counter, Mac was already reading through his notes. He glanced up when I sat down.

"Weird, right? Cloves down the victim's throat. I already called Lance and asked him to run a search of similar MO's in the area. I doubt anything will hit, but it's worth a shot." Mac told me.

"Yeah, I have to agree. I don't think anything will come of the search. Especially if, in the past, the killer has targeted high-risk victims like this one. Details on those cases always get lost in the shuffle. Good news for you, whoever killed her doesn't seem to be criminally sophisticated. Shit, he didn't even try and hide the body. I'd bet you a beer it turns out to be a drug deal gone wrong."

"Hell, man. That's no better. Feels like I have ten new drug-related cases hit my desk every day." Mac blew out a breath. He was a damn good cop and took every case personally. "Sure as fuck hope the Mayor makes good on his campaign promise to clean up the streets."

The laugh that ripped from my throat was loud, drawing the attention of nearby customers. "Goddamn, dude, that is the funniest thing I have heard all day. That dirty politician is more worried about covering up his mounting debt than the streets."

"Hey, guys, you need anything else?" Laura asked as she refilled our coffee.

"Yes, please," Mac replied.

Mac's eyes narrowed as he fixated on the pretty waitress.

I looked up at Laura to see her focus was firmly on

me, even though Mac had been the one to answer. Clearly, she was ignoring Mac.

"Please, Laura. In a to-go cup though if you wouldn't mind." I answered her. She quickly walked away. Mac had his phone out texting furiously.

"What was that about?" I asked.

He looked up from his phone. "What? What was what about?"

"Laura?"

"Nothing. Absolutely nothing is going on with Laura," he responded a little too fast.

"Right."

I had been watching those two dance around each other for the last six months. Something was going on there. If Laura was smart, she would steer clear of Detective Mackenzie. I loved the man like a brother, but he had *player* written all over him.

TITTY TWISTERS AND NIPPLES

Ava

I pulled up in front of JJ's school and waited in the pickup line. Why was there always that one parent that had to hold up the entire line by chatting through their window to the crossing guard? I did not have the patience to sit there and wait. I wanted to get JJ and go for ice cream. I missed my son. Summer couldn't get here fast enough. I wanted him at the café with me where I could visit with him all day.

I saw him running to the car, his book bag bouncing up and down, a huge smile on his face. That's my boy!

"Hey, Mama!" JJ threw his backpack into the back seat and jumped into the car. "Guess what?"

"What?" I knew, *what*. But I played along. We did this every week.

"I got a ninety-nine percent. I didn't even get the word wrong but Mrs. Smith said that my handwriting was sloppy on the word, *beyond*. She said she could see my eraser marks. I spelled it b-e-y-o-u-n-d, but then remembered what you said when we were studying, there is no *u*. I can't help it if I'm not a good eraser. Kendall is a good eraser. She sits next to me now. We moved our seats around this morning.

"Mrs. Smith said that I should ask Kendall to help me learn how to erase better. She's mean. Mrs. Smith, not Kendall. Kendall is pretty and smells funny, like she sprays that girl spray on herself like you do. Only, hers smells like peaches. The boys all say she has really pretty hair. The girls are mean to her. Mrs. Howard, the character counts coach, told her not to listen to the girls, they were just jealous because she was so beautiful, and she has an accident that is pretty to listen to. So, today can I get the extra scoop of chocolate since I got over an eighty percent?"

My head was spinning from the rush of information. He said all of that before we even drove out of the parking lot.

"Accent. Kendall has an accent, not an accident," I corrected him. "And I don't know. *Can* you have an extra scoop?"

"Oh, yeah. I meant, may I please have the extra scoop?" JJ corrected himself.

"Yes, of course, you may. I am very proud of you, little man. So, other than the big seat move today, the spelling test, you needing to learn how to erase better, and the pretty girl Kendall, what else exciting happened at school? Tell me everything."

JJ prattled on while I drove us to the ice cream shop. I could sit and listen to my son talk all day. He had always been animated. He spoke with his whole body. His arms moved and he gestured with every sentence. He reminded me so much of... no, I wasn't going to go there. I was going to stay in the moment and enjoy my son.

Two double-scoops of chocolate chunk later we were home, dinner done, homework completed, and I was beat. I still had household bills to pay and cleaning to do before I called it a night, but I could barely keep my eyes open. When I was at work, with the hustle and bustle of the café, I didn't have time to dwell on all that I had to do by myself, and how much had fallen between the cracks. I didn't have time to think about how lonely I was. I had JJ. He was my entire world and I loved him beyond measure, but I missed cuddling. I missed watching a movie and holding hands. Stolen kisses before work. And sex. I missed sex.

"Mama, why can girls give boys titty twisters but boys can't give them back to girls?" JJ asked.

Wow, that came way out of left field.

"Well, girls shouldn't really be giving them to boys, either. They hurt. And maybe we shouldn't be using that word, titty."

"Today Stacy gave Carver a titty twister. He screamed it hurt so bad. So, he gave her one back. A good one too, Mom. She cried and everything. Stacy was mad and told Mrs. Smith. Mrs. Smith told Carver that he cannot touch girls there because it was inappropriate. Carver asked why Stacy could grab his boy nipple, but he couldn't grab her girl nipple. He said a nipple is a nipple. I agree, a nipple is a nipple. My nipple hurts after Stacy gives me one, too. So, fair is fair, right? I mean if a girl gets to touch my nipple, I should be allowed to touch her nipple, too."

I tried, I mean I really tried to hold the laughter in, but I couldn't. It bubbled up and erupted. I knew I needed to tell him to stop saying, titty and nipple, but I couldn't. I couldn't breathe, I was laughing so hard. It felt good to laugh, sitting on the couch with my boy having fun. My sides hurt and tears were pouring down my cheeks as I tried to stop myself from laughing.

"You look pretty, Mama. I like it when you laugh."

I pulled my little boy, who was no longer so little, to me and snuggled him close.

"Thank you, little man. I love it when you laugh, too. Now, you cannot give girls titty twisters. Your teacher is right. It is inappropriate for a boy to grab a girl's breast."

"GROSS! No one was talking about grabbing a breast. I was talking about nipples. Stacy doesn't have boobs. She looks like me. I heard Kendall telling Stacy that her mom told her she was starting to bud. Why would she bud? I don't understand why Kendall's mom would tell her she was going to start growing flowers. Do you think she means she likes to plant stuff?"

Sweet baby Jesus, save me now.

I wasn't ready to have this conversation, especially right that very second.

"How about this? This weekend we will talk all about why boys can't grab girl's breasts, nipples, titty twisters, and why a girl buds. Until then, do me a favor? No more giving girls titty twisters." I was silently begging him not to question me any further.

"Okay. What are we reading tonight?" JJ asked as he got up and stretched.

I was blessed that JJ had always been the type of kid that liked his sleep. He was out the moment his head hit the pillow.

"Anything you want, my sweet boy." I kissed his cheek when I passed him to put my cup in the kitchen.

I was too tired to pay bills. I was too tired to clean up the rest of the kitchen. Hell, I was too tired to even shower. I wanted to get into bed with a good book and go to sleep. I was living the dream. Home in bed with a book by nine PM.

"I want to read Mr. Pine's Purple House. And you can call me 'sweet boy' in the house, but please don't call me that in front of Uncle Mac or Reid. I'm ten now. I'm too old to have my mom call me baby names in public." With those words, JJ stunned me into silence.

I had known this day was coming. He held my hand less and less in public. He never kissed me back if I was dropping him off at a friend's house. He switched back and forth from Mom to Mama. He never called me Mommy anymore. I wasn't ready for this, none of it. I wanted my baby boy to stay a baby. I already missed giving him a bath. I couldn't remember the last time I washed my son's hair. That day just came and went without notice.

I swallowed the lump in my throat and headed upstairs. Soon he wouldn't want me to read with him before bed.

I wasn't ready.

4

———

TROUBLE

Reid

"Not one more fucking step." In one well-practiced maneuver, I had the would-be robber pushed up against the stucco wall, both arms tightly secured behind his back. "Wanna tell me why you're lurkin' around here in the dark?" I whispered into his ear.

"Who the hell do you think you are?" the scrawny little punk slurred, too drunk to even think about struggling.

This idiot picked the wrong house on the wrong night to fuck with. Not that I would ever take kindly to some jackass prowling around my neighborhood, but tonight was especially bad. I was clean out of patience.

I had just spent the last nine hours up in Diablo National Park helping the local PD collect evidence. I was dirty, hungry, and tired. I was not in the mood for this douchebag.

"I believe I asked you a question. What are you doing?" Capturing both his thin wrists in one of my hands, I used my forearm to push his cheek into the stucco.

"Ava's my sister. I was checking to see if she was home."

My body locked at his mention of Ava's name. "Wrong answer, douchebag. Ava doesn't have a brother." I didn't like that he knew who lived here. I was pissed off enough when I thought this was a random break-in.

My gut told me that shit was about to go bad for my beautiful neighbor. And my gut was never wrong. I knew every last detail about Ava. She was an only child. In the last five years, no man had come over to her house, with the exception of me, Mac, and a few other guys from the precinct.

The porch light came on and I silently begged Ava not to open the door. I heard the deadbolt click and the door slowly opened. Did that woman have no sense of danger?

"Reid? What in the world is going on out here? I thought I heard banging around," Ava said as she started to step out the door.

"Ava, get back in the house! Call the station would ya? Ask the desk sergeant to send out Lance," I demanded, probably harsher than needed if the deepening scowl on her face was any indication.

"What happened? Who is that?" Ava questioned further.

I tried to hold my tongue, but my patience was slipping by the millisecond.

Before I could answer her, the douchebag started to struggle, trying to turn his face in her direction. Not a fucking chance was he going to lay eyes on her.

"Ava! Please tell this idiot to let me go!" the douchebag yelled.

"Jimmy, is that you?" Ava walked further onto the porch.

"Yes. Now tell the big ape to let me go."

"Reid, I know Jimmy. He's my brother-in-law," Ava explained.

And there it was, my gut was never wrong. Ava's brother-in-law, James Kelley, was a criminal. He still lived in Texas. How did I know that? Because I kept tabs on the little prick. Before Jacob died he had also kept tabs on his little brother. James had always been bad news. Why the fuck was he here in San Fran at three o'clock in the morning? My instincts screamed at me to have Jimmy taken down to the station and questioned. Who shows up at his dead brother's widow's house at three AM? Drunk?

A lying, scheming piece of shit, that's who.

Reluctantly I eased off the pressure allowing him to finally look in Ava's direction.

I slowly backed away, not for one second would I let this drunken fool have a chance to do something stupid, like take a swing at me. Not that I was worried he would even make contact, but him swinging on me would mean I would have to beat his ass. That, of course, would be followed by hours of paperwork. Paperwork and time, I did not want to waste on this idiot.

I just wanted a shower and my bed. Screw the hunger pains. I would wait until morning to eat. That would give me the perfect excuse to check on Ava before I hit the office. I could stop in at the café. It wouldn't be the first time I had stopped in there on my way to work. As a matter of fact, most mornings I was a fixture at the counter. Not because Del Mar's food was stellar or it was conveniently on my way to the office. It wasn't convenient. In fact, it was out of the way. Yet day after day I found myself sitting at her counter.

I watched in disgust as Jimmy wrapped his arms around Ava and gave her a sloppy kiss on the cheek. "I've missed you, Ava," he slurred.

Fucking douchebag.

"It's three AM, Jimmy. Have you been drinking?" she asked with the same sweet voice I had heard her use a thousand times before, but this time there was something different. Her tone was laced with hurt.

I had watched the sadness in her eyes fade over the years, but it was shining bright again. I had watched and waited. Waiting for the pain to lessen enough for me to make my move. I wanted Ava Kelley. I wasn't going to stand by and watch this douchebag bring the sadness back. Watching her grieve the first time was hard enough. If not for me, for her wellbeing, I wasn't going to allow Jimmy's presence to break her again.

I knew Jacob Kelley. It was hard for me to believe that this scrawny, drunk, little shit was his brother. Jacob was a good man and a great cop. When the case ran cold on his killer, the detectives called in a marker and asked my crew to take a look at the evidence. Within a week, we had the cop killer delivered to the station, only slightly worse for the wear. He was still breathing and could stand trial. That was all the district attorney asked for. We delivered. I don't think Ava knew that it was my guys that brought her husband's killer in. I liked it that way.

"Ava, a word in private," I requested.

"Sure, Reid." She pulled away from Jimmy. "Give me a minute to get Jimmy in the house."

She disappeared into the house with Jimmy. As the

seconds ticked by the more I thought this was not a good idea, Ava and JJ being in the house alone with a drunk criminal.

Just as I was about to go into the house and voice my opinion, Ava walked out.

"What happened, Reid? Jimmy said you came out of nowhere and attacked him," Ava asked.

"Really?" I chuckled, "Is that what he said? I suppose he would think that. I noticed him walking around your house as I pulled into my driveway. Obviously, I wasn't going to ignore someone wandering around your house in the middle of the night."

"Right. Thank you for checking it out." She stopped and smiled at me. "I really need to remember to leave the outside lights on, too," she added, more as a reminder to herself.

"Listen, are you sure it's a good idea, him being here?" I asked.

"Oh, sure. Jimmy is harmless."

No, he wasn't. But she didn't have the file I had on Jimmy, with his rap sheet. Over the last five years, he had been investigated for petty theft, robbery, illegal gambling, and grand theft auto. He was now running with a high-profile gang. It had been a few months since I had checked in on James Kelley. Him being here now, did not give me a warm and fuzzy feeling.

"It's after three AM and he is clearly drunk. He

certainly has not been around in the last five years." As soon as the words left my mouth I wanted to pull them back. The last thing I wanted to do was remind her of the last five years.

"We'll be fine," she snapped. "Thank you again, Reid." With that, she turned and walked back into her house.

I waited to hear the lock click before I turned to leave. Mentally kicking my own ass all the way back to my house.

I tossed my keys on the entryway table and headed upstairs. As much as I wanted a beer or ten after my night, I knew it was not a good idea. I needed a clear head, just in case Ava and JJ needed me.

I rushed through my shower in a daze. Today's events still plagued my mind. First, Sally's findings on the dead girl in the alley. Something wasn't sitting right with me. In my line of work as a private investigator, I had seen a lot of overdoses and investigated even more missing persons cases. Sadly, most of those ended up with my client's loved one an addict. I had never heard of addicts using cloves to help with the side effects of withdrawal. Second, there was the badly decomposed body in Mount Diablo Park. The more I ran through what I knew, the more questions I had.

I got into bed only to toss and turn. I prayed that

exhaustion would finally win out over the crime scene photos that were replaying over and over in my mind.

Then there was Jimmy. Why was he in San Francisco? And just how much trouble did he bring to Ava's doorstep?

5

WHITE KNIGHT—NO ARMOR NEEDED

Ava

"Hey, where is Jacob Junior?" Jimmy asked as he drunkenly stumbled to the couch.

My heart squeezed at the name. I hadn't called JJ by his given name in years. It was too painful. I had taken to using JJ on school and medical documents as well. I couldn't even write the name *Jacob*, let alone say it out loud. Hearing Jimmy use that name in such a blasé manner made me want to duct tape his mouth shut.

He had no right to say that name. None at all. Jimmy had completely checked out of our lives these last five years. If I was honest, he had checked out before Jacob died. When Jacob and I moved to California, Jimmy stayed in Texas. As much as Jacob tried to shield me from Jimmy's criminal behavior, I knew. I could see it in Jacob's eyes. He was heartbroken his little brother had followed in their father's footsteps and became a shit-bird criminal.

"It's the middle of the night, Jimmy. JJ is sleeping. He has school in the morning." I was trying to keep my cool. My initial shock of finding Jimmy on my porch with Reid was starting to wear off. Even though I would never admit this to Reid, he was right. This might not be a good idea. "How did you get here, Jimmy?" I hoped to God he didn't drive, as drunk as he was. Thankfully I didn't see a car out front, not that I looked all that hard.

"I'm starving, Sis. Do you think you could make me one of those grilled cheese and bacon sandwiches? You remember the ones you used to make when I would escape from Mom and Dad's house and stay with you and Jacob?"

There it was again. *Jacob.*

Jacob and Jimmy had a crap childhood. Their parents were absolutely horrible. My mother was horrified when I started dating the boy from the bad side of town whose father was a criminal. That might have been what pushed me to him in the first place. Anything to annoy my hoity-toity mother and her obnoxious band of snobs from the country club.

"I'm tired, Jimmy. How about I make you a peanut

butter and jelly? I need to get some sleep. I take it you're staying here tonight?"

I prayed he said no. That he was going to walk to a local motel. Bitchy? Yes! However, in the middle of the night when I was emotionally fried, I didn't care.

"Yeah, just for a few days. I thought I'd stop by on my way up north and check in on my favorite sister and Jacob Junior." His eyes were already closing as he sat upright on the couch.

Why was God punishing me? What had I done to deserve Jimmy showing up drunk on my doorstep after five years of not returning a phone call, a text message, or an email? Nothing. Not on a holiday, a birthday, or the anniversary of his brother's murder. He didn't even show up for the trial. I sat in the courtroom with no family. Only Mac and Reid stayed by my side.

The only days either of them missed during the two-month trial was if I needed someone to take care of JJ.

Jimmy had just abandoned us. Finally, I gave up trying to reach out to him. I had a life I had to piece back together. A child to raise, losses to grieve, and, for the first time in my life, I had to figure out a way to live on my own. I simply didn't have time to manage his feelings as well as mine. I couldn't help him if he was unwilling to meet me halfway.

"Why are you here?" I asked.

"I just told you, I wanted to see you." His eyes closed all the way and his head nodded off to the side.

"Right," I mumbled. I was too tired for this shit and he was too drunk to answer any questions.

I noticed my purse on the hook by the front door. I snagged it and my keys on my way to the stairs. I might be too nice for my own good sometimes, but I was not stupid. There was no way I was leaving my wallet and car keys unattended.

With a quick check on JJ, I was finally ready to get back in bed. I only had two hours until I had to be up and five AM comes fast. I wished I had a job where I could call in sick, stay in bed, all day, and veg out. How long had it been since I was able to take a lazy day and just lie in bed and read? Five years, that's how long. It had been five years since I was able to breathe.

I burrowed back into my warm bed, my eyes closing almost the instant my head hit the pillow. I would worry about Jimmy tomorrow.

The sound of loud banging woke me up. I was completely disoriented when I sat up in bed and threw the covers off. What the hell was that?

The sound of glass shattering finally pulled me from my stupor. My only thought was JJ. I had to get to him. I ran across the hall to his room.

Gone!

His bed was empty. An all too familiar feeling

started in my stomach and traveled out in all directions. The heat and panic I had grown accustomed to living with was coiled tight and ready to strike. It would be so easy to let it take over; fighting the panic attack was always so much harder. I couldn't let it consume me. I needed to find JJ.

Everything that Jacob had ever told me about personal safety and home defense came rushing back.

Do not scream and give away your location. Never call for JJ. If he is hiding he will run to you, giving away his location. Calm. Methodical in your movements. Never leave the bedroom unarmed.

Mother F'er! I broke that rule. I forgot to get the .38 I kept locked in a small gun safe in my room. Too late.

"MOMMM!" JJ screamed.

Downstairs. The yell came from downstairs. I took the steps two at a time, coming to a sliding stop in front of my son. He was standing in the living room surrounded by broken glass and a puddle of orange juice. Jimmy was standing in front of him pointing a gun at my son.

A gun!

"Jimmy! What the hell are you doing? Put the goddamn gun away!"

I was no stranger to guns. I, however, had never had one pointed at me, nor had I ever seen one pointed at my son.

All traces of my earlier panic were gone. Replaced with white-hot rage. I was going to kill Jimmy.

There was a movement to my left and before I could comprehend what was happening Reid was behind Jimmy. His own weapon was drawn and pointed at the back of Jimmy's head.

"Drop your gun, asshole." I watched Reid's mouth move as he spoke but his voice was unrecognizable. In all the years I had known, Logan Reid, I had never heard that menacing tone.

Jimmy didn't lower his gun. A wide smile pulled at his lips. "Ah, yes. The white knight has come to save the day again."

The dumbass must have a death wish. Why would he poke the bear who held a gun to his head?

"Please tell me this isn't happening! This cannot happen in my living room," I yelled. "Jimmy, swear to God, put that gun away."

"JJ, sweetheart, please go up to your room." As I gave him a gentle push in the direction I wanted him to go I noticed his bare feet and the broken glass around him. "Wait! I'll carry you to the stairs so you don't cut your feet."

"Both of you stay put," Reid's scary voice commanded.

Holy shit.

I was just about to argue when Jimmy suddenly fell

to the ground. The blow to the back of his head happened so fast I didn't even see Reid move. Jimmy's head hit the coffee table with a sickening thud and blood instantly began to pool.

"Close your eyes, JJ." When Reid spoke this time, his voice was gentle and coaxing.

Reid stepped around Jimmy's body, picking up the gun now laying on the floor. He reached around behind him and shoved both guns in the waistband of his jeans. He was taking slow and measured steps towards us, hands out in front of him. He must've thought I was a hysterical wreck the way he was approaching us, like he thought I might freak out at any moment.

I belatedly noticed he wasn't looking at me. Reid was laser focused on my son.

"JJ, I'm gonna pick you up and carry you to the stairs. I want you to wait until I bring your mama over to you before you go up. You with me, little man?" Reid spoke softly to JJ, a reassuring hand on his shoulder.

My heart squeezed at Reid's gentle care of my son.

"I'm with you, Reid." JJ's little voice trembled.

I was going to fucking kill James Kelley.

I remained silent as Reid scooped my son up and took him to the stairs. I was too afraid to speak. Now that guns weren't being pointed I could feel the adrenaline drop coming.

After setting JJ down Reid turned to me. "Look at me, Ava. You're safe. JJ is safe. Trust me. All you need to do is take JJ upstairs and I will handle the mess down here."

I nodded my head in response.

"Thank you," he acknowledged my nod.

"Thank you? For what? You're the one rushing in here saving the day," I whispered.

"For trusting me." Reid picked me up as if I weighed nothing, cradling me in his arms. I desperately wanted to snuggle into him and soak up every ounce of warmth he had to offer.

Wrong. This was so wrong. Not a single man had touched me since my husband died. I wouldn't even allow Mac to hold my hand at the trial. Nor had I let him hug me in five years. I didn't want anyone to touch me. Only JJ.

"I didn't see any glass in JJ's feet but you'll still want to check." Reid set me down on the bottom step next to JJ and I winced. For the first time, I realized I had glass in my feet. Damn, it hurt.

"Change of plans, little man. Go ahead upstairs, I'm right behind you." Reid picked me up again, adjusting my weight in his arms as he ascended the stairs.

"I can walk," I said in weak protest.

I could walk, that was the truth. It would hurt like

a son-of-a-bitch with the tiny shards of glass in the bottoms of my feet, but I still could make it.

"You're not walking." That was it, no further explanation.

Reid carried me into the master bathroom, JJ glued to his side. When he sat me on the edge of the tub I was a little confused. There was no way I was getting in the shower now. Was he crazy?

"Do you have Epsom salts?" he asked.

"Hmm, under the sink, I think."

"JJ, look under the sink, would ya?" Reid asked as he fiddled with the faucet, adjusting the temperature.

JJ silently handed the carton of salt to Reid and sat down next to me on the side of the tub.

"Mama, who is that man downstairs?" JJ asked.

I hesitated, not knowing how much I wanted JJ to know. In the end, I opted for honesty. "That is your Uncle Jimmy, Daddy's younger brother."

"That's Uncle Jimmy?" JJ was shaking again. "Why was he pointing a gun at me?"

Now that was the million-dollar question, wasn't it? I was going to kill James Kelley.

"I don't know, baby. He'll never do it again though. He came by last night after you were asleep. He said he just wanted to see us." I smiled brightly at my son, trying to be somewhat reassuring.

"Next time Uncle Jimmy wants to spend the night,

can you please tell him no?" JJ asked.

Reid chuckled at that.

I jumped when he touched my ankle, lifting my foot to get a better look.

"You're a smart little man, JJ." Reid continued to snicker as he set my foot in the warm water. "Let your feet soak a few minutes. I'll be back up with some tweezers and my kit. Stay put until I get back."

I cocked my head to the side and pursed my lips. It had been a long time since someone told me what to do. I wasn't sure I liked it.

"Please, Ava, stay up here. I need to know you and JJ are safe while I dispose of the trash downstairs."

It might have been the please, or the mention of keeping my son safe, or maybe the fact that he was handling my problems for me, allowing me to take care of JJ.

"Thank you, Reid."

"No worries. I'll be back. You watch your mama, little man." He winked at JJ and headed out.

"I was so scared, Mama," JJ admitted with tears in his eyes.

That is when I snapped and the dam broke. I sobbed, holding onto my son. The soles of my feet might have had a thousand shards of broken glass in them, but nothing compared to the pain I felt when my boy told me he was scared.

6

PACK A BAG

Reid

"I was so scared, Mama."

After hearing JJ's soft admission and Ava's sobs I was positively murderous. That motherfucker was going to pay. I knew I should've never let him stay here. This was on me. I knew plenty of guys on the force who would've come down here and hauled his drunk ass in.

Not to mention the fact that the name *Ava Kelley* had pull around the San Francisco PD. The widow of a murdered cop always got special care. She was on the watch list of every retired cop, watchdog group, and local PI. Even our not-so-friendly chapter of the Iron Claw MC had her on their radar. Everyone knew that Ava and JJ Kelley were to be protected.

I failed.

I pulled my phone out of my pocket, stabbing at the screen harder than necessary. When I found the number I was looking for I connected the call. "Yea," Austin grumbled on the other end of the line.

"Sorry to wake you, I need you at Ava's and call Rick and Dustin. I need them at the office ASAP. Tell them I want all of the information they can find on James Kelley's whereabouts and dealings since the last report. And tell them to dig deeper into the last five years, I want to know every hole this douchebag has ever crawled into."

"Copy that boss. See you in ten." The phone disconnected.

I jogged down the stairs, needing to make one more dreaded phone call. Mac. He was gonna kick my ass. And rightfully so. I should've called this in last night and made him aware that Kelley was in town.

"Mac here," he answered.

"We gotta problem. Call a unit out to Ava's and get here." As I rounded the stairs I saw that the douchebag was not where I left him. "Motherfucker! We need a *BOLO* out for James Kelley. He is injured and on the run. Last seen ten minutes ago, leaving Ava's. He is in dirty blue jeans and a red and black button up."

"Ava and JJ?"

I didn't need for him to finish his question. I knew what he was asking.

"Safe." I disconnected and shoved my phone in my pocket.

Drawing my sidearm, my training took over. I pushed all thoughts of JJ and Ava aside and cleared the downstairs, noting the black duffle bag that Jimmy had with him last night was near the dining room table. Douchebag was in a hurry to leave.

I heard the front door slowly creak open, I turned and leveled my weapon.

Mac.

"All clear," I informed him.

"What the fuck happened to Ava's garage?" he thundered as he holstered his weapon.

"Jimmy Kelley happened. He was on her doorstep last night when I got home, a little after three. He was drunk and peeking in the window. Ava heard the commotion outside and confirmed she was okay with him staying."

"Jesus H! Jimmy hasn't been around since Jacob's funeral. That piece of shit completely abandoned Ava and JJ," Mac boomed, not telling me anything I didn't already know. "Did I ever tell you I reached out to him? Six months after Jacob died. I offered to set him up in San Fran to be closer to Ava and his nephew. He declined and told me Ava and JJ were just as dead to him as his brother."

"He what?" Ava screeched from the top of the stairs.

Mac's eyes widened in shock, then slowly closed. He'd just fucked up. He had obviously never told Ava that he had reached out to Jimmy. I wouldn't have either.

The pain in her eyes was confirmation that news was best kept a secret. Only it wasn't anymore and, knowing Ava, she was about to blister Mac.

"Ava, how is JJ?" Mac asked.

Smooth. Try and change the subject to JJ. Normally that would work, Ava's only concern was for her son.

"Not gonna work, Mac! Why would you do that?" She narrowed her eyes, then winced when she put her full weight on her right foot.

Yep, Ava was pissed. But, now I was too.

"Thought I told you to stay put," I said.

"I wanted to see who was here. This is my house, after all," she sassed.

"I'll be up in a minute to check your feet and wrap them. After that, you'll pack a bag."

"Pack a bag? Why would I do that?"

She looked so beautiful with the sun shining in the windows behind her, highlighting her long, golden-blonde hair. It almost looked like she had a halo around her. The sun flare was only an illusion. Ava was no delicate, golden angel complete with a halo. She was strong, spirited, and by far the most stubborn woman I knew.

"You're not staying here." I was purposely vague. This was going to be an argument. Not only was I going to have to battle it out with Ava, but I would have an all-out war with Mac. He was not going to be happy.

"I agree, it's not safe here, Ava. Think about JJ. We have no idea why Jimmy is in town, and who followed him here," Mac put in his two cents.

Before Ava could argue further, there was a noise at the front door. Mac put his hand up, silencing the room. Ava quietly disappeared back into her room. Good girl. Mac and I both took cover behind Ava's overstuffed couch and reached for our weapons.

The door slowly opened and Austin's large frame came into view, weapon drawn, looking like he just woke up from a bender.

"We're good," Mac said.

"What the hell happened out front?" Austin asked as he walked over to us.

I glanced up the stairs to make sure Ava was still in her room.

"A little after five I heard banging. At first, I thought it was just trash pickup. Once I woke up enough to remember Kelley was in town, I grabbed my gun and ran outside. I didn't see a car leaving and no one was running down the street. My best guess is they used the mountain lake trail to come and go. To be honest, I didn't pay too much attention to the damage outside, I was more concerned getting inside to check on Ava and JJ."

"And, Kelley? Where does he fit in?" Austin continued to question me.

"Don't know that yet. I haven't had a chance to talk to Ava about him. I'm hoping by the time we get to the office Rick and Dustin will have a jacket prepped and ready for review. The douchebag isn't very smart, or good at covering his tracks. His duffle is in the dining room. There's a cell on the table too, but that might be Ava's."

"Reid..." Mac trailed off.

"Waste of time, Mac. I am investigating this. Either I can share my information with you or you can pretend I'm standing down. The play is yours. But we both know your hands are tied by rules and bureaucratic bullshit. Mine are not. I am going to find Jimmy Kelley, and when I do, that douchebag will be sorry he ever stepped foot back in San Fran."

"Tread easy," Mac gave in.

"Not sure about that, but I will make sure that nothing blows back on you." I blew out a breath and prepared for battle. "Ava and JJ are coming with me.

I'm going to take them to the cabin. It's far enough away that Jimmy and whoever is after him won't find us, but close enough if you need me I can be back."

Mac let out a boisterous laugh and I braced myself for the explosion.

"Brother, you calling that shack you have in the Tennessee Valley a cabin is almost as laughable as you thinking that Ava and JJ are going anywhere with you."

"Yeah? And why is that, *brother?*" I knew he didn't miss the sarcasm in my voice.

"This might not be the time or the place to have this conversation, but it is long overdue." Mac had easily slid into his Detective Mackenzie persona, talking to me like I was some perp he was getting ready to interview.

The Fuck!

"Remember who you're talking to, Mac. I am not a suspect. I don't appreciate the tone," I warned.

"You wanna do this in front of your crew?" He dipped his head in Austin's direction. When I nodded in the affirmative he continued, "It's not lost on me that you've been biding your time waiting to claim Ava." As I started to interrupt, Mac spoke over my objections. "Don't try and play me for a fool. I have watched you, watching her, keeping your finger on her pulse, waiting for her to be whole again. You're one of my closest friends and I would give my life for that woman, but she'll hurt you. I don't think that the hole Jacob left can ever be fixed, because she won't allow it. You have practically been a monk these last few years. Just leave it and move on."

Well, what could I say to that? If I told him how wrong he was, how I had watched the shine come back into her eyes, it would confirm that I had been doing exactly what he was accusing me of. Watching and waiting. Living like a monk, getting reacquainted with nightly self-love. Fantasizing about the day I could finally touch and taste and worship Ava. I had turned into a pansy-assed fool. I wanted to kick my own ass for being such a pussy!

"I'll take my chances," I replied.

"The unit's here. Mac, are we taking Jimmy's bag with us back to the office to analyze or are you going to have it tied up in the evidence locker at the station?" Austin asked, his tone was dripping with contempt.

Austin knew better than anyone how jacked the system was. He had been LAPD for fifteen years before he quit and came to work for me. He'd left the force after his sister's rapist walked on a technicality, resulting in her suicide. Now he skirted the letter of the law, making sure that the scumbags of earth paid for their crimes. No legal system needed.

"Fuck! Yeah, you take it. I'll handle my guys. I'll be at your office in two hours for a brief." Mac turned to me. "I know you don't need this, but you have my support. I love Ava like a sister. If you think you're up for the fight, go after her. Jacob..." Mac let out a breath and took a second to regain his composure. "Jacob would want her and JJ happy and protected. He'd be happy it's you. He respected the hell out of you, Reid."

"'Preciate that, Mac. Means the world coming from you." I reached my hand out. When Mac took it, he squeezed it a little tighter than necessary. "No need, Mac. Message received. Loud and clear."

"Good, glad we have an understanding. Now, how long ago did you receive the last intel on Kelley? Is he still running with Fuentes? Carjacking and running eight liners?" Mac asked.

"Six months, give or take. The last report said Kelley fucked up a car delivery. A new Benz was supposed to be taken from El Paso down to Juarez. The dumb fuck left the real registration in the car and was stopped at the border. He was out of custody within the hour. We all know those border quacks can be bought off faster and cheaper than a bunny ranch whore."

"Shit, that's the truth," Austin agreed.

"This is on me. I should've been keeping a better watch on Kelley, and had intel reports every three months instead of six. He never should've been able to get past me and to her door."

"You've been watching Jimmy?" Ava interjected from the top of the stairs.

That woman was like a super-stealth spy in her movements. She could've taught the guys in my Army unit a thing or two about light feet.

"Where's JJ?" I ignored her question.

"Why have you been watching him?" she tried again.

Damn, I wished she hadn't heard that. I looked around for help. Austin, the asshole that he was, had hightailed it to the dining room and Mac was already out the front door.

Cowards.

7

VODKA AND DIET COKE

Ava

This was too much! It was barely six AM and everyone had gone mad. I was officially living in crazy town.

Mac had talked to Jimmy behind my back. Reid was watching Jimmy or keeping tabs on him, whatever that meant. Apparently, my house was vandalized. I hadn't even checked on that yet. And the cherry on top of this shit show – Jimmy pointing a gun at my son.

I didn't have time to deal with any of these people. I needed to get to Del Mar's and open.

"Never mind. I changed my mind. I don't want to know. JJ and I are leaving. I'm gonna go open the café. We'll be back after lunch."

"You can't leave yet," Reid objected. "Call Suzie in to open today."

Was his eye twitching? Why was he annoyed? I wasn't the one barking orders at him. I wasn't the one who'd been keeping secrets.

"Why can't I leave? Mac can handle the police. You both have a key. Can't one of you lock up on the way out? I'll handle the insurance company when I get back this afternoon."

There it was again, the eye twitch.

"Ava. Let's start with we don't know where Jimmy is or why he is in town. It's not safe for you and JJ. Next issue, the cops are gonna want to talk to you about Jimmy having an illegal firearm in your house, not to mention he had it pointed at JJ. Your final issue is that at least two of your tires have been slashed."

Great, just great.

"Why is Jimmy here?" I asked.

"How should I know? I was hoping he may have told you something last night."

"You and Mac seem to have all the secrets," I quipped.

That reminded me, I still had a bone to pick with Mac. I was not happy he intruded on my life and spoke to Jimmy behind my back.

"What did he say to you last night?" Reid asked.

"I'll tell you that after you tell me why you've been watching Jimmy. Oh, and for how long."

I watched and waited for Reid to answer. The eye

twitch thing was in full force. He was obviously annoyed. Well, guess what, buddy, I was too. Mac and Reid had thought it was ok to take over my life. Okay, that might have been a minor exaggeration, but I was pissed. I was allowed to exaggerate.

"Go call Suzie and get the café taken care of. Grab a bag for you and JJ, we're leaving as soon as the detective speaks to you."

It was my turn to get annoyed.

"Who the hell do you think you are? Why are you barking orders at me like I am some child you get to command? I will decide who I call and when I leave. What is wrong with the two of you? Mac thinks it's okay to go behind my back in family matters and you think you can barge in and take over. Back off, buddy."

I started to make my grand exit by stomping out of the room when Reid caught my arm.

"You'll forgive me if I am a little on edge, sweetheart. I was woken up in the wee hours of the morning by someone trashing your house. Then I find you and JJ held at gunpoint by a douchebag that has been running with the worst kind of criminals in El Paso for the last five or six years. I don't think you are grasping what kind of danger you and JJ are in."

"You don't think I understand? *My* son had a gun pointed at him, *my* son is a wreck. I just want to leave this house and take my son somewhere he feels safe. I choose the café. He is going with me. You're acting like I am sending him to school today unprotected and pretending I don't have a major issue on my hands. I know I do. And I'll handle it."

"You'll handle it? How, Ava? How will you handle the criminal douche from El Paso?" Reid bellowed.

I had officially slipped past pissed to angry. The nerve!

"That is none of your concern. It is my problem. I will handle it. Since you don't want to give me any answers about Jimmy, I'll ask Damion. He seems like he's a man that can find answers," I taunted him.

I had no real intention of talking to Damion, our not so friendly local motorcycle club member. Truth be told, he kinda scared me.

"Damion? President of the Iron Claw motorcycle club? That Damion? The Damion that did a stint in San Quinton? Jesus Christ, woman, are you crazy?"

"I don't know Damion's prior living arrangements, but yes, he is the president of the Iron Claw MC. He told me if I ever needed anything I could ask him," I goaded Reid further.

"Fucking hell. Clue in sweetheart, Damion doesn't do anything for free. If he offered his services he expects payment. Either in ass or a favor. And since you have nothing he can use by way of favor, he'll expect payment in ass. Steer clear of him, Ava. Swear to Christ I will blister your sweet little ass if you go anywhere near him."

"Do you have to be so crass? Jeez! Damion has never been anything but respectful to me."

"And why do you think that is? Don't bother trying to think of why, I'll explain it to you. The president of the Iron Claw MC knows that Ava Kelley is off limits. You're untouchable. I have made it so. You and JJ are to be protected, always."

I didn't know what to say. I was untouchable because he made it so? I didn't even know what that meant. I didn't *want* to know what that meant. I was afraid of what the implications were of investigator and general badass, Logan Reid, telling the president of a motorcycle club I was off limits.

"Whatever. I'm going to call Suzie and tell her I won't be in...until later."

"Jesus H, she's gonna call Suzie...stubborn...pain in the ass," Reid mumbled under his breath. "You do that. I have some calls to make."

HA! I was a pain in the ass. I stomped all the way up the stairs.

"Bossy asshole." I made sure I said it loud enough for him to hear.

"Mama, who's the A word?" JJ asked.

"Sorry, no one is. There's been a change of plans. When you're done getting dressed, come down to the kitchen and I'll make you some breakfast. Looks like we're not going straight to the café after-all."

"Okay. Is Reid still here?"

I stopped scrolling through my contacts and looked at my son. "Yeah, baby, he is. Everything ok? Uncle Mac is down there too."

"Yeah, I just wanted to… I mean I was just wondering. No big deal, I'm fine."

There was something in JJ's voice I didn't like. He was hiding something. He was using his fake happy voice. Did he not want Reid in the house?

"You sure you're ok with Reid being here?" I asked.

"Yeah. I'm done getting ready. I'm gonna go find Reid." JJ was out of the room before I could even collect my thoughts.

He was going to find Reid? Not his Uncle Mac. That was strange, JJ adored Mac.

I went back to my phone and found Suzie's number. Her husband was gonna kill me calling this early.

"Hello," Suzie answered in her normal chipper tone.

"Hey, Suz babe, I am so sorry to call this early, but I have a huge favor. There's been a bit of an emergency here, is there any way you can open the café this morning?"

"Doll, I'm already at the café. Mac texted me

thirty minutes ago and told me there was an issue with your car and asked if I could open," Suzie informed me.

Son-of-a-bitch. That was it.

"Did he now? How...nice of him. Thanks for covering for me. You're the best."

"No problem. I hope you get your car situated. Listen I need to get these tables set up, but we are having a girl's night this week. I would say I'll bring a bottle of wine, but I know that tone. I'll bring the vodka. You supply the diet coke," Suzie laughed.

"Woman, you know me so well. It's a date. I'll call you as soon as I get rid of Mr. Pain In My Ass and Mr. Bossy Asshole."

"Oh boy, this sounds like it is gonna be a good story. Go handle your business. I got the café. Call me tonight. MUAH!" Suzie made several kissy sounds before hanging up.

I was so lucky to have her and her husband Michael. Outside of Mac and Reid, they were my closest friends.

Come to think of it, after today they were my only friends. Both Mac and Reid were now bumped off my friend's list. The overbearing baboons had slid firmly onto my shit list.

They both thought they could run my life. Wrong.

I was stomping down the stairs, ready to throw a

hissy fit of epic proportions, when I stopped short midway down the stairs.

Reid was kneeling in front of JJ. They were forehead to forehead, one of Reid's large hands on the back of JJ's head, holding him tight.

I could see the tears on my boy's face. JJ nodded the best he could at whatever Reid was telling him. I wished I was closer so I could hear what they were saying. Reid pulled away and patted JJ on the shoulder.

"...you and your mama are safe, JJ, I promise," Reid assured him.

JJ didn't answer. I watched him walk into the kitchen, shoulders hunched forward. He was scared and he didn't believe we were safe.

I was going to kill Jimmy Kelley.

I glanced back at Reid and my breath caught in my chest. He was watching me watch my boy. The look on his face was one of pure torture. He was feeling this; my boy being scared. That quickly took the wind out of my sails. I couldn't begin to summon up the anger and annoyance I had felt only moments before. Reid was trying to keep JJ safe.

"Thank you, Reid."

"For?" he questioned.

"For that." I motioned towards JJ. "For talking to him and wanting to keep him safe. I'm sorry if I was a little bitchy earlier. I am overwhelmed." And scared, but I wasn't ready to say that out loud yet.

I still needed to know what Jimmy was up to and why he was in San Francisco.

"It's not just for JJ," Reid said.

"Oh, yeah right. I'm sure Mac asked you to help too."

I misread the situation. Of course, Mac would ask Reid to help watch over us. He was an overprotective, nosy baboon.

"It's for you, Ava." Reid met me at the bottom of the stairs. He leaned in and pulled my forehead to his, the same way he had done with JJ. "You and JJ. I want you and your boy safe."

I felt his breath fan across my lips, so close, his lips were so close to mine.

He wanted us safe.

FRIEND'S LIST

Reid

With her forehead against mine, I could feel her every exhale. I was literally breathing her in. The fresh scent of lavender filled my senses and my body hardened. The visceral reaction was unstoppable. This was not the time or place, but in all the years I had known Ava I had never touched her, not like this. Not in any intimate way.

My hand on the back of her head fisted her beautiful blonde strands. It took all of my self-control not to tilt her head back and take her mouth. I was desperate for her. The reality of this moment was so much better than my nightly fantasies.

She was trembling, and I could feel the war that raged inside of her. She wanted to melt into me, but she would resist. The cinderblock walls she lived behind would need to be carefully chipped away. Not so fast that she would lock up and run, but fast enough she wouldn't be able to patch the cracks I made.

"Reid," she started.

"I am going to ask you to trust me. I know this is hard for you. You are the most independent, self-sufficient woman I know, but you need help. Let me keep you safe."

"I don't understand what is even happening. Do you think Jimmy will hurt us? Maybe we should just go to Texas for a while." Her voice was low and soft, but she didn't try to pull away.

"That is the worst thing you could do. I need to find out what went down in Texas that made Jimmy run to California. I don't know why he is here yet. Do I think he'll hurt you? Not on purpose, and not him directly. But whoever followed him to San Fran wouldn't bat an eye at hurting you to get to Jimmy. We have a few options. I have a safe house in Ventura or a cabin up north..."

"No," she interrupted. "You have cases. I can't pull you away from your work. You need to be close to your office."

"My cases are not important. Besides, you do realize I have employees that can handle my business in my absence, don't you? You and JJ are more important."

"I can't ask you…"

"You're not asking. I'm offering. More than that, I'm not taking no for an answer."

Was she nuts? Did she really think that my caseload was more important than her safety? Than JJ's?

"Thank you," Ava whispered.

"You keep saying that. Sweetheart, there is no need to thank me. I would do anything for you and JJ."

Her tears were my downfall. I wrapped my arms around her and pulled her to me. She burrowed in, tucking her head under my chin. She was a perfect fit. I held her tight and let her cry into my chest. No words were needed.

The front door opened and Mac walked in, followed by some uniformed cops. Great, the whole fucking nosy block would be talking about this before lunch. The neighbor to Ava's right was a busybody. I'd be surprised if she wasn't out there already in the skimpiest nightie she owned, trying to get information from the cops. So much for keeping this low key. Ava was not going to be happy about being the gossip of the day. If I was smart, I could use it to my advantage to get her off the block and somewhere safe for a few days.

Ava lifted her head and stiffened in my arms. Our moment was ruined and reality rushed back. Before I could stop her, she was out of my arms and marching across the room towards Mac.

Oh, shit! She looked like one pissed off woman.

"Mac, I am going to try and say this the nicest way I can. Back the hell off! I know you're trying to help, but you way overstepped this morning calling Suzie. Del Mar's is my business. Mine, not yours. You had no right making arrangements for my café," Ava shouted, her hands flying out to her sides.

Oh yeah, she was pissed. Mac glanced my way, his eyes pleading for help. I shook my head and looked down, admiring Ava's newly refinished hardwood floors. Payback's a bitch. He was on his own.

"Ava, I was trying to help. This morning has been jacked. I didn't want you to have to worry about Del Mar's. Michael is on duty this morning. He knew about the vandalism, so I didn't think I was breaking confidence by asking your best friend and manager to open so you could handle your house and JJ," Mac tried to explain.

Bringing up JJ was smart. It normally worked. If Ava was the slightest bit mad, you could turn the topic to JJ and she would normally relent. Not today. Manipulative? Sure it was. But with women, especially this woman, you had to use every tool you had to your advantage.

"Not cool. Don't do it again. You should've asked me. I didn't like hearing it from Suzie. One more bonehead move and you're off my friend's list!" Ava seemed to calm down.

"I'm sorry. You're right. Lance is here to ask you a few questions about Jimmy. It shouldn't take that long. I'll call the insurance... I mean, would you like me to get the adjuster out here to look at your car and the front of the house?" Mac caught himself at the last second.

"Baboon," Ava whispered under her breath. "Yes, thank you. Jenny's number is in my phone."

"I've got it in mine," Mac chuckled.

Of course, Mac had it. Mac had the number of every semi-attractive woman in a fifty-mile radius. I had no doubt he knew Jenny... in the biblical sense.

"Mom? Breakfast?" JJ yelled from the kitchen.

Every man in the room laughed at JJ's outburst.

"Crap, I forgot breakfast. Lance is gonna have to wait." Ava started to walk into the kitchen.

I cut her off before she could get very far. "You handle this. I'll get JJ. Breakfast burritos okay?"

She stared at me and her eyes said it all. She was overwhelmed. The stresses of the morning had taken their toll on her. That was completely unacceptable.

I lowered my forehead to hers, so only she could hear me, and whispered, "You're not going to like what happens next. I apologize in advance. I asked you to trust me, this is one of those times."

I straightened to my full height and tucked her in close again. This time when I held her, she was stiff as a board. I didn't know if it was because we were in a room full of police officers or if she just didn't want me to hold her. I was hoping it was the former.

"I'm shutting this down. Ava's done. I'm taking her and JJ to get something to eat, then to my office. Lance is welcome to come there to interview her, but give us a few hours."

Is there something stiffer than a board? Whatever that was, Ava became it after my declaration.

"Copy that, Reid. I'll bring Lance over when I come for my brief. I'll handle Jenny and lock up. Just a suggestion, you might want to go out the back." Mac turned to the cops, "You guys take off."

"Don't I have a say?" Ava asked.

"Nope," I replied.

"But I want a say," she continued.

"Not this time. You're exhausted. You need coffee and little man needs to eat. Both of you need out of this house. There will be plenty of times when I'll ask your opinion or you'll have a say, but this is not one of those times."

"I don't think I like that. No! I know I don't like that. I am not happy about being bossed around and told what I am gonna do," Ava huffed.

If she didn't like that, I'd bet my savings she wasn't going to like what was coming next.

"I'm sorry you're not happy, but sweetheart, right now I don't give two shits if you're mad at me or not. I am more concerned about taking care of you."

"Mom! I'm dying I'm so hungry," JJ whined.

I waited for one of Ava's witty comebacks. I loved listening to her and JJ's banter. It was a thing of beauty when they were together.

Nothing. She remained quiet, just staring at me.

"Hey, little man, get your stuff. We're headed out to breakfast and to my office for a little while."

"Cool. Can I play Minecraft when we get there?" JJ's face lit up. All thoughts of dying of starvation were forgotten.

"That's up to your mom."

"Oh goodie, I get to make a decision," Ava sassed. "JJ, we don't have time to unhook your Xbox to bring with us."

The kid threw me under the bus. "We don't need mine. Reid bought me one for his office."

"He what?"

Jesus H. I couldn't catch a break this morning. Every time I put out one fire a new blaze was lit.

"It's no big deal. There have been times when I had JJ and had to stop by my office. I didn't want him to get bored while we were there. I got the Xbox and a few games. Before you ask, there are no shoot-em-up games," I tried to explain.

"Mom, it's awesome. Reid made me my own office. I have a desk for homework, too. He said that I was an honorary member of the crew. He said that since I was a member of the crew all the guys had to watch my back and I had to be a receptacle man. I want to be receptacle." JJ was bouncing up and down as he told Ava all about his space in my office.

"Respectable. You want to be respectable," Ava corrected.

"Yeah, that. I want to be that. Can we please eat now? I'm still dying."

"Yes. Go get your stuff," Ava directed. As JJ ran up the stairs she turned to me. "You bought him an Xbox and gave him an office?"

"I did buy the Xbox, yes. His 'own office' is a bit of an overstatement. I had one of the guys bring an extra desk into my office and gave him a corner so he could do his homework. I didn't like it when he was in the conference room and I couldn't see him. It's really no big deal." I didn't know which way this was gonna go.

"Thank you. I'm sorry you had to go to all that trouble. I guess I never really thought about how much I asked you for help. I'm really sorry I put you out so much."

I didn't like the far-away look in her eyes. Guilt.

"You're pissing me off, sweetheart. You've never put me out. Having JJ with me is not an imposition and he is never any trouble. I love having him with me. And honestly, I would be mad if you didn't ask me."

"Ready!" JJ came to a skidding halt in front of us.

"Let's go out the back so we don't bother Uncle Mac," I suggested. "Where should we eat? Pinkcos? They have your mom's favorite vanilla coffee."

"Yes! It's Mom's favorite," JJ agreed.

9

BASKETBALL AND PANCAKES

Ava

Reid knew my favorite coffee. He had watched JJ so often that he had bought my son a video game system.

Where had I been? How did this happen, me relying on Reid for so much? Sure, he asked to take JJ to play basketball almost every Saturday I had to work. And if I couldn't get out of the restaurant in time to get JJ from school, Reid, more often than Mac, would watch him until I could leave. I just never realized how much I had asked.

I thought back over the last week. Shit. Reid had JJ three times. It was only for about an hour, but three times Reid had left work to get JJ for me. I was a horrible mother.

After...well, after I became a single mom, I opened

the café so I could make my own schedule. I only served breakfast and lunch so I could close in time to get JJ from school. Me! I was his mother. I should be the one to get him from school. I should be the one to take him to play basketball. Me. Not Reid.

I was failing. I realized I couldn't do this on my own. Too many things came up after I closed; late deliveries, things that needed to be repaired, cleaning, the list was endless.

Much to my mother's dismay, I had used most of Jacob's life insurance to pay off my house and buy the restaurant. She had her financial advisor and investment banker friend try to counsel me on the error of my ways. She had him plan out my financial future, my investment portfolio, and explain why I needed my mortgage interest as a tax write-off. Blah, blah, blah. I ignored their advice and did what I felt was right.

Maybe I should've listened to them. Between my family trust fund and the life insurance, I wouldn't have had to work. At the time, I thought I needed something to keep me busy. I couldn't stay home. I would've sat and dwelled on all I had lost.

"Ava." Reid startled me. "We're here."

"Right." I quickly unbuckled and looked in the back seat. JJ was vibrating with excitement, his smile infectious. I couldn't help but return it. "You ready for some chocolate chip pancakes?"

"I love Pinkcos' cakes. But don't tell Dale. It will hurt his feelings. And he makes me special chocolate chip cakes on Sundays." JJ was referring to the retired police detective who worked in the café on Sundays. He jokingly said it was to give his wife a 'Dale free day', but I'm sure he was a little bored in his retirement. He was also the handyman I used around the café.

"Your secret is safe with me, kiddo. I wouldn't want Dale to stop making you cakes."

This kid!

Thankfully, Pinkcos wasn't that busy and we were seated immediately.

Just as we settled into our seats a spunky, twenty-something waitress came bouncing over. "Hey, Reid. Nice to see you on a weekday," the woman beamed.

"Hi, Melanie," Reid said, giving her a wide smile.

I narrowed my eyes at Reid, then glared at the woman through squinted lashes. Who the hell was she and why did her spunk piss me off so badly?

"What can I get you all to drink?" Miss Bouncy asked.

Before I could answer, Reid ordered for us. "A large vanilla latte, a hot chocolate with extra whip and chocolate sprinkles on it, and a black coffee."

She jotted down our order and flounced off, adding

a little extra sway in her hips. All for Reid's benefit, no doubt.

My mouth dropped open at his audacity. "I can order for myself," I hissed. Yes, I actually hissed at the man.

"No need, I knew what you'd order," he answered.

"What if I wanted hazelnut today? Sometimes I like to change things up."

"Would you like hazelnut today? I'll ask Melanie to change the order."

He was missing the point. "No need to bother *Melanie*. Vanilla is fine," I huffed.

Reid threw his head back and laughed. Jeez, he had a beautiful smile. His dimples were on full display. I had never seen them up close before. They only appeared when his smile was wide and deep. In all the time I had known him, how had I missed how handsome he was when he laughed? He was downright gorgeous. No wonder Melanie was swaying her hips like a cat in heat, trying to get his attention.

Reid leaned close to me and whispered, "You alright this morning?"

"Yes, I'm fine. Why do you ask?"

"Oh, no reason at all." He chuckled again and turned his attention to JJ.

Crap. I had forgotten JJ was sitting across the table

from us, listening to me carry on about drink orders. Where the hell was my head today?

"Have you thought any more about joining the rec basketball team? Summer tryouts are coming up," Reid said.

"No. I haven't asked Mom yet. If I go to summer camp again this year I won't be able to make practices," JJ answered.

Summer basketball? I silently chastised myself for not knowing my son wanted to play basketball. What else was I missing out on? When did I become this mother? The one that had no clue what her own child was doing? Was JJ a latchkey kid without the key?

"I didn't know you wanted to play rec ball."

"I really like playing when I go with Reid, and the coach says I am getting really good. It would be fun but..."

Melanie the hip-swayer came back with our drinks, not allowing JJ to finish his thought.

"Here you are. Do you all know what you'd like or do you need a minute?" Melanie looked around the table.

Reid put his hands out in front of him like he was trying to ward off an attack. Smart man.

I put down the menu. "I think we're ready. I'll have the ham and cheese omelet, extra bacon. JJ will have an order of chocolate chip pancakes with extra bacon as well." When I was done, I glanced over at Reid. It was his turn to have his mouth hanging open. "What?"

"You know how big that omelet is?" he asked.

"Yes. What are you trying to say?"

"Nothing, sweetheart, just wondering. I'll have…"

Miss Know-it-all hip-swayer interrupted, blurting out, "Your usual three egg whites scrambled, hash browns, sausage links, and bacon. With an everything bagel toasted. Got it."

There she went, swishing her ass for all to see.

Trollop.

"Isn't that sweet? Little Miss Melanie knows your order," I said before my brain re-engaged and I thought better of my snarky comment.

"Why Ava, is that jealousy I detect?" Reid spoke directly in my ear so JJ couldn't hear.

"As if!"

Wow! That made me sound like a silly teenager. Jealous? Was I jealous of the beautiful, twenty-something waitress? There was no way, not that I could even remember what jealousy felt like. Reid must've had a screw loose.

"Anyway, please continue what you were saying before we ordered." I motioned for JJ to continue his thought.

"Oh, nothing. I forgot what I was gonna say." JJ

looked down at the table and started ripping little pieces off his napkin.

Reid honed in on JJ's habit of picking at things when he was nervous. "It sounds fun, but... That's where you left off. But what? Are any of the boys giving you a hard time at the Y? Is there something I should know about? I know all of the dads there."

"No. All the guys are great, their dads too. It's just that, there's this fundraiser at the beginning of the season. It's a big one. All the rec teams get together." JJ continued to pick at the napkin.

Had I neglected my kid so much that he thought I wouldn't make time to help with a fundraiser? "Okay, what do I need to do? Bake cookies? Sell those candles or Joe Corbis pizza kits? Whatever it is, if you want to play, I'll help with the fundraiser."

I did this. I had never hated myself so much as I did at this very moment. I was the worst mother in history. I was failing.

"Just forget it. You wouldn't understand," JJ snapped.

My eyes widened in disbelief. Sure, JJ was a normal ten-year-old boy and I got some backtalk, but he had never been overtly disrespectful before.

"JJ!" Reid warned, his tone leaving no room for argument.

JJ pushed his lips together and contorted his face.

He looked as if he had swallowed a whole lemon. "I'm sorry, Mom."

After a moment, Reid continued, "Are you talking about the pick-up game at the beginning of every season?"

JJ pushed the ripped-up pieces of napkin around in front of him.

Reid waited him out, his eyes never leaving JJ's face. The man had the patience of a saint. I wanted to hurry this along. I was anxious to know what pick-up game they were talking about.

"Yeah. The father-son game," JJ muttered, barely above a whisper.

Tears gathered in my eyes and spilled over my cheeks. I angrily swiped them away. It had been years since we had come up against a father-son activity. I was emotionally wrecked from Jimmy's visit and this morning's fiasco. It was times like these that I missed Jacob so much. Not only his physical presence, but also his guidance. He would know what to do in a situation like this. He was the strong one, not me.

Reid spoke softly. "JJ, look at me." He waited until JJ's damp eyes came up to meet his. "I've been waiting to ask you if you would let me play in the pick-up game with you. I know I'm not your dad. I could never replace him, buddy, but I would like to stand in for him if that's all right with you. I didn't want to bring it up to you if you weren't interested in playing, but if that's what's holding you back, I'd be honored to play alongside you. I got your six, remember? You're part of the team. I'll always have your back, little man."

JJ's face lit up. "Is that alright, Mom? I wanna play. Would it be alright if Reid played with me?"

Reid would be *honored* to stand beside my son.

I tried to swallow the lump in my throat and blink away my tears. It was no use. They just kept coming. My shattered heart felt a little less jagged at that moment. Reid had just put a sliver back in place. I was nowhere near whole, but at that moment I was a little less broken.

I opted not to speak, nodding my head instead. In an attempt to cover up my breakdown I used my napkin to cover my mouth.

Damn. In a restaurant, no less.

10

A HUNDRED LARGE

Reid

"Here you are, enjoy. Is there anything else I can get you?" Melanie placed our plates on the table and tilted her head to the side as she studied Ava crying next to me.

I shook my head and gave her a reassuring smile. The last thing Ava would want was any attention drawn to her tears.

"No, we're great, Melanie. Thanks. Is that wife of yours at work today?"

As much fun as it was teasing Ava about her jealousy, and that is exactly what it was, now was not the time nor the place. Melanie's wife, Roni, worked for me as an office manager. If Ava thought Melanie was pretty or flirtatious, she would think doubly so of Roni.

It was ironic. Melanie wasn't flirting with me, she was innocently flirting with Ava.

"Yes. The flu bug seems to have passed, thank the Lord. I was ready to send her to her parent's house," Melanie laughed.

"Bullshit. You love taking care of her," I shot back.

"You're right, I do. I just like teasing her. I don't want her to know how soft I really am. I have a rep to protect. Give her a smooch from me when you see her." She winked at me. "And little man, I snuck you a couple extra pancakes on that plate. Enjoy."

"Really? Thanks so much, Melanie. That's really cool of you." JJ looked at his plate and counted the pancakes.

There was no way he would be finishing that stack.

My phone vibrated on the table. Before I could silence it, the office number came across the screen.

"Yo," I answered.

"How long until you're in the office?" Austin asked.

"Food just got here. Not that long, depending on bridge traffic."

"Shit," Austin grumbled.

"What's the rush? Is Mac there already?" I tried to use a nonchalant voice. I didn't want any added stress on Ava and JJ. They'd had enough for a lifetime.

"There's a hundred large in the duffle."

Shit. Fuckity fuck. I bit the inside of my cheek to prevent myself from uttering a string of colorful language that Ava would no doubt chastise me for using in front of the little ears. Mother shit! Whoever owned that hundred thousand would want it back. This had just gone from fucked to completely FUBAR'd. Fucking Jimmy Kelley would die.

"Anything else of interest?" I asked.

"No dope. There's a notebook you're gonna want to look at. If I'm not mistaken he's running a book."

Christ Almighty, the shit storm kept getting better and better. Gambling. What would be next? Was he running women and guns too?

"Copy that. See you soon. Do me a favor? Make sure that the notebook and anything else of interest are in my personal safe. The rest needs to go in the vault until Mac can pick it up."

"Already done." Austin disconnected. He was a thorough son-of-a-bitch. I was lucky to have him on my crew.

"Everything alright?" Ava seemed to have pulled herself together.

Earlier, when I saw the tears well in her eyes I desperately wanted to pull her soft body into my arms and hold her, comfort her, take all of the pain away from her. But I knew that even if she let me comfort her now, she would be horrified later. Damn if this woman didn't try to do it all. Trying to get her to let me help was like pulling teeth. She was the best mother I knew. She juggled her busy schedule with ease, always cool under pressure. I wondered if she knew how much JJ bragged about her, how much he adored her and looked up to her. Her strength and determination were unparalleled.

"Yep. Austin was just checking in. No need to worry about anything."

"Reid, did the popcorn machine get delivered yet?" JJ asked.

"Little man, if you keep throwing me under the bus like this, I won't be able to buy you anything else." I shook my head and the laugh I was trying to swallow down won out. Damn kid.

"What popcorn machine?" Ava gave me the stink eye and twisted her mouth. She really had the scolding mother routine down pat. If I was honest, it was hot as hell watching her try to reprimand me. *That's a no-go sweetheart.*

"Oops. Umm... nothing, Mama," JJ tried.

"It's nothing. All the guys in the office love popcorn but they always seem to burn the microwave shi...stuff. JJ had a great idea about a commercial popper. It was brilliant. Now I don't have to smell the burnt crap." None of that was true, I hoped that burnt popcorn really did smell bad. The truth was that JJ loved popcorn. He saw the popper machine on TV and said it looked cool, so I bought him one.

"Yeah, right. I can see a bunch of ex-military types and general badasses not being able to handle microwave popcorn. He suckered you, just admit it." Ava's face lit up and she let out a laugh. The kind that brightened her whole face, and made her look carefree. What I wouldn't give to be the one that put that look on her face every day.

"Hey, I didn't sucker him. I just said it would be cool," JJ said while shoveling the largest bite of pancakes I had ever seen into his mouth.

Ava continued to giggle. "He used the look, didn't he? The one where he gives you those big, brown, pleading eyes."

"I was played," I agreed.

Ava was right. When JJ wanted something, he cleverly mentioned it and acted like it was your idea to buy it for him in the first place.

"Popcorn is a healthy snack. No one wants me to starve, do they?" JJ asked, laying on the innocent look.

"Well, after you finish inhaling those pancakes, no one will have to feed you for a week," I joked, pushing my empty plate off to the side.

I must have been shoveling my food in just as fast as JJ had been. I was eager to get to the office. I wanted a chance to look at the contents of Jimmy's duffle bag before Mac got there. I would share information with him, but there were always a few details that I left out. He knew how I worked. Anything that would tie him up in red-tape got left out of my report. I never wanted to put him in a position of having to lie or be charged with evidence tampering.

"So, Melanie's married, huh?" Ava asked.

"Yep, her wife works for me. Roni. You'll meet her today."

"Um." Ava pushed the food around on her plate.

"Um what? Still jealous?" I leaned into Ava. I could pretend it was so JJ didn't hear me teasing his mother, but truthfully, I just wanted an excuse to touch her.

I had waited for what felt like a lifetime to be this close to her. I wasn't going to waste a minute of it. I knew it was only a matter of time before she was buttoned up tighter than a nun again.

"You wish." Ava playfully knocked my arm with her shoulder.

What I would give to know what was going on in that pretty little head of hers. I was happy to see that the tears had dried up and she was smiling.

"I'm stuffed! Next time we come here, I want Melanie to be our waitress again. She's the best. I think she told them to put extra chocolate chips in, too. Is she really married to Roni?" JJ spoke around a forkful of pancakes.

"Yes, her and Roni are married," I replied.

"That's so cool. Roni is really nice and super-hot too."

Ava reprimanded him. "JJ, it's not polite to call a woman super-hot. She may be beautiful, but it is more important that she is kind and intelligent."

"Oh, she is, Mom. She is really smart. I hear her on the phone bossing the guys around. They all listen to her. And she is always nice to me. She sneaks me Jolly Ranchers when no one is looking. But she is still super-hot. I hear the guys say that, too. Austin thinks that she is the perfect woman."

Whelp, JJ heard way more around the office than he should. I'd have to remember to tell the guys to keep their traps shut when he was around. If I wasn't care-ful, Ava wouldn't let me spend time with JJ and that just wasn't an option. I loved the time I got to spend with him.

Melanie appeared next to me and started clearing the plates. "You must be talking about Roni. She has an endless supply of Jolly Ranchers. They are her favorite and she doesn't share with just anyone. You must be pretty special if she sneaks you some. She won't even share with me. You want a box for that, Ava?"

"Sure. Umm, you know my name?" Ava asked, pushing her plate towards Melanie.

"Of course, I do. I've heard all about you from Roni. She loves JJ, thinks he is just the best little kid ever. We've been talking about starting a family. She was reluctant until she started spending time with him. She told me we could have five kids, as long as they're all like JJ. She also told me that you own Del Mar's and you're a fantastic mother—she knows this because your son not only tells her how great you are, but because it shows in how well-behaved he is. She said you were beautiful. She knows *that* because she has seen a picture of you in Reid's office. And, I'd have to say, she was wrong. You're not beautiful. You're stunning. That's about all I know about you."

I really wished that Melanie had left the part about the picture out of her monologue.

"I don't know what to say."

"Nothing to say, sweetie. My Roni makes it her business to know everything about everyone. As a matter of fact, I'm gonna call her now and tell her I got to meet you first, even if it's only by thirty minutes. She's gonna shit bricks when she finds out you're on your way in." Melanie winked at Ava. "I'll box this up for you."

I handed Melanie my credit card in an effort to

expedite her departure. The longer she spoke, the more freaked out Ava looked.

My phone vibrated on the table again, reminding me I had bigger problems than Ava freaking out over my receptionist being a huge gossip.

"Yea?" I answered Austin's call.

"Hey man, sorry to bother you, but you need to get here sooner rather than later. He's here."

"Fu…" I caught myself just in time, "Yep. We're leaving now." I angrily stabbed at the end call button on my phone.

"That doesn't sound good," Ava said.

I battled with myself over telling her the truth or not. On one hand, I didn't want her any more upset than she was. On the other, she needed to know how much danger she was in with Jimmy Kelley being near. In the end, the truth won out.

"It's not. We'll talk about everything when we get to the office. No need to bore you with the details now."

"Okay." Thankfully, she understood why I didn't want to discuss the details in public or in front of JJ.

Melanie came bouncing back to the table with my card. "Here you are. You're all set. It was nice to finally meet you, Ava and JJ. I hope this isn't too forward, but we'd love to have you over for our Sunday family dinner and game night. Roni and I do it every Sunday.

It's a ton of fun and totally kid friendly." She looked so hopeful as she spoke to Ava.

"But we're not family. I wouldn't want to intrude," Ava declined.

"PSHH," Melanie breathed. "You and JJ are totally family. You're Reid's, that makes you family, whether you want to be or not."

Holy fuck. Melanie needed to stop talking!

"Well, in that case, thank you. JJ and I would love to come."

"Great. I'll get your number from Roni and call you, I'm not a texter, I call. Too many emotions are lost in a text, I like personal interaction, not some stupid text, alright, back to work I go, tootles, give Roni a smooch," Melanie rushed out all in one breath.

That woman should be an Olympic swimmer with her breath control. Jesus H., she talked too much.

I stood, and pulled out Ava's chair in an attempt to move things along. "Alright. Well, let's go. Nice seeing you, Melanie." God only knew what Melanie would say next if I didn't stop her. She'd have Ava running for the hills quicker than a jackrabbit on a date.

"Jeez, Reid. We're coming." Ava grabbed her to-go box and purse, motioning JJ to come along.

I could tell by the way Ava was worrying her lip as we walked out to the car, the questions would be rolling in any second now.

"What did Melanie mean when she said 'I am yours'?" Ava asked.

And there it was.

"Who knows? Melanie is kooky, you just have to ignore her half of the time. You don't have to go to Sunday dinner if you don't want to. She can be pushy, too. Kooky and pushy, that's Melanie."

"We'll see."

11

JIMMY FUCKING KELLEY

Ava

There was a whole lot of yelling going on in the conference room.

JJ was showing me around Reid's office, talking about all the cool awards and pictures on the walls, but I was only half paying attention. I was more curious about the yelling. I was trying not to let my temper get the best of me, but I knew they were in there discussing Jimmy. I should've been in there.

"...and this one is of Reid when he was in Iraq," JJ said, tapping a framed photograph on the wall. "It's hard to tell which one is him, because they all have on camo and face paint, but he's in the middle."

My attention snapped to the picture. I knew that Reid had been in the Army, but I had never seen any pictures. He didn't keep any in his house. At least, none that I'd ever seen.

I stared at the picture of him and his team. He looked sexy as hell dressed in his uniform. Where did that thought come from? Sexy? I hadn't said that word in years, hadn't even thought it. What was wrong with me?

I looked at the rest of the pictures. Reid in various locations. In some he was holding his gun, in others, he held an American flag. One picture caught my attention; he was kneeling in front of a pair of boots. A rifle was standing vertically with a helmet resting on top.

"That was taken when his friend Peters died. It's a memorial. You know that black metal bracelet that Reid wears?" JJ asked.

Sadly, I had to think about it. I guess I'd noticed Reid wore a bracelet, but I never really paid attention. God, I was a selfish bitch. I knew very little about Reid's personal life. I had never asked him about his service, or even what his job was in the Army. He knew my favorite coffee and JJ's favorite breakfast. Reid knew every facet of my life and I knew nothing about his.

"Yes, I know the bracelet," I said, stretching the truth a tad.

"That is Peters' hero bracelet. It has his name, where he died, and dates on it. Reid said that he never takes it off. That every time he looks at it, he says Peters' name out loud. He also said that no hero should ever be forgotten, that no one should forget their name. Reid says that's his way of making sure that Peters is remembered." JJ sure seemed to know a lot more about Reid than I did.

Quite possibly that was because, on top of being a selfish cow of a friend, I was a crappy mom who had other people watching her kid all the time.

"Ava!" Mac yelled from down the hall. "Can you come in here?"

"A please might work!" I yelled back.

"Please," Mac ground out.

I could practically hear his teeth clipping as he gnashed them. Jerk! I was still pissed with him about his behavior this morning at my house.

"I'll go into Reid's office and play my Xbox," JJ said.

I needed to count to ten before I entered the conference room; calm my nerves so I didn't fly off the handle at the men who had undoubtedly just made decisions on my behalf. Jimmy was right on one count; they were overgrown apes!

When I walked into the room, five sets of eyes snapped to me. Mac, Reid, Austin, Rick, and Jimmy fucking Kelley.

"What the hell is he doing here?" I screeched.

There was no other name for the sound that came out of my mouth. "Why is he here?"

"Ava, calm down," Mac had the nerve to say to me.

"You want me to calm down?" I yelled back. I stalked towards Jimmy. "You son of a bitch, you showed up at my house drunk in the middle of the night. You pointed a gun at my son. You scared my son, you piece of crap. And you insulted my friend." I threw my arm out, pointing at Reid. "You called him an ape, you asshole. And, and you made my boy cry. Someone needs to kick your ass for all of that." I turned to look at the rest of the room. "Why hasn't someone kicked his ass?" I asked the room at large.

"I'm sorry, Ava. You're right. I fucked up big time. I shoulda' never come to San Fran. I only came to Reid's office to get my stuff back. Tell your friends to give me back my duffle bag and I'll be gone. Promise you'll never hear from me again. I fucked everything up this time, but I need that bag."

"Why? What's in that bag? Is it important enough to point a gun at your nephew?"

"I didn't mean to point the gun at Jacob Junior. He happened to be walking past the couch when the banging outside woke me up. I jumped up and grabbed my gun. It was just instinct. I know I scared him and he dropped his glass. I never touched him. I swear it. I would never hurt my nephew." Jimmy actually looked like he felt bad for scaring JJ. "I just need my bag and I'll leave."

"Enough, you sniveling douche. You're not getting the bag back. It's going down to the station as evidence." Mac turned to me. "Does this belong to you?" He handed me a manila envelope.

I opened the metal clasp and let the contents spill onto the table.

"You no-good prick. My wedding rings? You stole my wedding rings? Is someone please gonna kick his ass?" I didn't know if the tears spilling down my cheeks were from frustration or from the heart-stopping pain of seeing my wedding bands. I had taken them off a year after Jacob died and I'd never opened the jewelry box since that day.

"Wait just one freaking minute. You were in my room? When I was asleep you came into my room and looked through my stuff?" I was back to screaming.

Piece of shit.

"I didn't..."

I cut him off before he could finish. "Liar! Don't you go pissin' on my leg and tell me it's rainin'. You damn well went into my room. Fuck you! Fuck your bag. Fuck you forever. I never want to see your face again. Your brother was right about you. You're no better than your useless, low-life scum of a father. He knew you'd never be any better than the shit you grew up in. Freaking cowardly dick."

I was spitting mad! I couldn't remember the last time I had used that many cuss words at once.

"Ava, I need the bag and I'll leave," Jimmy said. He didn't have the courage to even look me in the eye.

"You're about as worthless as tits on a bull. Are you deaf? You're not getting the bag."

"Oh hell, her Texas is showing. The twang only comes out when she is scary mad," Mac laughed.

I didn't see anything worth laughing about. The whole situation was beyond screwed up.

"They'll hurt you if I don't give them that bag," Jimmy announced.

There was a moment of shocked silence in the room, then everything happened at once. Four men jumped up and moved so quickly that I didn't understand what was happening. Mac had Jimmy on the floor, knee on his back and yelling in his face. Reid was at my side shoving me behind him like a bear was getting ready to attack and he would stand between me and any harm. Austin had his phone up to his ear, already talking into the receiver. Rick had his laptop open, furiously pounding on the keys.

"Austin, I want this building locked down," Reid yelled.

"JJ!" I pushed away from Reid and ran for the door.

I was panting when I threw Reid's office door open with such force it hit the wall and bounced back, almost hitting me in the face.

Just as I stepped in the door I caught a glimpse of a beautiful, petite blonde. She was kneeling under a popcorn machine, but she moved with lightning speed as she drew her gun and pushed JJ behind her.

"Shit, Ava, I'm sorry! You scared me pushing the door open like that. It was natural instinct to draw," she said as she lowered her gun.

"Why me? Why do people keep pointing guns at me? Oh, I know why. Jimmy Fucking Kelley!"

While it might have been natural for Miss Badass over there to draw a gun, it was my natural instinct to stomp my foot and throw a tantrum.

"Swear jar, Mom," JJ chimed in. "That's a dollar for the F word."

"I'll give you a twenty and we'll call it a day."

"What's going on?" the blonde asked, looking over my shoulder.

Reid was right behind me. "We're on lockdown, Roni. Would you mind staying in here with JJ while we finish up? It won't take but a few minutes."

"Sure thing. It was nice meeting you, Ava. Again, I'm really sorry."

"What's wrong, Mama? You look scared," JJ asked, running to me and wrapping his arms around my waist.

I hugged my son tight and tried to be as reassuring as I could. "Nothing, baby. I'll be back in a flash. Everything will be just fine. Let me finish up with Reid and Uncle Mac. Are you cool staying in here with Roni?"

"Yeah, I'm fine. Roni is super cool. She got the popcorn maker all set up. We were gonna pop some and she was gonna watch me play Minecraft." JJ pulled away and smiled. All worries were forgotten when he remembered he had popcorn coming up.

"Awesome. Save some for me." I kissed the top of his head before he ran to the machine. "Thanks, Roni, I'll be back in just a minute. And thanks, for... protecting him."

"Of course. You guys are family. It's what we do."

There was that word again. Family. I hadn't thought about family outside of JJ and I for a long time. The thought of having family around gave me butterflies in my belly. The kind that makes you a little queasy. I wasn't quite sure if it was a good flutter or not.

By the time we walked back into the conference room, Jimmy was back up in his chair. This time he was handcuffed.

Dirty, lying, no-good bastard.

There was so much testosterone in the room I could smell it. I was about to get steamrolled. They wouldn't be able to help themselves. Fixers. They were all fixers, and today they thought they were going to fix my life.

"Before anyone says anything, I have a few things to say." The men in the room stopped what they were doing and gave me their attention. "First. Mac, I am still mad at you about this morning, but we don't have time for that now. Just know that I'm pissed. Don't take over my life again. You ask before you trample."

This next part was hard. But, in light of what was going on, I knew it was necessary.

"I know I am about to get bossed around." I put my palm up to shush both Mac and Reid as they simultaneously started to protest. "Please listen. I now fully understand that Jimmy has put me and JJ in danger. I will not take any chances with my son. I concede. Reid, I will do whatever you tell me needs to be done to protect JJ. I may be stubborn but I am not stupid or reckless when it comes to my son's safety."

I closed my eyes for a moment to gather my thoughts. It stung to look at Jimmy. The Kelley brothers, one a good honest decent man, the other a low life criminal. One dead, one breathing.

God took the wrong one.

"Jimmy, I never want to see you again. We are dead to you. You said that to Mac five years ago when I buried my husband. Now I'm saying it to you. We do not exist for you, we are nothing. You're dead to me. I have never been thankful that Jacob was dead, but in this moment, I'm glad he's not here to see what you've become. This... this would break his heart. I hope you rot in hell, you piece of shit."

I turned to leave. I was emotionally and physically exhausted. "Reid, just tell me what you have planned. I'm going to sit with JJ. One more thing. I'm not staying in that shack you call a cabin. That's a no-go for me. There are copperheads up there. Do you know what happens if you get bit by a copperhead?"

The room erupted in chuckles. Reid cleared his throat to cover his laugh. I was glad I could be so amusing.

"No, Ava, I don't know what happens when you get bit by a copperhead. Why don't you tell me?"

Smartass!

"I don't know either, but it can't be good. Your leg probably swells up and it might even eat away at your flesh. I like my legs the way they are. No shack."

"Alright, sweetheart. No shack. Let me finish with this trash and we'll leave."

I closed the door behind me and bent at the waist to catch my breath.

What was I thinking, allowing Reid to make decisions for us? That was so out of character for me. It was like aliens had taken over the earth. My whole life had been turned upside down. I lived a boring life. Hell, I didn't even speed. Jimmy, that's what happened. And now I needed to protect JJ. Reid was the best way to keep him safe.

With one last exhale, I made my way to Reid's office and plastered my best academy award winning smile on.

"Hey, guys! Watcha playin'?"

"Hi, Mom. I was just showing Roni all the new mods in Minecraft. I made a new house. Wanna see it?" JJ set a gigantic bowl of popcorn on the side table and picked up his controller.

"Absolutely, I wanna see."

Roni moved over to make room for me on the couch and patted the seat next to her, inviting me to sit.

"Thanks," I smiled at her.

"You're doing fine. I know there's a lot to process. When you need to talk, you come find me. In the meantime, we'll just chill and eat some good ol' fashioned popcorn. Extra movie theater butter." She playfully knocked my shoulder with hers and handed me her bowl. It was worth noting that hers was bigger than JJ's.

Extra movie theater butter sounded good.

Reid

"If Jacob would've just minded his own Goddamn business, none of this would be happening," Jimmy muttered under his breath.

"The fuck you say?" Mac shoved out of his seat and was on his feet stalking Jimmy.

"At least uncuff him before you beat his ass," Austin encouraged Mac.

"Mac, sit down." I needed to get control of this before Mac broke Jimmy's jaw. It's kind of hard to get someone to talk when their jaw is wired shut. "Jimmy, explain what Jacob has to do with this."

I caught Rick's attention and gave him a nod. We'd worked together for so long he understood my nonverbal request.

"Nothing. Please just give me my money and let

me leave. Everyone's problems will go away. You'll never see me again."

Mac just growled. He was known around the precinct for having a short temper. The inch of patience he normally had was cut in half when dealing with Ava. This was personal for him. Jacob had been his best friend and he thought of Ava like a sister.

Rick slid his tablet across the table to me, my notes from Jacob's murder investigation pulled up on the screen. I quickly scanned the document looking for any names that jumped out at me.

Alexander Jenkins pled guilty to the murder of Jacob Kelley. The detectives hadn't been able to find any ties to organized crime, drugs, or even petty theft. He was a drifter. I continued to read over my notes, finding nothing of use. I had kept Jenkins at the safe house for two days trying to break him before I handed him over into custody. He gave me nothing. He immediately admitted that he shot and killed Jacob and after that not another word. He was one tough son of a bitch. I wished I could've had another shot at him, but he was killed by another inmate two weeks into his life sentence.

I swiped the screen, bringing up photographs of Jenkins. White male, average height, and average build. Completely unassuming. I swiped again. The next set of images were of his tattoos. I stilled my finger on the screen just as I was about to move to the next page. I enlarged the image and zoomed in on his hand. He had tattoos across his knuckles.

Earlier I noted that Jimmy now had two full sleeves of tattoos and tattoos on his right hand and knuckles.

"Let me see your hands, Jimmy."

"Let me have my bag and I'll leave. You have no idea what you're getting yourself into. I am begging you, leave it be," Jimmy pleaded.

"Not gonna happen. Why don't you tell me about the tattoos on your knuckles?" I asked.

"Leave it. Give me my bag. If that money is not delivered by tomorrow, no one is safe. Why the fuck do you think I came to your office? It wasn't to chat, Reid, I just came here to pick up my bag."

"Who is no one? Who won't be safe?" I needed Jimmy to start talking. We didn't have time for twenty questions. Jimmy was scared and that meant that Ava and JJ were in grave danger.

Jimmy remained silent.

"Austin, pull his hands up onto the table." Best not to ask Mac, he looked like he was ready to kill Jimmy.

With Jimmy's hands on the table, I inspected the markings on his knuckles first. I enlarged the image of Jenkins' even further and, sure enough, they were the same. A thick outline of a diamond with the center empty on his ring finger. The other three fingers had various designs. All crosses, but different markings around the cross. I was most interested in the diamond. This shit just kept getting worse and worse. How had I not remembered that Jenkins had the diamond tattoo?

"Who are you dropping the rake off to?" I asked.

"I don't know what you're talking about," Jimmy said. But he did know. His posture gave him away. He was now on alert. He sat up straight, his jaw locked. He tried his hardest to keep his face blank, but he couldn't control the twitch under his left eye.

"The rake, Jimmy. You know, the money you're transporting. The house's take on illegal gambling. What's the going rate these days? Ten, twenty percent? Who the fuck are you delivering the motherfucking rake to?" I slammed my hands on the table.

Jimmy was dumber than I had originally thought. He remained quiet.

"Okay, you stupid little shit, let me break this down for you. In the five years since your brother's murder, I've learned a thing or two about the Diamonds. Five years ago, they were low-level nobodies trying to make a name for themselves. Naturally, vice would've never made the connection between Jenkins and a bunch of thugs in Texas. I didn't make the connection either. Since then, they have slithered their way up the food chain. You wear their brand. So that tells me that you run with the very men that called a hit out on your brother. That leads to me having to ask, what your role was in his murder? How would a bunch of nobodies in Texas know anything about a San Francisco cop?"

Mac sucked in a breath and it felt like all the oxygen in the room had been used up. The calm before the storm.

"Lock that shit down, Mac. A dead bird cannot sing. And Jimmy, I suggest you start singing. This might be your only shot to save your own life. You'll be lucky if Mac doesn't kill you himself. If he doesn't, I'll put the word out on the street that you gave up Fuentes. That's who's runnin' the Diamonds right now, isn't it? The dumb little fuck tattooed *'Thief in law'* across his damn forehead trying to pretend he's badass. He couldn't even come up with something original, he had to quote a fucking Russian. Can you believe that lame shit? Stupid ass thinks he's as badass as the Vor."

"You wouldn't!" Jimmy yelled and started to thrash around in his seat.

Good, emotion. We were finally starting to get somewhere.

"Why is that, Jimmy?"

"You think you're so smart. You don't know shit. You won't do anything you just threatened me with. If you do, Ava and JJ will die. They're collateral. The Diamonds know everything about them. Fucking Jacob started all of this! I had one delivery to make to

Redding, thought it would be nice to stop off and see my brother. Nosy prick searches my car and finds three keys of coke hidden in the trunk."

"Holy fucking shit. Three kilos." Mac was putting the pieces together. "A week before Jacob was killed, an anonymous tip was called in about some cocaine that was found in an alley. Jacob was the first on the scene, which was odd because we were off duty. He said he heard the call and was close by. There were three kilos."

"Three kilos of my coke. You don't steal three keys of coke without being put in the ground. I told him not to do it. That I would not die because he was a goodie two shoes sellout pig. I told him! He knew I would tell my crew who stole the drugs. Jacob just laughed at me. He was a cocky prick and he thought that stupid badge he wore would protect him. All it did was get him dead."

Rick interrupted. "You need to hear this, boss. Dustin unwrapped all the money bundles. There were trackers in two of the bundles. No doubt it's been tracked. Jimmy's crew knows what a fuck up he is. There is no way they wouldn't've been trackin' that shit on an hourly basis. I would expect more company soon." He closed his laptop.

"Fuck. Just give me the money back." Jimmy was sounding more and more like a parrot.

"Have the trackers been disabled?" I asked Austin.

"Hell, no. Everyone knows better than to disable them here."

Mac tried to get Jimmy to give up something. "Hey, dip-shit, do something right for a change. Give Austin the address in Redding where the money is supposed to be delivered."

"Go fuck yourself, pig. Remember when Ava and Jacob Junior die, just like Jacob did, their blood is on your hands." Jimmy sat staring at the wall.

I had never wanted to kill another man in cold blood before, but at that very moment, I wanted to put the animal in front of me down. He didn't deserve to be breathing. What kind of man allows his blood to be killed? He might as well have been the one pulling the trigger.

"Have Dustin drive the trackers up to Redding. Tell him to leave them anywhere that is abandoned. Reformat the security footage drive, smash it, then take the shredded paper bin out back and burn it along with the drive. Lots of lighter fluid," I instructed Austin then turned to Mac, knowing he was struggling with what he was going to do next. "You do what you need to do. I'm taking Ava and JJ out of here. Roni will be leaving for the day. Austin and Rick are at your disposal. The trash dump is vacant and ready for use. It's yours if you want it. We all have your back, brother. You know I would love nothing more than to help you, but Ava and JJ are my priority."

Mac didn't answer. He didn't need too. I knew that within the hour James "Jimmy" Kelley would no longer be breathing. Justice would be served and another rabid cop killer would be put down. Good riddance.

"One last thing, Jimmy. Who else did you piss off? Vandalizing Ava's house seems like someone just wanted you to know you're being watched. If the Diamonds were here already and they thought you had double-crossed them, you'd be dead."

"I have no idea what you're talking about," Jimmy answered.

"Piece of shit!" With that, I left. I couldn't stand to spend another minute in his presence.

My only concern was protecting Ava and JJ from the shit show Jimmy Kelley brought to town. I knew a way to buy us some time, but I didn't know if it would be enough. The Diamonds had power in El Paso and it was far reaching. Not to mention there was already a threat in San Fran.

I had a call to make before I took Ava and JJ to the safe house. I ducked into Rick's office and shut the door. I needed a burner phone and privacy. I shook my head at all the pictures Rick had taped to the metal storage cabinet in his office. All pictures of him and his girl, April. Them at the park, skydiving, and sailing. I noticed a new one that must've just been taped up. The ring. He had finally proposed. Rick was a lucky man, April was a great girl, a great partner to have in this life. I wanted that.

I powered up the burner and made my call. "Hey, I need a favor. You good with a marker?"

"Room is secure. I'm putting you on speaker. You know I am, what do you need?" the man on the other end of the phone asked.

"You know the Diamonds out of El Paso? Fuentes is running them now."

"I'm familiar with them, yes. They've been moving quite a bit of product out of Juárez, and the eight liners they run are doing well. Illegal poker games are all the rage with the kids these days." His voice was dripping with sarcasm.

A whole new generation of thugs who thought that illegal poker was a new thing that they themselves had just thought up. Fucking idiots.

"Long story, and I will fill you in another time, but they are after my woman and her son. I need them gone."

"How long do we have until they're in San Fran?" a woman asked. *Nightstalker*, one of my oldest friends. We served in the Army together. She was human intel as well, and one badass chick. There was no one I would rather have cover my six than that woman.

"Best guess? Twenty-four hours tops. James Kelley showed up. I have other problems, too. Someone vandalized her house this morning, slashed her tires, looks like a warning. Not the Diamonds style. They don't warn, they just kill," I informed them.

Another voice came on the line. "Motherfucker, piece of shit is like a bad fart. He lingers and stinks up the room."

"Always so colorful, Ghost. I'll send Panther and Breeze out to Texas now, see what they can dig up. You just hold tight and keep that woman of yours safe. I take it you finally claimed Ava?"

"Damn right, I did," I answered.

"'Bout fucking time. No marker. Ava Kelley is off limits."

"Thanks, Viper. Appreciate it, man. When all this shit is over, I'll bring Ava and JJ out to Maryland. I could use a vacation for sure."

"You do that. My door is always open. You keeping this phone open?" Viper asked.

"Yep. My personal cell is powered out. Ava's will be as well."

"Copy that. I'll hit you back when I have something. Stay safe. Out."

Viper disconnected the way he always did, with the last word. Zane Lewis owned and operated the top security contracting firm in the United States. Hell, him and his team had a direct line to the President of the United States. I was lucky to be friends with a man like Zane. This was not a case he would normally take on. This was piddly shit. He ran black ops missions in foreign countries. There were even rumors that he was the one who brought down the dirty CIA director.

I locked my personal cell phone in the safe, pulled out a bundle of cash and a few extra magazines. I couldn't take the chance of using anything that could track my movements. Only a select few would know our whereabouts.

I had heard the laughter before I opened the door to my office. Beautiful! The sound of Ava and JJ's giggles soothed my soul. I loved nothing more than to hear them banter with one another. They were like two peas in a pod. As close as a mother and son could be. I was amazed at how well she was keeping everything together. Damned impressive.

After I opened the door, I couldn't help but to laugh with them. Ava was sitting on the floor cross-legged, making the funniest face I had ever seen as she concentrated on the Xbox screen. She had the controller in her hands at eye level and was moving it around as if that would make the character on the screen go in the direction the controller was moving. Her tiny pink tongue was ever so slightly pushed out, licking her lips as she jerked the controller.

"You do know that no matter how far you lean to the side, the little man on the screen doesn't follow, don't you?" I asked.

"Mom's trying to chop down trees to get wood. We needed more pickaxes. She won't kill the sheep though, even though we need wool to sleep on," JJ informed me.

"I'm not killing the cute little sheep. Or the pigs. I like the pigs," Ava said.

"You guys about ready to get out of here?" I waited for JJ to complain about wanting to continue to play Minecraft but to my surprise it was Ava.

"One more minute, I almost have enough trees."

"I can't believe you're playing that game. You finish up and I'll get Roni squared away." I motioned for Roni to follow me.

"It was great to finally meet you, Ava. Please don't forget to call us about family dinner. JJ, my main man, I'll see you soon. Awesome popcorn makin' skills, by the way." Roni gave JJ a fist bump and followed me to the door.

"It was nice meeting you as well. Thanks again for the chat," Ava called out, never looking away from her game.

Roni knew the drill. She'd been around long enough to understand what was going on without me telling her. "I'll wait for Rick's call and get a clean-up crew out to the cabin. I'll grab a burner cell before I leave. What number did you take? Oh, did someone already handle the security feed?" Roni asked. Gone was the playful woman who had been hanging out with Ava, and back was the professional I knew her to be.

"I took phone three. The feed has been taken care of. Text me when everything is handled. I'll be at the industrial park apartment. Please make sure Mac knows that when he's done." I turned to leave, "And thank you, Roni. I appreciate you taking care of Ava and JJ."

"She's your one, isn't she?" Roni asked, smiling.

"No, *they* are my one. The both of them."

13

IN COLOR

Ava

"Can we stop by the café?" I asked when we got to the car. "I need to pick up the deposit."

"I'm hungry," JJ said from the back seat.

"How is that even possible, JJ? There's plenty of food at the house, little man. Roni stocked it, so I'm sure there'll be lots of good stuff for you," Reid answered JJ. "I'll send Rick or Austin to get the deposit for you."

That was it. The idea of Austin or Rick getting my deposit put me over the edge.

"No, Reid. I have to stop and get my deposit."

I might have agreed to allow him to make decisions for me about where we were going to stay until the whole Jimmy situation was sorted, but there was no way he was making decisions about my business.

He didn't answer, so I tried again. "Is this how it's going be?"

"How what's gonna be?" he asked, only half paying attention to me. His eyes darted around the parking garage.

"What did Jimmy say to you? You weren't acting like this when we went to Pinkcos." I wasn't as naïve as he thought I was. I could see the change in his behavior.

He didn't speak for long moments. He just continued to check his mirrors, navigating out of the parking structure. I was starting to lose patience with his silence when he checked the rearview mirror again.

"JJ?" he asked, an odd tone in his voice.

I looked over my shoulder at JJ. He was playing a video game with his earbuds in. There was no answer.

After a few seconds Reid spoke again. "I'm struggling with how much to tell you. But I think it's important you know a few things. Jimmy is running with a gang in El Paso. He's lost a large amount of their money. They're not gonna be real happy when they find out. He's obviously pissed off more people than just his gang, made evident by your tires being slashed. The biggest problem is that the gang knows about you and JJ."

I swallowed the lump in my throat and prayed I could keep my tears in check. God knows Reid had seen me cry enough for one day. This was way worse than I thought.

They knew about JJ.

"Fuck." I was losing the battle against my tears. I had to clear my throat. "So, it's worse than you thought?"

Reid reached across the center console and grabbed my hand. I closed my eyes to savor the warmth that spread over my body.

"Yea, sweetheart. Fuck about sums it up."

"I'm really scared," I admitted.

"You have to know that we'll keep you and JJ safe. You have my word. Why don't you call Suzie and tell her one of the guys will be in to get the deposit? Also, she's gonna need to cover for you for at least a week," Reid suggested.

Screw my business. At this point, all I wanted was for my son to be safe. I had enough money in my trust fund to live comfortably for the rest of my life. I had never wanted to touch it and give my mother the satisfaction of knowing I needed her money. But if my café had to close down for a week because I didn't have coverage, I would swallow my pride to keep my son safe.

"I don't have my phone. I don't think I grabbed it when we left the house."

Damn, I couldn't believe I forgot my phone. I had a

million thoughts running through my head. My house, JJ's school, appointments I had to cancel, how I was going to kill Jimmy Kelley with my bare hands.

"No worries, you can't use your phone anyway. Use the burner." He motioned to a flip phone in the cup holder.

My eyes widened in disbelief, was that what I thought it was? "Seriously? A flip phone? What is this, a bad 1990's Bruce Willis action flick? It's 2017. You couldn't spring for the new and improved pay-as-you-go smartphone? You know they have those now, right?" I couldn't stop the laugh that broke free.

I didn't know why I was laughing as hard as I was. It really wasn't that funny, but I couldn't stop. All the nervous energy that was bottled up inside of me bubbled up and exploded.

"You done yet?" Reid chuckled.

"I don't know... Sorry... I must be exhausted, that just hit me the right way. I can't stop." Another round of laughter exploded. The harder I tried to stop, the more I laughed.

I blew out a breath and tried again, "Okay, I might be done. Sorry."

Reid kept sneaking sideways glances at me. He was smiling so wide both his dimples were out again. Wow. Twice in one day. I let go of his hand to grab the phone, leaving his now empty hand to rest on my thigh. I jolted at the sensation. He gave my thigh a squeeze and I tried to ignore the tingling that was traveling up and down my body. For the first time in five years, I felt alive. All my nerve endings were rapid firing, coming back to life.

"You remember how to use one of those? You have to flip the cover open and use actual buttons to make a call," Reid joked.

"I think I can manage this relic. The first thing we're gonna do when this is all over is upgrade your burner phone selection. This is truly pitiful. You, being the badass investigator you are, cannot be seen with low-tech gadgets. It has to be bad for your street cred," I quipped.

"Ah, funny girl. Tell you what, when this is over, you'll have full access to Rick's burner stash. Make all the upgrades you'd like."

I opened the phone and dialed the café.

"Hello, Del Mar's. How may I help you?" Suzie answered.

"Just the person I needed to speak to. How's the day going, sweets?" I asked.

"Oh fine. Jam packed all morning, you know, the normal. The lunch rush was just as crazy. Al called about the delivery. He was missing the eggs on the order. I called Ginos. They had the twenty-five dozen you ordered, those have been delivered, better price too. Other than the eggs it has been smooth sailing. I am finishing putting the last of the order in the walk-in and I'm outta here."

Thank God for Suzie. She was an awesome manager.

"Thank you so much for handling everything for me. Listen, I have a huge favor to ask you, and if you can't do it I'll understand." I felt horrible having to ask for her help.

"Anything. You know that," she replied.

"Well, I'm not... with everything going on, I won't be able to come into the café for about a week."

"A WEEK?" she interrupted me, "What's going on? Are you okay? Where are you? What do you need me to do?"

"We're fine. Reid is handling everything. I don't really think I should get into any details at the moment or over the phone. But I promise I will tell you everything soon. I was wondering if you could cover for me the next seven-ish days? I can't come in at all."

"Reid, huh? Nice, 'bout time that boy pulled up his big boy britches and made his move. I'll cover Del Mar's. Don't worry about anything. I take it the plain clothes cop sitting in the corner drinking cranberry and sprite all morning is because of your...situation? Hold on, that cop is knocking on the front door he may have left something, don't hang up."

What in the Sam hell was she talking about? Big boy britches? Making his move? She along with everyone else had gone kooky.

"Sorry, I'm back." She sounded out of breath when she picked the phone back up.

"I have no idea why there is a cop in the café, I would assume that is Mr. Bossy Asshole's doing. He is in overdrive this morning. I'll ask Reid to talk to Mac about it. And thank you for taking over. You have no idea how much better I feel knowing that you'll handle my business."

"Where are you going?" Suzie asked.

"Umm, I'm not really sure."

That was a weird question, she was married to a cop, she knew better than to even ask.

"Right, I'm sure Reid has plenty of places to put you."

This conversation was getting stranger and stranger.

"Hey, you alright? If taking over the café is too much, it really isn't a problem. You really should ask Michael anyway."

"Nope, everything is peachy. Listen I'll let you go. I love you, Ava. Please remember that. Be safe."

Suzie disconnected before I could say anything else.

"Everything alright?" Reid asked.

"Yea, she just sounded tired and a little stressed. A busy morning at Del's will do that to you. Oh crap, I forgot to tell her about the deposit."

I tried to call back but there was no answer.

"Damn. Oh well, she must be in the walk-in and can't hear the phone. It can go into the bank tomorrow, I guess."

"Austin can swing by and get your keys and alarm code. He can make the drop tonight."

"Okay, I really do need it to go in tonight. I wish I could tell you not to bother him, but I can't have checks bouncing."

"We're here. Let's get settled and I'll call Austin."

I didn't understand. We were in the warehouse district. There were no houses around here. Reid drove up to what appeared to be a loading dock. The large, industrial metal door rolled up, and Reid drove in.

The space was huge and completely empty.

"Um, are we staying here? There's nothing here. I don't mean to sound ungrateful, but where are we going to sleep?"

"You'll see. Wake JJ up and we'll go upstairs."

I glanced behind me and sure enough, JJ was asleep. "Wake up, little man. We're here."

JJ stretched and yawned. When his eyes opened, he pressed his face against the window and looked all around.

"This place is so cool! Reid, can we come back so I can ride my rollerblades in here? I bet I could go really fast in here."

"Tell you what, I'll ask one of the guys to bring you over a pair," Reid offered.

"Oh, no. No more buying JJ anything. He has a pair of brand-new ones at home." Reid had to stop spoiling him. I didn't want JJ to get used to getting everything he wanted. We had rules and chores. If he wanted something extra, he had to earn it.

"They can go by the house and pick them up," Reid said.

I didn't believe that for one second. There was not a snowball's chance in hell that Reid would take the chance of someone being followed from my house to here.

"Sure..." I let my words hang.

"Come on, let's get upstairs. I wanna show you around." Reid got out of the car and waited for JJ and I to follow.

The place was huge. We navigated through a series of doors and hallways, then made our way to the service elevator.

"This is way cool. I've seen these kinds of elevators in the movies. Can I pull the door down? How does it go up?" JJ rushed into the old elevator.

Truth be told, I was a little worried. It didn't look like this elevator had been serviced in about forty years.

"It's safe," Reid whispered in my ear. "Here, little man, let me pick you up so you can reach the handle."

Reid picked JJ up and helped him with the door. I watched as Reid explained how the elevator worked and pointed out the pulleys. Thankfully, the elevator stopped when Reid started to explain the physics behind how the lift worked. JJ was still a little young to grasp Newton and Einstein.

"Holy wow! This is totally radical! I love this place. Can I go check it out?" JJ was already running in the direction of the wall of windows.

The upstairs was wide open. It was straight out of an HGTV renovation show. Modern kitchen, concrete floor, whitewashed brick interior walls. It was absolutely the coolest apartment I had ever seen.

"I've only had this place a little over two weeks. The security systems are still not fully installed, but it is the only safehouse I have in the city. It has never been used, so I am not concerned about the location being compromised," Reid explained. "Come on, I'll show you around."

"This is really great, Reid. Thank you again for letting us stay." I followed him further into the huge room and noticed the partitioned off area to the left of the entryway. "What's over there?" I asked.

"The bedrooms, bathroom, office space, and a vault," he answered.

"A vault? Why in the world would you have a vault in an apartment?"

"It was here when I purchased the property. During the demo and renovation, I asked my contractor to leave it there. The guys will retrofit it as a panic room."

"Gotcha."

The severity of the situation hit me yet again. I was in a safe house, potentially hiding to save my son's life. I hated Jimmy fucking Kelley. I hoped he rotted in hell for all of eternity for putting JJ in danger.

The rest of the afternoon was uneventful. We hung out and played Uno and Monopoly. And more Uno. I could almost pretend that we weren't locked away in hiding. Reid and JJ joked and laughed. I was surprised how natural it felt. A couple of times Reid brushed up against me or squeezed my leg when I won a round. I wasn't sure if it was a "way to go, bud" kinda squeeze, or if he meant more by it.

By the time I had put JJ to bed, my head was spinning. I was so confused. I was analyzing everything Reid said, every move he made, every thought I had. This was new to me. Why was I so worried about why Reid was doing what he was doing? When we were making dinner, his chest brushed against my back when he reached for a glass in the cabinet above me. Was it on purpose? Did I feel him flex his hips more than necessary? I was obsessing over every last detail.

A five-year fog had been lifted and suddenly things were in color. My life had been monochrome for so long I had stopped feeling anything. The only joy I had allowed myself was my son. I had seen him in color, but everything was bland and boring. I had been faking my way through life. Why was I questioning Reid's every motive now? Maybe it was the fear and stress. Maybe everything would be back to normal by tomorrow; me living my life with blinders on, not noticing anything or anyone around me.

Only, I wasn't sure I wanted that anymore. Maybe I wanted to feel again; feel the tingling when Reid touched my leg, or the way my breath caught when he put his forehead against mine. Maybe I had been wasting my life away because I was afraid.

"Do you want to watch a movie?" Reid asked from the living area.

I was drying the last of the dishes. Reid told me to leave them, but I needed to do something to burn off nervous energy. If I was at home, I would've had the entire house cleaned by now.

"Sure, whatever you want is fine with me," I shouted back.

I swear the apartment needed an intercom

installed. It would be easier than shouting room to room.

"Are you almost done?" he asked, suddenly right next to me.

My heart skipped a beat and I jumped at his close proximity. I hadn't heard him come into the kitchen. My hip banged against the counter, causing me to lose my balance. Just as I started to stumble, Reid reached out and caught me, pulling me tight against his body.

I closed my eyes and savored his strong arms around me. When I opened them we were face to face, a mere inch separating our lips. I wondered what his lips would feel like pressed against mine. Would he be gentle and soft, or would his kiss be hard and demanding just like he was? I wanted to know. This might have been the most uncharacteristic thing I had ever done. I was not bold and I was not brave, but right there and right then I had to know.

I lifted up to my tippy-toes, giving me the extra height I needed to lean in and press my lips to his. His full lips were soft and gentle. He didn't move a muscle as I gave him the first experimental peck. I pulled back a centimeter and licked my lips before I tried it again, this time with a little more confidence. I brushed my lips against his. He met me halfway and added his own peck.

Wow.

My body was alive, flooded with sensations I had long ago forgotten. I was hot all over from one chaste kiss. He pulled me in tighter, not allowing our lips to pull apart. I could feel his erection on my stomach. I wasn't sure if that scared me or excited me more. Emboldened by his reaction, I licked the seam of his lips, begging him to open.

His tongue brushed against mine in a timid swipe, almost as if he was testing the waters. He had not moved other than to pull me closer. He made no attempt to deepen the kiss or to rush me along. He was allowing me to control the pace. As much as I appreciated what he was doing, I needed him to take over. I didn't know what I was supposed to do next.

"Please, Reid," I whispered against his lips.

"Are you sure?" he asked as he licked my bottom lip.

"Yes."

14

MINE

Reid

Her soft plea was all I needed. One hand went low on her back, locking her in place. The other worked its way up her back and into her silky hair. My fingers massaged the back of her scalp until my need took over. With a soft tug of her hair, I tilted her head to the angle I needed and thrust my tongue into her mouth. The meet and greet was over. All niceties flew out the window the minute she gave me permission to kiss her. It was my turn to take.

I had waited and longed for this moment for years. Her lips were pillow soft. She tasted like desire, need, and hunger all rolled into one. It was a flavor I wanted to savor for the rest of my life. The soft noises she was making made it so hard for me not to take this any further. Her kiss was perfect. Our tongues danced and my cock begged for me to take her. I slowed the kiss and sucked her tongue into my mouth. One more small nibble to her bottom lip and I broke the kiss. Ava continued to peck the corners of my mouth. I allowed her to explore and loosened my grip on her hair. I had no doubt her desire would be pooling in her panties.

The thought of her pussy getting wet from my kiss was heady. My cock was throbbing in my jeans. One more brush of my cock against her hip would have me exploding in my pants. I couldn't wait to have her naked and spread out before me, mine to touch, to lick, and own.

Soon.

The first crack in her fortress had been made. I needed this first chip to be deep and lasting. Strategically placed for maximum impact. As badly as I needed her, she wasn't ready. I had already taken advantage of the stressful situation, any further than this and I would never forgive myself.

The loud shrill of my phone broke the moment. Normally, my phone was on vibrate, but, in light of the situation, I couldn't afford to miss a call.

Ava pulled back and opened her eyes. I was worried I'd see regret. She smiled at me and I was elated to see the gleam in her eyes. Her hair was beautifully tousled and her lips were swollen and red. My heart swelled and I beat back the urge to pound on my chest like a Neanderthal. I caused that. I mussed up my woman and reddened her lips.

"Go. You better get that. It could be important," Ava suggested.

With one last peck on her lips, I reluctantly let her go and went in search of the still ringing phone.

"Reid," I clipped.

It was Roni. "Hey, boss, Sally Levenson from the medical examiner's office called. She said it was urgent. I also wanted to update you. Rick and Austin are on their way back to the city and the cleaners are en route to the garbage dump. Rick took phone one, Austin took two, and I have four," she informed me.

She was damn efficient and, not for the first time today, I was thankful to have her.

"Shit, I forgot about Sally. I'll call her back. Thanks for the update. Can you please ask Austin to go to the café and pick up the deposit? He knows what bank to drop it at. Any issues taking out the trash?"

"Nope. Everything is five by five, boss man. I'll let Austin know. Speaking of Ava, how's your woman holding up?" Roni's nosiness knew no bounds. She might be asking under the pretense of concern, but I knew her. What she was really asking was had I made any progress with Ava this evening. She wanted the intel before anyone else.

"Everything is five by five," I threw her own words

back at her. "I better call Sally. If she's calling me after hours, it must be important."

"Right. Have a good night," Roni drew out the last word in a singsong voice. The call disconnected and I shook my head. Nosy broad.

I could feel her before I could see her. The invisible tether that had always tied me to her was even stronger now. Clichéd? Yes. Made me sound like a pansy-assed-pussy? Probably. Did I give two shits? Fuck no.

"I have to make one more phone call. Pick out a movie and we'll watch it when I'm done."

Her hand on my back alleviated any fear I had about her regretting our kiss. The soft touch was reassuring and comforting. I loved that she was freely touching me.

"Is everything ok?" she asked.

I turned to pull her into me, bending down to gently touch my lips to hers. A soft peck on her lips was all that I could allow. My need to take her was great and my control was holding on by the thinnest of threads.

"Yea, sweetheart, everything is fine. I have to call the coroner back about a case. No worries, though." I gave her one more peck and pulled back. I wanted to gauge her reaction to our newfound closeness.

"Alright, go make your call. I'll wait to start the

movie." She made no move to pull away from me. "Are you okay?" She tilted her head to the side and studied me.

"I am more than fine. I am fucking fantastic. How are you?" I asked.

She closed her eyes and breathed in deep. After a long exhale, she answered. "I am more than fine, too. I'll be honest, I'm not sure exactly what is happening here. I'm a little scared and a whole lot nervous. I'm not real good with people and reading between the lines."

The message alert on my phone beeped, breaking the moment once again. Fucking phone.

"Go. Handle your business. I'm fine, I promise." She pulled away from me and wrapped her arms around her middle.

That bothered me, I didn't want Ava in a protective posture. I unwrapped her arms and held both hands.

"We'll finish this conversation after I make my call. Everything will be fine. We'll take it one step at a time. Nice and slow. The only thing I want you to promise me is that you won't run. If you get scared, we talk about it."

"Okay, I can do that."

I pulled the phone out of my pocket and read the text:

on my way to handle the deposit. Mac has your whereabouts. Trash is handled -A

Perfect. One less thing for Ava to worry about. I knew she was putting on a front that she would be okay if she had to close the café for a few days. The rent on that place had to be a mint. The café was in an upscale area. It would be devastating for her if she had to shut down for any amount of time. I wouldn't let that happen if I could help it. Her world was already turned upside down because of Jimmy Kelley. I'd be damned if she lost her business because of him, too.

I dialed Sally's personal cell phone. I doubted she would still be in her office.

"Sally Levenson," she answered.

"Hey, Sally, it's Reid. Sorry to call so late, but Roni said it was urgent."

"Hey, thanks for calling. It's been a day." Sally exhaled loudly.

"Don't I know it. Whatcha got for me?"

I grabbed a pen, and looked around for something to take notes on. A to-go menu caught my attention. That would have to do for now.

"I've got a weird one for you. I'm sorry to bother you, but Mac's not answering his cell. This one pushes weirdness to the nth degree."

That was weird. Mac always picked up when Sally called.

"It'll be hard for you to top the cloves, Doc."

"You'd think. But you'd be wrong," she said with a sigh. "This guy was stabbed in the gut. It's what killed him. But the freak who did it...I dunno...but he poured condensed milk into the wound."

I absentmindedly jotted down notes as she spoke. The fuck, *condensed milk?*

"Condensed milk? Are you sure? Like the perp opened the wound and dumped milk into his stomach?"

"I didn't believe it myself. And at first, I thought it was just poured over the wound. But no. This whack job stabbed the victim, opened the wound, and funneled that shit into the body. I've never...I mean never, seen something like this. It's beyond freaky. It's Hannibal Lecter insane." Sally sounded as perplexed as I was.

"First, we have a body with cloves shoved down the throat, and now this? Do you think we could have a serial killer on our hands?" I asked.

"I don't know, but I'm scared. Serial killers are methodical. Practiced. They have rituals. There's nothing really similar between that addict and this guy. The girl was strangled, then stabbed. This guy took a knife to the gut. It could be? But it's not typical."

"Remind me again, the cloves were placed in her throat postmortem correct?"

"No. She was alive. She breathed them in sometime before death. This guy was most definitely dead...or dying. There's no way to tell," Sally corrected me.

Something was wrong here. I underlined the words, cloves and condensed milk. I needed to remember to have Austin run another search.

"So, other than both victims having some sort of food placed in the body right before they died, or as they were dying, we don't have any other connection. I gotta tell you, Doc, that is one hell of a coincidence. I don't like this. When do you think you'll have your report ready?" This wasn't a coincidence, but I didn't want to freak the doctor out any more than she already was. For now, I would keep my opinions to myself. Besides, it was best I talked to Mac before I made too many assumptions.

"I'll finish it up tonight and shoot it to you and Mac. I agree, it's weird. That's why I wanted to talk to you. Call me if you need me. I might not answer right away. I've got plans this weekend, but if you need me, just shoot me a message."

"I appreciate the heads up. Plans, eh? Wouldn't happen to be with Derek from the cafe?" I taunted her.

That reminded me, Austin said he'd run that check on Derek Lemar. He came back spotless. No priors, independently wealthy, it seemed he was well respected in his circle. He also supported the arts which I knew was a big deal for Sally.

From the very first case she worked for us, Mac and I both took an immediate liking to her. A few years back, I'd thought Mac was going to ask Sally out. Then, in a passing conversation, Sally mentioned her husband had passed away. I watched Mac's eyes cloud over in pain, and much like he did with Ava, he now religiously watched over Sally.

There was one issue that Austin said he wanted me to look at and had emailed me a dossier on Derek. Now that it sounded like Sally would be spending more time with Derek, I would have to look back over that email. I should've felt bad for prying into her life, only I didn't. When Sally was in her role of ME, she was commanding and competent. But, when Sally was just *Sally the woman*, she was shy and reserved. It was a shame, the woman had no clue how beautiful she was.

"Ha! Don't be prying into my life. Not unless you want me asking you about that waitress you had your eyes on," she ribbed me back.

So, Sally did catch me staring at Ava's ass yesterday at the café.

"Touché. Have a good evening, Doc. Enjoy your weekend."

"You too, Reid. Goodnight."

I quickly disconnected the call and tossed the

phone on the kitchen table. Clove buds in the Jane Doe's throat? Condensed milk, in vic number two's gut? Something told me that this shit was going to get worse. Doc wasn't lying, this was creepy as fuck. As perplexed as I was about the dead girl in the alley, I was eager to get back to Ava. I scribbled a few more things I wanted to remember on the menu and left it on the counter. I would worry about cloves and milk tomorrow.

Tonight, I wanted to concentrate on Ava, and Ava only. I was still reeling from our kiss. I wanted more of those. I was desperate to touch her again, feel her soft body pressed against mine. I wanted to hear more soft moans as she lost herself in our desire.

I found her curled up on the couch with a far-away look in her eyes.

"A penny for your thoughts?" I inquired.

"Crap, you scared me. I didn't hear you end your call. Everything okay?" she answered.

It didn't escape my notice she had changed the conversation to me.

"Nothing that can't wait a few days. Did you pick out a movie?"

I didn't want to push her to talk, but I wouldn't allow her to curl into herself and try to close me out.

I sat in the corner of the couch and pulled her close to me, forcing her to stretch out her legs. I wanted her close. I wanted to touch her as much as possible. If I wanted to have any chances of breaking down her walls I couldn't allow her to go into her own head.

She rested her head on my shoulder and relaxed into me. We sat there in silence so long I thought she had fallen asleep.

"Tell me about the Army?" she asked.

That was the last thing on earth I thought she'd ask about. In all the years I had known her, she had never asked me a single personal question. I doubt she even knew I had a brother.

"Not much to tell, really. I started out as infantry, got recruited into a scout unit my second year in. When it was time to re-enlist, I changed my MOS to human intel. I served eight more years and got out."

There was no reason to bore her with all the details. I didn't want to fill her head with all that I had seen during my deployments. Hell, I didn't want most of the memories in my head either.

"Tell me about your bracelet?" she whispered.

My body stiffened and my breathing picked up before I could stop myself. Peters. He died saving my life. He should be here, with his wife and son.

"Another time," I answered.

"Sorry, that was rude. I shouldn't have asked. I just realized today at your office I don't know anything about your past. I'm sorry I have been such a selfish bitch. I've been walking around like an ostrich these last five years." She paused and took a deep breath. "But I want to know. I want to know everything about you. You already know everything about me. I think…I think I'm ready."

She was ready. Thank fuck! It was time for me to open up to her just a bit.

"Peters. That's who this bracelet is in memory of. I promise to tell you the story another time. But he died saving my life. I was injured in a firefight, he rushed out from behind cover to pull me to safety. When he did a sniper…a sniper…he was killed."

I couldn't bring myself to say the words 'head shot'. Peters was shot in the head while trying to pull me to safety. It is amazing what your mind will protect you from remembering. For years and years, I had wished I could remember the moment Peters died. I thought if I couldn't remember that moment then I wasn't honoring him or he would be forgotten. When my nightmares started, bits and pieces slowly came back.

Then I wanted nothing more than to forget the memories of my best friend's head exploding in front of me. Brain matter hitting me in the face, me covered in his blood. All because he wanted to save my sorry ass. His son was an orphan because of me.

"I'm sorry, Reid. Thank you for sharing him with

me, and with JJ. He thinks your bracelet is real special. Thank you for that, for showing him what a hero is."

I was a little choked up and at a loss for words, which was a first for me. I didn't know what to say to that.

"I don't say it enough, but you have to know I appreciate you and everything you do for me and JJ. I couldn't ask for a better role model, you and Mac both. I know how much he loves you."

"I love him too, Ava. I would do anything for him."

"I know you do, Reid."

The phone rang again. Someone better have cut off a Goddamn arm. Or they'd better be bleeding, at least. The fucking interruptions were killing me! Every time Ava started to open up, the phone ruined the moment.

"I'm sorry, sweetheart, I have to get that."

She shifted her weight so I could stand and I instantly missed her soft body tucked into me. I was going to kill whoever was calling.

I snatched the phone off the table and brought it to my ear.

"What?" I growled.

"Fuck, Reid! We have major problems. Suzie's down, she's barely breathing. I have a bus on the way. Michael has been notified and is on his way," Austin said, out of breath.

"The fuck?" I roared. "Where?"

"Del Mar's. I came in to get the deposit. The door was locked but, the alarm wasn't set. No sign of a struggle in the dining room, kitchen is clean too. Ava's office is a mess. Suzie fought like hell. She's beat to a bloody pulp. Money was still in the deposit envelope on the desk, with more cash on the desk. This wasn't a robbery. Rick is on his way to you to sit with Ava. You're needed here."

"Motherfucker! Shit. Okay, ETA on Rick? Has Mac been notified?" I asked.

"Five minutes, tops, on Rick. No, I thought you'd better call Mac," Austin answered.

"I got Mac. Out."

"What happened? Who's hurt?" Ava asked.

I shouldn't've been surprised she heard that conversation. I wasn't exactly quiet.

"Sweetheart, I need you to take a breath. I'm not gonna lie. This is gonna fucking hurt, but you need to know." I took a deep breath myself. "Suzie has been badly beaten."

Please, God, don't let her ask me details.

"WHAT?" she screamed, "Where? How? How bad?" She was rapid firing all the questions I didn't want to answer.

"Ava, baby, calm down."

"Don't call me that. Don't ever call me that again. That is not yours. I'm not your baby." I was surprised by her outburst.

"Okay, Ava. I won't, but I need you to calm down."

Her tears were killing me. I wanted to pull her in to me and hold her, but I was afraid to. "I don't know who did it or why. She has been beaten, that's all I know. There is an ambulance on the way now."

"Where is she? Was Michael there? Is he okay?"

"Michael is on duty tonight. He's on his way to her now."

"You're not answering me, where is she?" she tried again.

Fuck.

"At the café," I answered.

She launched herself at me and wrapped her arms around my neck. I hugged her back as tightly as I could and let her sob into my neck.

"It's all my fault. She is hurt because of me."

"No, Ava, it is not your fault."

My phone beeped in my hand. I flipped it open and held it up to see Rick's message without letting go of Ava. He was in the garage downstairs.

"Rick's here, Ava. He's gonna stay with you and JJ while I go to the café."

"Please, don't go," she begged.

"Sweetheart, I have to go and check on Suzie and the café. Rick will be here, you're safe."

I heard the lift doors open and Rick walked into

the room. He looked like he was getting ready to kill someone. When he saw Ava in my arms, he quickly softened his scowl and stopped in the doorway.

"You're right, you need to check on Suzie. I want to go to the hospital," Ava said, wiping her face and nose on my t-shirt.

"Okay, sweetheart. When she is settled in, I'll see what I can do," I lied. There was not a chance in hell she was leaving this safe house, but there was no reason to argue with her now.

"Please hurry, Reid." My heart was breaking seeing her in pain, but knowing that she didn't want me to leave her made me the happiest I'd ever been.

"I will. Promise." I quickly kissed her before she could pull away.

I didn't give a shit Rick was in the room. I didn't care that I could taste her tears. I poured every ounce of my soul into that kiss. I couldn't say the words yet, but I wanted her to know that I loved her.

"Please be safe, Reid." She rested her forehead on mine, the same way I had done to her and JJ earlier at her house. "I need you to come back to me safe."

Just as I was about to promise her I would, it hit me. She had been promised a safe return in the past. Only, he didn't return.

"Ava, listen to me. I swear to you; I will do everything in my ability to be safe. I will be back as quickly as I can."

"I know you will. I trust you," she whispered.

I pulled away and walked to the door, I passed Rick with a chin lift, no words were needed. He would protect my woman. And my boy.

That's what they were, even if she didn't fully understand yet.

My woman, my son. They were mine.

15

THE PAST COMES BACK TO BITE

Ava

Reid had been gone for hours.

I tried sitting in the living room with Rick, making small talk, but I couldn't do it. My nerves were frayed. I finally gave up and came back to cuddle with JJ. I tossed and turned, waiting for JJ's soft breathing to lull me to sleep, but it wasn't working.

Reid called to check in with Rick and give him an update. Rick's responses were clipped and short, his side of the conversation gave nothing away. When Reid got on the phone with me, he told me that Suzie was at the hospital and Michael was with her. She wouldn't be allowed visitors tonight. He asked me a bunch of questions about Suzie and if anyone had given her a hard time, or if someone had threatened her. Of course, no one had.

The last twenty-four hours played in my mind. How had this become my life? I turned onto my side and willed myself to go to sleep. My mind would not turn off as I thought about my last conversation with Suzie.

Shit.

I threw the covers off and ran into the living room.

Rick flew off the couch and reached for his gun. "Damn, woman, you scared me," he chastised.

"The plainclothes cop!" I blurted out. "Did Mac stick a cop in the café?" I asked.

"What? Today?" Rick asked.

"Yes, today. Did Mac order a cop to sit in my café all day today?"

"Not that I'm aware of," Rick said, his phone already out of his pocket.

"Last time I talked to Suzie she was checking in the rest of today's order. She said that there was a plain clothes cop sitting in the corner all day today. He just sat there drinking cranberry and sprite. She didn't bother with him because she figured Mac had ordered it. She's a cop's wife, she knows better than to blow someone's cover," I rushed out. "And then she asked me to hold on because the cop was knocking on the door, she thought he had left something. When she got back on the phone she sounded different. I missed it. She knows better than to ask where Reid was taking me. Shit, Rick, she sounded scared."

"Did Mac order an undercover to sit on the café today?" Rick spoke into his phone.

"Shit, Reid. Ava said Suzie told her there was a plain clothes cop sitting in the café all day." He paused a second. "No, Suzie didn't give her a name, just said that he sat in the corner drinking cranberry and sprite." Another pause. "Yep, he also came back after Suzie locked up, she let him in." Rick walked to the windows and looked out. "Fuck, Reid. I hear you. I've got Ava. See you soon."

Rick pocketed his phone, and looked at me. "You did good, Ava. That was good information."

"What did he say?" I asked.

"Mac didn't order an undercover, neither did Michael. They're gonna ask around," Rick said.

Shit, shit, shit, this was not good news. I was praying I was overreacting.

I heard the elevator come to a stop and started to run towards it. Thank God Reid was back. I needed him. I didn't want to but I did.

"Ava! Get in the room with JJ. NOW!" Rick whisper-yelled.

"What, why? Reid's here," I said, taking a step back.

"No, he's not. He's at the hospital. No one is

supposed to be here. Get JJ and get in the vault. Hurry."

Rick had his gun drawn and pointed towards the elevator. I turned to run when I heard the gunshot.

I winced at the sound. My ears instantly started ringing. Another shot rang out and I had to close my eyes at the sound. I covered my ears with my hands, trying to get the pain to subside.

I dropped to my hands and knees. I had to get to JJ. As soon as I uncovered my ears to crawl, the ringing was back. I looked over my shoulder as I started to crawl. Rick was on the floor, blood pooling around his head.

"No!" I cried. "No, no!"

I tried to move, but my body was no longer going forward. Someone had grabbed my foot. I tried to kick the hand off but their grip tightened. I turned to my back and tried kicking with both feet.

"Carl?" I screamed. "What the fuck?"

"Be still, Ava." He twisted my ankle. God almighty, that hurt.

"What are you doing?" I was still struggling to get away.

"Stop moving," he demanded.

"Are you fucking nuts? You killed Rick."

I kicked as hard as I could and made contact with

his stomach. I took advantage of his momentary shock and yanked my foot out of his grasp.

I twisted and got to my feet, making a beeline to Rick. I needed his gun. It was on the floor next to his body. Blood. There was so much blood. I needed that gun.

Please, God, keep JJ in that room.

"I wouldn't try that bitch, or I'll shoot you here and now. Then I'll kill JJ," Carl sneered.

My blood went cold and my heart was pounding in my ears. I was paralyzed. Did I go for the gun? Did I risk JJ's life?

Ava, baby, don't move.

Had I completely lost my mind? I closed my eyes and tried to shake my dead husband's voice from my head.

"Good choice." Carl walked over to me, shoving his gun in my back and grabbing my arm with his free hand.

"Why are you doing this, Carl?" I didn't understand what was going on. Carl was a cop. He was Jacob's first partner when he joined the force.

"Oh, come on, baby, I know you've been waiting for me. I remember how you looked at me and flirted with me before Jacob knocked you up," he scoffed. "I know you wanted to be with me, but then Jacob trapped you with that brat and you had to stay with him. But I will not have you tramping around now."

"What the hell are you talking about?"

"It's okay, baby. I understand. You needed to raise the kid. Well, he's old enough now to be without you. Mac can have him. We can be together now." He licked from my jaw up to my ear. "I have been patient and waited, but I will not have other men showing up in the middle of the night."

I shook at the disgusting feel of his nasty tongue on my face

"That's right, baby. I know you like that. It's our time now." He misunderstood my shiver, sick bastard. "That man showing up at your house last night made me very angry."

"You've been watching me?" I felt like I was going to throw up. "You... you vandalized my house?" I asked.

"It's time to go, baby. No more chit-chat." Pain radiated from the base of my head and down my spine.

Please, Reid, help me.

My world went black.

16

IRON CLAW

Reid

Something was wrong. Very wrong. Rick wasn't answering his phone. Mac and I were in Mac's SUV racing to the safe house. Austin was following behind.

After Rick's call, Mac and I tried to find out who had been sitting on Ava's café and why. We had nothing to work from. 'Cranberry and sprite' wasn't a whole lot of information. No physical description, no name, nothing. Cranberry and fucking sprite.

After what seemed like hours we pulled up to the warehouse apartment. Wordlessly, exiting the vehicles, we were perfectly in sync as we navigated the emergency stairwell without a sound, our weapons drawn and ready. At the top of the stairs I stopped, placing my ear on the door that led into the apartment. No sounds. I cracked the door open and waited. Still nothing.

We entered the apartment and white-hot rage shot through my body. Rick was lying in the middle of the floor, blood pooled around his head.

"FUCK!" I roared. All of my training flew out the window. I did the worst thing I could've done and ran for the bedroom. I had to find Ava and JJ.

I entered the room Ava and JJ planned on using. Empty. The bed was a mess, the sheets and comforter half off the bed. My heart rate spiked, someone was going to die for this.

I heard Mac and Austin yell "clear" from the other room.

Fuck! Gone! They were gone.

Falling to my knees, I grabbed my head and screamed.

"Reid?" I barely heard the whisper.

"JJ?" I called out. "Where are you, little man? It's safe." I quickly swiped my tears away.

I watched as JJ crawled out from under the bed. Fuck. I forgot to check under the bed.

As soon as he cleared the bed he jumped into my arms and started screaming for Ava.

Mac and Austin rushed into the room. Austin stopped short when he saw me shake my head at him. His shirt and hands were covered with blood, the last thing I wanted JJ to see.

"I want Mama," JJ cried.

"I know, little man. We're gonna get your mom." I held my own tears back.

"He took her. She was crying and there was gunshots."

"Who took her, JJ?" I asked.

"Carl," he answered. A fresh wave of tears started.

"Do you know Carl?" I continued to question JJ.

"No. I was at the door listening. Mama called him Carl. He yelled at her that they could be together now. He said that my dad knocked her up."

"Wait, he mentioned your dad?" Mac asked from the door. He was vibrating with anger.

"Yes. He said my dad knocked her up and made it so she couldn't be with him. I wanted to help Mama, but my dad told me to get under the bed and hide."

"Your dad?" Mac asked.

"Yes, Daddy told me to get under the bed and hide. He said that's what Mama would want me to do." JJ stopped and pulled my head to his and whispered in my ear, "You believe me, right?"

"Yes, little man, I believe you. I believe your daddy was protecting you tonight. You did the right thing."

"I didn't help Mommy," JJ admitted.

"Yes, you did. You did exactly what your mom wanted you to do. You stayed safe. You also listened and gave us all the information we need to help your mom."

"Are you going to get Mama, Reid?"

"Yes, little man, I am. First, I need you to do me a favor. I need you to stay here with Uncle Mac..."

"No. No. No. Don't leave me, Reid. Please don't leave me," JJ blurted out.

I knew it was killing Mac that JJ was clinging to me and not to him. He was JJ's uncle in every way. He was Jacob's best friend.

"Little man, I need to make a phone call. I'm gonna step right outside the door."

"Right outside the door where I can see you," he demanded.

"Yes," I agreed.

JJ climbed off my lap and sat on the floor.

I got to my feet and approached Mac. "Who's Carl?"

"Carl Allen. He was Jacob's first partner. Jacob fucking hated Carl. Not only is he a shit cop, but he was always making lewd comments about Ava. Jacob kicked his ass then asked for the reassignment. He was my partner after that," Mac explained.

Motherfucking douchebag.

I pulled out my phone and dialed the only person I knew would help with no questions.

"Yo," he answered.

"Damion, it's Reid. Marker."

"Whatcha need?" he asked.

"Tonight Carl Allen killed one of my men and took my woman, had my boy hiding under a bed."

Before I could even finish he was mobilizing.

"Iron Claw, let's ride." I heard yelling and grunts in the background. "Where we headed?" he asked.

"I'll have an address for you in a minute. I'll meet you there."

"No, Reid. You stay clean. Your woman and son are gonna need you. We got this. Family, bro."

"Appreciate that, brother. But I know you heard me. This motherfucker came into my house, killed my man, took my woman, and scared my boy. I will be the one to slit his fucking throat."

"I hear that, we'll wait for you, my men are ready."

"Copy that. Out."

I disconnected and glanced at Rick. Fuck.

I closed my eyes and gathered my thoughts. How had tonight turned to such shit? A few hours ago, I finally had my woman in my arms. Now she was gone, and I'd been outsmarted by a Goddamn psychopath.

"Here's Carl's last known address. Start there, and I'll work with Dustin to find any other locations he could've taken her to," Mac said as he walked up beside me.

"The motherfucker beat Suzie, knowing that one of my men would lead him right to Ava." I blew out a breath trying to hold in my temper. "How could I have been so damn stupid? He had to have been watching. How in the fuck did we miss that?"

"This is not on you, Reid. None of us thought about that. We were all concentrating on Jimmy." Mac tried to make excuses for my lapse in judgment.

"FUCK!" I roared. "If one hair on that woman's head is hurt his death will be slow and painful."

I watched as Austin covered Rick's body with a bed sheet. He died trying to protect my woman. Another good man dead because of my inadequacy.

As much as I wanted to be here when Rick's body was picked up, I had to get to Ava.

"No one call April. I need to be the one to notify her." I instructed, referring to Rick's fiancé.

"You ready?" Austin asked.

"Almost," I answered him. I turned to Mac, "I need you to take care of my boy."

I didn't give two-shits at the moment if I offended him by my statement. I didn't have it in me to care about hurt feelings.

"Not even a question. You know I will," Mac replied.

I walked back into the room to JJ. He was sitting on the floor, rocking back and forth. Jesus Christ, how was I going to leave him? In all my life I had never been so torn. JJ needed me, yet I had to find Ava.

"JJ." I waited for him to look up at me. As soon as

he did, he was on his feet running to me. I caught him when he hurled himself into my arms.

"Did you find her?" he asked.

"Thanks to you, we have a good place to start. Uncle Mac is gonna take you somewhere safe so I can go get your mom," I told him.

"No! No Reid. I want to be with you," JJ yelled. He grabbed my shirt with both of his little fists and pulled me to him. "Bad things happen when you're not here," he whispered.

"I want you to listen to me carefully, little man. Uncle Mac will not let anything happen to you." I didn't know how to make JJ understand I had to be the one to get Ava. "I love you, JJ. You and your mom are the two most important people in the world to me. I would never leave you with anyone I didn't trust with my life. Do you know why?"

JJ shook his head no.

"Because you and your mom are my life." I waited for him to digest what I had just told him. "Your mom needs me right now. I need you to do me a favor and go with Uncle Mac. I promise I will bring your mom to you as soon as I have her."

"You promise?" JJ asked.

"Yes, son, I promise. I will get your mom," I assured him.

"Okay, I'll go with Uncle Mac."

Mac was standing in the doorway and spoke for the first time, "Come on, JJ. Let's get out of here, buddy. Reid will be home in no time with your mom." Mac tried to smile at JJ, but it looked like a cross between a scowl and grimace.

I knew Mac was feeling this almost as badly as I was.

Mac took JJ's hand and started to lead him out of the room when JJ pulled free and ran back to me.

"I love you, Reid." JJ wrapped his arms around my middle.

"I love you too, little man."

I closed my eyes and hugged him back. *Please God keep him safe.*

With a chin lift, Mac and JJ were out the door. I heard the elevator squeal to life and knew they were gone.

"Let's roll," I yelled to Austin.

I'm coming for you Ava Kelley, and when I find you, you are mine...

17

HUSH

Ava

I slowly cracked one eye open, then the other. Unconsciously I blinked trying to get the gritty, sandy feeling to subside. *What is wrong with me?* Lying there in the dark, my eyes open but unseeing, I tried my hardest to focus on my surroundings. It was difficult to concentrate with my head throbbing and the metallic taste of blood in my mouth. I was definitely moving, and I had no control over my body as I swayed with the motion. Bile rushed up. I quickly swallowed it down as I struggled to move my arms and legs. Nothing worked, I couldn't move. Panic surfaced, my breathing was rapid and choppy. My body jerked, and my head slammed into something hard, pulling me from my fog.

Memories came rushing back. Carl. Gunshots. Rick dead. JJ! I hoped to God that Carl didn't find JJ and take him too. I moved around as much as I could in the confined space to check if I could feel anyone else in here with me. Nothing. I was alone the best I could tell.

The smell of rubber and musk filled my senses. Trunk. I was in the trunk of a car.

"JJ," I whisper-yelled.

I strained to hear anything over the loud swooshing of tires rushing over the asphalt. I blew out my breath in a long sigh when no one answered. I had to believe that Reid had found JJ and would keep him safe until I could get out of here.

The car came to an abrupt stop, rolling me to my side. My head once again banged into something hard. If I didn't have a concussion before the trunk ride, I certainly had one now. Excruciating pain bloomed on my forehead, traveling behind my eyes and temples. Sweet mother of God that hurt.

I heard the car door open, I had a choice to make. Did I pretend I was still unconscious or did I scream my head off as soon as the trunk opened? I remembered what Jacob taught me; if I ever needed help from a crowd of people always call out, "fire." He drilled that into my head over and over. Onlookers will always turn to see a fire, but if you called out for help, most of the time people didn't want to get involved and would ignore you. Sad, but true.

I never thought I would ever be in a situation where I would need to test that theory, but there I was, locked in the trunk of psycho Carl's car. I had no idea if I would be in an area where someone would even hear me.

The door slammed, and I was down to milliseconds, I had to make my choice.

Hush, Ava baby. Don't make a sound.

Jacob!

The truck opened, and cool, crisp, fresh air hit my face. I kept my eyes closed, and my lips sealed tight. It was harder than you think, not screaming and fighting once the trunk was opened. And when I was lifted out and thrown over Carl's shoulder it was even harder not to bite him and spit in his face. But my hands were tied, literally tied, behind my back and my feet were bound. I was completely and utterly defenseless. Jacob was right. I needed to wait, be patient, and my opportunity would arise where I could take him off guard.

I opened my eyes when I was securely in a fireman's carry, and Carl couldn't see my face. My field of vision was limited from the angle. But what I could see was familiar. It was my house.

Carl kidnapped me and took me to my own house? Was he crazy? Reid and Mac would find him straight away. Well, of course, he was crazy, only a crazy person kills someone and kidnaps another.

I heard keys clinking and the sound of metal sliding into the deadbolt. Where on earth did he get keys to my house? Reid and Mac were the only two people who had spare keys.

He had keys to my fucking house!

My mind was racing with all sorts of sick scenarios. Had he been in my house when I was sleeping? Did he let himself in when I wasn't home? I tried to think if there was ever a time something was missing or out of place. I was coming up empty. But Carl was a cop, and if he had been in my house, he would know how to leave without a trace.

He gently laid me down on my oversized couch and went to work untying me. Perfect, when these bindings came off, I was going to claw his eyes out. Never in my life had I wanted to inflict so much pain on another person. Not even Jimmy. And Jimmy was a despicable human being, but I just wanted him out of my life for good. I never wanted to see him again. And after Mac takes him to the station and has him processed, I never would. That chapter of my life was over.

I couldn't stop the tears from falling when I thought about poor Rick. His fiancé was going to be devastated. I knew that feeling all too well. Losing the person that you thought you would grow old with. I knew what it was like to have everything stolen from you, there would be no raising children together, no watching the man you love walk his daughter down the aisle, no grandchildren to spoil. All of her hopes and dreams would be ripped from her hands and her heart. She will be left with nothing but a fractured half-life.

"Oh good, you're awake. We're home now," Carl said as he licked the tears off my cheek.

Disgusting pig.

I remained quiet, I didn't know what I was supposed to say or do in this situation. My legs were still bound, I couldn't do anything but bide my time.

"Eva, will you please bring Ava a glass of water? And I want a Sprite with a splash of cranberry," Carl yelled. "You must be so thirsty, and we cannot have that." He brushed my hair out of my eyes, and his face came into focus. His nasty breath skirted over my face and I flinched at the foul odor. Either he didn't notice my grimace, or he knew he had stink mouth and didn't care.

And who the hell was, Eva?

"I am so happy you finally get to meet my wife, Ava." Carl smiled brightly.

I didn't know if he was addressing me as *his* wife, or if he was saying he was happy I finally got to meet his wife. Either way, this man was a few tools shy of something or other. I didn't know how the saying went, and I didn't really give a shit at that point. Carl was crazier than I thought.

I waited for someone to bring me a glass of water or answer back, but no one did. My feet were almost undone, and I was fast losing my cool. I needed to know if there was someone else in the house before I made my move.

Hush, Ava baby. Just wait.

"I see that look in your eyes, Ava," Carl snarled. Whoa! Talk about a change of mood. "Don't even think about trying to leave me. If you run, that son of yours dies."

"No, Carl I wouldn't." I tried to placate him.

"Yes, you would, you lying bitch. You have a lot to make up for. I have waited a long time, and you should be grateful. I let you raise that little bastard child until he was old enough for you to pop your titty out of his mouth. Now he's someone else's problem."

That was it. I couldn't hold it in anymore.

"Fuck you! You crazy piece of shit. You're delusional if you think there has ever been a time I ever looked at you with any kind of attraction. I loved my husband. And only my husband. And if you ever call my son a bastard again I will fucking kill you, do you understand me?" I screamed back.

"Fuck me?" Carl smacked me across the face, and blood immediately started pouring out of my nose into my mouth and onto my couch. "Watch your dirty little mouth before I wash it out with soap. Where is Eva? Stupid woman. Now you need to clean up. Get up."

Before I could get myself off the couch, Carl had me by the arm and was yanking me to my feet.

"Good there you are, go and get Ava some clean clothes. And hurry up next time, would you?" Carl said.

I looked around the room, but we were alone. Who the hell was he talking to?

Let it go, Ava baby. Don't make him angry.

I bit my tongue to prevent myself from calling Carl out on his crazy. I was beginning to question who was actually crazier here, me or Carl? After all, I was the one hearing my dead husband.

After being pulled up the stairs, undressed and pushed into the shower, I stood under the lukewarm water horrified. Wasn't it now I should've been fighting? Carl was distracted, having some make-believe argument with an imaginary woman. But I was afraid. He seemed too agitated, frantic even. If he still had the gun from earlier, I needed to wait until he was asleep, or not so anxious. I needed the upper hand. If I could just play along for a little while and get him to drop his guard I could figure out a way to call for help or get out of here.

Just wait. They're coming.

"Stop being a jealous bitch and get my wife some clean clothes," Carl yelled.

Holy shit, we had both lost our minds. I was officially crazy too.

"Are you ready for me Ava? I have waited too long to consummate our love. The time has come, I get to finally have my wife," Carl said as he stepped into the shower stall with me fully nude. His small erection pointing right at me.

I couldn't stop the tremors from wracking my body when he reached for me, there was no way this man was going to touch me.

"Don't fucking touch me! You'll have to kill me before you put your filthy hands on me," I spat out.

"Funny, Eva said the same thing. But she quickly learned her place." Carl grabbed a fist full of hair. "You will too, my beautiful bride."

18

RIVERS OF BLOOD

Reid

I watched Mac leave with JJ, and my heart was literally pounding in my chest. I didn't want JJ out of my sight. I know that made me a dick, Mac would always protect JJ, but it felt wrong watching them leave. I had to get the hell out of here and find Ava.

"Let's roll," I yelled to Austin.

I looked around the loft again, Rick's dead body was still lying on the floor covered with a sheet. The blood stain was like a beacon not allowing me to forget that Rick gave his life for my woman and son.

I was being pulled in two different directions. I wanted to be the one to handle Rick's body. He was more than an employee, he was a close friend, and I didn't leave men behind, ever. I owed him the respect of personally taking him to the medical examiner's office.

The only comfort I had was I knew Rick, he would want me to go after Ava. Hell, if my sorry ass was lying on the floor dead and his woman was taken, I would expect him to leave me and go after his woman. Yet, I still couldn't stop the guilt.

What a cluster fuck. I am so fucking sorry, Rick.

My phone vibrated in my pocket, in my haste I fumbled the phone and almost dropped it. I needed to calm the fuck down and get my head right. My woman needed me, and I would be of no use if I was clumsy and unfocused.

"Yeah," I answered.

"CCTV shows Carl's car turning onto Ava's street," Dustin answered.

"The fuck? You sure?" I asked.

"Absolutely. I dialed into the security cams outside your house. And sure as shit, the dumb fuck took Ava to her own house." Dustin paused. "Reid, he carried her into the house over his shoulder. She looked unconscious. I texted Mac and told him to keep an ear out, in case any of the neighbors call it in. Hopefully, everyone on the street is already asleep."

"Goddammit. Thanks for the update, Austin and I are on our way there now. I have to call Damion." I quickly disconnected the call.

My hands were shaking as I dialed Damion. What if Carl had already hurt Ava? What if he had already killed her, or... the more my mind played the what if's, the more my hands shook. I was going to rip Carl's balls off and feed them to his crazy ass.

She needs you calm, Reid.

My body locked tight. I hadn't heard that voice in over five years. I quickly glanced around the room then at my phone to see if maybe I hadn't disconnected my call with Dustin.

She is safe for now. Go and get our girl.

Please, Jacob, keep her safe.

I must've lost my mind, talking to my dead friend, but, at this point, I was willing to do, or try, anything to keep my woman safe. Even if that meant pleading with her dead husband.

"Damion, Carl was spotted at Ava's house. We can't all roll up in the neighborhood. Those bikes of yours can wake the dead. You know the Mountain Lake trail behind the house?" I asked.

"I know the trail. I will get some of the guys to hang back. You got an idea how long they been there?" Damion asked.

I moved to the elevator where Austin was already waiting for me and stepped in.

"Hour tops. I'll wait for you, we'll go in together. I'll be there in ten," I told Damion.

"On my way. Don't fuckin' roll in there on your own dammit. You don't know what kind of fucked up shit he's doin'," Damion instructed.

I closed my eyes and prayed to God, Carl was not doing any of the fucked-up shit Damion was talking about.

"Copy that. Out." I disconnected and shoved my phone back in my pocket.

"We got this, Reid," Austin said. "She'll be fine. You know that we all have your back, and Ava's. I guarantee you will have your woman in your arms in the next twenty minutes." Austin tried to calm me down as the old elevator vibrated as we descended.

"Twenty fucking minutes too long, Austin. You know what he can do to her in twenty minutes?" I asked, still thinking about what Damion said.

"You can't do that to yourself. Ava is smart and strong. She will do everything she can to keep herself safe until you get there. She knows you're coming for her."

I knew what Austin was trying to do, I also knew that Ava was a strong, smart woman. But, Carl was a lunatic, completely unhinged, and I couldn't predict what someone like him would do. He could be torturing her right now, or he could simply be trying to play house. I had no idea what his intentions were.

"Why do you think Carl brought Ava back to her house?" I asked once we got into the car.

"Who the fuck knows why that piece of shit is doing anything he is doing? What you cannot do is drive yourself crazy trying to get in his mind." Austin stopped for a minute, and I was worried this was bringing up bad memories for him. His sister was taken by her ex and held for a day. She'd been raped repeatedly during those hours. Just the thought of that happening to Ava made me want to rage and put my fist through the windshield.

"Listen," Austin continued. "I know this is only going to worry you more. But, I also know if I don't tell you, you'll put your foot up my ass when you find out."

"Find out what?" I asked. I snuck a look at Austin, but in the dark, I couldn't make out his expression.

"Dustin sent over Carl Allen's file. He had a girlfriend, Eva Martin. They dated for just over a year. Apparently, Eva's parents got worried last month when they hadn't heard from her in over a week and called around asking if any of her friends had seen her. No one had. They've filed an official missing person's report. The local detective's notes say that the Martins' called Carl. He told them that he and Eva had broken up, and that Eva had told him she was going to move home to Tennessee. But she's never shown up in

Tennessee, and there is still no trace of her in San Francisco."

"Fuck!"

This shit just keeps getting worse.

"What do you think? Did Eva leave him and then he snapped? Or did he kill Eva and go after Ava as a replacement?" I wondered out loud.

"I don't know. We don't have a whole lot to go on. Without more information, I can't give you anything more than a gut feeling. And my gut is telling me Ava has always been Carl's end game. That Eva was a stand-in until he could get to Ava," Austin theorized.

"Why?" I hated not having all the information. I loathed going into a situation without a plan of attack based on up to date intel. I trusted Austin and was interested in why he thought Carl wanted Ava.

"I briefly skimmed Jacob Kelley's request for a partner change. Either Mac didn't remember this or Jacob never told Mac. But, Jacob found pictures of Ava in Carl's locker. The pictures were taken without Ava's knowledge. They were all candids of her; at the grocery store, walking into the gym, her going to work. Creepy stalker shit. The Captain questioned Carl, but he explained it away by telling the Captain that he thought Ava was cheating on Jacob. Carl said he took those pictures while he followed Ava to get Jacob proof of the affair."

"How in the hell is this sick bastard still a cop? Christ almighty, he is a complete fruitcake. The SFPD better hope to God that my woman is not harmed. This shit is whacked."

I pushed on the gas and wished I was in my Camaro LZ1 rather than the Rover. I finally turned onto West Pacific Avenue and followed it until it dead-ended at the Mountain Lake Trail. Three Harleys were parked next to the guardrail, I wasn't sure how Damion and his guys got there before me, but I was grateful. Austin and I would have to take the last three blocks on foot.

I slammed the Rover into park and jumped out, not even bothering taking the keys out. I tapped my right hip to ensure my Sig Sauer P226 9mm was secured in my holster as I took off in a full sprint.

Damion, Trig, and Blaze were waiting just outside Ava's side yard fence. Goddamn, they looked like a bunch of scary motherfuckers. Each over six feet, all of them wore full beards, add their black leather cuts and guns, and no one in their right minds would fuck with them.

As I stepped in front of Damion, he pulled me into a one-armed bone crushing hug.

"You straight?" Damion asked.

"Yep," I stared into my brother's eyes.

He studied my face, nodding his head when he

found what he was looking for. "We take front. You got back. Meet in the middle. You see anything call that shit out."

"Copy that." We didn't waste any more time on pleasantries. "Austin, follow me."

We hopped the low cinderblock wall that separated Ava's side yard and the running trail that ran between the golf course and the housing track. I checked back over the wall, Damion, and his guys were already out of sight.

As Austin and I silently made our way around the house, I noted the living room and kitchen lights were both on. I tried the kitchen door, and it was locked. Austin continued, moving ahead of me and around the corner of the house. I heard a whistle and hurried around the corner to find Austin picking the lock of the slider. So much for being quiet.

Austin had the sliding glass door open just enough for us to slide through. I gently closed the door behind me and cleared the kitchen to my right, while Austin went left into the main room. Both of us turned and leveled our weapons when we heard the front door crack open.

Damion strutted into the living room, his guys following closely behind like he owned the fucking room. No regard for finesse or trying to be quiet. He didn't give the first fuck if someone heard him or not.

In his world, if he entered your house you are dead anyway, there wasn't a need to be sneaky.

I stopped at the couch, and white-hot rage coursed through my veins. There was blood on the cushion and floor.

"They are just droplets, Reid," Austin said. "Cool your shit. That is barely a bloody nose." He tried to be reassuring, but even a single drop of my woman's blood was too much.

A loud crash above our heads, had us all looking at the stairs. I started to take off, but before I could take my first step a large hand wrapped around my bicep, bringing me to a stop.

Damion shook his head before he whispered, "Don't do nothin' stupid. We don't know what we're up against and you don't want nothin' to happen to her. Stay focused."

Fuck he was right. My head was all over the place. I had to play this smart before I screwed up and got someone else killed. I blew out a breath and allowed my training to take over. I knew better than to rush in. Ava needed me, on point and focused.

"Austin, you stay down here with Blaze. Trig, Damion follow me." I started towards the stairs. "One more thing, Carl is mine."

"Heard that. Trig, you secure the area once we move in. I'll look after your girl. You do your thing."

"This goes without saying, brother, but you…"

Damion cut me off before I could finish. "Believe me when I say that I'd take a bullet for somethin' you care about," Damion reassured me.

No further words were needed. I knew Damion would take care of my woman. I was going to gut this fucker, and the last thing I needed was Ava seeing that.

Another crash upstairs pushed us into action. With Damion and Trig right behind me, we bolted up the stairs. Ava's bedroom door was open, and I could hear water running. I threw my hand up over my shoulder motioning for the guys to wait. I slowly stepped into the room and peeked around the corner into the master bathroom.

Carl was naked on the tile floor struggling to find purchase with the shower curtain half wrapped around his legs. Ava was fucking naked on her knees trying to scramble away.

"Don't fucking touch me, you disgusting pig," Ava yelled.

"Motherfucker!" I shouted.

I felt Damion at my back, vibrating with anger. I knew my brother well, this was not going to play out as planned. Once he was in a rage, there was no stopping him. Your only hope was to pray you are not on the receiving end of his fury.

"Son of a bitch!" Damion roared.

Before I could even register what was going on, Damion stepped around me and had Carl by the hair, pulling his flailing body across the wet floor away from Ava. The sound of bone cracking rang out right before the sickening thud of flesh hitting tile.

"Get her outta here, Reid! This motherfucker is meetin' the basement at the clubhouse," Damion said.

"Oh shit. Blaze is gonna like that," Trig added.

Before I could protest reminding Damion I was taking out Carl, Ava untangled herself from the mess on the bathroom floor and launched herself into my arms. The force of the collision had me taking a step back. Trig grabbed a wet towel off the floor and draped it over Ava's back covering her naked body.

"I got you, Ava. You're safe." I hugged her to me tightly. "Thanks, man." I gave Trig a chin lift.

"I knew you'd come," Ava whispered. "I knew you'd come. Where's JJ?" Ava continued to shake in my arms, and for the second time that evening I was torn. Ava needed me, but every part of me wanted to rip Carl's dick clean off his body and make him choke on it.

"Safe," I answered.

My woman had been naked on the floor with a crazy man.

Take our girl home, Reid. She needs you.

Jacob was right. I had to take care of Ava, and JJ.

All thoughts of Carl's torture flew out the window. My woman was my only concern.

"Trig, get this motherfucker out of here." Trig moved to get Carl's body off the floor while Damion wiped the blood off his fists.

"Don't worry sweetheart, he won't be comin' near you again," Damion told Ava.

Ava stiffened at Damion's voice. She was in shock, and I doubted she'd even realized there were other men in the room. "Damion? What are you doing here?" Ava asked.

"Your man will fill you in later. Let's just say it's family lookin' out for each other."

I squeezed Ava tight and turned to my brother. "Rivers... you hear me D? I want rivers of blood."

Damion laughed, "You know me better than that, Logan. There will be oceans."

"Appreciate it. I owe you."

"You don't owe me shit. Family, brother. Family."

I knew Damion would handle Carl. There was no doubt he'd be praying for death long before he drew his last breath.

With a lift of my head, I turned to leave. "Wait. You gotta cage here? I got someone coming to pick up Carl's car out front unless you need it, and I can leave Austin here if you need another driver."

"I got this brother. I always come prepared. Take care of your girl. Let me handle the rest."

"Of course, you do," I laughed. I pulled a throw blanket off the end of Ava's bed and tossed the wet towel back on the floor and started for the stairs. I wrapped the blanket around Ava's back and made sure she was completely covered. "Close your eyes sweetheart, I'll have you outta here in just a minute."

"I knew you'd come," Ava repeated.

"Always," I answered.

I jogged down the stairs with Ava still in my arms and found Austin and Blaze covering their posts. One at the front windows looking out, the other at the rear sliding door.

"George already came and got Carl's car. Do I need to call clean up?" Austin asked.

"No, Damion and his crew will handle it from here." I turned to look at Blaze. "My brother has a present for you upstairs. Toy with the motherfucker for me. I want him begging for you to end his miserable life."

"It will be a pleasure," Blaze answered. His features hardening when he saw Ava wrapped around me. "Your girl okay?"

"No. But she will be," I answered honestly. Ava was trembling in my arms, her face was already bruising, and I still didn't know why she was in the shower in the first place.

"You want me to pull the car around?" Austin asked.

"No, I want her outta here now. I'll carry her back to the car."

"I knew you'd find me," Ava whispered into my neck.

"I will always find you."

19

IN COLOR

Ava

He came.

Reid found me, and just in time. I didn't know how much longer I could've fought Carl off. I swallowed hard, hoping I wouldn't throw up on Reid. But between the memories of Carl's dirty hands on my body and the bouncing from Reid jogging down the dirt trail, my stomach was rolling.

"Please stop for a minute. I feel like I am going to throw up," I told Reid.

"We're almost there sweetheart. Try and hold it, we can't stop," Reid answered.

I closed my eyes again and really tried, but I couldn't hold it in. "Reid..." before I could warn him bile rushed up and I barely turned my head in time.

I threw up. Vomit splattered all over his shoulder

and the blanket he used to wrap me in. Reid stopped running and waited for me to finish emptying the contents of my stomach. Uncaring that I was throwing up down his back. Tears mixed with the acidic taste of vomit. I was horrified.

"Sorry," I mumbled.

"Don't be. You good?" Reid smoothed my wet hair and adjusted my weight in his arms.

"I think so."

Without another word, he took off into a jog again. I let my head fall on his chest and watched the golf course pass by.

I was safe.

Austin was already at Reid's SUV holding out a clean blanket. The cool crisp air hit my naked back and ass when Reid pulled the soiled blanket off my body. Mortification set in. There I was wrapped around Reid like a spider monkey, my bare breasts against his chest. I had no idea how many of his men were in the house when he found me. A clean blanket was once again wrapped around me, and Reid carefully tucked the ends in between our bodies.

Damion. Crap, Damion was there too. My face and neck burned with embarrassment. Maybe I should've been thinking more about the fact I was found, and less about who had seen me naked, but I couldn't control my racing thoughts. Was Reid mad at me? Would he believe me about what happened?

"I didn't want him to touch me. I promise," I blurted out.

"Motherfucker," Austin roared.

Reid stiffened and tightened his grip on me.

"I know you didn't, sweetheart. You're safe now. He will never hurt you again." His voice sounded angry, furious even.

Crestfallen, I rested my forehead on his shoulder. I knew he would be mad at me. I was tainted now. What man wanted to see the woman he had kissed only hours before rolling around on the floor naked with another man?

Carl ruined everything.

Reid opened the back passenger door and moved to set me down on the backseat. I lifted my head trying to look around at anything but his face. I wasn't ready to see the disappointment and disgust in his eyes. Twenty-four hours ago, he had me convinced I could be happy again. He had woken me up from a five-year slumber, with one single press of his lips.

Now it was gone.

All the beauty and color he had shown me was gone. Carl Allen took everything away from me in the blink of an eye.

For the second time in my life, my whole world

was destroyed because of someone else's actions. This had to be the Universe's way of telling me I was destined to be alone.

I lost Reid's body heat when he had me secured in the backseat. He stood in the door frame of the Rover and pulled his shirt over his head and balled it up throwing it to Austin. I was so lost in my own misery I missed when his strong arms picked me back up, and he slid in the seat settling me on his lap.

"Ava, I don't know what thoughts are swirling around in that pretty little head of yours, but I won't let you shut down on me," Reid said, his tone still hard.

I remained quiet when Austin got into the driver seat and started the car. I kept my eyes averted, unseeing as the street lights and buildings rushed by. I didn't want to think about what would happen when we got to where Reid was taking me. I just had to concentrate on JJ, and making sure he was okay, knowing once again we would be alone. I would have to move. Carl took that from me too. I could never step foot back into the house I loved. All the memories JJ and I made in that house, us making it a home after we lost Jacob. The comfort I felt when Reid bought the house next door. It wasn't quite so lonely knowing he was a few yards away if we needed anything.

We pulled in front of a nondescript, one-story white building. I should've been paying more attention to where we were going instead of having the pity party I had been indulging in.

"Where are we? Is JJ here?" I asked.

"We are at Doc Chesterfield's clinic. You need to be checked and clean up before I take you to JJ," Reid answered.

Of course, I must've been a mess. Reid was right, I didn't want JJ to see me like this. And I needed a shower. I wanted to scrub my body with bleach to wash away Carl's repulsive touch and putrid scent. I hoped the bruising on my face and nose wouldn't be so bad, I couldn't cover it with makeup. I didn't want JJ to be scared, or have a reminder of tonight for weeks to come.

Who the fuck was I kidding? I'm sure tonight would be burned into my son's memory for all of eternity. God knows what JJ heard back at the safe house. Tears spilled down my face, my poor baby boy. He must've been so scared, and I was completely helpless to comfort him.

I failed again. Always failing. No wonder Reid was so angry. I was weak, and he had to come in and save the day again.

Reid opened the car door and stepped out with me in his arms. I allowed myself just a few more seconds of his warmth and comfort. But even in those final seconds, something felt different, the uncertainty and anxiety had already curled in my belly fighting to break free.

"I can walk," I snapped.

I didn't want to walk, I wanted Reid to wrap me in his warmth and never let me go.

"I'm sure you can, Ava, but you're not going to," Reid replied.

"Put me down," I tried again.

Please don't let me do this, I screamed in my mind.

"No. Stop fighting Ava." Reid's angry voice was back.

If I was smart, I would've closed my mouth and conceded, but all those toxic emotions swirling around in my belly broke free. And standing in the middle of Doc Chesterfield's parking lot, the Python in my belly threatened to choke me from inside out if I didn't let him loose.

"I said, let me down. Now Reid." I struggled with all my might until he finally lost his grip on me and had to settle me on the ground. "I don't know what the fuck is wrong with you and Mac, but you both think you can swoop in and take over my life anytime you think I need your help, but it ends here," I yelled. I might've stomped my barefoot on the pavement for full dramatic flair. "Thank you for finding me and saving me from that bastard Carl, but I know what is happening here. I know you hate me, I got Rick killed, I pulled you into my disastrous life. And, in your misplaced obligation, you think you need to continue to take care of me until you can let the poor, used up, soiled woman down. I get it, I'm dirty now. You don't need to pretend. I will see the doctor, scrub Carl's filth and slime off my body, and you can just drop me off with JJ. I won't bother you again."

When I was done with my temper tantrum all I heard was two angry men growling. It sounded something like a mix of a bear and a wounded lion. Austin stomped away muttering a string of curse words that would make the devil himself blush. Reid, well, he just stood in front of me staring. I wasn't sure if it was relief or anger that flashed in his eyes.

"All of what you just said is jacked. Totally fucked up. I know you needed to spew out all that shit and get it off your chest. I'll give you that, Ava. What I won't give you is you talking about yourself that way, ever again." Reid grabbed me by both my shoulders and shook me so hard my teeth rattled. "Don't you ever call yourself, soiled, used up, or dirty again. Do you hear me? Don't you ever talk about my Goddamn woman that way. Whatever Carl did to you, it's not your fault. You may not get it now, but you will, Ava. I'll make sure of it. Nothing that piece of shit did is your fault. And Rick, he died protecting my woman, my family. I can never repay that, but I will not ever allow you to disrespect his sacrifice. He died so I could live another day loving you. Do you get it yet, Ava?" Reid stopped again and searched my confused eyes. "No, I see you don't. But mark this, you fucking will. And one more thing. No woman of mine is walking barefoot in a parking lot with a Goddamn blanket wrapped around her. I don't give a flying fuck if you're in tip-top health and want to skip to my Lou. Not ever gonna happen, sweetheart. So, get over yourself."

With that, he scooped me up and marched us into the clinic. There was so much he just said to me I didn't know where to begin.

"Did you say you loved me?" I whispered.

"Jesus Christ, she's getting it," he mumbled.

"That's not an answer, Reid," I snapped.

"Now, she's breaking my balls... yes, sweetheart, I love you."

And with those words, with the sun coming up over the horizon in the early morning hours my world was filled with a little more color.

Maybe, just maybe, the universe was wrong.

20

RELIEF

Reid

Jacked.

Every fucked-up word she spoke tore me to shreds. I needed to be patient with her, and handle this with care, but I snapped when she called herself 'used up.' What the fuck? It was a slow build up, one I tried to control, but the more she spoke, the harder it was to contain my fury.

I wished I could be there when Damion ripped Carl's last breath from his body. Making sure that Ava was taken care of was more important than disposing of the scum that Carl was, but there was still nagging in my gut. A nagging feeling that my brother would have the pleasure of killing the man that hurt my woman.

Doc Chesterfield met us in the lobby of his clinic dressed in casual blue jeans and T-shirt. I was relieved he didn't have his white doctor coat on. Maybe if this was less formal, Ava would feel more comfortable. Who the fuck was I kidding? No amount of casualness would ease the shock and pain of being violated. That was just a lie I was trying to convince myself of. And this was not about me, this was about getting my woman the treatment she needed to ensure she was safe.

"Logan," Dr. Chesterfield greeted. "Follow me."

He motioned for me to follow him into a small exam room. When I tried to place Ava on the exam table her grip around my neck tightened.

"No." That's all she said, a single syllable that spoke volumes. Maybe she was getting it now. I wasn't going anywhere.

I found a chair and settled myself with Ava still in my arms. The doctor looked at us but didn't make a comment about Ava not wanting me to let her go.

"Ava, I need to ask you if it is okay for Logan to stay in the room while we talk. Once I begin my exam, if you prefer, he may stay in the room, but I will need you to move to the table," Dr. Chesterfield said.

His voice was calming and soothing. I had never heard him use that tone before. When he patched up my crew, he was the gruff Med Corps Officer I knew him to be in the Army.

"I want Reid to stay with me. Can't I sit on his lap

while you look at my face? I don't think my nose is broken," she whimpered as she pulled the blanket tight around her body.

Check yourself, Reid. Our girl is strong.

I bit back a curse and tried to tamp down my anger. Jacob was right, Ava was strong, and she didn't need me losing my temper. I had to get my head straight and prepare to hear her say the words that would make me want to tear apart San Francisco.

This wasn't about me.

The doctor sat on his stool and rolled himself closer. He gently used his thumb to touch Ava's cheek and nose. Once he had checked both sides and swept his thumb under her eye and over the bruised area, he sat back.

"I agree. Your nose is not broken. You're going to have one hell of a bruise for a few days though. I'm interested in hearing about your head injury. When Austin texted me, he said you had possibly been knocked unconscious?" Dr. Chesterfield jotted something down on a notepad and tossed the pad onto the exam table looking back at Ava.

"When..." Ava stopped and cleared her throat. "When Carl took me from the safe house he hit me in the back of my head. I think... I think he hit me with his gun. I must've passed out because the next thing I remember is being in the trunk. I hit my head on something hard while I was bouncing around in there. Maybe a tire or something? And, I think I hit my head when..." Ava stopped again, closing her eyes. Doc Chesterfield patiently waited for Ava to pull herself together. "When we were in the shower. I can't remember if I did for sure or not. We were struggling, and I was trying to get away from him. In the struggle, I slipped, and we fell out of the shower onto the floor. I might have hit my head when I fell, but nothing hurt."

"Okay. Let me check the back of your head." Dr. Chesterfield rolled closer again and maneuvered around the chair.

I'm sure the exam would've been easier if Ava was on the table and he could check her head without having to move around me as well. Though, I was grateful he was allowing her to sit on my lap.

"Ouch, there," Ava said and grabbed my hand holding it tight.

"Oh yeah, you have a goose egg back here," the doctor chuckled. I wasn't sure what there was to chuckle about, but I appreciated the gesture. "I'll get you an ice pack and a Tylenol. We are going to treat this as a concussion. I don't see the use in a CT scan tonight. I understand you've already been nauseous. What about a headache, do you have one now?"

"No. And after I threw up I felt better," Ava admitted.

"I can imagine you did. All that adrenaline pushing through your body. I will go over the instructions on how we treat a concussion, though I'm sure Logan here has them memorized with the number of times one of his crew has come in here with a head injury." Dr. Chesterfield took a moment and jotted down another note. When he looked back over, his eyes bore into mine. A silent communication, preparing me for what was about to happen. I took a deep breath and blew it out. Ava smiled up at me and squeezed my hand. Even in her darkest hour, she was trying to reassure me. Christ, this woman unmanned me. She never ceased to surprise me with her strength.

"Ava, before we begin your exam, let's talk a little bit about what happened in the shower, and go back from there," the doctor coaxed.

"What about the shower? I already told you what happened," Ava replied.

"Would you feel more comfortable if we maybe talked alone?" Dr. Chesterfield asked.

"What? No. I want Reid with me. I don't understand what else you want me to tell you." Ava's response was fast and sure.

The doctor cleared his throat, and I braced myself.

"I understand this is hard. I'll be as gentle as I can be, but there are certain details I need. And I am sorry if they seem intrusive. When you were in the shower, did Carl wash your vagina?"

"WHAT!" Ava screeched.

Her eyes were as wide as saucers, and she was shaking again.

"I'm sorry Ava. I am only trying to gain insight into whether or not he tried to wash away fluids. Sometimes, after a sexual assault, the assailant will try and wash his victim..."

Sexual assault. Assailant. Victim. I didn't hear the rest of what the doctor explained to Ava. Those four words replayed in my head over and over again. I hoped Carl was screaming like a bitch in Damion's basement. I hoped Blaze was disemboweling him, and using his intestines as a noose. Sick motherfucker.

"He didn't rape me," Ava yelled.

"What?" the doctor and I asked in unison.

"He... Carl... he didn't rape me. He licked my face. He kissed my mouth, he undressed me and saw me naked." Ava's cheeks turned red, and she lowered her head. "... and he tried to grab my breast. That's when we struggled. Jacob told me not to make him mad, to be patient and you would come and get me." Ava gripped my hand tighter and raised her eyes to meet mine, tears brimming. "I tried. I really tried, but when he reached out to touch my breast, I had to stop him. You came into the bathroom as soon as we fell out of the shower.

He didn't rape me. You got to me in time," Ava explained.

Relief. Pure relief flooded my body. I would like to say that it was all for Ava's sake, that I was a good man and I was only thinking of her. But that would've been a lie. The relief was for all of us.

"Why did he take you to the shower? And who is Jacob?" Dr. Chesterfield asked.

"Jacob is... um... my husband. He was killed, but I could hear him in my head," Ava explained in a rush, "Carl was being crazy, he was talking to some woman named Eva. Only there was no one there. I was confused, and Carl accused me of planning to run. That made him mad, and he slapped me in the face. My nose was bleeding, and he took me to the shower to clean up. He yelled some more at Eva then got in the shower with me. Talking about consummating our love, and he called me his wife." Ava turned herself in my lap and looked me square in the face. "Do you believe me?"

"Yes, every word, sweetheart. I am sorry I assumed. But, I needed to make sure that you were safe and taken care of." I kissed her forehead.

"I knew you were coming," she said. "Jacob told me. I could hear him."

"I know he did, sweetheart. He talked to JJ too." I

wasn't ready to admit that Jacob had spoken to me as well.

Dr. Chesterfield looked at me and nodded his head.

"Great. Well, Ava, I'll get you the instructions for your concussion. Reid, you know the drill; wake her every two hours, headaches or vomiting, any more swelling I want to see her."

The doctor grabbed his notepad and left the room. With a gentle click of the door, we were alone.

"Thank you," Ava said snuggling in close. "And I'm sorry."

"There is nothing to be sorry for," I replied.

"Are we just going to pretend I didn't have a complete meltdown in the parking lot? And two point five seconds later my mood swung the other way and I was back in your arms?"

"Yep."

I could feel Ava shaking, only this time I smiled brightly. I knew what was coming next. She wouldn't be able to stop it. A cute little snort came from Ava followed by a full belly laugh. There it was, my woman, in my arms, her head thrown back laughing.

This was how I was going to make sure every day was like from now on. Only we would not be sitting in a doctor's office. And she would not be wrapped in a blanket. No, my woman would be on my lap, in our bed with nothing between us. And her head would be thrown back, only it would not be laughter I heard, it would be her soft moans of pleasure.

"Can we get out of here? I want to see JJ." Ava glanced up, a horrified expression crossing her face. "Oh my God, I forgot about Suzie. Where is she? Is she okay?"

21

DARK CHOCOLATE WITH RASPBERRY FROSTING

Ava

It's official, I was the worst friend ever.

"Don't start that shit, Ava. I know that look," Reid scolded me.

"I can't believe I forgot about Suzie. Is she okay? Where is she?" I repeated starting to get off Reid's lap now in even more of a hurry to get out of here.

"Slow down." Reid held me tight and settled me back on his lap. "Suzie's still in ICU. Michael is with her. I will get you there tomorrow. Right now, you're gonna get cleaned up, and we are headed to Mac and JJ. I promised JJ I would get you back to him as soon as I could."

"How is he?" I asked.

My poor boy had to be so scared. I knew Mac

would take care of him, but I needed to see him and hold him. Pepper his handsome little face with kisses.

"Mac texted that they are both safe. He told JJ that I found you, and we would be on our way in a little while. JJ is a little shaken up. He heard a lot of what Carl said to you. We tried to shield him from as much as we could at the safe house. But, your boy is smart. He had that shit figured out in two seconds."

I had been trying to block out what Damion said about taking Carl to his basement. And what exactly he meant by, 'Blaze having fun with Carl.' Damion's reputation preceded him. His MC was brutal. You'd have to have been living under a rock not to know about Iron Claw MC. But now, thinking about all that my son heard, all that he saw, and how scared he must've been, I hoped Blaze was removing Carl's fingernails one by one. I knew that Reid would never give me details, and I would never know exactly what happened to Carl. I was okay with that. Damion told me I was safe, and I believed him.

"Thank you for taking care of him. And me. You seem to be rescuing us a lot lately." I glanced at the door making sure it was still closed. "May I ask you a question?"

"Anything," Reid replied.

"Damion called you brother, and family. Is that

brother as in by blood, or brother like guys say to each other?"

I knew Reid had a blood brother, but he never talked about him, and I had never asked. Yet another thing I had to feel like crap about. I had been pretending to be an ostrich the last five years. Sticking my head so far in the sand I allowed the world to go on around me. Never really getting too involved with anyone except JJ. Hell, Suzie was who I considered my best friend, but I was only on the outskirts of her life too. We got together for a movie and wine often, but all the conversation was kept on an acquaintance level. She never brought up Jacob, and certainly never brought up my miscarriage.

No, Mac was the only one who made me talk about it. Every year on the anniversary of Jacob's death he forced me to visit the baby's memorial marker he had placed in the children's section of the cemetery Jacob's buried in. I didn't want the marker, I didn't want the reminder, and I more than anything never wanted to talk about it. But he did. He never let me forget I killed my child. My stupidity. If I had just listened and sat down, I wouldn't have fallen and hit my belly on the table. Every year Mac rubbed it in, that I didn't listen.

I secretly hated Mac a little more every time we visited for making me remember. It was coming, the anniversary, and I knew he would drag me there kicking and screaming. I was already trying to freeze him out. Mac was the master of emotional blackmail. He used Jacob's love against me. Each year I said no, and he coaxed me into going by telling me that Jacob would want me to remember our child.

"Damion is my blood brother. We share the same mother but have different fathers. Not many people know," Reid answered, pulling me from my musings.

"Does Mac know and his club?"

"Mac knows. There are some guys in his club that know, but only his most trusted men. That is for both our protection." Reid stopped, and a pained look crossed his face. "I love my brother. He's a good man. He lives his life by a strict code of honor, family is always first, he protects and takes care of what is his. Do I wish he had chosen a different path? Yeah, I do but I understand why he chose the club, and I respect his decision. He always protected me when we were growing up. My mom tried the best she could in the beginning, but my dad was a piece of shit. Damion took that for me. As soon as I turned eighteen, he drove me to the Army recruiter and told me to go."

Reid looked like he was transported back to another time and place. I didn't want to bring up bad memories but, if he was being forthcoming, I was going to take advantage of it.

"Why did he tell you to go?" I asked.

"Damion was already running with a club. By that time, he was the one supporting us. My dad was long gone, and Mom had become useless. Damion refused to allow me to work when I was in high school. He wanted me to play sports and keep up with my grades. It all fell on him. More days than not, Mom didn't get out of bed. There was always some man slithering out of our trailer in the morning. Damion shielded me from that too. Making sure her dealers were out of the house by the time I got up. He thought I didn't know, but I did."

"I'm so sorry. I can't imagine what that was like for you... and Damion."

"It was fucked. Damion's only a few years older than me, but he was always more of a dad than a brother. He dropped me off, told the recruiter to make something of me, and he never wanted to see me again."

"He never wanted to see you again?" I whispered.

Holy crap! That had to have hurt Reid badly. I was an only child, so I didn't understand a sibling bond, but I did know what it felt like to have someone so close leave you.

The pain of loss. Poor Reid. That actually explained a lot about him, and why Reid was always protecting those around him.

"At the time, I was pissed. I thought I was gonna

join his MC and stay with him. The moment I mentioned prospecting for the club he ran me out of town. He said he wanted a better life for me. I joined the Army, a pissed off resentful kid, with a huge chip on my shoulder." Reid was still staring at the wall unblinking.

"I think I love Damion," I blurted out. "He protected you, saved you. He taught you to protect those you love, even when it is painful. He made you into the man you are today. You live by that same strict moral code he showed you. He is a good man, I'm glad you have him."

Reid's laughter boomed through the tiny room. "Don't ever tell Damion you think he is a good man. He has a reputation to uphold. And he would likely disagree with you."

"Please, don't you know me at all? I can be very persuasive. Besides, you'll be taking me to his club-house in a few days. I owe him and Blaze a plate of cupcakes."

Reid continued to laugh, the hilarity of my statement getting the better of him. He wiped his eyes before he asked, "Cupcakes?"

"Yes. Dark chocolate with raspberry frosting. Maybe I'll put JJ's favorite sprinkles on the top too." I thought for a minute, trying to calculate how many cupcakes I would have to make.

"You're gonna make cupcakes for a bunch of bikers?" he asked still smiling.

"Yes, of course. He helped you save me."

I didn't see what was so funny. Everyone liked cupcakes, especially my dark chocolate with raspberry frosting. Surely bikers liked sweets.

"You're a nut. Let's get you cleaned up so we can go get JJ," Reid suggested, patting my thigh signaling for me to get up.

"Yes, please. I want to see my son. Is there a place I can clean up here? I want to try and cover this bruise, so JJ doesn't see it."

I was anxious to get to JJ. What I was not looking forward to was facing Mac. Our friendship was strained at best, these days. It was all one-sided, I was the one that was mad at him. He just continued to take my ire and never said a word. Some days I thought it would be easier if he would just call me on my shit, and tell me he was done with me. Easier for me, harder for JJ.

"Come on, I'll take you to the bathroom. Austin should have some clothes for you by now."

Reid gently took my hand and led me out of the room and down the hall. Austin was sitting in the waiting area deep in thought with a bag on his lap. When we approached, he looked up, and the pity and grief that crossed his face made my belly hurt. He looked so lost. When his face softened, he didn't look as big and tough like he normally did.

I don't know why I did it. Maybe it was the mother in me, the nurturer, the need to comfort those around me. I let go of Reid's hand and ran to Austin. He stood just in time to wrap his arms around me as we collided.

"Thank you. Thank you for coming to find me," I said into his chest.

I didn't like seeing this big strong man downcast and distraught.

"No worries, Ava. Just doing my job," Austin said into my hair.

"Don't do that. You were right there with Reid and Damion saving me. You didn't have to. And no matter if it is your job or not, I appreciate it just the same."

Austin cleared his throat. "You're welcome. You're Reid's that means you are always protected. I'm sorry it happened in the first place."

"Nothing to be sorry for. It's not your fault Carl is crazy," I explained. "I'm grateful he only wanted me, and left JJ alone."

I wondered if Reid felt the same way? Like it was his fault that Carl had fallen off the coo-coo truck and came after me.

"I should've known. Researched more. It is my job to know. I failed, and you were hurt because of it." Austin tried to push me away from him.

"No. You had no way of knowing about Carl. You all thought that the danger was Jimmy. And you took care of that. The doctor said the only thing wrong with me is I may have a concussion. Nothing serious. Nothing that all of you guys haven't had in the past. I'll be fine in a few days."

Austin's body stiffened, and the air around us changed. He maneuvered me in front of him careful not to move the blanket still covering my naked body.

"Ava, you have to find a way to deal with this. I know it is hard. I know because it happened to my sister. She couldn't deal. JJ needs you, we will all help you figure this out."

I cocked my head to the side not understanding what he was talking about. Weirdly I was alright. Maybe, once the relief of being rescued wore off, it would hit me I was kidnapped by a deranged lunatic, but for now, I was okay.

When I didn't respond, he continued. "Sexual assault is..."

"I wasn't raped," I blurted out.

"But I thought... you said in the parking lot..." Austin stumbled.

"I felt dirty, and used up. Carl saw me naked. He put his mouth on mine. He tried to touch me. No man has seen me with no clothes on since Jacob died." I closed my eyes feeling even sillier now for my display in the parking lot. "Until yesterday, the last man I kissed was my husband. For years, I hadn't thought of another man. Never dreamed I'd touch another man. Then, I share this one incredible kiss with Reid. It wasn't just any kiss. It was life-changing, excruciating, unbelievable. I was afraid Carl ruined that, that he took that away from me and Reid. That is why I said that. You guys saved me in time. He never touched me like that. I promise."

I don't know what compelled me to admit that to Austin. Maybe I was stronger than I thought. Maybe with Reid by my side, I was ready to start living again. What I did know was, it felt good to find a little piece of the old me. The person I was before... Jacob was taken.

22

READY

Reid

I watched Ava and Austin from across the room. I was so fucking proud of my woman. There she was being strong for Austin, sensing he needed comfort. She pushed past her insecurities and reservations, and shocked the hell out of me when she opened up to him. In all the years I had known Ava, I had never seen her be so vulnerable.

So Goddamn strong.

The same relief I felt washed over Austin's face. He pulled her into another tight hug and laughed.

He whispered something into her hair that I couldn't hear; she nodded and looked up at him.

"Go. Your man is waiting for you," he said.

She didn't respond, just took the bag Austin held out and walked back to me. Her face open, beautiful whiskey colored eyes shining brightly. Yeah, my woman was strong, and if she had a moment of weakness, I would be there.

It was definitely time. The cinderblock wall she had built was about to crumble. Not only was it going to crumble but it was going to happen fast. Now that I had a taste of all the sweetness that was her, there was no taking it slow.

I took her hand again and led her to the bathroom. "I'll wait right outside the door. Get dressed, and we'll leave. I know you said you wanted a shower but that's gonna have to wait."

"Okay, Reid." Without any argument, she closed the bathroom door.

I caught Austin's stare from across the room, he still had something on his mind. I gave him a chin lift and motioned for him to come down the hall. I needed to talk to him, but there was no way I was leaving my post. If Ava opened the door, I wanted her to know I had not moved.

"What's going on?" I asked Austin when he stopped in front of me.

"Talked to Dustin and asked him to pull the CCV feed from Lake Street and 5th. He only had access to the last month. But Carl has been down your street at least once a day. Sometimes more. He had to have parked down the block, because when Dustin pulled your outside cameras he's nowhere on them. Another thing, Dustin looked at the footage again from the night Ava's house was vandalized. He had to of hacked your system and deleted that day's recordings."

"Motherfucker! How the hell did a fruit loop like Carl Allen hack my system? That is impossible." There was not a snow ball's chance in hell Carl hacked it without help. I designed that system myself, and had asked several hackers I knew to try and break through. Only one could and with a great amount of time and difficulty.

"Don't know man. But your hard drive was wiped clean. I had Dustin double check. We're still looking into Eva Martin. So far..."

I cut Austin off before he could finish. "I guarantee she's dead. Ava said that Carl was talking to Eva when he had her. Only Ava never saw anyone else in the house. She certainly wasn't there when we went in. The question is, where'd he stash her?"

"Sick fuck. Dustin and I will hit his house after I get you to the beach house. Mac said that JJ is itchin' to see you and Ava." Austin paused and gathered himself. "When you gonna talk to April? I'd like to go with you."

Guilt hit my gut. I told Ava the truth, I would forever be grateful for Rick's sacrifice. He died protecting my woman. It was only right I did the same in return. April was now my responsibility. A responsibility I would gladly take care of.

"Damn, Austin, I don't know what the fuck I'm supposed to do. I have to get home to JJ. He wants his mom. I am so damn torn. My family needs me, but shit man, I have to talk to April."

As luck, would have it, Ava opened the door just in time to hear the last of my statement. Dammit. Her face paled and sucked in a breath. "You need to go to April, Reid. She needs you. Believe me, I know how much."

"Sweetheart, look at me." I waited for her to meet my eyes before I continued. "I will handle April. I'm gonna be honest with you. It is killing me that I haven't already been to see her. But, you and JJ? You are my priority. That might make me a dick, but I have to know my family is okay." I hoped she understood.

I glanced at Austin wishing he had the answer. Before we could continue Doc Chesterfield walked into the hallway.

"Here is the information on concussions, Ava. I know that Logan is basically an expert on head trauma, but I want you to read through this information yourself. Please call me if you get a headache, you feel nauseous, or you get dizzy." The doctor handed Ava a stack of papers. "And, nothing stronger than extra strength Tylenol." When he was done talking to Ava, he handed me a single dose packet of Tylenol, a bottle of water, and an ice pack.

"Thank you, doctor," Ava said when she took the paperwork from his hand. "Will you bill me for the visit? I don't have my purse."

"Silly woman. Logan has me on retainer. There is no payment," Dr. Chesterfield responded with a broad smile.

"Thank you." Ava reached her hand out. When Doc Chesterfield took it, he pulled her in close.

"You take care of yourself. Please let me know if you need anything," Doc Chesterfield said to Ava. He released her hand and faced me. "Logan, Austin nice to see you both. While I appreciate a beautiful woman in my office instead of one of your grumpy men I hope next time I see Ava it's at dinner." He winked at Ava and continued, "I'll expect an invite, and soon. Don't waste time Logan."

Without waiting for my response, Doc walked down the hall disappearing into his office. Crazy old man.

I welcomed the silence as we drove to the beach house. I needed a few minutes to gather my thoughts and form a plan. I was undecided on what needed to happen next. I was running out of time. April needed to be told.

Ava was snuggled into my arms in the back seat. I looked up and caught Austin's eye in the rearview mirror, he was watching us. Tonight had to have taken a toll on my friend. I'm sure all the fucked-up memories from his sister's kidnapping and rape flooded his head. How could it not? Another thing I needed to do, was get Austin alone so he could unload.

"I'll go." Austin broke the silence. Ava lifted her head off my chest and looked towards Austin. "I'll drop you and Ava off at the beach house and go talk to April. Carl's house can wait," Austin said.

At that, Ava pushed herself up further, a scowl marring her beautiful face. "What's at Carl's house?" Damn that woman never missed a thing. Not that Austin was real smooth in his declaration.

"Nothing for you to worry about," I answered, trying to brush any further explanation aside.

"He had keys to my house," Ava announced.

"He what? How do you know he had keys?" Austin inquired, taking his eyes off the road and looking at us in the rearview mirror again.

"I didn't have my keys with me. I left them and my cell phone on the counter when we left for breakfast Friday morning. I wasn't really thinking straight, and I wasn't driving. Carl let himself into my house," Ava explained. "He said we were home."

Austin looked at me, damn, he was right. Carl was playing house with Ava.

"What else did he say about Eva?" I questioned Ava. Something was nagging me. Why now? If Carl had been stalking Ava for years why make his move now, instead of say, two years ago? What changed?

"He called her a jealous bitch..." Ava trailed off. "Nothing else really. He called out to her a few times telling her to bring me water and clean clothes. Told her to hurry up. That was it. I spent most of my time in the trunk, thankfully. Is Eva real? That's weird right, him having an imaginary friend named Eva. So close to my name."

"Eva is real. She was his girlfriend until a month ago. Her parents are worried they haven't heard from her since her break up with Carl," I explained. I didn't want to give Ava any more detail than that, or tell her Austin's theories.

"So, what? She left him, and he snapped and came after me to replace her?" Ava questioned.

"We don't know yet, that's why Austin and Dustin are gonna look around his house. Try and find some answers."

The beach house came into sight, and I had to

make my decision. "You sure you're good going to April's by yourself?" I asked Austin.

"Yeah, I'm sure. I don't want to overstep, but man you cannot leave your family. Let me help." Austin pulled in front of the house and turned his body completely around in the seat. "I owe this to Rick. Without getting into detail, he helped me a fuck-ton. When my head was screwed up, he pulled it outta my ass for me. I promise I'll handle April with care."

"Man, this is not about whether or not I think you'll handle this. It's fucking with my head because I feel like I am fucking off my responsibility," I admitted.

"You know Rick would want you to take care of your family," Austin continued.

"I know you're right. Ava and I will be around April's tomorrow. I'm taking her to see Suzie in the hospital then we'll be over. You're staying there, right? She cannot be left alone."

"Of Course. I'll check in with you in a few. Ava, I am happy you are home safe and sound. We'll see you tomorrow. This goes without saying, you need anything you call me. I know your man will take good care of you, but the offer is always on the table. We take care of family."

"Thank you, Austin," Ava whispered.

I don't know what the two of them talked about when they were in the waiting room. I really didn't need to know, I trusted Austin, he was a good friend. I was thrilled as fuck my woman's circle just grew one more person. He was a good person to have on your side. He needed an Ava, and I hoped like hell when that woman came along, he opened himself up to all the goodness she had to offer. He had deep scars that only the love of a good woman could heal.

"Thanks, man. Later." I climbed out of the car with Ava in my arms, using my hip to check the door closed.

"Sweetheart, I am gonna let you walk. As much as I want you in my arms, I think it is important that JJ sees you walkin' on your own," I told Ava as I set her on her feet.

"Thank you, Reid. You're right." She stopped and turned towards me. "I can never repay you for all you have done for me." When I started to protest, she reached her hand up to quiet me. "I know you don't want payment, I know you don't even want a 'thank you,' but I need you to know something." Ava came in close, so close I could feel her breath fanning across my neck. "Life is short. It can be taken from you in seconds. I am done living in fear. I am done being a bystander in my own life. I am just plain old done. I am telling you that to tell you this... I am ready for you, Logan Reid. I cannot promise I won't screw up. I cannot promise I won't try and run. But, I am counting on you not to let me go. I will hold on as tight as I can if you promise when my grip slips you'll be strong enough to hold on for both of us."

Those whiskey colored eyes I loved so much were clear and bright, glassy with moisture. She stared up at me with so much love and trust it scared the hell out of me. I prayed to God I wouldn't let her down. Now that I had her I was scared to death I was gonna lose her.

Kiss your girl, dumbass.

I threw my head back and laughed. Before I grabbed both sides of Ava's neck bringing my face to hers.

"What's so funny?" Ava asked.

"One day, I'll tell you. But right now, I need to kiss my woman."

Before she could argue, I took her mouth. This time, it was slow and gentle. I poured every ounce of love I had into that kiss. There was not another woman out there for me. Ava Kelley was it.

"Let's get you inside to the boy." I broke the kiss but let my lips linger on her mouth.

23

UNBROKEN

Ava

"Momma," JJ yelled as soon as Reid opened the front door.

His little body hit mine like a freight train, and I stumbled back. Before I could fall, Reid's strong hand righted me, holding me in place.

I wrapped my arms around my son and thanked God, the stars, the universe, Jacob, and anything else I could think of for keeping my son safe and getting me home to him.

"I'm okay, baby." I plastered a fake smile on my face.

When my son looked up at me with his big brown eyes, eyes that were identical to mine, he had tears brimming over his lids. Guilt and shame mixed together in one swirling emotion that took hold in my belly. My poor son. He has gone through so much in his ten years.

"I'm okay," I repeated. "We are all gonna be okay. I promise."

"I was so scared," JJ cried. The sound of my son crying was more than I could bear. I pulled him down to the floor and into my lap rocking him back and forth. "I heard it, I heard him taking you. Daddy told me not to move. I wanted to go with you, but Daddy told me not to. I'm sorry, Mama."

I was speechless. We sat in the entryway of the house for what seemed like an hour. Me holding JJ, and him crying into my neck. I didn't know what to say to make this okay.

"JJ, I want you to look at me," I said. When JJ lifted his face out of my neck, I allowed him to see my own tears. "You did the right thing. You listened to Daddy. I needed you safe so I could worry about keeping myself safe until Reid could come and get me. If you had tried to come out of the room, Carl might have tried to hurt you. Do you understand that?"

I stopped and waited for JJ to nod his head.

"You did the right thing. You were brave and smart and waited for help. Momma is strong, and I knew Reid would come and get me. Do you know why I could be strong baby?" I asked.

JJ just shook his head.

"Because I knew you were safe and waiting for me to come home. I knew Uncle Mac had you and was protecting you until I could get back to you. I promise you, Jacob, I am okay."

JJ's eyes widened, and I sucked in a breath. I don't think JJ remembered me calling him Jacob. He was only five the last time I used his full name.

I know you are Ava baby. You're gonna be just fine now.

A chill rushed over my body, and fresh tears fell over my cheeks. Yeah, I was going to be just fine. We were going to be just fine.

"Let's get up off the floor and find a cushy place to cuddle," I suggested.

"Are you really okay, Mama? I'm not a baby anymore you can tell me the truth," JJ asserted.

There's my son, quick with the 'I'm growing up routine.'

"I promise JJ, I am fine. Reid took me to see a doctor before we came home, even he agreed that I am okay. I have a bump on the back of my head. That's it. Reid got to me in no time flat, kiddo." I smiled at JJ.

After long minutes of him studying my face, he nodded. "Uncle Mac said that Carl was a crazy son-of-a-bitch, but Reid would find you and dispose of Carl like the trash he is," JJ announced.

"Did he now?" My eyes cut to Mac. I was so tired,

and happy to have JJ in my arms, I couldn't summon up the energy to be annoyed.

"Yep. He also said that now that Reid had finally pulled his head outta his own butthole..." JJ dropped his voice to a low whisper. "Uncle Mac didn't really say butthole, he used the A-word. He would never let anything happen to you. Because you are his woman. And a man always protects his woman."

Both men let out a chuckle. Reid walked over to where JJ and I were sitting on the floor and reached his hand down to pull JJ up. "Come on, little man, let's get your Mama off the floor."

Once JJ was standing, I looked up, and I had two hands reaching down. One big strong hand that offered me security and protection. And one little boy hand that offered me the sweetest, purest love. I stared at both their hands, then their faces.

Mine.

I reached up and took both their hands and pulled myself to a standing position. I had to talk to Mac. Reid might have been the one to save me, but Mac kept my whole world safe so Reid could come and get me.

"Can I have a minute alone with Mac?" I asked.

"Sure thing. Come on, little man, let's see what's to eat in this house. I'm starving." Reid guided JJ out of the room, leaving me alone with Mac.

"Thank you," I whispered.

"Nothing to thank me for, Ava." His voice was clipped and hard.

"Of course, there is. You kept JJ safe for me."

"There's where you're wrong. I kept JJ safe for me. You seem to forget that I love JJ too. You think you're this one woman show, who has to do it all alone. You're not alone. You never have been. You seem to forget, I promised you and Jacob the day JJ was born to love and protect that boy as if he were my own flesh and blood if something were to happen to either one of you. Fuck Ava, something did happen, and you have slowly stolen that from me. Made me break a promise to my best friend. So, no you do not need to thank me. You wanna thank me, pull your head out of your ass and open your eyes. It. Is. Time."

Holy crap. Mac had never spoken to me like that before. He was always calm and placating.

"You're right," I returned.

There really was nothing to argue. I had done the things he accused me of, and he had made the promise he said he did.

"You finally ready?" he asked.

"Yes," I answered honestly.

"Thank fuck! You gonna stop pushing me away now too?" Mac challenged.

"Are you going to stop making me go and visit the baby's marker every year?" I pushed back.

That was the crux of the problem. Every Goddamn year he insisted on ripping my heart out again.

"No," he stated matter of fact.

"Then no, I'm not ready to stop pushing you away. Every time you take me there it fucking hurts, Mac. Why do you want to continue to remind me that I killed my baby? I don't want to remember it," I growled.

"That is why I take you. Every year, I will drag you there until you finally understand that you did not kill your baby. You did nothing wrong. You heard what the doctor told you. You falling down had nothing to do with having an ectopic pregnancy. You didn't plant that embryo in your fallopian tube. You continue to blame yourself for no reason. And one day when your head is finally out of your ass I do not want you to beat yourself up for not honoring your baby."

I stared at Mac. He stared back. We were engaged in some sort of adult version of a staring contest. Screw him. What did he know about losing a baby? Nothing, that's what.

"Ava, that baby was loved. Jacob knew..." Mac stopped. His words hung in the air like a plume of thick smoke ready to choke me.

"He knew? About the baby?"

"Yes," Mac confirmed. "He knew you were pregnant. You know Jacob though, he would've never ruined your fun. He was excited and happy to have another baby. That's all he talked about the whole day was getting home to you so you could tell him. He loved that baby, Ava."

My head was spinning, Jacob knew, and Mac kept another secret from me. "Why didn't you tell me?"

"You weren't ready." That was it. That was all Mac offered.

"I wasn't ready? And that was your call to make? Who gave you that right?" I yelled uncaring that Reid and JJ were in the other room.

"You can be as mad as you want. I wouldn't change a thing. You can yell, think I'm a dick, but I know..." Mac stepped closer and lowered his voice. "I know I was doing right by Jacob by protecting you. That's what he would've wanted. You were not ready to know certain things. Jacob knowing about the baby was one of them. You would've twisted that shit in your head somehow. Me not telling you that I reached out to Jimmy was another secret I kept. He was a criminal and a jackass. I tried to help him clean his shit up so he could be an uncle. He refused. That was not something you needed to worry about. So again, be as pissed as you want, but Ava, I will always do what I think is right when it comes to you and JJ. You know who gave me that right? Jacob did when he asked me to watch over you and his son."

"I hate you," I spit out.

"Doesn't change a thing for me, Ava. I love you both. You are my family. Nothing you say will change that. I only want what is best for you."

Mac had a Goddamn retort for everything. Why couldn't he just tell me to screw off and leave me alone?

"What's best for me is you not pushing me to do things I don't want to do and keeping secrets from me," I told him.

"I beg to differ," he answered.

Whatever. I didn't want to argue with him anymore. I wanted my son and a cuddle. I was all out of fight for the night.

"Thanks again, Mac."

I walked away. I was so over the conversation.

"Anytime, Ava," Mac said to my back.

Infuriating man. He always had to have the last word. I heard the shrill ring of Mac's phone and hoped he got a call out so I wouldn't have to talk to him anymore.

"Hey baby, whatcha got?" I asked JJ when I found him and Reid in the kitchen.

"Reid said you needed to eat. So, I made you your favorite turkey sandwich and a hot chocolate, with extra chocolate sauce and mini marshmallows." JJ held out a plate for me to see.

"Yo, Reid a word," Mac called out from the other room.

I breathed a sigh of relief and took the plate from JJ.

"Thanks, honey. You wanna come sit down with me on the couch while I eat?"

Reid skootched past me in the tiny kitchen kissing the top of my head as he went. I didn't miss JJ's smile as he watched Reid. Oh hell, I think I needed to have a talk with JJ.

"I'll bring your hot chocolate." JJ followed behind me as I made my way into a cozy nook off the side of the kitchen that overlooked the South Bay, with a perfect view of the Golden Gate Bridge to my right.

I wondered whose house this was. It had to have cost a mint. Real estate in Sea Cliff was so far out of my budget I didn't even know what these houses started at. A house on 25th street with this view at the end of a cul-de-sac had to be at least three times, if not more, what my house in Lake Street was worth.

That reminded me, I would have to start looking for a new house. JJ and I could rent an apartment for a while. I would take JJ's furniture and the keepsakes I had stored in my garage, but I wanted nothing else from that house. Not my favorite overstuffed couch, not my comfy bed I shared with Jacob, nothing. I'd be happy to burn the rest down. Carl ruined it, all of it.

For the second time in my life, I had to start over.

"Listen JJ, we need to talk," I started.

"Reid told me," JJ informed me.

"Told you what exactly?" I asked.

"That he loves us. You and me. And he wouldn't leave me with Uncle Mac unless he knew I was safe. Because me and you are his life. And he trusts Uncle Mac with his life. Reid told me he would bring you home to me. I wasn't as scared after that because Reid always keeps his promises. That is what being a man is about, keeping your promises."

I was stunned. Was my son ten or thirty? I looked at JJ, really looked at the young man he was becoming. He looked so much like Jacob, acted like him too. But now, in his mannerisms, and the way he spoke, I saw a little of Reid in him. Mac too.

I swallowed hard and remembered Mac's words. I wasn't alone. I never had been. Mac and Reid had always been by my side. They were both molding and shaping my son into a man that Jacob would be proud of. Jacob had five years with his son. Five years to plant the seeds, but Reid and Mac would be the ones to help those seeds grow.

Damn, I am a bitch. I still didn't want to go to the baby's marker. But, Mac was mostly right. A man kept his promises. I had been fighting him every step of the way. Jacob would be mad, Reid will be mad, and I was flat out wrong. Damn, I hated when I was wrong. A big plate of crow looked to be in my near future.

"How do you feel about that?" I asked.

JJ sat for a minute not answering. I thought it might've been too soon to be discussing this in light of the last 48 hours. Maybe this was a conversation best shelved until we could get past this latest crisis.

"Is it wrong that I love Reid and wish he could be my dad?" JJ peeked up at me.

I sucked in a breath, but it still felt like there was no oxygen going to my brain. That was not what I thought JJ was going to ask.

"No, sweetie, it's not wrong. You know that Reid loves you too," I reassured JJ.

I wasn't sure what the swelling in my chest was from, if my heart was breaking for my son, or if Reid had inadvertently glued another piece back together. I wanted nothing more than my son to feel love and peace. I didn't want him to live with the heavy burden of loss. Even if that was what I had made myself live with.

"You know I will always love your daddy. He was a good person, a good husband, he was the type of man I want you to grow up to be. Your dad will always hold a piece of my heart. But you know what I've learned?" I waited for JJ to acknowledge me. "That my heart is big enough to love someone else too. That the part of my heart that I thought would be broken forever is unbroken, and Reid did that. He did that by loving you, he did it by being gentle and patient with me. But most of all he did it when he told my son that he was his whole world. Because, JJ, you are my world too. I only want you to be happy."

"Do you think Uncle Mac would be mad at me if he knew I wanted Reid to be my dad? I don't want Uncle Mac to be disappointed in me," JJ whispered.

"No," came from the doorway. JJ and I both jumped a mile and turned to see both men filling the entrance to the kitchen area. "I am not mad at you, and JJ you could never disappoint me by loving Reid." Mac's voice was sure and hopeful. "Your dad was my best friend. We were as close as brothers. I know your dad would want a good man in your life. A strong man to take care of you and your mom. There is no other man I would trust to love you and your mom the way you deserve to be loved. It's time to be happy. Moving on doesn't mean forgetting. Your mom is right, there is more than enough room in both your hearts."

"Okay," JJ said, and his face heated red. He was still a little boy that needed guidance and encouragement, but was embarrassed talking about feelings.

"Come here, little man." That came from Reid. He sounded unusually gruff and quickly cleared his throat.

JJ went to Reid on his command and stopped in front of him.

Reid went down on a knee making himself level with JJ. I loved it when he did that. He never made my son feel like he was being talked down to.

"I want you to understand something. I can never take your dad's place," he started.

JJ's head fell forward. I couldn't see his face because I had his back. What the hell?

"Look at me, son." JJ's head slowly came up. "I can never take your dad's place because your dad was a better man than I could ever hope to be. But, I will promise you this, you let me in, and it's okay with your mom, I will try my best to live up to his memory and be the best dad I can be. But you have to promise me something, yeah?"

JJ nodded his head enthusiastically.

"Well, two things. First, you never feel bad about talking about your dad to me. If you miss him, if you're sad, if you just want to hear stories about him. We talk about him. He is the reason I have you, JJ. I will not let him be forgotten in my house."

"We say his name out loud because a hero should never be forgotten," JJ interjected.

"Damn right. And your dad is a hero. The second thing, when the time is right, you gotta convince your mama to marry me."

"Okay," JJ said jumping up and down.

It was truly amazing how resilient my son was. In the space of an hour, he went from crying on my lap to jumping up and down in excitement. I wasn't sure if that was how all ten-year-olds were or if that was the power of Reid.

Somehow, I think it was the latter.

24

AFTERMATH

Austin

Across town...

I used the drive to April and Rick's house to try and convince myself I could do this. The last time I had to break the news that someone's loved one had died was when I told my parents Loren was dead. My palms were sweaty, and my heart raced. Damn, I missed my sister. The last 24 hours had fucked with my head. When Reid brought Ava downstairs naked wrapped in a blanket, I thought Carl had violated her. After her outburst in the parking lot, I was positively murderous. Loren had said pretty much the same thing after she was raped. Goddamn, I hated that word. Hated what it meant. I watched as my sister blamed herself. Loren's decline was fast and furious. First with alcohol to numb her mind, then drugs. Once she started, there was no stopping her.

I had to get away from Ava and let Reid handle his business before I overstepped and said something that I would regret. I knew Reid wouldn't let Ava get away with the shit talk. I knew he would set her straight, but all the memories and emotions came rushing back. Like a freight train, I couldn't stop them. Ava wasn't Loren, and in the end, Reid had gotten to her in time.

The more I thought about what I was going to say to April, the more I started to doubt myself. Put me in a five-on-one bar fight, not a fucking problem. Clean up a crime scene after a scumbag takes one to the head, non-issue. A grieving woman crying... that had my gut in knots. I had never done well with a crying woman, but after I watched my mom grieve and cry for years, I could no longer handle it.

I couldn't fuck this up. April needed to be taken care of. I couldn't disappoint my friend. I had to do this. Rick was one of my closest friends, and I had to do this for him. For Reid.

Fuck.

All too soon I pulled to a stop in front of the house. It was barely dawn, and the house was still dark. I sat in the truck and stared at the house. It was a cute little starter house in an older hood of San Fran. Rick bought it only six months before. When he asked April to marry him, he moved them out of the one bedroom apartment into this three-bedroom home. He wanted her to have this. I only know a little about her past, but I do know she had a shit childhood and Rick was determined to make sure she never had shit again.

I wondered if I should wait just a few more hours? Give April a few more hours of peace before I ripped her life out from under her.

You know, the thing is, minutes before your whole world is shattered - when you're going about your daily life without a care in the world, you don't know that your life is about to be in ruins. You don't know you should take those last minutes and savor them, remember them, try your hardest to hold on to that feeling. Because it is about to be gone, forever.

I wanted April to have just a few more minutes. Even if in her sleep, she didn't know any better. She didn't know that the man she was getting ready to marry was gone.

I hoped Blaze and Damion were killing Carl Allen in the most painful way possible. And what I wouldn't give to be in on the action. I knew if I called Damion and asked if I could join them, he'd tell me where they were and gladly give me my shot at him. But, April needed me.

I pushed my thoughts of revenge aside and started towards the house. I wiped my sweaty palms on my pants and blew out one last breath before I knocked. I flinched when my knuckles rapped on the hardwood.

No answer.

Fuck, I hoped I wouldn't have to stand out here and bang on the door, trying to wake her. Just as I was raising my hand to knock again. April threw open the door, her short blonde hair messy from sleep. She had on her glasses, that I knew she hated wearing because she said they made her look twelve. She was not wrong. Standing in front of me in a pair of rolled up boxers and a T-shirt, she indeed looked years younger than her twenty-four.

Twenty-fucking-four. She was a kid.

"Austin? Hey, you okay? Rick's on a call out," April said, her voice rough with sleep.

"Hey, April. Listen, can I come in a minute?"

"Rick okay?" she whispered.

"April, let's go in the house," I tried again.

I saw it. The minute understanding started to dawn. The very second, she went from the blissfully not knowing to the building panic.

"How bad is it this time? Fuck. Just tell me. I'll be ready in two minutes can you take me to the hospital?" She turned to leave, presumably to go get on clothes so I could take her to Rick.

Jesus Christ.

I used the opportunity to step into the house and

close the door. When she turned her head toward the sound of the door slamming, I shook my head no. In two long strides, I ate up the distance between us and pulled her into me, wrapping my arms around her as tight as I could. "April, I am so sorry. So, fucking sorry."

"Please don't say it, Austin." April's tears were almost my undoing, they had already begun to soak through my shirt.

"I'm sorry," I said again and continued to rock her in my arms.

In a manic motion, she pulled out of my arms and pushed me away. "Take me to Rick. I want to see him."

"April, I can't do that." Fuck it to hell. Not only would I never take her to see Rick in his current condition, he left explicit instructions not to allow her to see him no matter what condition he was in.

"I don't believe you. I wanna see him. What hospital is he at?" Her eyes were wild with panic and grief. I didn't know if she didn't believe me he was gone, or she couldn't believe I was being a dick and saying no to her. Either way, she wasn't leaving this house.

I read Rick's instructions. We all had a trust on file at the office. As morbid as that sounded, in our line of work, it was necessary. We didn't have the luxury of thinking about death in the abstract. If something happened to one of us, there was a detailed plan of action. Each of us knew our wishes would be carried out to the letter. Rick's stated that April was not to see his body. No one other than the crew was to see him. He wanted to be cremated immediately.

"April..."

She cut me off before I could finish. "No. No. No. Stop saying my name. Where is he?"

Truth time.

"He has been taken to the County Coroner's office. He will remain there until Dr. Sally Levenson can examine him and give us an official death certificate. After that, Huffin and Burrow's funeral home will pick him up. He will be cremated immediately. Per his wishes."

"Take me to him," she begged.

"I can't April. He doesn't want you to see him like that."

This was not what I was expecting. I thought there would be tears and sobbing. Not this much anger this fast.

"Well guess what, Austin? Rick doesn't get a say anymore," she yelled. Bending at the waist, she put her hands on her knees and started bawling.

I didn't let her push me away this time when I scooped her up in my arms and carried her to the couch. I settled us both in and let her use my tee as a Kleenex. Her trembling body started to relax into me, and when the sobbing turned into a soft hiccup, she finally gave me all her weight. I thought she was asleep when I heard a soft whisper.

"What was that? I couldn't hear you." I wiped her hair away from her face and glasses.

"I don't want him to be alone in a drawer in the morgue." I still could barely hear her.

Jesus, I didn't know what to say to that. If I was telling the truth the thought of that bothered me as well.

"April, you're killing me, honey. I can't let you go to the coroners. If it makes you feel any better, Sally is the best medical examiner in the state. She is also one of the most gentle and caring women I have ever met. Trust me when I tell you, Rick was taken to Sally's office because we trust her to take care of Rick with the utmost respect and dignity."

"I miss him already," she sobbed.

"I do too."

I was still in shock. I myself still had not processed that my friend was gone. Rick was a damn good person and friend. Over the years he had helped me through some fucked up shit. Whenever my head would go to a dark place, and I felt myself starting to slip dangerously to the edge, Rick would pull me back.

I welcomed the silence as we both sat there lost in our own thoughts. April was resting peacefully on my chest, her rhythmic breathing calming my frayed nerves.

"I'm pregnant, Austin." She started crying again burrowing her face further into my chest.

Oh, Fuck.

25

GODFATHER

Reid

JJ's smile lit up, and my soul filled with hope. I had claimed Ava and JJ a long time ago. But there was a difference, me claiming them in my mind, and them claiming me back. They had claimed me.

Mine. All fucking mine.

"You askin' me to marry you?" Ava smiled from across the room.

"You gettin' sassy with me woman?" I joked back and threw a wink in for good measure.

"Me? Never. But, just so you know that might've been the worst proposal in history if you were." Her smile grew bigger than I had ever seen it.

Over the years, I had watched Ava and JJ joke and banter. I had watched her smile brightly. But those smiles were reserved for JJ. The smile she gave everyone else was shy and guarded. Now she was beaming, all that goodness directed straight at me. I knew JJ was a lucky kid having Ava as a mom, but right then and there I realized just how lucky. He got that smile, all that goodness from her daily. I'd only had it once, and I wanted to bow down and hand her the world.

"And if that was a proposal what would your answer be?" I shot back, not wanting the fun to end.

"No."

"No? Well damn, looks like I'll have to come up with something good then." I laughed.

"Better hurry up. Time's a tickin' away..." Ava let her words trail off.

"She always this impatient?" I asked JJ.

"Yes," Both JJ and Mac said in unison.

"She can't even wait to open her birthday presents on her birthday. She opens them the day before," JJ told me.

Of course, I already knew that. The woman hated to wait. If you told her you had a present for her, she'd nag the hell out of you until you gave it to her. The last two years I got smart and just showed up the day of her birthday to give her, her gift.

"Sorry to have to bail, but I got a call out," Mac said.

"Bye, Uncle Mac." JJ wrapped his arms around Mac's middle. "I love you," JJ whispered.

"I love you too, buddy. I'll see you soon." Mac hugged him back.

"Thank you, Mac. I'll...um... I'll call you in a bit," Ava said from across the room, not getting up.

I knew they had some shit to work out. I heard most of their conversation from the kitchen. It was hard not to when Ava started yelling at Mac. I'd have to talk to Ava. I don't think she realized what she was doing to Mac. He put on a tough guy front, pretending the reason he screwed every woman in San Fran was because he was some hotshot playboy. But the truth was Aiden Mackenzie had the biggest heart of anyone I knew. He was loyal to a fault and took his obligations seriously. Not that Ava was an obligation in the bad sense of the word. And every time Ava pushed him away, he felt like a failure. I knew this because one drunken night he admitted it. The next day he either didn't remember the heart to heart or pretended not to. Either way, we'd never discussed it again.

"Sure thing. Pleased as fuck you're home safe and sound."

"Swear jar, Uncle Mac. That's a dollar for the F-bomb," JJ called out, doing some weird fist bump into the air.

This kid.

"I gave you a fifty-last night, kid. I think I'm covered," Mac responded and ruffled JJ's hair.

"A fifty?" Ava yelled out from across the room.

"He swears a lot mom. The fifty only covered the first hour. After that, I gave up. I wasn't sure if douchebag was a bad word, so I didn't count those," JJ explained.

"YES! It's a really bad word you don't get to repeat," she answered JJ and turned to Mac. "Nice mouth," she hissed.

"What is a douchebag?" JJ asked.

Ava bent down and whispered something in JJ's ear that made is eyes go big.

"Gross, Uncle Mac. You're calling someone a vagina cleaner," JJ yelled to Mac.

I lost the battle and belted out a laugh. Damn this kid. Ava looked like she was getting ready to have a shit hemorrhage. She didn't find anything funny about Mac's choice of words in front of JJ.

Mac bit back a smile. "I would say I was sorry. But I had bigger things to worry about than JJ hearing me cuss. And there wasn't a chance in fu..." Mac caught himself. "There wasn't a chance JJ was gonna be out of my sight. Don't repeat those words, kid, or I'll take my fifty back." Mac patted JJ's head one more time and took off for the door.

Smart man, Ava wasn't done with his dressing

down. And if Mac stood there a minute longer she'd let him have it with both guns a-blazing.

I walked Mac to the door.

"Everything okay with the callout?" I asked.

"Shit man, another body was found. The Chief is up our asses to get this solved before the feds are brought in. We can link all the bodies to one killer. At least that's what it looks like. Either that or we have a copycat running around too. We haven't released any information about the mutilation to the victims, so I don't see that as a real concern. But there are always leaks. Shit, we have three bodies tied together. We officially have a serial killer on our hands," Mac explained.

"The cloves, the condensed milk, the cinnamon. What the hell? The sick fuck making a pie or something?" I joked.

"Holy fuck. You might be on to something. Goddamn, I'll have to run that by the Chief, and see what else Sally has for us. And to top this shit storm off, the media has been swarming the station snooping around. Jesus Christ the last thing we need is for some reporter wanting to make a name for themselves and put this information out there and get the public in a frenzy."

"Let me know if you need anything. I've been fucking wrapped up in everything here, I had forgotten a world even existed outside of us. Sorry man. And the whole Jimmy thing, you need to talk about that?" I asked.

"Nope. I'm straight. You take care of them, and I'll handle the case. If shit goes sideways and I need your skillset, I'll call you in," Mac said, his voice tight.

Yeah, he needed to talk about what happened with Jimmy. But he wouldn't, he'd keep that shit bottled up tight. Austin said that when Mac came up from the basement he was afraid Mac was going to throw up. Mac might be quick-tempered, but he also went by the letter of the law. He took his oath seriously. The fact that Mac had committed a crime, had to be weighing heavily on him.

"Listen, I need to thank..." I started.

"No, you don't. I get that you love them, I know they are yours. I could not be happier for all of you. But, you do not need to thank me. Just tell me, is Carl handled?"

"Yes." I wouldn't give him details, and he'd never ask. If I told him it was done, he knew it was done.

"Did he... was she..."

I saved Mac from having to say the word. "No, he didn't. He kissed her, he saw her naked, and he tried to touch her. But she stopped him. We showed up in the middle of the struggle, and that's it."

Mac let out a colorful string of curse words that

would've had him owing a C-note to the swear jar if not more.

"One more thing. Carl was talking to Eva Martin, only she wasn't in the house. Crazy fuck. Austin is at April's right now telling her about Rick. Dustin is doing some more digging, Austin will help with that too. Can you get me Carl's service record from the PD without raising any red flags? Or should I ask Royston to help? I don't wanna pull Dustin off Eva."

"Crazy motherfucker. You know what bothers me? That someone as crazy as Carl can be a cop. How does that happen?" Mac shook his head. "I'll get you his service records. By the way, Dustin told me about your security system being hacked and the feeds being deleted. That might be something for Royston to look into."

"Yeah, that's a good idea. Royston was the one who finished the system for me. I just don't understand. He's the best fucking hacker I know, and it took him days to break into my system. After that, he went back and patched up the weak links. How in the hell did an idiot like Carl Allen hack my system? There is no way he did it on his own. And the bastard had keys to Ava's house. He was planning this shit for a long time."

Another long string of cuss words flew from Mac's mouth. Carl was lucky he was dead or on his way to being dead, because Mac looked like he was ready to tear him from limb to limb.

"Did you know he had pictures of Ava in his locker and Jacob found them?" I asked Mac, and watched as his face turned red.

Guess that was my answer.

"No. He never said anything. Though that's not surprising. Jacob had already given him a beat down. Had he told me that, I might've broken a leg for good measure."

Good to know that Jacob handled Mac the same way I did. Always trying to protect him from his own damn temper.

"I'm taking Ava to see Suzie in a few hours. I'll check in with you when I get everyone settled."

"You want me to come back and stay with JJ?" Mac looked hopeful. Damn, he missed the boy. Yet another thing I had to talk to Ava about. She had to stop cutting Mac out of JJ's life. I understood why she was doing it, but it had to end. Mac didn't deserve it.

Without even bothering to discuss it with Ava, I answered Mac, "Yeah. That'd be great. Go handle your shit and call me when you're done. Maybe I can convince Ava to take a nap. And if you have JJ, I can take Ava to go see April."

"Sound's good. See ya in a few." Mac started to

walk away before he stopped and turned back. "You know I'm JJ's Godfather, right?"

That was an odd question.

"Yes, I knew that," I answered him.

"You know I expect to be the Godfather to any more rug-rats you two spit out?"

I let out a peal of laughter. "Sure man. Though I wouldn't tell Ava you think she can spit a baby outta her vagina. I think women get pissy about shit like that."

"Noted. One more thing. You know I want to stand up for you when you marry her. She loves you, Reid. So does that boy in there. You are one lucky son-of-a-bitch. And before you say it. I know what you're thinkin', that you're the lucky one. And that right there is why I know you are the man that will love them the way they deserve. Thank you for that."

Mac didn't give me a chance to answer, he was down the walk and almost to his car before I had processed all of what he said.

I was the lucky one.

I shut and bolted the door, and went in search of Ava and JJ. I found them in the breakfast nook looking out the large bay window that gave you a perfect view of the Bridge and the Point Bonita Lighthouse. At night, you could see the light flashing, guiding ships past the point. One of the many reasons I bought this house.

"Whatcha guys looking at?" I asked coming up behind Ava, wrapping my arms around her from behind and kissing the top of her head.

"There's a huge sailboat. It's so cool," JJ exclaimed.

"That's a Townsend and Downey. She's a beauty, isn't she? It's too bad they're on power and don't have the sails up," I told him.

"Look there's another boat," JJ enthusiastically pointed out.

We stood in silence and watched the early morning boaters taking advantage of the still waters. It was a clear morning, the normal morning fog absent. I took the opportunity to give thanks to the universe. Thankful that I had Ava back in my arms.

JJ yawned loudly, reminding me that none of us had slept.

"Why don't we try and get some rest?" I suggested.

"I'm not tired." JJ yawned trying to cover it up with his hand.

"Well I am," Ava said, yawning herself.

"Why don't you and JJ head upstairs? I'm gonna check the house and lock up." I let go of Ava, taking her plate and cup with me into the kitchen.

"No," JJ all but shouted. "We'll wait here for you."

"What's wrong?" Ava asked JJ. She turned to study

his face.

"Nothing. I just want to wait for Reid. Um, how do we know what's upstairs? He should show us."

JJ was panicking, and Ava's face paled.

"Alright JJ. Let's go lock up the house," I suggested, "Is it ok if your mom goes upstairs and gets changed?"

"Yeah, okay. But you're just going upstairs right?" he probed.

Ava's eyes cut to mine, and she tilted her head to the side. Obviously confused by my suggestion.

I nodded my head, and she answered, "Yes, I'm going straight upstairs."

"Okay, I'll go with Reid." JJ quickly made his way to my side and grabbed my hand. "Can we hurry?"

"There should be something for you to sleep in, in the master bedroom. Help yourself to whatever you find in the drawers."

Ava's confusion grew. I knew she wanted to question me, but she remained silent as she left the kitchen area. I waited until she was out of earshot before I addressed JJ.

"What's goin' on, little man?"

"Nothing, I just want to help," JJ lied.

"Alright, I'm gonna lay it out for you. You, me, and your mom, we're a team. The three of us. Being part of a team means you're always honest, even if it is uncomfortable or embarrassing. If something is bothering you,

you tell me." JJ's eyes widened. He obviously didn't think that Ava or I had caught on that something was wrong.

"Okay," he responded.

"So, I'm gonna ask you again. What's going on?"

"I'm scared," he whispered.

"Of what?"

I knew this was costing him, me making him be honest with me. Making him talk about how he felt, and what he was scared of. But I couldn't let this slide. JJ had to understand that if something was wrong, he could always trust me to help him.

"I don't know." Now he was being honest. I believed he couldn't put to words why he was scared.

"Do you think I'm going to leave you?"

"No. I know you wouldn't leave me. I'm scared that he'll come and take me next," he murmured.

Motherfucking, Carl Allen.

"He won't. I promise you will never have to worry about Carl Allen again. Ever. He will never touch you, you will never hear his voice again, and he will never get near your mom again. He is gone. Forever." JJ looked at me, but he still didn't look like he was convinced. "JJ, do I break promises?"

"No," he answered.

"I promise you, son, that man will never hurt you or your mom again. It is okay to be scared. We'll work through that as a family, a team. But, you have to tell us if something is bothering you so we can help you."

"Okay."

"Let's get the house locked up so we can check on your mom. Do you know where the garage door is?" JJ nodded his head. "Go check that door is locked. I'll check the front door and meet you at the stairs."

I watched as JJ tried to work out if he was going to check the door by himself. Just when I thought he was going to tell me no, he nodded his head and ran towards the back of the house.

Brave.

I checked the door and armed the alarm. JJ was waiting for me at the bottom of the stairs. He was out of breath, and red-faced. I didn't bother to acknowledge either. He did it, left my side, and proved to himself he could do it.

"Door locked?" I asked.

"Yep."

"Good, let's go find your mom."

We found Ava in the master bedroom wearing a pair of sweats that were three times too big for her. She had them rolled up and still had to hold them up. She looked like she was wearing... well, my clothes.

"Can I stay in here with you two?" JJ requested.

"Reid's not..."

"Yes. Of course, you can. Hop up little man," I cut

Ava off.

If she thought for one second, that she and JJ would not be in here with me, she was crazy.

"Reid, maybe..."

"Nope. Not a chance. Get comfy, sweetheart, I'll be right back."

I grabbed a pair of sweats and a clean tee and headed to the master bathroom. I'd give her a few minutes to make this adjustment. It was non-negotiable, she would be in my bed from here on out.

When I came out, she and JJ were cuddled up, taking up half of the king-sized bed. The sight was breathtaking. JJ snuggled safely in his mom's embrace, Ava kissing the top of his head.

I couldn't stop the vision from playing out in my mind of Ava sitting in bed nursing our baby with JJ snuggled up to her side. The more I thought about it, the more I wanted it. Soon.

I crawled into bed, so exhausted my eyes were closing as soon as my head hit the pillow. I wasn't even lying there a minute when I felt it. JJ turned in Ava's arms, both facing me. One little boy hand reached out and grabbed mine. A second later, a soft warm, woman hand reached out and grabbed our hands.

My eyes closed and sleep started to take me.

"My boys," I heard muttered softly.

I fell asleep with a smile playing on my lips.

26

WE'RE A TEAM

Ava

I cracked my eyes open, and I was alone in bed. Panic set in, then I remembered where I was. I was safe. Reid found me. I sighed and laid back down. I needed a few minutes to myself.

I was emotionally exhausted, and my nerves were shot. The relief of being found had dissipated, and guilt had set in. I felt like I was going to have a nervous breakdown any moment. Jimmy showing up, Carl, Suzie in ICU, Rick, April. All of it, my fault.

I had to go see Suzie today, but I was afraid to face Michael. He must hate me. It was my fault his wife had been beaten. And April, poor April, the man she was getting ready to marry was dead. Again, because of me.

I turned my head and let my pillow absorb my

tears, muffling the sound of my sobs. I didn't even want to think about the untold effect this was having on my son. He looked so scared last night when Reid told us to go upstairs. JJ didn't even want to be alone with me, not that I blamed him. I was a walking disaster. But, it still hurt like hell.

I gave myself a few more minutes before I sat up and wiped my tears away. I needed to go and find my boys.

A quick trip to the bathroom to clean up and fix my face before I went in search of JJ and Reid.

They were in the kitchen nook, eating a pizza talking with Mac.

Fucking A, I couldn't catch a break. I had hoped I could push the Mac situation out of my mind for a few days.

"Hey," I greeted when I walked in.

"Hey, Mom. Uncle Mac brought us a pizza. He brought your favorite. Garlic knots! They're on the counter. Oh, and a diet coke," JJ rushed out.

"Good Morning to you too." I smiled at JJ. "That was nice of your Uncle Mac. Did you tell him thank you?"

"Of course, I did." But, judging by the look on JJ's face I doubted he remembered to say thank you.

"Good Morning Mac. Thank you for breakfast... er...lunch. Reid, is there a coffee maker?"

Both men laughed. My need for coffee was real. Reid stood up and came to me, as soon as he was close enough his hand shot out, and he tagged me around the stomach pulling me into him.

"Hmmm." He inhaled close to my neck. "Good morning, sweetheart. Go sit. I'll make you coffee."

"Thank you." I lifted on my toes and kissed his cheek. That was all I felt comfortable with in front of Mac and JJ.

Before I could get very far, Reid grabbed both sides of my face and brought his lips to mine.

It was a chaste kiss. Just the touching of lips. But my body caught fire, and all sorts of images played through my head. I remembered what it felt like having his tongue stroking mine. I wanted more of that.

"You're welcome," Reid said against my lips.

"Hey, bud you done eating yet?" Mac asked JJ snapping me out of my wayward thoughts.

"Yeah." JJ wiped his mouth and pushed his plate away from him.

"Good. If you're ready, let's hit the road." Mac stood, picking the plates up off the table.

I must've missed the planning of our day. I hadn't even had coffee yet, and my stomach was growling. I needed at least an hour before I was ready.

"I'm not ready. Can I at least have a cup of coffee?" I grumbled.

"Uncle Mac is taking me to the skateboard park so you and Reid can run errands," JJ informed me.

Say what? I was instantly on alert struggling to keep my temper in check. It's not that I didn't appreciate Mac wanting to take JJ so we could go to the hospital, but I would've liked to have been consulted.

"Can I talk to you? In private." I wasn't quite sure which man I was speaking to. I didn't know which one of them had made the plan without talking to me first. But, I figured whichever one made the plans would follow me out of the room.

In the end, it was Reid that followed me into the living room.

"You have something you want to tell me?" I quizzed him.

Reid looked thoughtful for a moment and shook his head. "No."

"What the hell? Mac is taking JJ out to the park? Did anyone think to run that by me?" I challenged.

"No."

I was getting ready to strangle Reid. "How about an answer that is more than one word?"

"We have things to do today. Things that JJ should not see. Mac offered to spend some time with him this afternoon so we could do those things. I took him up on the offer. That's it."

"Don't you think you should've asked me?"

"No."

Holy shit. We were back to the single syllable answers.

"No? And why is that?" I was a millimeter away from losing my patience. "So help me God, if you answer with one word I'm gonna throat punch you, Reid."

I didn't miss the flash in Reid's eyes before he stepped close invading my space.

"I didn't ask you because it's Mac. Again, he offered. I took him up on it so we can go visit Suzie and April without JJ seeing and hearing things that would further scare the shit out of him. I also didn't ask because I'm not gonna bother you with petty shit, that I know you're gonna say yes to. You trust me?" He stopped speaking apparently waiting for my answer.

I wasn't sure what I was supposed to say. Yes, I trusted him. But...that wasn't the point.

"Me trusting you is not the issue. You made a decision about JJ without talking to me first."

"You miss the conversation we all had last night?"

I thought back, trying to recall last night's conversation. Did I miss something? Was I so tired that I forgot we talked about Mac taking JJ?

"What conversation?"

He lowered his face to meet my eyes and held them for a minute.

"The conversation where that boy in there said he wanted me to be his dad. The conversation where I explained to him in no uncertain terms that not only did I claim him as my son, but you as the woman I am going to marry. Did you miss *that* conversation, Ava?" His voice hardened, and his eyes narrowed.

"Well, no. I didn't miss *that* conversation." My voice sounded shrill even to my own ears.

What the hell was wrong with me?

"Then the problem is what? I am not stupid Ava. I know, for now, there are boundaries. Mac, however, is not one of those boundaries. You have to trust me."

Shit, he was right. I was making a big deal out of nothing. Mac taking JJ for the day wasn't the issue. Reid overstepping was not the issue. The issue was me. I was used to being the only one that made decisions regarding JJ.

"Fine." Reid chuckled at my answer and kissed my forehead. "I need coffee," I informed him.

"Yeah. Ya' do." Reid continued to laugh.

"What is that supposed to mean?" I snapped.

"Goddamn, woman, you are sexy as hell when you are feisty. Let's get you some coffee before I take you upstairs and show you just how sexy I think you are."

As tempting as that sounded, I didn't think that was the best plan with my ten-year-old son waiting for us in the kitchen.

Without answering, I walked away leaving Reid standing in the living room laughing.

Asshole.

When I made it back to the kitchen, Mac and JJ were both standing waiting to go. Both had identical smiles across their faces. I hoped like hell they hadn't heard that conversation.

"Thank you, Mac." I didn't know what else to say. Yes, we needed to have a long conversation, one where I admitted I had been a royal bitch and I was wrong. But now was not the time for that.

"Anytime. Now, my Godson and I are gonna go rip shit up at the skate park," Mac announced.

I rolled my eyes in annoyance. There was no use trying. As many times as I reminded him about his mouth, he ignored me. I should just be thankful he wasn't dropping F-bombs. JJ laughed beside him before he tried to cover it up with a cough. Cheeky brat and he knew it too.

I smiled at JJ and winked. "Love you, kid. Be good. And please wear your helmet. You have a pretty head. I'd like to keep it that way."

"Sure, Mom. I'll see you later." He waved tugging Mac's shirt as he walked out of the kitchen.

I didn't miss that he didn't tell me he loved me back. This was one of those times JJ had told me about.

Where when he was in front of the *guys* he didn't want me embarrassing him.

Sigh.

"See ya, Ava." Mac waved.

I stayed rooted in the kitchen. I wanted to go after them and kiss my son goodbye, but JJ would be embarrassed. I started to stir the creamer into my coffee watching it turn a 'blonde' color, putting another splash in for good measure. Coffee taste was nasty, the more creamer the better.

That's when I felt it. My son wrapping his arms around me from behind, squeezing me tight. I didn't move. I closed my eyes and appreciated the moment.

"I love you, Mama," he whispered to my back.

I didn't answer. I just let his words seep in, spreading warmth as they went.

God, I loved my little boy, who was no longer so little. As fast as he ran into the room he ran back out.

I took my coffee to the nook, enjoying the view of the South Bay. The cloudless sky a deep blue. It looked to be a beautiful day out. Unusual for this time of year, it looked like spring might come early. I welcomed the warm weather. JJ loved the summer when we could be outside all day, enjoying all the outdoor activities San Fran had to offer.

I was planning a trip to Fisherman's Wharf in my head when Reid came in.

"How are you feeling today?" he inquired.

I plastered my fake smile on before I turned to face him.

"Great." The lie rolled easily off my tongue.

"Bullshit. I'll tell you the same thing I told JJ last night. The three of us... we're a team. We don't bullshit each other. Honesty, always," he replied.

"You said that to JJ?"

"Ava!"

He wasn't going to let me get away deflecting. Damn him. I didn't want to talk about this. I remained silent in hopes that he would understand.

"How. Are. You. Feeling?" He enunciated each word in his impatience.

Jeeze.

"My head is feeling fine. No headache. And nothing hurts." There, that was an answer.

"Good to know. What about the rest?" He pushed.

UGH!

"I'm fine. Really,"

"Is that why you came down this morning with your face blotchy from crying?"

"That's nice. You saying I look like shit?"

"Like shit? No. Did I know you'd been cryin'? Yes. You forget woman, I know you. I am not new. Mac is walking on shaky ground with you. He knows this, so he'll keep his mouth shut and won't press his luck. I'll press."

He was infuriating. I didn't want to fucking talk about this. So, I announced, "I'm going to take a shower."

I stomped out of the kitchen, and up the stairs. All the while I was waiting for him to follow me. Demand I answer him.

He didn't.

I grabbed my new clothes from yesterday and brought them into the master bathroom with me. I turned the water on full blast and as hot as I could handle before I stepped in. I stood there for a long while, letting the water wash away my tension. I rolled my neck under the hot water and relaxed even more.

One moment I was standing in the steam enjoying a peaceful shower and the next I was screaming down the house. The memories snuck up on me, the last time I was in the shower a madman was in there with me, threatening to violate me. I thought I might pass out. I couldn't stop it, I couldn't catch my breath.

Strong hands grabbed my shoulders, my naked back hit a wall of muscle. I continued to scream and struggle with all my might. He wouldn't touch me. He would never, ever touch me.

"Ava!"

In the abstract, way far away, I could hear my name.

"Ava!"

This time a little clearer, but still in the fringes of my mind.

"Ava, sweetheart. You're safe."

"Reid?"

"Right here, sweetheart. Slow down. Breathe with me."

I waited, and after a few beats, I could feel his chest move against my back. I mimicked his breathing, slowing mine.

"That's it, sweetheart. Just breathe," he spoke softly near my ear.

I continued to breathe in slow deep breaths until my mind cleared and could feel the roughness of Reid's jeans on my backside. Then I was panting and breathing heavy for a whole new reason.

I wanted Reid to erase the memory of Carl in the shower. Replace it with something better.

"I need you," I admitted.

"I'm right here, sweetheart."

I had never done this before. I had never been the one to initiate any sort of intimacy. I wasn't sure how to do it.

"I *need* you, Reid." I tried again, this time interjecting flirtation in my tone.

His body stiffened behind me, and his fingers on my hips tightened.

Now he understood.

"You're not ready yet." He rejected me.

I should've expected that. He probably still had the same images I had of Carl touching me in his head. He might say that he didn't think I was dirty, but another man had touched me.

"Stop, Ava."

"Stop what?" I asked. "I understand, it's... a... um... it's okay." Great now I sounded like an idiot.

As much as I understood, his rejection still stung.

"That, right there, you don't understand. You think just because I won't throw you up against the shower wall and fuck you, I don't want you."

"What if I want you to fuck me against the shower wall?" Jeeze, that was uncomfortable to say.

"You don't. You don't want me. You want to use me to wash Carl away."

Shit, when he said it like that, it sounded bitchy and dirty. I was disgusted with myself.

"I'm sorry. You're right." I turned in his arms, uncaring that he would have a clear, unobstructed view of my body. "That's not fair to you."

"Sweetheart, if I thought for one second that me fucking the hell outta you in this shower would help you, make no mistake I would. But, trust me, it would only make it worse. The first time I finally have you, it will be because you simply cannot wait to feel me inside of you."

I might've been halfway to feeling that way already. Hearing him say, 'feel me inside of you' was doing strange things to my body. A good strange. I had never had anyone talk dirty to me before.

Jacob and I had a healthy sex life, it was good sex. He was my first, and my only. He was always gentle with me. He had good stamina and always made sure I was taken care of. But, he never used coarse words with me. He would've never picked me up and fucked me against anything. Hell, he would've never called it fucking. It was always in the bed. Either him on top or me. Never any other way.

"Can I ask you for a favor?" My request was met with a twitch of Reid's lips.

"Anything," he replied.

"Will you take off your clothes and just stand here with me?"

I don't know what made me ask him that. Maybe I didn't want to be alone in my vulnerability.

"Sweetheart, you're making this real hard on me."

I blinked my eyes confused. "Why?"

"I am trying here. I have self-control, but only so much. You standing here naked in front of me. Your perfect tits on display. Your pretty pink nipples pebbled, looking like they need to be licked and tasted. I'm holding on by a thread here."

"Oh." I didn't know what else to say. Again, no one had ever spoken to me that way. So open in expressing their appreciation for my body. I was a little shocked, and a whole lot turned on.

"Yeah. *Oh*. Are you starting to understand yet? I have waited years, to touch you, see you, kiss you. I am using every ounce of control I have."

"What if I told you, I was ready to beg to have you inside me. That I was a hundred percent sure."

His only response was to growl before he took my mouth. His kiss took my breath away. He could have it, because at that moment I didn't need it. The only thing I needed was him. My hands tore at his shirt. Breaking our kiss long enough to pull it up over his head. Next, my hand reached for the button of his jeans. I made quick work, getting them down to his knees before the wet fabric bunched up making it impossible for me to remove. He took pity on me, and in some ninja move, he kicked his pants off and into the corner of the shower, never taking his lips from mine.

"Can I?" I started. I had to stop and clear my throat. I wasn't sure how to ask this. "May I touch you?"

I had kept my hands firmly on his biceps, afraid to move them. First, I needed to hold on to something to keep my balance, and secondly, I wasn't sure what to do with them.

"Ava. You're killing me," he panted.

I looked up and was shocked to find his pained expression.

"I'm sorry. I don't know what came over me."

I was acting like some horny teenager who couldn't control her hormones. But, holy shit I had to touch him.

"Fuck it. I tried. I tried to take this slow, but I see that's not gonna work. You have a choice to make here and now. We talked a bit about this last night. We talked to the boy about it, and I know where he stands. I want this real clear, Ava, so there is no misunderstanding. When I take you. You're mine. And I mean that in a forever kinda way. Not that I am your boyfriend and we are gonna date to see where this goes. It means I put my ring on your finger ASAP. You and JJ are in my house from now on, you making it our home. If you need time to think this over, let's slow this down. Take a few days. Because the moment I slide into you, there will be no stopping. I have waited years. I can wait a few days more."

Holy wow. My head was spinning. Did I want that? Did I want Reid's ring? Did I want JJ and me in his house? The answer came faster than it should've.

"I can't," I blurted out. "I can't wait. I don't want to

wait. I meant what I said earlier. The part of my heart that I thought would always be shattered and broken, it's not anymore. You fixed it, pieced it back together. It is unbroken. I'm ready. I love you, with every part of me."

"Unbroken?" he asked.

"Unbroken," I confirmed. "You fixed it."

"You ready?"

"More than," I answered.

"You gonna say yes when I slip my ring on your finger?"

I scrunched my face up and tapped my chin pretending to think about the answer. Reid wasn't having any of that. He picked me up, and I wrapped my legs around his waist. My back hit the tile wall, his face now inches from mine. "You gonna say yes?"

"Yes." I giggled as his strong hands flexed on my ass.

27

TWISTED...AGAIN

Reid

The word, yes, echoed in my mind, over and over again.

My mouth came down on hers, and it was a duel for ultimate supremacy. Our tongues danced, and my cock ached. I should've won the Goddamn Guinness Book World record for the best self-control. Her tight ass was in my hands, bare tits pressed against me, and her pussy was less than an inch from my cock.

And I still hadn't taken her.

I reached around and shut the water off, uncaring if she had actually washed or not. The first time I had Ava wasn't going to be in the shower. And as much as this was going to piss both my cock and Ava off, I was not going to fuck her in some hurried frenzy. As a matter of fact, I wasn't going to fuck her at all.

Not right now.

I heard her words. I even believed that she thought she meant them. But I wanted to wait. As much as my cock begged to differ, another few days wouldn't kill me. I would have her for a lifetime.

But just because I wasn't going to fuck her, didn't mean I wasn't going to give my woman one hell of an orgasm, my cock just wouldn't be involved.

I navigated us out of the shower, through the bathroom, and into the bedroom all the while continuing to kiss her.

We both came down on the bed. I gave her my weight and slid my hands through her wet hair, holding her at the angle I wanted.

I broke the kiss and nearly came when she moaned at the loss of me.

Oh fuck, this was not going to go well for me. The truth was I hadn't had sex in a very long time, hadn't touched another woman in well over a year. At the risk of sounding like a pussy whipped monk, it was actually closer to three.

The last time I had a woman in my bed, Ava witnessed the morning after, when I walked my date out to her car. Regina looked a mess, dress back on from the night before, no shoes, no makeup, no false eyelashes. The pretense had washed off during our activities, and she was not that attractive in the daylight. Ava was out watering her flowers in the early morning hours and watched in horror as Regina basically dry humped me by the side of her car.

I only tried one woman after that. I had taken that one back to her place, with no Ava to witness the walk of shame the next morning. That was a non-starter, my cock refused to cooperate when all I could focus on was Ava's look of disgust.

As much of a bastard as this made me, I knew six months after Jacob's murder that I wanted Ava. What started out as a physical attraction fast grew into an emotional one. I stayed away, because she wasn't ready, and there was no way I could've competed with Jacob's ghost. The first eighteen months after I made that realization, it was business as usual. A revolving door of women graced my bed. None of them were Ava, none of them came close, and none of them had a chance at my heart because it was taken. They were a release and nothing more. Dick move on my part? Absolutely. I didn't know any better then. I had no clue that the empty sex would leave me feeling even emptier. Until Ava saw me. I was giving away a part of myself that belonged to Ava to meaningless women.

Even if she didn't know it. I knew it. I knew that I was in love with Ava, and one day I would have her. That made me a prick, so I stopped. Hadn't touched another woman since. It was not a chore, and it was not hard. I knew the payoff would be well worth it.

My lips continued their slow glide over her jaw, down her neck, making sure I paid special attention to the hollow of her throat.

She arched her back and tilted her head giving me better access. The move only thrust her tits closer to my mouth. I had had a lot of women. None, not a single one, had tits as nice as Ava's. They were full and sagged just enough to remind me she was all woman. Not a young girl with perky little boobs. But, all woman with big full tits. They were Goddamn perfect. And nice big nipples. Just the sight of them made me want to pinch and bite them.

I continued to stare and wasn't sure what I was waiting for. Ava was spread out in front of me mewing like a kitten waiting to be licked, and here I was musing about how I'd like to taste her tits instead of actually doing it.

Fucking idiot.

"Scoot down the bed sweetheart. I want your ass right at the edge."

Wordlessly she complied, and I was back to staring again. This time because I had a full unobstructed view of her entire body. I looked her over from top to toe.

Sweet Mary mother of God. I had to close my eyes, the vision of her was too much. My cock twitched, pre-come now dripping from my head. I wouldn't have been surprised if I had actually just came a little. Her toned, tanned legs lay draped over the bed, thighs spread just enough to see her trimmed pussy lips were puffy and slick with her own excitement.

I opened my eyes to find her now staring at me. "Hi," she whispered. Her voice shy and unsure.

I wondered how much it was costing her laying here in front of me. Letting my greedy eyes eat her up. For the first time in my entire life, I was unsure what to say to a woman, and I began to doubt myself.

"You are so beautiful, Ava."

Her lips tipped up into a smile, and her cheeks began to pinken.

"Thank you."

She jumped when my hand hit her knees, and I spread her legs farther apart. I watched her eyes closely and saw trepidation behind them. Confirming, I had made the right call. We were going to take this nice and slow.

My hands traveled up her inner thigh, missing her pussy, over her belly, under and around those tits. I was torturing us both. My hands itched to touch more of her, but I'd make her wait. I glided my hands back down to where I had started, and back up again. Over and over again, slow and gentle working her up. Her skin felt so good under my palms, everything and more than I ever imagined.

Her back arched again, and she spread her legs on her own accord. There it was. I lowered my mouth and took one of her pebbled nipples into my mouth.

"Oh my God, LOGAN," she screamed.

I didn't answer. Not verbally anyway. I took advantage of her shock and pushed a single finger into her pussy. So Goddamn tight. I pulled my finger out using her moisture to wet her clit before I pushed two fingers in this time. My thumb went to her clit and made slow circles, timing them just perfectly with my tongue on her nipple.

She wiggled her ass around and moaned again.

"Logan," she panted.

I still didn't answer. I just gave her more pressure on her clit.

"Logan. Please."

"What do you need, sweetheart?" I asked, slowing my ministrations.

"I don't know. You. More."

My control snapped, and I gave her what she asked for. More. More of my mouth and more of my fingers.

"Let go, Ava. Relax."

Her body had gone stiff, and she was fighting it.

"I can't. I... don't," she stuttered.

"You don't what, sweetheart?" I asked, continuing to work her pussy with my fingers.

"I don't know how. I've never... not this way," she admitted.

Surely she didn't mean what I thought she meant.

"You've never come on a man's fingers?"

"No," she confessed.

My excitement rose ten-fold.

"Relax, sweetheart. I'll walk you through it."

She nodded in response, I didn't wait for her words of confirmation before I took her mouth. Working her back up with a smoldering kiss. I slowed my thumb on her clit and gave her more of my fingers. I could hear how wet she was every time I plunged my fingers into her snug pussy. The sound was fucking hot.

Soon she was panting and had to break the kiss to catch her breath. I stayed bent over her, my lips near her ear.

"You're almost there, Ava. I wanna feel you come all over my hand."

"Oh God..."

"That's it, sweetheart. So Goddamn sexy. Your cheeks are flush, your nipples erect, I can feel your pussy starting to convulse."

"Oh my God..."

"You like my fingers, Ava? Do you like when I finger fuck you and bite down on your pretty little nipple?" Her pussy spasmed, she was almost there. "Ah, yes, sweetheart, so fucking close. I cannot wait to taste you. I'm gonna lick your pussy until you scream. And after that, you're gonna watch me as I jerk off, watching you play with your beautiful tits."

"Fucking hell! Logan."

Her orgasm broke free, and it was a thing of beauty. I'd like to say it was sexy, but it looked painful, like years of buildup and need had finally shattered. It was spectacular to watch.

I slowly brought her down, when her eyes opened they were filled with tears. Yeah, I made the right call. This needed to be handled with care. Us going slow, I would take her step by step.

I kissed the tears that had started to roll down her cheeks and removed my fingers. Though I still cupped her sex and gently stroked her. This wasn't a quick get off, and move on. I gave her more of my weight and held her close to me. I figured after her first sexual experience in five years, she would need a moment. Hell, I needed a moment. My cock was nestled between us, pushing painfully into her hip. It was primed and ready to go off. I needed to excuse myself, and soon, to go and take care of it.

Her breathing slowed, I thought she had fallen asleep until I heard her relaxed voice.

"May I touch you now?" Her breath tickling my ear as she spoke.

She brought her legs up around my hips and locked me to her, moving my cock against her skin in the process.

"Be still, Ava, or we're gonna have a mess on your belly," I warned. She didn't stop, and I lifted my head out of her neck staring down at her. "Ava. Please. Be still."

"I don't want to be still. I want you."

Oh no. Oh hell no. She couldn't look at me with those big brown imploring eyes with my cock begging and pleading with me to take her.

"Sweetheart, you have me."

"Inside. I want you inside of me."

"Not yet."

"Now," she insisted and moved her hips to grind into me more.

I had to suck in a breath and count to ten to stop the rushing sensation. Next thing you know, I was going to make a deal with myself like I would just put the tip in like some high school boy. This needed to end. I had to get control back and stop her. Because I was a hair's breath away from going back on my word and giving her the tip, then the middle, then my whole fucking cock as I drilled the hell out of her.

Slow down, asshole.

I stood to my full height and palmed my cock.

"You wanna mess, Ava? Is that what you want?"

She didn't answer just tightened her legs around me. I glanced down at her pussy and groaned.

"Grab your tits." She did immediately and gave them both a squeeze. "I want your thumbs to brush over your nipples. I want them both hard," I instructed.

I gave my cock a few hard pulls with my right hand and massaged her pussy with my left.

"You like watching me stroke myself while I play with your pussy?"

Her thumb continued to work over her nipples, her chest was reddening, her breathing was getting choppy.

"Oh yeah, you like to watch. You gonna come again for me, baby?"

"I wanna feel you," she told me.

I took my cock and positioned it at her opening rubbing the head up and down through her wetness. I was playing a dangerous game.

"Please," she begged.

I teased her entrance with the head of my cock putting pressure at her opening. A small shift of my hips and I would be inside her. I needed her to hurry and come again before that happened.

"Pinch your nipples, sweetheart." She did and closed her eyes. "I want your eyes on me. I want you to watch while I jerk myself off all over your pussy. You're gonna come with me. I need you to hurry, Ava. I'm almost there."

And I was. So fucking close I was going to blow and leave her behind.

"Almost," she panted.

"Tell me, Ava, you wanna feel my cock?"

"Yes."

"Say it," I demanded.

"I wanna feel your cock."

"You wanna feel it here, in your slick warm pussy?" I gave her more pressure, my cock starting to breach her opening.

"I'm there, Logan."

I gave myself a few more strokes before I pulled away from her pussy. I tensed as heat rushed through my body, and I let go on her hip and belly.

She looked startled as my come marked her flawless skin. After long moments, my shoulders and neck began to loosen, and I searched Ava's face for any signs of unease. None was present, just pure happiness.

"That is a mess." Her giggle started soft and sweet, but quickly turned into a full belly laugh.

Beautiful.

"Yeah, sweetheart, you certainly made a mess."

"Me?" She batted her eyelashes. Trying but failing to look innocent.

"You know exactly what you did. Don't play miss innocent with me."

As much as I didn't want to rush this, the day was slipping away, and unfortunately, we had things we had to take care of. I was glad that in the middle of this shit storm she could still laugh.

"Let's get cleaned up."

I didn't wait for her reply when I picked her up off the bed, her legs still wrapped around me, and walked us back into the shower.

Not much was said when I washed her. She understood why we needed to hurry and clean up. I didn't push her, she needed time in her own head to work out what today would bring. I'd allow it, as long as she didn't start pushing me away, or spewing whacked shit about things being her fault.

None of this was on Ava. She didn't ask to be pulled into James Kelley's bullshit, or be stalked by Carl Allen. I didn't want to bring up that we were still not outta the woods, and I had to check in with Zane Lewis in a few hours to see what he'd found out about the boys Jimmy was running with in El Paso. If there was going to be any sort of blowback or retribution for Jimmy, I was taking Ava and JJ and we were leaving town. I wasn't taking any more chances.

The ride to the hospital was quiet. Ava was pulling

into herself, shrinking back into her seat the closer we got.

"Stop," I demanded when we pulled into the hospital parking.

"I'm not doing anything, Reid."

"Yeah, sweetheart, you are. You're twisting all sorts of shit up in that pretty little head of yours. I'm afraid to even ask what kind of fucked up shit you're making up in there."

Ava's body went solid in the seat next to mine. I threw the Camaro in park and pocketed the key fob. Before she could start speaking, and by doing so piss me off, I got out of the car, rounded the trunk, and opened her door.

She woodenly walked beside me through the parking structure. By the time we had made it to the elevators, I'd had enough.

"Say it," I urged her.

"Say what? Anything I say, you'll tell me it's jacked or fucked up."

"Because it is. But I need to know what parts you're twisting, so I know what to untwist."

"You know it's kinda mean to tell me how I feel is jacked."

"No, it's not. It's real. I'm not gonna blow unicorns up your ass, just so you don't think I'm mean. I'm really not gonna stand here and let you blame yourself for shit that is not on you. I gave you time, I didn't push. I let you go in that head of yours hoping that you'd work it out yourself. You didn't. I see that was the wrong thing to do."

"You let me?" she screeched.

"Absolutely."

"Really. And pray tell how you let me."

"Ava, I can be real persuasive when I want something, and real creative in the ways I get it. If I didn't want you in your own head, you wouldn't be there. I thought you could sort yourself out. You can't, so now, I'll sort you out."

Ava's face was fire engine red, if I had to guess, I'd say that smoke was seconds away from coming out of her ears. I didn't want to do this, but I now knew it was necessary.

28

OUR GIRL

Ava

"Reid..." I tried to stop him from saying whatever it was he was going to say. I was already pissed, and he was only going to make me angrier.

"No. There is no nice way to say it, so I'll just say it." Reid grabbed my hand and pulled me to him. What came next pissed me the fuck off. "Nothing. I'll repeat nothing that has happened is on you. Jimmy Kelley was a piece of shit. Always had been. Everybody knew it. Mac knew it, you knew it, and Jacob knew it. Carl Allen was a fucking lunatic that should've been locked up a long time ago. He's taken care of now, and you don't ever have to worry about him. What he did to Suzie, is fucked. What he did to Rick, and that bleeding over to April, is even more fucked. But, again, none of that is on you. Rick died protecting my family.

He made that choice. And Ava, make no mistake, that was a choice. He died for me. He knew what he was doing. April is gonna be devastated, destroyed, and you're gonna have to help her with that. You're a good woman, so I know you will. What I need from you now, is for you to get the hell out of your head and deal. There is nothing we can do about changing the past. I knew Jacob. Not well, but I knew him. I know he was good through and through, a good dad, and a great husband. I know he was gentle with you. But I also know, if he was here, he'd be standing here telling you the same thing."

I didn't know what to say to all of that, so I blurted out the first thing that came to mind. "Don't say his name. You don't get to say his name."

"Yeah, sweetheart, I do."

"No. You. Don't. You don't get to use Jacob's name." It was coming, the famous Ava temper was boiling to the surface. Who the fuck did he think he was, using Jacob against me? He didn't know shit. Jacob would've never said any of that to me.

"I do. And I will. Wanna know why? That night you were taken, the very same night both you and JJ heard Jacob. I heard him too. While he was whispering to you and JJ keeping you safe, he was leading me to you. You know what that tells me? I have his blessing.

He called you 'our girl' and told me to take you home and keep you safe."

My breath caught in my throat, and I felt light-headed. I needed a moment to catch my breath but Reid wouldn't allow it, he just kept laying it out for me. Only now he'd grabbed the back of my neck and forced me to look at him. "Your woman's dead husband tells you to take our girl home and keep her safe. A man like me, Ava, I take that real serious. I know I'm nothing like Jacob. I never was, I never will be. That isn't bad, just different. He might've sugar coated this for you, cushioned the blow more than I did. But the outcome would've been the same. Neither one of us are gonna let you tie yourself in knots and blame yourself for some shit you didn't do."

"He talked to you?"

"Yes."

"Wow."

I was shocked. I thought I was crazy when I had heard Jacob talking to me, a little less so when JJ told us he had heard Jacob too. Now knowing that he spoke to Reid, I wasn't sure how to deal with it. Reid tucked me under his chin and let me cry into his chest. This poor man must think I am a babbling idiot as much as I cry on him. My mind was all over the place. I didn't know what to make of any of it.

In the recesses of my mind, I knew Reid was right.

"I'm not ready."

"Come again?" Reid's grip on my neck tightened and I felt his muscles under my cheek jump.

"Logically I know. I know that what's happened isn't my fault. I'm just not ready to stop blaming myself," I explained.

"You are now."

"It doesn't work that way. Just because you tell me that, doesn't mean I'm ready."

Reid held me tighter and I realized this was him trying to protect me, even from myself. Only he didn't understand that protecting me from outside threats would be easier than protecting me against my guilt. He was right. Jacob would've cushioned his words. He was always thoughtful and gentle with me. He was a different sort of man. Not better, not worse, just different like Reid said. But Reid was wrong about something. While Jacob would've protected us from any outside force, he would've allowed me to live in my head. He would've never forced me out of it. He was too kind to tell me what I was thinking was fucked.

I wasn't ready to give up my guilt yet, and Reid was going to have to deal. There was nothing he could do to change that.

"Can we go see Suzie now?" I asked.

"You done blaming yourself?"

I thought about lying to end the argument, but

when I thought back to what Reid had said about us being a team, I decided on honesty instead. "No. Not yet, but I'm closer."

"Good. We'll get you there."

With a kiss to the top of my head, he pushed the button on the elevator. He didn't let go of my hand. Not in the elevator, not in the lobby, not in the corridor leading to Suzie's room. And especially not when I clocked Suzie's husband coming out of her room with grief clear on his face. Reid held on tight, giving me all the strength he could.

The knot in my stomach was expanding, the impending explosion was near. Maybe this wasn't a good idea. I doubted Michael would want to see me, and I didn't know if I was ready to face Suzie.

"Ava, honey, come here," Michael called out.

I froze. His tone was full of understanding not venom like I'd expected. Reid gave my hand a squeeze and started to let go. As soon as I lost Reid's hand, I ran into Michael's awaiting arms.

"I'm sorry. I am so sorry. It's all my fault, Michael," I sobbed into his neck.

He was nowhere as tall or broad as Reid. Michael couldn't tuck me under his chin and cocoon me with his arms. My face rested on his shoulder and my tears rolled down his back.

"Hush, Ava. Nothing is your fault."

"Suzie..." I cried louder.

Michael continued to hug me and rock me back and forth. I felt Reid come up beside me and Michael passed me over to him. I tucked in and let my tears soak Reid's shirt. More damn crying. I was so over crying, only I couldn't stop.

"How is she today? Any updates?" Reid asked over my head.

"The doctor performed a procedure last night to relieve the subdural hematoma. They drilled a burr hole into the side of her head for drainage. The swelling is still worrisome, but to be expected. They set her arm, but when she recovers from the hematoma, she'll need surgery to fix that. She has an orbital rim fracture, but we won't know if that will require surgery until the swelling goes down," Michael explained.

Oh, my God. Oh, My God. Drilled a hole into Suzie's head. I couldn't understand how Michael could be so calm, and matter-of-fact when his wife had a hole drilled into her head. Sweet Jesus! I thought I was going to hyperventilate.

I lifted my head off Reid's now drenched tee and asked, "What is an orbital rim fracture?"

"Her eye socket is broken. It's the lower edge of the eye rim which affects her cheekbone. All in all, she is lucky. Austin found her in time, and the doctor was able to drain the hematoma. Another few hours she might not have made it," Michael continued.

I put my head back on Reid's chest. Thank God Austin was going to get the deposit and found her. Suzie must've been so scared.

"Is it done?" Michael weirdly asked, his tone had taken on a hard edge.

"It is," Reid returned, and hugged me close.

"Can I see her?" I whispered.

"Of course, you can, Ava," Michael answered.

"Sweetheart, I think you should know..." Reid started.

"I'll be fine, Reid." I cut him off and pushed away from his chest.

I looked at the glass wall behind Michael, the curtains were drawn. I couldn't see in, which was good. That meant the guys wouldn't be able to see me while I was in there. I was fairly certain I was going to have a breakdown when I saw my friend. I didn't need them witnessing me crying again.

Michael hit a button on the wall, and the glass door slid open. The first thing that hit me was the sound. Now that the door was open I could hear the monitors beeping and whooshing.

I stepped into the room and put my hand up to stop Reid from following. "I need a moment alone with her."

His lips pinched together, and he nodded. The door shut behind me, and I was glued in place. Afraid to take a step towards the bed. I needed a moment to fortify myself against the pain of seeing my dearest friend.

When I finally made my way to Suzie's bedside, I was in total shock. A small patch of hair was shaved around her left ear, I assumed that's where the doctor had drilled into her head. Her right arm was wrapped in a temporary cast, tubes and wires seemed to be everywhere. But what was most shocking was her face. Suzie was unrecognizable. And for a moment I hoped that I was in the wrong room, that this was not my friend. I wouldn't have known. I couldn't distinguish a single feature on her swollen and bruised face.

There was a single chair in the room, next to Suzie's bedside. Michael had to have pulled it close, sitting there all night long in a bedside vigil for his beloved wife. I sat in Michael's chair and picked up Suzie's uninjured hand, careful not to disturb the IV.

"I am so sorry, Suzie. So fucking sorry. This should be me, not you. I don't know how you'll ever forgive me." I held her hand and lowered my head to the bed, crying again. It was a wonder I still had any tears left. "So sorry, Suzie. I know Michael hates me for what happened to you. Please, Suzie, forgive me. I love you."

"Nonsense," came from the doorway. I lifted my

head seeing both Reid and Michael, the word, however, came from Michael. "I do not hate you. Never could hate you, Ava. This is not your fault. Carl Allen beat my wife. A man I fucking worked with, a man I considered a brother in blue. This is not on you."

I nearly jumped out of my seat when a monitor came on hissing and beeping.

"Blood pressure cuff. She's okay," Michael explained.

Neither of them moved, allowing me time with Suzie while they stood guard at the door.

"Detective Jones. How is she this afternoon?" a doctor asked, walking past Michael and Reid.

"You tell me, Dr. Sanchez," Michael replied.

The doctor looked up from the tablet in his hand and smiled at me. "It looks worse than it is," he said to me. Then he turned back to Michael. "Her vitals look good. Her latest scans show the Decadron is doing its job reducing the swelling. That is very good news. The next twelve hours are still critical. I explained to you last night the risks of the burr hole procedure, but so far, she is responding well. I am highly optimistic. You have a fighter here, Michael. I will start lowering her dose of propofol."

"What is the propofol used for again?" Michael asked.

"It's a sedative. Right now, she is heavily sedated.

With any brain injury, it is important that the patient not become agitated. We need her comfortable and not feeling any pain, give her some time to rest and heal."

I no longer tried to keep up with the conversation as the doctor went on about cerebral pressure autoregulation and hypertriglyceridemia. My brain couldn't even begin to comprehend what he was explaining. I zoned out and held on to the words I could understand, *highly optimistic, fighter, good news.* I needed those words.

Please God, let Suzie be ok. Please, please, please.

I stared at my friend, guilt and regret tangled in my belly and heart. Why had I kept her at arm's length over the years? Why was I so fucked up that I never let anyone fully in? No more. As soon as Suzie was better, I was going to open up, be a better friend.

"You ready to go, sweetheart?" Reid gave the back of my neck a squeeze.

Was I ready? No. I wanted to sit here all day and watch over my friend. But I knew it was time to go. Reid and I had another painful stop to make, and I was sure that Michael wanted to be alone with his wife.

We said our goodbyes, and before I could walk away, Michael stopped me. "I want you to listen to me, Ava. Suzie is strong. You heard the doctor, she's a fighter. We have to hold on to that. She will fight, but we have to give her the strength. When she wakes up, she'll need you strong. I need you strong. Get it out of your head now that any of this is your fault. I don't blame you, and I know Suzie would never blame you. You are her best friend. She loves you."

"Thank you for that, Michael. I'm trying."

"Good. We'll see you tomorrow." Michael smiled at me and exchanged some look with Reid that I couldn't make out.

Thankfully Reid gave me some space as we exited the hospital, but just as he did when we entered, he held my hand. His silent comfort was all I needed.

He remained quiet on the way to April's. We pulled into an older neighborhood full of nice houses. Bicycles and toys left on front porches suggested it was a block full of children and young families. Reid's features turned from thoughtful to hard.

Now it was my turn to offer him support. I just prayed I was strong enough to hold us both together. No. Fuck that, I was strong enough. I would be strong enough because Reid deserved it. He wrapped me up tight behind the shield he created and made me feel safe. I would damn well do the same for him. Even if it broke me later, now was the time he needed me.

Reid parked the car and stared at the house for a moment. I noticed his Range Rover was still parked in front of the house. That had to mean that Austin was still there. Good. April would need a friend. Someone strong that she could lean on.

"She'll be ok," I broke the silence.

Reid just nodded his head, his eyes never leaving the house.

"It'll take time, but she'll get through it."

Still nothing from Reid. No words, no movement, nothing.

"We should go in," I told him.

"How do you know?" he asked.

"Know what?"

"That she'll be okay."

"Because she'll have you by her side to help her pick up the pieces and heal. She'll have Austin to give her strength when she has none. She'll have me and JJ to show her there is hope and peace on the other side. I know she'll be okay, because I am."

I didn't need Reid to answer. I only wanted him to know I would also be there for April.

Reid knocked on the door and quickly lowered his hand like the hardwood had burned him. We waited several long seconds before Austin answered. Shit. He looked like hell. His eyes were bloodshot and puffy. He looked like he still hadn't slept, and his nerves looked to be shot.

I don't know many men who were emotionally equipped to deal with a grieving woman. I suspected

Austin was one of those men who could. But it didn't mean it wouldn't take a toll.

Both men stood locked in some sort of manly silent communication that only badass men knew. While they had their telepathic superhuman conversation, I sprang into action. I could be useful here. With Suzie, I had no power to do anything. With April, I knew what she was going through. Been there, done that, had the fucking t-shirt and wall plaque.

"Why don't you boys go outside and talk? I'll find April," I suggested.

"Ava, I don't think that's a good idea," Austin said.

"It is, trust me."

"She's not doing well. I think maybe you and Reid should come back."

"No." I blurted out. "I know you both are big badasses that think you're always right. I'll give you that ninety-nine percent of the time you are. But right now, you need to trust me."

Reid nodded his head, and Austin moved to the side, allowing me entrance to the house.

The first thing I noted was the curtains. They were closed. The house was in near darkness.

Wrong. Way wrong.

I found April curled on the couch, a t-shirt hugged to her chest. Shit. She had to get up.

"April?" I called out softly.

Her eyes opened, but she made no attempt to move.

"I'm Ava."

Still nothing. I wondered if Austin had given her a sedative. Mac had threatened to have me sedated days after Jacob's murder.

Now that I was in front of April, I didn't know what to say. All the confidence I had when I charged past the guys escaped me.

"Reid and Austin will be right back. They're just outside talking."

"Will you take me to him?" she whispered.

Shit, crap, damn. I didn't know what to say to that.

"No, honey. Not yet. We'll ask Reid when you can go to him."

She closed her eyes. I wondered if this was how I looked after Mac told me that Jacob was gone. Small, broken, lost.

"Have you eaten?" I inquired.

If I hadn't been watching her closely I would've missed the slight shake of her head.

"You need to. I'll look in the kitchen and see what you have."

"No. I don't want food."

"I know you don't. But you need to eat, April."

"How do you know what I need? I just lost my

fiancé. How the fuck do you know anything?" April lashed out.

I waited to reply until I could gather my thoughts. I had two ways of going about this. Jacob's way, sugar coating the truth and treating her with kid gloves. Or Reid's way, laying it out for her. Either way was a crapshoot. I didn't know April from Adam. I'd never met her.

"I know because I've been the one laying on the couch clinging to my husband's tee after he was murdered. I've been you, lost, broken, and in so much pain I felt like my insides were being ripped out. You and me, April, we are the same. Women who've lost their whole world. Now I'm telling you, you have to get up and eat something." April's face paled, and she sat up. "Another thing, we're opening the curtains and the blinds. You need light in here," I added as an afterthought.

"I don't…"

"I know you don't. I didn't either. I wanted to lie in the dark and be left alone to my thoughts. I was a one-woman pity party, hating the universe for taking my husband, my son's father, my unborn child. I lost big… huge. I wanted to lie in the dark and never get up."

April nodded her head, a fresh set of tears rolled down her eyes. She made no attempt to move or let go of Rick's tee, but she also didn't stop me when I opened the curtains flooding the room with light.

"April, I will not lie to you. This is gonna be hard. The hardest. This is gonna hurt like hell. All you'll be able to do is pray you can get through the day. Do not make it tougher on yourself sitting in the dark. Every day, you have to make the choice to get up. In the beginning, it will be a chore, it will take all of your energy. But you have to get the fuck up, no matter what. As the months pass, it will get easier."

"Does it ever go away?" April asked through her tears.

"What, honey? Does what ever go away?"

"The pain, the hole in my chest."

"Yes and no. Over time the hole will close, the pain will ease. But there will always be a twinge. And that's okay. I don't want that twinge to ever go away. It is a reminder of the man I loved and lost. The love we shared. But, I promise you, April, one day you will find joy again, and it will burn out the searing pain in your heart. But you have to be kind to yourself. Let yourself heal. You are not alone." I winced at my choice of words. How many times had I heard Mac tell me I wasn't alone? "I know you won't believe that right now. It's taken me five, almost six years, to believe myself. But I have finally realized, I'm not alone either. I never was, I always had people who loved me by my side. I just chose to not allow them to take care of me. Don't do what I did. Lean on them, and trust that they are strong enough to carry your burden when you can't anymore."

Man oh man, I had a lot to make up for. With both Mac and Reid. I had been so very wrong. In that moment, I fully comprehended how blessed I truly was. Neither of them ever quit on me or gave up. Even when I gave them no reason to continue.

I would make this right.

I heard the men enter the house, and turned to watch both of them walk into the living room. Shock was evident on Austin's face. I can only assume he, too, had tried to get April to sit up. Probably even tried to open the curtains. He was sugar coating it for April, though I would bet he too would slide into laying it out for her. He wouldn't be able to help it. He was too much like Reid.

Without a word, Reid walked to the couch and pulled April up and into his arms.

"I am so fucking sorry, honey."

I watched as my big strong man held April in his arms, wrapping her in that shield, holding on to her, willing to take whatever pain she would give him.

"I miss him so much, Reid," she sobbed.

And that's when it happened, a tear rolled down Reid's handsome face. I had to turn away. I was intruding on a private moment. I took a chance and looked at Austin, his face was contorted, anguish clearly written all over it. Austin felt this loss, and deep. I wondered what would happen to April now that Rick was gone.

"We...I... we were going to wait a few more weeks to announce this, but I need to tell you now. I'm pregnant."

Holy shit.

29

JOHN 15:13

Reid

Fuck me.

This could be a really bad thing, or just what April needed to get through the pain of losing Rick. I quickly looked at Ava, afraid this was all too much for her. This had to be digging up some painful memories for her. Maybe it wasn't such a good idea having her here.

"I'm gonna make April something to eat," Ava announced and left the room.

Shit.

Austin caught my attention and motioned in the direction Ava went with his head. I gave him a chin lift in return. Fuck, but Austin was intuitive as hell. He knew my woman was gutted and he would go and check on her for me. Good man.

"Let's sit down," I suggested and let April go. "How far along are you?"

"I'm only twelve weeks. We wanted to make sure everything was ok next week at my ultrasound before we announced it. I had some problems in the beginning, nothing major, but enough to cause pause."

"How are you now? I mean the baby, is everything ok?" I asked.

Fuck me, the last thing April needed was to miscarry.

"Everything seems to be fine now. My progesterone levels were a little low. My OB prescribed me Prometrium, so far everything looks good."

I'd have to remember to do some research on low progesterone. I had no idea what that even was and how it could affect pregnancy.

"Good, glad to hear that, honey."

"I miss him already."

"Fuck, I know you do. So do I," I answered.

"When can I see him?"

Damn. Austin had texted me and told me she kept asking to see him. I was hoping that Austin had explained that Rick had left explicit instructions not to let April, or anyone other than the crew to see him.

"He didn't want that, April. His instructions were clear. He didn't want that for you."

"Austin already said that," April stated, her voice

getting louder. "But guess what? Rick is not here to get what he wants. He's gone. I should get what I want."

"No honey..."

"Do not *honey* me, Logan Reid. I want to see Rick. Either you or Austin takes me to him, or I'll find him myself."

Austin had also said that April was being combative. When I read Austin's text I couldn't believe April could ever be combative. She had to be the most passive woman I had ever met. A perfect match for Rick. Damn, I wish Ava was in here, maybe she'd know what to do.

"Reid?" April shouted pulling me out of my thoughts.

"Honey, I know you just lost Rick. Fuck, we all did. But I know that you're feeling it the most. I'm gonna tell you this in the gentlest way I can. Not only did Rick not want you to see him, but you simply cannot. Even if Rick hadn't let his wishes be known, not a man on my crew would let you see him in the shape he was in."

April's face turned a shade of red before all the color drained out of it. It happened right before my eyes. I had crushed her. Understanding was starting to kick in.

"Was it that bad?" she whispered.

"Yes, honey, it was."

"Did he... did he suffer?"

Holy fuck I did not want to get into the details of Rick's murder with her. There were some things I would never tell her, things that would haunt her for the rest of her life.

"No, he did not."

"Will you tell me?"

"Fuck no."

She flinched at my outburst. That came out a little harsher than it should have.

"Sorry. But no, I will not give you details." I blew out a breath and settled in for the hardest part of the conversation. "This is what you need to know. Rick died a hero. Rick gave his life to save Ava. And by doing so, he saved mine. He saved JJ the sorrow of losing both his parents. Shit, April, I can never repay what his sacrifice means to me. Not to him, not to you and not to the baby you're growin' in your belly."

I heard a whimper from the other side of the room and looked up to see Ava with her hands over her mouth.

She slowly walked over to the couch and knelt in front of April.

"I am so sorry, April. I am so, so sorry Rick died because of me," Ava told April tears brimming in her eyes.

"It's not your fault Ava. I know Rick. If he died

protecting you, then he considered it an honor. He lived by a code, he believed the words he had tattooed on his forearm."

Ava tilted her head, not understanding about Rick's tattoo. She had probably never gotten close enough to read it.

"It read, *greater love has no one than this: to lay down one's life for one's friends,*" I explained to Ava. "It is a bible verse, John 15:13."

She lost the battle trying to hold back her tears. "I know that verse. Officer Barnett recited that verse to JJ when he presented Jacob's flag to him."

"Then you understand. Your husband served so others could be safe, protected, and live. Just because Rick didn't wear blue doesn't mean he didn't live and breathe to protect and serve. I am proud of Rick's sacrifice," April told Ava taking her hand and holding it.

This was the April I knew, always giving, always taking care of everyone around her. She was a good woman, I was happy Rick had that in his life.

I watched as both women stared at each other. Both had tears in their eyes. One in the beginning stages of her grief, one that had finally let go of hers. I prayed that it didn't take April five years to find the happiness she deserved.

"I made you a BLT. I couldn't find your prenatal

vitamins. If you tell me where they are, I'll get them for you." Ava broke the silence.

"I ran out, Rick was... Rick was going to pick them up for me on his way home."

"Okay. I'll get you your sandwich and a glass of milk. Austin and Reid can run out and go pick them up. If you don't mind, I'll make them a list of things to pick up at the grocery store. When they get back, you and I can make a few things to keep in your fridge, so you won't have to cook. But, April, you have to remember to eat."

She was spectacular. My woman was brilliant. Give April something to focus on, even if it was for a few hours.

"Okay," April agreed.

"Good. I'll be right back." Ava got up and hurried back to the kitchen.

Austin was still standing in the doorway, arms crossed across his chest like a sentry standing guard watching over April. I liked that for April, and Austin too. He needed something to keep his mind occupied. The last few days had to have fucked with his head.

"So that's Ava, huh?"

My eyes cut back to April. She had a smile playing at her lips. I liked that too.

"Yeah, that's Ava," I answered April.

"You know, Rick has been talking about her for like

freaking forever. Did he know, you know, that the two of you finally got together? I mean, you two are together right?"

"Yes, I am going to marry that woman. And yes, he knew," I replied.

Jesus this was hard. So damn hard talking about Rick in the past tense.

"Good. He was happy then. You know, he wanted that for you. What we had. He wanted you to have a good woman in your life. He was worried about you." April lowered her voice so only I could hear. "Austin too. He said that only the love of a good woman would sooth Austin's soul. He was worried about him."

Fuck. I knew that. Rick and I had talked at length about Austin. Rick was always worried, that was just him. He was a protector, and he was a fierce friend.

Before I could answer, Ava came back with a huge BLT, and a glass of milk.

"Here you go." She handed the plate off to April. "Here's the list of stuff for the grocery run." She handed me a piece of paper. Then back to April, "Are your prenatals a prescription or do you get over the counter vitamins?"

"Over the counter. The empty bottle is on the vanity in the bathroom," April cried.

I looked at Austin, he nodded his head and started down the hall towards the bedrooms.

"Thank you, Ava. Thank you, both. I don't know what I would do without the three of you. I feel so lost. I don't know what to do, where to start, what I am even supposed to do. I just want to curl into a ball and die."

"We'll get through this. Step by step. Word of advice?" Ava asked April, she nodded and Ava continued. "Don't do what I did. Don't turn away the help, and whatever you do, do not shut down. It will seem like the easy thing to do, but trust me, it will take years and years to recover from it. You'll have to fight. But when the burden is too heavy, give it to one of us. We'll carry it for you."

"Thank you." April wiped her face. "I'm sorry I am such a blubbering mess."

"Don't. Don't you apologize. And there is no thank you needed, ever. I owe you my life."

"Ava..." April began.

"I do. I owe you and your baby a debt that I can never truly payback. But I fully intend to do my best to make sure that I give you whatever it is you need to get through this. I promise you, I will not leave your side."

And for the millionth time, Ava proved she was remarkable. God, I loved this woman.

Austin came back with a vitamin bottle in his hand and resumed his guard post.

"Alright. We're gonna run to the store real quick.

We'll be back soon." I stood and dropped a kiss on Ava's head.

"April?" Austin spoke for the first time. "You gonna be okay here alone with Ava?"

I stiffened at his question. What the fuck?

"Yes, Austin. Thank you, I'll be fine."

Austin met me at the door, and I bit my tongue trying to hold my temper until the door was shut behind us.

Austin beeped the locks of the Rover and tossed me the keys. Once we were both inside, I couldn't hold it in anymore.

"What the fuck was that back there? Asking April if she was okay to stay with Ava. What do you think Ava is gonna be a bitch to her? Seriously, what the fuck?"

"All due respect, Reid, fuck you. You think that low of me that you'd think I would ever imply something like that about Ava? I'm gonna chalk that shit up to lack of sleep and stress. I was asking April if she was gonna be okay with me leaving. I promised her I wouldn't leave her alone."

"Shit man. I'm sorry. You're right that was a dick move. I wasn't thinking."

Austin didn't look like he was ready to accept my apology. He kept his eyes down on the vitamin bottle in his hand.

After long moments of silence, he finally let go. "FUCK," he roared. "Fucking Goddamn. Reid, man, I'm lost. April, she is hurtin'. I was shocked as hell when she let Ava open the curtains. I'd been trying to do that all morning, but she wouldn't let me. I was about to go out of my mind sitting there in the dark. And she's pissed. I wasn't ready for her to be so angry when I told her she couldn't see Rick. No fucking way, April seeing Rick with half his face blown off."

I flinched at his words. My mind immediately drew up the image of Rick lying on the floor.

"No, she's not. Not a Goddamn chance is she seeing him. She asked me, too."

"Yeah, I heard. Ava seemed pretty shaken up when she heard about the baby, but recovered quickly," he informed me.

"She'll deal. I'll talk to her about it tonight. I really wish I'd known so I could've prepared her for that. A baby. Shit man, a new life being brought into this world without a dad," I mused.

I'd have to check Rick's will and life insurance. Make sure there was enough there to take care of April and the baby. I'd already put in motion the house to be paid off. Over the years, I'd been lucky in the investments I'd made. I had funds set aside for emergencies such as this. April and the baby would be taken care of. Any of my guys would be if something were to happen.

My phone vibrated in my pocket, I glanced at the dash display before I hit the answer button on the steering wheel.

"Yo. Zane, what's up," I answered.

"We secure?" he asked.

"You're on speaker in the car. Austin's sitting next to me, we're good on my end. But, no, the line is not secure."

"Heard about your woman. You got that under control?" he asked, skipping all pleasantries. That was Zane Lewis. Always straight to business.

"Yeah, we're good."

"Update on the El Paso situation. I sent Panther and Breeze, the Diamonds are neutralized. They will not be an issue for you."

"Anything I should know about?" I asked

"Nope. Everything is five by five," Zane informed me.

I knew Zane would never give me details.

"Thanks, Zane, I owe you, man."

"No, you don't. Make that woman happy, and live a good life. We'll be square."

That was also Zane, always watching out for everyone else.

"I'll send you a bottle of Knob Creek. I know you like your whiskey like you like your women; cheap and with a long slow burn as they go down."

Zane chuckled before he added. "Not all of us can be as lucky as you and that fucker Ghost. Both you men are so pussy-whipped, I'd be surprised you didn't already shred that man card."

"Say what you want, but knowing that Ava's crawling out of my bed every morning only to be crawling back in every night is a beautiful thing, brother. If that means I need to shred my man card, consider it done."

"I hear that. Be well, Reid. I expect you and Ava in Maryland this summer."

"Copy that."

The line disconnected and I was amazed. In all the years, I'd known Zane Lewis, I think that might have been the first time he didn't get in the last word before he hung up.

"Glad to hear that situation is handled," Austin commented.

"Shit. You and me both."

Austin went back to staring at the bottle in his hands while I was lost in my thoughts.

Maybe, just maybe the storm had passed. Jimmy and Carl had been disposed of. Suzie was on the mend. We'd all pull April through, though that was going to be a long road.

"I called the funeral home, went over the arrangements for Rick. The coroner hasn't released him yet, but they know what to do once Sally is done," Austin said on our way back to the house.

Vitamins picked up, and grocery shopping done, we were almost back to April's. Austin added about a hundred things to the list Ava had made. Anything that looked healthy went into the cart. He was on his phone the whole time searching for what pregnant women could and couldn't eat and drink. I think he may've ordered a pregnancy guide off Amazon while we were checking out, but I didn't ask. If this is what he needed to do to get through losing Rick, I was keeping my lips zipped. There were worse things he could be doing than obsessing over the baby. Like drowning his sorrow in the bottom of a liquor bottle.

"Thanks, man. I appreciate you double checking. The payment has been wired. Roni took care of it. She's also gathered all the pictures and personal items from his office to pack up for April."

The rest of the drive was in a comfortable silence, each of us caught in our own heads.

When we walked into the house, both women were on the couch. Ava was laughing at something April had said. Her head thrown back, smile on her face. April was laughing too holding her stomach.

Indeed, I would live a good life.

If in the wake of tragedy my woman could take a grieving woman who had just lost her man and make her smile and laugh like that. That meant good things for me.

Ava turned her head to me and smiled; it was a shot straight to my gut that traveled down and hit my cock. Goddamn, my woman was beautiful.

"Hi, honey," Ava smiled.

I liked the way that sounded. Her calling me honey. Many women have tried to use pet names with me, but I cut that shit out quick. My name was Reid, they could use that or Logan, but nothing else. However, when Ava used the pet name, it warmed me from the inside out.

"Hey, we'll unload and let you women put everything away," I announced.

"Should you be putting groceries away in your condition, April?" Austin asked.

Oh, Lord. I bit back a laugh, the look on the women's faces was priceless. Both their jaws dropped open. Ava actually laughed, and April looked pissed.

"Yes, Austin I can put away groceries. I'm pregnant, not an invalid. Thank you very much."

"Don't get your panties in a twist woman. I don't know what a pregnant woman can and cannot do, and my pregnancy guide doesn't get here until tomorrow," Austin advised.

Oh shit, I was right. He had ordered a book.

Ava laughed again, wiping the tears from the

corner of her eyes. April, however, was not laughing, but she no longer looked pissed either.

Her face softened. "You ordered a book?" She sounded shocked.

"Of course, I did. How else am I gonna know what to do? I don't know anything about babies, or growing them. Shit woman, you know I don't have any kids. Hell, I didn't even know there were things you *couldn't* eat. Who knows what else there is?"

Ava had now stopped laughing and was looking at Austin like he had hung the moon. April however, looked at him like he had just grown two heads.

"Thank you, Austin," she murmured.

By the time we left April's, Ava looked dead on her feet. Mac texted he had a call out and had to drop off JJ, which was a perfect excuse for me to get Ava out of there. She would've kept going if I'd let her.

April had enough food pre-made for a week, plus all the extra food Austin had stocked her cabinets with. Dustin had come by and dropped off a bag for Austin, but didn't come in. He simply texted Austin his bag was on the porch. When Austin said he was going to run home to get some clothes, April paled and started to panic. Austin calmed her down and opted to just ask Dustin.

It looked like Austin was sticking around for the

long haul. When Dustin offered to take a shift at April's, Austin turned him down.

After a teary goodbye, both Ava and April promised to call each other. I loaded my woman in the Camaro and headed home.

"Do you wanna talk about it?" I asked Ava.

"Nothing to talk about. She's grieving. She's going to grieve for a while. In some weird twisted way, this baby will make it easier for her. She'll have a piece of Rick. I'm happy she has that. Not happy the baby will never know his father, but happy for her."

"Yeah, I get that. The baby will never meet his or her father, but Ava, they will know Rick. We'll all make sure of it," I assured her.

"Good."

"You wanna talk about the baby? I'm sorry about that, I wish I had known. I hate that you were taken off guard."

"I won't lie; it was like a kick to the belly. I needed a minute, but then I was okay. It just took me back. You know, to the day Mac told me Jacob was dead, and the day my baby died," Ava admitted.

"I know, sweetheart. I'm sorry. Thank you for being so good to April."

"You don't have to thank me for that. I've been where April is, if I can help her I will. I owe her that. But more than that, I really like April. I want to do it."

"If it gets to be too much, you'll tell me," I demanded.

"Okay." Her answer was too fast. She might've agreed, but she wouldn't tell me. She'd keep it to herself and help April no matter what.

We picked up Chinese on the way home. There was no way Ava was cooking anymore today. JJ talked nonstop through dinner, telling us all about his day with Uncle Mac.

"He did what?" Ava hissed.

"Uncle Mac bought me a new board, and wheels too," JJ repeated.

Man, I was going to have to talk to JJ about not throwing his Uncle Mac under the bus. Mac wasn't even there to defend himself, and JJ had not only run him over, but backed up over him too. Ava looked furious.

"Ava," I tried.

"Don't Ava me. JJ didn't need a new board."

"So? Maybe he didn't need a new board, and Mac just wanted to buy him a new one."

"Just buy him a new one?"

JJ looked like he was watching a tennis match, his head bouncing back and forth between Ava and me.

"Yes, sweetheart. Mac is his uncle. Uncles have been known to spoil their nephews. As a matter of fact,

I think it is in the rulebook. All uncles must spoil their nieces and nephews."

JJ laughed at my sarcastic response. Ava not so much, instead she gave me the death glare. So much for trying to defuse this with humor. "Ava, leave it. Mac loves JJ and wants to buy him things. He has the money to do so. Let him. It's not hurting anything, and JJ is happy and smiling. Win, win."

"I don't want JJ to think he's entitled to new things for no reason," Ava explained.

She had a point, and I fully understood that.

"JJ, you think you're entitled to new stuff all the time?" I asked.

"No. I have to earn stuff. I have to get good grades on my tests and report cards. And I have to go through my room every Thanksgiving and give the toys I don't play with anymore to the homeless shelter before Santa comes," JJ told me.

"Don't think you have a problem, Ava. Let Mac buy things for JJ, and for God sakes, let the kid enjoy them."

Ava sat and looked thoughtful for a moment.

"You're right. I'm sorry JJ. That was really cool of Uncle Mac. I didn't mean to get so upset about it, I'm just really tired. No excuse, but that's the reason. I hope you remembered to say thank you." Ava spoke softly to JJ, grabbing his hand off the table.

"It's okay, Mama. I did tell him thank you. And then we tried out my new board. After that, it was really hot, so we got Italian Ice at that stand by the park. Uncle Mac let me get two flavors but no more. He said he didn't want you mad if he ruined my dinner."

Jesus, the kid did it again. It was hell holding back my laugh as Ava's face contorted into what she tried to pull off as a smile.

"Well, that was nice of him," she said.

I lost the battle and belted out a laugh.

JJ joined in and when he finally caught his breath he turned to Ava. "I was just pulling your chain, Mama. Uncle Mac only bought me one flavor," JJ laughed.

Oh shit. That was funny. JJ was sounding more and more like Mac and me as the years slipped by. I guess we were okay until he started dropping F-bombs.

"You think you're funny?" Ava surged up and grabbed JJ around the middle pulling him from the table. Before I knew what was happening Ava and JJ were on the floor, Ava was tickling him as JJ struggled to talk.

"I'm gonna pee," JJ screamed.

"Should've thought of that..." Ava continued to tickle JJ.

He continued to complain he was gonna pee his pants as he and Ava both laughed.

Yeah, life was good.

AFTER DINNER WAS FINISHED and cleaned up, we settled in for a movie in the living room. It didn't take long for JJ to knock out on the couch. Ava was more than a little worried about him sleeping in his own bed away from her. It had taken a little convincing before she agreed that we needed to set a precedent of normalcy. If JJ needed us, he could come to us. But he needed to sleep in his own bed.

Ava grabbed another one of my tees to sleep in even though some of her own clothes had been brought over today. Dustin had gone to Ava's with Roni and packed her and JJ a few things. We would have to sort out the rest of her house. There was no way in hell that she was ever stepping foot back on that street. However, now was not the time to have that particular argument with her. She needed a few days to process all that had happened.

When I finished my shower, Ava was already in bed. She had the covers pulled up to her neck, and she was staring up at the ceiling lost in thought.

"Cold?" I asked.

"No. Not at all. Why?" She turned her head to look at me.

"Well, you have the sheet pulled up like you're a mummy," I replied.

"Um, no. Just thinking." I searched her face, but she gave nothing away.

Fuck. Between visiting Suzie and seeing April, who knew what crazy shit was swirling around in her head.

I crawled into bed, yanked the covers down, tagged her arm, and pulled her to me. When she settled in, she was fully pressed against me, her arm over my gut, tits pressed against my side. I had to immediately remind my wayward cock that this was not the time to get overly excited.

"'Bout what?" I asked.

"This morning. Actually, this afternoon." I thought back to this morning and the argument we had about Mac taking JJ without me talking to her first. Before I could remind her that we had already discussed that she continued. "I was thinking about our shower and what you said."

My body tightened, and I readied myself for her to tell me I had pushed her too far, too fast. Goddamn it. I should've waited. I shouldn't have allowed anything to happen. I didn't want her to regret a second of our time together.

"What part are you thinking about?"

"All of it. What you said about us being together in a forever kinda way. Us moving in. It's a lot to take in," she answered.

Now my body was tight for a whole new reason. Her fingertips were gently grazing over my abs, and she was circling my belly button.

"Let's break it down. You good moving in here with me?"

"I am. But, I'm still scared," Ava admitted.

"Scared? What are you scared of?"

"Mostly JJ. So much has happened in the last week. I'm afraid everything is moving too fast for him. I don't want to make a mistake with him." She lowered her head to my chest and continued to trail her finger up and down my abs.

Her touch was so soft it sent chills through my body. Never had I lain in bed with a woman while she gently touched me. Hell, I couldn't remember a time I allowed a woman to cuddle next to me and tell me her fears, or anything for that matter.

Cuddling and talking gave the wrong impression. Even before I had my eyes on Ava, I never found a woman that truly made me feel anything past lust.

"Ava, you are a wonderful mother. JJ is a great kid. I have been in his life and yours for a long time. I am not some man you just met. This, what we have, is not just some fling. If I wasn't a hundred percent sure that what we have is solid I wouldn't have asked you to move in with me."

"Asked?" Ava chuckled. "You didn't ask. You told me that we were moving in. I didn't have much of a choice."

"I'm not sure how to say this, other than to just lay it out for you. I want you in my house and in my bed every night. I want JJ in his room surrounded by his things in this house. I want us to make this our home. I want my ring on your finger, and you and JJ to take my last name. And I want that soon. But, if you need time, I understand. As long as we continue to move forward, I won't push too fast. I know JJ is ready too. The only thing that is non-negotiable is; that once I take you, there is no going back. No going slow, no taking time. It will be full steam ahead. I know myself, Ava, I know that once I finally bury myself in you, I will never be able to let you leave. If that scares you, I'm sorry. But that is me, that is real.

"JJ doesn't want to be alone with me," she whispered.

That was a quick change of subject.

I quickly thought over the day and was coming up blank. "What? Why would you think that?"

"When you went to lock up the house, he wanted to stay with you. He wouldn't even go upstairs with me." I felt the first tear hit my skin and my heart hurt. JJ was everything to her.

"Sweetheart, that was not about him not wanting to be alone with you. He was scared that Carl would come and take him next. We had a word, and I explained to him that Carl Allen would never touch either of you again. That he would not ever have to see or hear his voice again," I explained.

"Stupid bastard," she spat out.

"He's gone. You never have to think about him again. As a matter of fact, his name is not to ever be uttered while we are in this bed. This is ours. This is a place where I want you to feel safe and secure. Only happiness in this bed."

"Happiness huh?" she giggled.

"Oh yeah, happiness. I plan on giving you lots and lots of happiness in this bed," I teased.

I was pleased to hear the playfulness in her voice. I knew it would take time before the scars that Carl Allen left behind would fade. But I was determined to make that happen sooner rather than later for both her and JJ.

"Am I allowed to touch you now? I didn't get to this morning." Ava's voice was soft and unsure.

"Ava, I don't think...."

"Oh no. You said that you would know I was ready

when I begged. And I already did. You got to touch me today. Turnabout is fair play."

This was going to kill me.

Maybe it was the flirtation in her tone that convinced me, or maybe I was just a selfish son of a bitch. Either way, I clasped my fingers together behind my head and readied myself for her exploration. "I'm all yours."

And explore she did. She must've been well versed in the ancient ways of Chinese torture because she had me ready to give her anything she wanted if she would just grab my cock. She ran her hands all over my chest and stomach, going just low enough to be a hair's breath away from my sweatpants before she started her journey back up.

"You're killing me," I whined. Yes, I whined like a little bitch. My cock was gonna have permanent damage if she didn't grab hold of it. Or stop and let me excuse myself and take care of it.

"Am I?" she laughed.

Her soft little hand made its way under my sweatpants, and she wrapped her fist around my cock, giving it a few firm tugs.

My eyes rolled back, and muscles jumped at the contact. A few more minutes of her pulling on my cock like that and I was going to come like I was fifteen getting my first handjob. Something that lasted all of sixty seconds.

I had almost regained my composure when I felt her lips graze my nipple.

"Ava." Her name came out like a plea.

Thankfully she took pity on me and slowed her hand as she kissed down my chest, over my tight stomach muscles. Stopping every few inches to snake her tongue out and lick where she had just kissed. It was slow and painful and so fucking sexy. My cock was jumping at the thought of her mouth getting closer.

Her lips found the waistband of my sweatpants, and she stopped to lick just above the fabric. I lifted my hips when she tried to tug them down. Next, she pulled my tee over her head. Her tits bounced, and her nipples pebbled the moment the cool air had hit them.

Spectacular.

Ava's mouth found my cock, and I found ecstasy. She sucked me down to the base of my cock in one fluid motion. Her throat swallowed around my head before she pulled back up. Her tits grazed my thighs, and her fingernails dug into my stomach as she balanced herself over my cock. Up and down she went.

"Slow down, sweetheart," I warned.

Ava ignored me and doubled her efforts. Fuck, I was too close to exploding in her mouth, and as appealing as that sounded, I wanted her pussy more.

I rolled up, caught her under her pits, and pulled her to a stop. Her mouth disengaged with a loud pop and her questioning eyes found mine.

"Was that not okay?" she whispered.

"Sweetheart that was so fucking good I was ready to blow down your throat. As much as I would love to watch you swallow me down, I need to feel you around my cock more."

Her beautiful blonde hair was hanging loose, curtaining her face. She tried to hide behind it as a pretty blush covered her cheeks and neck. I couldn't take it anymore; I needed her right this very second.

"Get up here," I demanded. She immediately got to her knees and started to crawl over me. "Take off your panties first."

She wordlessly complied and straddled my lap. I needed a moment to take in the beauty of her sitting astride me. And it wasn't the physical beauty I was taking in. It was the beauty of what was about to occur. The gravity of what this next step would mean.

"You good?" I asked.

The smile that played on her lips was nothing short of breathtaking.

"I'm good," she confirmed.

"And we're clear? What this means. What this means to me, and for us. I won't ever be able to let you go."

"I don't ever want you to let me go."

I tagged her around the back of the neck and pulled her in for a kiss. Her tongue came out to meet mine. It was shy and timid at first, gently stroking mine. We kissed a long while with a tenderness I had never known.

Kissing for me had always been a means to an end. I had never fully understood what could be conveyed in a kiss until my lips met Ava's for the first time. But this, this was something else entirely. I could actually feel with heart-stopping intensity what Ava was telling me.

I broke the kiss and searched her eyes, nothing but love and need shone back. She was ready.

I grabbed my cock and positioned the tip at her pussy, and watched as she slowly lowered herself onto me. Ava was only able to take a few inches of me before she pulled herself back up, and started the process all over again. Even as wet as she was, it was a struggle for her to take me.

There were no dirty words as she took me. Our moans mixed together, and our eyes locked. We were finally bound together, and our bond was complete. She was finally mine. A warmth that I had never known spread over my body. This was not fucking. For the first time in my life, I was making love to a woman. My woman. God help her because there wasn't a chance I was letting her go.

She pulled herself back up, using my chest for leverage, and slammed back down, her tits swaying with her swift movement. Holy fuck that felt good.

"Slow," I choked out.

"Logan," she moaned.

I gripped her hips and guided her up and down, slowing her pace.

"Logan."

Her thighs tightened at my side, and she tried to break free from my grip.

She was so snug around my cock, she had me panting, "You okay?" I asked.

"Harder. Please," she moaned.

I pulled one of her hands off my chest and took it in mine.

"I want you to feel this." I brought Ava's hand to her pussy, her fingers brushing my cock as I slid in and out of her. "You feel that? The connection. My cock inside of you." Ava slid her hand further down, rubbing the side of my cock with her finger every time she pulled up. "So fucking sexy, Ava." Her eyes left mine, and she looked down watching as my cock burrowed in and out of her wetness.

"Harder, please," she begged.

"I don't want to hurt you."

"You won't. I don't want slow, I need you to fuck me, Logan," she pleaded.

Who was I to deny her what she needed? At least that is what I told myself as I let raw need take over. I stopped holding myself back and gave her what she asked for. More. Harder. Deeper. I flexed my ass pushing further into her every time she slammed down on me. My hands on her hips set a relentless pace, giving her every inch of my cock. Her pussy was spasming and tightening. She was almost there.

"Holy fuck, Logan." Ava threw her head back and let out a guttural moan. Music to my ears.

Holy fuck was right. I was so close to exploding I could barely hold it back any longer.

"Lean forward, sweetheart. I want your tits in my mouth."

She did as I asked and continued to rock herself back and forth. I needed just a little more before I brought us both off. I needed to taste her nipples, just a minute longer. I needed to feel her ass in my hands, as she shook with need when she tried to grind her clit harder. I didn't want this feeling to end.

"Please, please, please," she begged.

My thumb found her clit at the same time I gently bit her nipple, and that was all she needed.

"I'm...I'm .... there," Ava stuttered.

I watched with rapt attention as her orgasm took

hold, and stopped fighting my own need. With a few more thrusts, I buried myself fully inside her slick warm pussy and joined her.

Nothing was better than this, right here. The beautiful look of pleasure on Ava's face. The sheen of sweat on her tits. The hooded look of desire in her eyes. The pretty flush of her cheeks.

I would remember this moment for the rest of my life.

30

THE NEW AVA

Ava

We were lying in bed, Reid just finished giving me the business, and he did it well. I was exhausted, he had been energetic. He started by giving me an orgasm with his fingers and mouth, it was magnificent. By the time he gave me his cock, my body was on fire and ready to explode. It was brilliant, fucking superb.

I grabbed his tee and rolled to him, throwing my arm over his gut. He pulled me in close and kissed the top of my head. I loved when he did that. Kissed my head, and let his lips linger like he never wanted to move them.

I was counting the beats of his heart under my ear, thinking about how glorious our week had been.

Normal.

No kidnappings, no death, no beatings. Suzie was

improving by leaps and bounds. She now was awake most of the day and had been moved from ICU to a regular room.

April was still a mess, but she was dealing. She was pregnant and had just lost her man. I knew from experience that kinda pain doesn't go away after a week. But, she was making herself get up every day, opening the curtains and letting the sun shine in. She was also allowing us to take some of her burden when she felt like she needed a break.

In the span of a week, April had become just as close to me as Suzie. The new Ava, Reid's Ava, let people in. I didn't keep them at arm's length. I pulled April in and spilled my life story. She knew everything about me, every last detail, down to the baby I'd lost and what a bitch I had been to Mac over the years.

I was learning, I was growing, and it felt good.

JJ was JJ. He was funny and happy. Reid moved us into his beach house, and it was like we had always lived here. JJ was thrilled. Reid explained that he bought this house as a rental. We would now live in this house, and he'd use his place in the Lake Street district as the rental. He knew I'd never go back down that street. Mac and Reid handled the contents of my house, it was now empty. I let them manage the move, including putting my house up for sale, and I did it without making a fuss. Improvement. The things I wanted to keep were in storage, I'd sort that out later. I wasn't in a rush. I still needed to talk to Mac, and I was working up the courage to do so.

I was just living. Enjoying every day. Maybe the universe was finally giving me good. God knows I had earned it. I'd gone through hell to get here, and I was determined to suck every bit of happiness I could out of life. Just like I had told April, the day Rick died; joy was now burning out the pain.

It was beautiful.

I had something I needed to talk to Reid about. I had been swirling the idea around in my head the last few days. I hoped he liked it. I hoped I wasn't over-stepping.

I traced the tattoo on his chest, even though I couldn't see it in the dark I didn't need to. I had every tattoo memorized, every scar too. I knew Reid's body better than I knew my own. That was okay because Reid knew my body well enough for the both of us.

"I wanna get a tattoo," I announced.

I felt Reid's silent chuckle under my cheek, "Really. What do you wanna get, sweetheart?"

"Umm..."

"Ava, spit it out,"

"Umm..."

"Alright, how 'bout this, as long as it isn't some

stupid cartoon character or some girly crap, I think that'd be hot."

"I was thinking…" This time he didn't say anything, he let my words hang in the air. "I wanna get the same tattoo you and the guys have," I rushed out.

Reid's body went tight. "Which one?"

A few days ago, while I was at the Café, Reid and his crew had gone and all got Rick's memorial tattoo done. Reid's was the biggest, placed on his left pec over his heart. Reid said that Rick had given his life to protect mine. Therefore Rick had given him the world. He wanted Rick near his heart, always.

He also got JJ's name and mine on his left side down his ribs. Reid asked me to sign my name on a piece of paper, JJ's too. When I wrote out JJ's name, he asked me to expand it to Jacob Jr. I didn't understand why until he came home with the tattoo in my hand-writing. He explained he wanted Jacob Jr.'s full name because he wanted to make sure he included Jacob in his tattoo. After all, Jacob was a part of our family too. What man did that? Wanted to include his woman's dead husband in his family. A good man, that's who. A man who was not threatened by the memory of another good man. I loved that about Reid. True to his word, he spoke to JJ about Jacob. Not often, but his name was spoken. Reid had also insisted that a picture of JJ and Jacob be placed on the shelf next to all the other photos. I loved that too.

"The bible verse. I don't wanna overstep. I don't want to hurt anyone's feelings. But that one means something to me. It means something to April. It meant something to Rick. He lived by those words, and I never want to forget them. I never want to forget his sacrifice for our family. I want those words on me, so I can look down and remember. Remember what he gave."

Reid was quiet for a long time. Damn. I screwed up.

"I'm sorry. I don't have to get it. I understand if you don't want me to. I know that is something special, maybe I overstepped. Forget I said anything," I rambled.

"Shut it," Reid said his voice thick with emotion. "I think that is the perfect tattoo. I love that you want it. I get why those words would mean something to you. I'll take you to my guy, tomorrow I'll make an appointment."

"You have a guy?" I questioned.

I didn't know anything about tattoos. I thought you just looked in the phone book and called around until someone had an opening.

"Yeah, I have a guy. Best fucking artist in San Fran.

He owns Motor Quill, name's Ivory. I've known him a long time. Met him in prison."

I sat up, pulling out of Reid's arms. "You were in prison," I shrieked.

"Quiet sweetheart. Jesus Christ, if your moaning earlier didn't wake JJ, you did now."

"I wasn't loud earlier," I protested.

"Sweetheart, I had to cover your mouth with my hand to shut you up. That was right after you begged me to fuck you harder, and I was worried the headboard was gonna go through the wall. That reminds me, the headboard? It's sweet and all, but it has to go. I can't have it bangin' on the wall every time I take you rough."

He was probably right. I was loud. And he was definitely right about the new headboard I purchased. As much as I loved using it as leverage when I was on top riding him, it did hit the wall. It had to go.

"Whatever. Tell me about prison."

"I was undercover. The warden was having an issue with contraband, he asked my crew to take a look into it. The guys worked on the outside, and I went in. Spent about thirty days in lock-up. Turned out, Ivory's cell mate was the leader. He had one hell of a racket going. Everything from cigarettes and girly mags to drugs and weapons. Ivory was smart, didn't wanna get caught up in that shit.

He just wanted to keep his head down, do his time, and get the fuck outta there. Ivory caught on pretty quickly who I was and why I was there. He kept his mouth shut, and never ratted me out. Even when it looked like shit was gonna go bad for him with his cellmate, he still had my back. In exchange, I made sure that when the sweep came down, Ivory's name stayed out of it, and I kept him clean. Good fucking guy. He caught a raw deal. Shit childhood, did some shit he shouldn't have, and took responsibility."

"You let a felon tattoo you?"

"Abso-fucking-lutely. Like I said, Ivory is good people. It's not my story to tell, but trust me, if I didn't think he was a good man, and a great artist, I wouldn't let him near you. I respect the hell out of him."

I thought about what Reid said, and if he respected Ivory, that meant something. I settled back down on Reid's chest and crowded his side. This is how we slept, maximum contact. If I tried to roll away in the middle of the night, Reid pulled me back and held me tight. Even in my sleep, he had that shield of protection around me.

Life was good.

"Sorry, that was really judgmental and bitchy. If you trust Ivory, then I trust him. I would love for him to tattoo me."

"Good. Now let's get some sleep. I'm fucking beat. You wore me out."

"Me? I wore you out? I didn't do anything, you did all the work."

"I know, sweetheart, that's why I am worn out. You're greedy. Every time I thought you'd had enough, I felt your pussy tighten, and you were ready for more."

"Reid," I snapped.

"Anything I just said not the truth?"

"I'm not greedy!"

"You're not? So, that wasn't you who begged for my cock after I brought you off with my mouth twice? That wasn't you who begged me to put you on your knees and fuck you from behind after you had already screamed another orgasm? Because sweetheart, I know for a fact that when I put you on your knees, smacked your ass, that greedy little pussy of yours quivered around my cock, and you let go again. So yeah. I'd say you are greedy. And I have to say, I am pleased as fuck you are."

Well, when he said it like that, I couldn't argue. I had done all of that. Though he had forgotten one detail. I also begged him to let me suck his cock, which he turned down, in between orgasm one and two.

"Fine."

"Fine? Just fine?" he taunted.

"Fine, you're right," I admitted.

"Yeah, I am."

Smug bastard.

REID PICKED me up from the café. I still hadn't worked a full day. Poor Laura was picking up the slack, acting as the manager while Suzie was in the hospital. She said she didn't mind and was happy for the extra pay. She smiled like always and hustled around the café, upbeat talking to customers, but it didn't reach her eyes. Something had changed in my friend. And the new me was going to get to the bottom of it. As soon as I had time.

We made small talk on the way to the tattoo shop. When Reid said he was going to call his guy, Ivory, and get me in, I didn't think it was going to be the next day.

So, today was the day I was going to get my very first tattoo. I was both excited and nervous it was going to hurt.

Reid told me about the memorial service for Rick. It was this coming weekend. The guys had decided to wait to have the service until after April had some time to adjust. They all wanted to make sure she saw her doctor first, and she and the baby had a clean bill of health. Actually, it was Austin who insisted on that.

I think his words were, *"Rick's not going anywhere. April and the baby are more important than any fucking service. Rick wouldn't want that shit anyway. He'd be just as happy to have us all go down to Red's, grab a beer, toast him, and dump his ashes in the South Bay."*

Reid agreed, so they were waiting.

April had seen her doctor. She asked me to go with her to the ultrasound. It hurt like hell seeing the baby in her belly. It reminded me of the one I had lost. But I pushed those thoughts down deep, and I was there to hold my friend's hand. The baby was perfect. Healthy, with a strong heartbeat.

Austin stood in the corner of the room, arms crossed, with his eyes never leaving April. I knew that he was still staying at the house. First, because April begged him not to leave, she was afraid to be alone. Now, I think it was as much for Austin's benefit as it was April's. I was worried about Austin. It was in his eyes, they looked wild and full of sorrow. I wish he'd open up to Reid. But he hadn't.

My legs were all but shaking in my seat, I was so excited.

"You're gonna wear a mark on the floorboard if you don't stop that bouncing," Reid laughed.

"I'm excited," I explained.

"Yeah, I can see that."

We pulled up in front of a nice building, Motor Quill, proudly displayed in the front window. Reid parked, rounded the hood, and opened the door for me.

"Yo," Reid called out when we entered the shop.

"Reid. Twice in one week." A man stood from a stool and started towards us. "This must be Ava."

I was thankful that Reid had me tucked to his side, with his arm around my middle or I might've stumbled back.

Holy wow. I didn't know who this man was, but he was hot, as in, movie star hot. Reid might've been the sexiest man I had ever laid eyes on, but this guy... he was a close second. I wasn't sure if he belonged on some TV show that centered around hot badass bikers, or if he should be on the cover of a men's fitness magazine.

He was big; tattoos covered his arms, all bright colors that seemed to come to life right in front of your eyes. The closer he got the more detail I could see, and my eyes honed in on his muscular forearm. He had a tattoo of a bloody ear, dripping blood, into an object I couldn't make out. You would think the ear would be grotesque, but it wasn't. The outline and the detail looked to have been done with great care. It seemed to have pride of place on his arm, I'm sure there was a special meaning behind it.

"Hey, man, thanks for doing this on such short notice," Reid said to the man.

Now only feet away from us, I gave him one more look from top to toe. Yeah, he was definitely hot.

"Hey, sweetheart, you done checkin' out Ivory yet?

I'd like to introduce you, and preferably not have to kick my friend's ass because my woman's eyes are buggin' out of her head."

I closed my eyes in horror, shit, I was totally caught. That's when I heard it, a deep rumble of laughter coming from both men. I wasn't sure what was more embarrassing, that they were laughing at me or that I'd been caught. I figured it was a good thing that Reid was laughing at me.

"It's all good, babe. I'm used to it. Women just can't help themselves around me." Ivory's voice was full of laughter.

My eyes popped back open to see Ivory laughing. Reid, however, was no longer laughing. "Friend or not, you might wanna not flirt with my woman," Reid told Ivory.

"Flirting? Man, if you think that is flirting, friend, you have been doing it wrong. This is flirting..."

Reid let out a low guttural growl that made Ivory bust out into another round of laughter.

"Dude, that was just too easy." Ivory was shaking his head, smiling at Reid, before he turned to me. "Hi Ava. I'm Ivory, nice to meet you."

"You too, Ivory. Reid speaks very highly of you. It's a pleasure to meet you."

Something changed in Ivory. It happened so fast I

couldn't place it. It played across his face for just a moment before he masked it.

"Highly, huh? Then he's yankin' your chain." Ivory smiled at me again. "I drew up some pieces for you to take a look at. Different scripts for you to choose from." Suddenly he was all business.

"Okay," I mumbled, scared I had offended him.

A sudden movement over Ivory's shoulder caught my attention. Holy shit, I knew that fedora. The man walked fully into the entryway where we were standing, sure as shit, it was the whistler.

"I...I...I-vory. Did y...y...you o...o...order the d... d... door g...g...gasket for the a...a...autoclave?" the whistler stuttered out.

"Yeah, Kevin, the gasket will be here tomorrow," Ivory answered him.

I glanced up at Reid, his eyes focused on the whistler. When Kevin turned to walk away, Reid looked back at Ivory.

"Who's that?" Reid asked.

"Kevin? That's my brother. You've met him before, haven't you?"

"Not here. Didn't know that was your brother, man. I have seen him before. He frequents Ava's café, Del Mars," Reid explained.

Ivory let out another belt of laughter, "Best fucking pumpkin pie in San Fran. I know all about Del Mars."

That felt nice that someone thought my café had the best of something. Even if it was just my pumpkin pie. What a small world.

"What happened to his face?" Reid questioned Ivory further.

"Nothing, man. Sometimes he's got a short fuse. Got into a little altercation."

Obviously not wanting to elaborate on what altercation meant Ivory turned and started to walk back to his workstation.

All thoughts of the fedora-wearing whistler, now known as Kevin, went from my mind, as the bouncy excitement came rushing back.

I was getting my first tattoo.

Everything was perfect until it wasn't.

SURPRISE

Reid

I had no fucking clue that the pie eating guy that came into the café was Ivory's brother. I tried to think back if he'd ever been in Motor Quill while I was here getting tat'ted. I was coming up blank. I would certainly remember Kevin. Something about the man was a little off. Mac had been curious about him too, but only because he is curious about anyone who spends a lot of time in Ava's café.

Ava and Ivory were going over the pieces Ivory had drawn up. The scripts he used were outstanding.

"Which one?" Ava asked, looking at them all spread out over Ivory's workstation.

"Sweetheart, it is your body. And in my opinion, you can't go wrong," I answered her.

And she couldn't. Each one was feminine, with

swirly font. Ava had chosen to get the tattoo on her forearm, just like Rick. All the men in my crew had this tattoo, all in various locations.

"This one," Ava exclaimed proudly as she pointed to one of the pages.

Ivory got Ava situated, wiping her forearm down with alcohol. I could hear them talking, but my mind was still on Kevin. Soon, I heard the gentle thrumming of the tattoo gun. Surprised that Ava hadn't even flinched when Ivory started.

"It's not too bad," she said.

Ivory was just about half-way done when the front door chime went off. I looked over at the door and watched a pretty young woman walk in. She was gripping a little girl's hand, almost dragging her along to keep up with her fast stride.

I vaguely heard Ivory slow the needle and come to a stop. I continued to study the woman. Memories came rushing back.

Valerie.

It was the night of her twenty-first birthday. I was guarding some up and coming new band, Shadow & Flame. They were opening for the headliners, some Abel... or something. I can't remember the details. It wasn't something I'd normally did, but a friend asked me for help. So, I'd spent the night playing babysitter.

That was the first time I had met Rhianna Rains and her band.

Valerie was trying to get backstage. She didn't have a pass and offered to blow me if I'd let her through. No, I'm not that big of a dick that I'd let some girl blow me to get backstage, but I did end up taking her home that night. Where she did indeed blow me, right before I fucked her.

She was still pretty. Her brown hair shorter than it had been, she looked a little older now. Not in a bad way, she just looked tired. Shit, she had to be somewhere around twenty-six maybe seven.

As soon as she saw me, she skidded to a halt, and her eyes widened. Oh fuck. She better not cause a scene with my woman. We had one night together over six years ago. I was honest about what I wanted, and she was more than happy to take what I was offering. She didn't ask for my last name, or my number.

Now that she was closer, she looked frazzled and in a rush. She quickly averted her eyes from mine and stared at Ivory.

"Hi, um, I'm sorry to interrupt, Ivory. I was just stopping by to give you this," Valerie said to Ivory.

I didn't hear anything else. I caught a good look at the little girl shyly standing by Valerie. The little girl locked eyes with me, and all sorts of warning bells were going off.

We continued to look at each other, my green eyes staring, into an identical pair. Hers were even complete with the darker green outline. I knew those eyes. I saw those same eyes every time I looked in a mirror.

Oh fuck. Oh fuck. She looked to be about six. Her hair was a little browner than her mother's, more like my color.

"I...I...Ivory." I heard the strangled stutter.

I looked up to see Kevin walk back into the main room. I followed Kevin's eyes as they went from Ivory over to Valerie.

Valerie jerked back and tossed Kevin a dirty look.

I must've missed the whole conversation between Ivory and Valerie because the next thing I heard was. "Come on, Melody, we have to leave." And Valerie was pulling the little girl out the door.

"I'll be right back." I jumped up, not waiting for Ava or Ivory to answer.

By the time I had made it outside, Valerie was buckling the little girl in the backseat. I waited until she slammed the door closed before I spoke.

"She mine?" I asked.

Valerie jumped before she turned around. She didn't need to answer me verbally. The answer was written all over her face.

"Val, I asked you a Goddamn question. Is she mine," I repeated.

"Yes, Logan she is," Valerie confirmed.

Oh, fuck!

"You didn't think it was pertinent for me to know that you were carrying my kid?" I spit out.

"I tried."

"Obviously not hard enough. Seeing as you had my kid, and I'm just now finding out about it."

I was being a dick. I knew I was, but fuck, I just found out I had a daughter. My fucking daughter had been floating around San Fran for the last six years, and I never knew.

"What did you expect me to do, Logan? Call the fucking FBI to find my baby daddy? I didn't know your last name. I didn't know your number, and if you remember, we went back to my place, so I didn't even know where you lived. And I did try, asshole. I called the venue, tracked down who was in charge of Shadow & Flame security, but they wouldn't give me any information on a Logan. They thought I was some groupie trying to get your information," she fired back at me.

"Fuck. I'm sorry I'm being an asshole," I apologized, "I'm a bit in shock, Valerie. I don't know what the hell I'm supposed to do or say here. I have a thousand questions running through my head, but I can't sort them enough to ask. Her name is Melody?"

"Yes, Melody Susan," Valerie answered.

My daughter's name is Melody.

"How old is she?"

"Five. She'll be six at the end of summer."

"I want to know her, Valerie."

"We're leaving, Logan. That's why I'm here. I was saying goodbye to Ivory."

"Leaving?" I questioned.

"We're leaving San Fran. There is too much going on. And after what Kevin did, I'm done. I have to leave."

"What the fuck did Kevin do? Did he hurt Melody?" I roared.

I was going to fucking kill that guy if he hurt my daughter. I didn't care if I didn't know she existed until five minutes ago. I knew now. And if that bastard laid a finger on my daughter he was dead.

"No, he didn't hurt Melody."

"What'd he do?" I questioned. "Does it have something to do with the marks on his face? The altercation he got into?"

Valerie's face paled, and she started to tremble.

"I don't wanna talk about it. I'm just not safe here anymore," she whispered.

"I can make you safe. You're not taking my daughter, Valerie. I just found out I have a kid after almost six years. You're not taking her from me again."

I watched as Valerie worried her lip and thought about my offer.

"Promise you won't tell Ivory or Kevin?" I nodded my head, and she continued. "I'll stay. But only a few days until we can work something out, Logan. I still have to leave. But, you're right, you deserve to know your daughter, and she deserves to know you."

Thank God, she agreed to stay a few days. I'd be able to convince her to stay permanently once I had a chance to talk to her. I just had to figure out what had her so scared.

"My kid in danger?" I asked.

"Not at the moment. That's why I need to leave before she is."

Mother fucker.

"Where are you living? Same place?" Not that I remembered where that was so it was actually stupid to bring it up.

"No, I have an apartment over by the Java beach café."

I knew where that was. Decent hood, not great, but not a shit hole.

"Here." I handed her my phone. "Call yourself, so you'll have my number."

She took my phone, and once her phone rang, she handed my phone back to me.

"We're the first building after the Café on Judah Street, apartment 3160. I'll wait for your call."

I glanced in the backseat, where Melody was happily playing on a tablet with earbuds in.

"She's beautiful, Val."

"She is. She looks just like you."

"Fuck. Okay. I'll text you tonight," I told her.

"I'm sorry, Logan. I didn't know your last name. I promise I tried to find you."

"I know, babe. It's all good. Reid. My name is Logan Reid."

"Nice to meet you, Logan Reid." Valerie laughed out.

She was a pretty girl, even prettier when she smiled. Not quite as beautiful as Ava, but pretty nonetheless.

Shit Ava.

How the fuck was I going to explain this to Ava?

"I'll call you tonight. Be safe. And if you need anything, you call me. If you hear something funny, you call me. You get scared for any fucking reason, you call me."

"Okay. Thanks."

She rounded her car and slid in the driver seat. I watched as she drove away. Taking my daughter with her.

Holy fuck, my daughter.

When I walked back into the shop, Ivory was finishing up Ava's tat. I'm not sure how much of that they heard, but by the looks on their faces, they had seen a lot.

Damn.

"What was that about?" Ivory asked.

"Nothing," I clipped. "You done already?"

"Don't look like nothing to me." Ivory went on ignoring my question. "You know Valerie?"

"Yep. Val and I go way back."

"That so? She tell you why she stopped by?" Ivory inquired.

"Nope. Just shootin' the shit, catchin' up."

Ivory wasn't buying any of that shit, but he did stop pressing me.

"Yeah, we're done."

He held out Ava's arm for me to inspect before he covered it with plastic wrap.

"Turned out great, man, thanks again for doin' it."

And it did. It looked awesome. Ivory did great work.

Ivory rattled off the aftercare instructions to Ava while I scanned the room looking for Kevin. What the fuck was going on.

Ava tugged on my shirt causing me to look down at her. "You ready?" she asked.

"Yeah. Sorry, sweetheart." I dropped a kiss on her forehead and followed Ivory to the entrance. I handed him a wad of cash, thanking him again.

"See you soon, Ivory. Take care."

"You too, Reid."

I was distracted all the way to the car. I couldn't stop thinking about Valerie and Melody, and where Ivory fit into the mix. Was Valerie his woman? Had he been daddy to my daughter? Fuck this was a Goddamn mess. I had to hurry and text Mac. I needed his help.

"Who was that?" Ava started in as soon as the car door shut.

"We need to talk," I told her.

"I gathered that. Who is Valerie?" she asked again.

"Fuck, Ava, we need to have a conversation, but I don't think the car is the best place to talk about this."

"Reid, you're scaring me. Is everything okay?"

I didn't know if there was a right way or a wrong way to do this. What was the protocol when you were about to tell your woman you just found out you had a kid?

"No, everything is not okay. But it will be. You sure you want to do this now in the car?"

Maybe I should wait until we were home, where I could lock her in the bedroom if she tried to run.

"I want to know now," she answered.

"I need you to promise me you'll listen to the whole story, and you won't run."

"I won't run."

"Fuck. Okay, I met Valerie years ago at a concert. I

was working security for Rhianna's band. Valerie wanted backstage. Shit. This was a long time ago, Ava. You need to know that. I won't give you details, all you need to know is that she decided not to go backstage, but went home with me. It was one night. No numbers exchanged, no last names, just one night." I explained.

I chanced a look at Ava, she did not look happy. But then what woman would look happy hearing about a woman her man had fucked. Didn't matter how many years ago it was.

"I haven't seen or heard from her since that night..."

"Oh. My. God," Ava whispered and covered her mouth.

"It was about six years ago," I rushed out.

"The little girl?" Ava paused. "Is she..."

"Yes," I answered.

"Holy crap, Reid. I don't know what to say. Why didn't she tell you?" Ava asked.

"No last names, no numbers. She said she did try and track me down, but had nothing to go on," I explained.

"Do you believe her?"

"Yes. She really didn't know anything about me. As much as this makes me sound like a douche, we didn't do much talking, and I didn't make a habit of giving out personal..."

"I get it." She cut in, stopping any further explanation. "So, what now?"

"I don't know. Valerie said she was leaving town, that's why she came to the shop, to say goodbye to Ivory."

"What? No. She can't just take your daughter. You just found her. That's bullshit. Absolutely not. She can't take that little girl away from you."

Damn, I loved this woman. She was fierce and protective.

"She agreed to stay a few days. I didn't get a whole lot of information from her. I gathered that there is something going on between her and Ivory, since she went out of her way to see him. And I have a feeling that the marks on Kevin's face have something to do with her. Either directly or indirectly. I need to talk to Mac and Damion and see what they can dig up."

"Did Kevin hurt her?" she gasped.

"No, I don't think so. I asked Valerie if Kevin hurt Melody, and she said no."

"Melody." Ava smiled. "What a beautiful name for a beautiful little girl."

I didn't know what to say. It was surreal. I had a daughter.

"How are you with all of this?" I asked.

"Me? How am I? I am a little shocked. I am more than a little pissed on your behalf that you've had a daughter out there that you didn't know. But, that's alright, you know now. We'll make it right. How are you?"

Every day, twenty times a day, Ava's compassion and thoughtfulness impressed the hell out of me.

"Same as you, I guess. I'm in shock. I'm mad, not at Valerie per se, but mad I missed out on a lot of years. And honestly, I'm a little scared," I admitted.

"Scared? Of what?"

"I'm worried about what this does to Melody. How do we introduce me to her, as her dad? I'm worried about JJ and my relationship with him. I don't ever want him to think that just because we found out about Melody that it changes anything between us. He is my son, and nothing changes. I'm worried about you, well us I guess."

"First, Melody will adjust fine. We'll just have to take it slow. As for JJ and me, we will love her. She is yours. She is a part of our family now. Remember what I told JJ? There is enough room in our hearts to love more than one person. We'll make room for her. She will fit right in, and in no time flat, it will be like she's always been there. You'll be a good dad, Reid. I know because you're already a good one to JJ. There is nothing to worry about. We'll talk to Valerie and work something out."

I might've had to pick my jaw up off my lap. My fucking woman was spectacular.

"Goddamn, I love you woman. There is no two ways about it, you are simply unbelievable. Thank you. I want to know her. I want her in our lives as much as possible."

"And she will be. I have no doubt you and Valerie can work something out. Invite Valerie over so she can get to know us all. Melody will feel more comfortable if Valerie is there for the first little while anyway. We need to welcome Valerie into the family as well. This is gonna be hard on her too, Reid. She's had Melody to herself all this time. She's never had to share her child. We're gonna have to think about her feelings as well," Ava explained.

"Shit, I didn't think of that. You're right. This is gonna be hard on both of them. You think JJ is gonna be okay?" I asked.

"Oh, yeah. He'll be just fine. The only thing JJ wants is for the people he loves to be happy. He will love her."

I hoped that Ava was right. I didn't want any setbacks with JJ. That boy was my heart, and this might make me a dick, but I already had a tight bond with that boy. He felt more like my blood than my own daughter. Maybe that would change over time. Jesus, I hoped it would, but if Valerie took off and ran with Melody I might never get the chance to know her.

"We'll talk to him tonight?" I didn't want to push this, but I wanted it out of the way. If there was any fallout, I wanted to be able to handle it quickly.

"Yep. We'll talk about it at dinner."

"Thank you," I said.

"For?"

"For understanding. For being so great about all of this. Most women would be throwing a hissy fit right about now."

"A hissy fit, huh? Good thing I'm not most women," she answered.

"No, you're not most women. You're my woman."

"We'll love her, honey. We will bring her into the family and wrap her up with so much love she won't know what to do with it all. I promise."

"Yeah, we will."

MY SISTER

Ava

Once again life had thrown us a curve ball, not any old curveball, the five-year-old daughter variety. So much for the peace and quiet I had been enjoying.

I wasn't sure what to make of all of this. I hoped for Reid sake, Valerie was reasonable about allowing Reid to be a part of Melody's life. I didn't want to voice my concerns just yet and freak Reid out, but there was a possibility that Valerie would fight him on custody. Depending on the kind of woman she was, this could go bad fast. I was just going to hope to God she was not that kind of woman.

There was also a real possibility Valerie would be the kind of woman who didn't want her daughter around the 'girlfriend.' That would destroy Reid. I'd like to say I was the type of person who would be the bigger person and step out of the way if Valerie had issues. But, I'm not. I found my joy, and I wasn't giving that up for anything. I would fight like hell to keep my new family intact. Hopefully, it wouldn't come to that, and Valerie was being honest with Reid. I would give her the benefit of the doubt for now.

We pulled into the driveway just in time for the carpool to drop JJ off. That was another thing that had changed. Once JJ found out a friend from school lived on the block, he wanted to start riding home from basketball practice with him. It was working out well. I took the boys to school, and Betty would bring JJ home. The new Ava was trying to let people in and take them up on their offers of help.

"Bye, Mrs. Stevenson. Thank you for the ride," JJ said and slammed the car door.

I waved my hello as JJ came running up the driveway.

"Guess what?" JJ asked holding out a blue slip of paper.

"What?" I answered and took the paper. I already knew what this was, but I wasn't going to ruin his fun.

"I got my progress report. Look at it." He was so excited he was practically bouncing.

"Oh, maybe later. Did you have a good day?" I teased him and kept the paper folded.

"Mom!"

"Oh alright, let me have a looksy." I smiled.

I slowly unfolded the report card and brought it up it to read.

"Mom!" JJ yelled.

"Not bad," I told him trying to hold in my smile.

"Not bad? What do you mean not bad?" He stomped his foot, a pout playing across his face.

"I'm just yankin' your chain, son. It's excellent." I laughed and handed Reid the paper.

"Not funny," he whined.

"Straight A's. Good Job, little man," Reid said, giving JJ a fist bump. "Proud of you. What do you say we drop your bag, go get a bite to eat, and after we'll get an ice cream?"

"Double scoop of chocolate chunk?" JJ asked.

"Anything you want, you earned it," Reid told JJ.

"Yippy." JJ took off towards the door.

"Hey wait a minute," I called out to JJ. He stopped skipping and waited for me to catch up. "I'm proud of you. You worked really hard to get those B's up to A's. Good work." I kissed the top of his head, and he smiled so wide and big it made my heart happy to see him like this.

"Thanks, Mama."

Once we dropped JJ's bag in the house we headed out to dinner. JJ picked a Mexican restaurant that was famous for its giant taquitos. Over dinner, JJ filled us in on his day and an upcoming science project he had. He and Reid went over the details of photosynthesis, bouncing ideas back and forth. I sat back and watched, enjoying the normalcy of their father/son banter. I prayed nothing came between them.

After dinner, we stopped at our favorite ice cream shop. It was a beautiful night out, still a little chilly, but nice enough to sit outside and enjoy our celebratory cones of chocolate chunk. Reid looked lost in thought while JJ went on and on about everything that had happened at school. God, I loved how animated JJ was when he spoke.

I debated whether or not to talk to JJ now about Melody or wait until later. Reid looked like he had the weight of the world on his shoulders. I knew he was worried about how JJ would respond. I hoped I was right and JJ would be happy to welcome Melody into our family. Maybe if Reid knew that JJ was going to be okay, he would be a little less worried.

"Hey kiddo, we have some... unexpected but exciting news we want to share with you," I said.

Reid looked at me in shock, his body went rigid, and he looked like he had just swallowed a lemon. Damn, he needed to relax. I reached over and took his hand in mine and gave him a reassuring squeeze.

"Oh yeah?" JJ asked as he took another lick of his ice cream barely paying attention to me.

"This is important. I need you to look at me for a minute." His eyes came to mine and all of a sudden, I was at a loss for words. What seemed like a good idea a minute ago, no longer felt like one. I hadn't thought out how I was going to explain how Melody came to be. "Today we found out that Reid has a daughter. Her name is Melody. She is five years old. She has been living with her mom, but now that we've found out about her, she's gonna be spending some time with us too."

"A daughter?" JJ murmured. "Where has she been? How come she's never been around? Did you not want her?"

JJ suddenly looked horrified.

"No, JJ. Reid didn't know about her," I tried to explain.

"I didn't know she existed until today. Do you think I am the type of man who would turn my back on my child and not want them?" Reid asked. He looked hurt that JJ would even think that about him.

"No, I know you wouldn't do that. I'm confused. How do you have a baby and not know?" JJ turned fully to Reid and implored.

"I dated Melody's mom a long time ago. We lost touch before she found out she was pregnant and she didn't know how to contact me to tell me. None of that is important right now. The important thing is, I know

now. I want to get to know Melody and I want to have her be a part of our family. How do you feel about that? Is it okay with you?" Reid asked JJ.

"Can I... will I... still be your son? I mean you'll have Melody now. Do you still want to be my dad if you have her?" JJ whispered.

Reid mumbled a curse under his breath and quickly got up from his chair, stomped around the table and got down on one knee. Eye to eye with JJ, his hand shot out and went around the back of JJ's neck, and he pulled him in, forehead to forehead.

"I want you to listen to me, and listen well. You. Are. My. Son. Nothing, and no one changes that. My love for you is yours and yours alone. I love you differently than I love your mom. My love for your mom belongs to her. And I will love Melody differently as well. Nothing will ever make me not want to be your dad. Do you understand that?"

"I understand," JJ replied.

"You sure? I need to know that you're a hundred percent on this topic. It's important you completely understand that I will love you no matter what. That just because I found out about Melody doesn't mean anything changes between us. I am your dad, always."

"I am a hundred percent. Will Melody be upset if I call you dad too?"

"No, she will not be upset," Reid answered JJ.

"Does that mean she'll be my little sister?"

"Yes, it does." I watched as Reid gave JJ's neck a squeeze when he answered.

"When can I meet her?"

And there it was, all was right in JJ's world. He needed some reassurance from Reid but other than that he was ready to meet her.

"Soon, buddy," I answered. Both my boys looked at me and smiled. The relief on Reid's face was evident. "She is beautiful, JJ. She has long brown hair, and is a cute little petite thing. I can't wait to have her over."

"We have to buy her a bed if she is gonna spend the night. And she'll need some girly toys too. I mean, she can play with my boy toys. But girls like pretty pink stuff, not Power Rangers. Kendall and Stacy both wear girly stuff in their hair, too. Does she have girly hair stuff? She'll need some. Oh, and they talk about an American Girl doll, we need to get her one of those, too. Can I pick that out for her? I want her to like me. If I give her one of those and the hair stuff, she'll really like me." JJ rushed out in a hurry. He was looking at Reid with a hopeful expression. I thought I saw moisture in Reid's eyes as he stared back at JJ.

"Little man, she'll love you no matter what. You're gonna be her big brother," Reid said and cleared his throat.

"I want to be the best big brother. We need to get

her the doll just to make sure. It will be a welcome to the family gift," JJ explained.

"We'll get her a doll and some pretty hair stuff, too. We'll wait until she comes over before we decorate a room for her. That way she can help pick out what she wants," I suggested.

"Yeah, that's a good idea," JJ conceded. "Dad? Are you happy?"

Holy shit. That hit me like a ton of bricks. JJ had talked about wanting Reid to be his dad, and Reid had called him son. But I hadn't heard JJ call a man 'dad' since Jacob died. The reality of that slammed into me. I tried to choke back the tears, but a few fell down my cheeks.

Reid tried his hardest to look unaffected, but he was unsuccessful. "Yes, JJ, I am more than happy. I have you, and your mom, and now we will have Melody. Life is good, son."

"I'm happy too. Can we please go buy her the doll now?"

A low rumble of laughter came from Reid. "Sure thing, little man. Finish up your ice cream and we'll go get Melody a doll."

"You mean my sister. We'll get my sister a doll," JJ corrected.

"Yes, your sister," Reid amended.

We quickly finished our ice creams and looked up

where to buy American Girl dolls. Seeing as the closest store that sold them was an hour away at the Stanford Shopping Center, we decided to wait until Melody could go with us to pick out the doll. JJ settled for buying his new sister a variety of pretty hair bows and a few no name brand baby dolls.

As soon as we walked in the door JJ bolted up the stairs to the guest bedroom. "Mom," JJ called from upstairs.

"Coming," I hollered back.

Reid and I both went up to see what JJ was doing. There was a whole lotta ruckus coming from the bathroom.

"What are you doing?" Reid asked when we stepped into the bathroom.

"Making room in the cabinet for my sister's stuff," JJ replied. "She can have this side since it's closest to her room." He pointed to one of the sinks in the Jack and Jill bathroom. "That way she can keep her girly stuff in here. Mom, do you have more of that spray that makes your hair pretty? Melody may need some."

"Honey, Melody is five. She doesn't need hairspray yet. But it's really kind of you to make room for her," I told him.

JJ looked up at Reid completely perplexed. "Don't look at me, little man, I don't know anything about hairspray."

"Well, just in case, you should put some in here," JJ suggested.

"Alright, I'll find some," I relented. "Come on it's already late, homework time."

"Alright," JJ grumbled and ran out of the bathroom.

"Told you." I turned to Reid. "JJ is excited."

"That's an understatement." Reid laughed. "Thank you."

"Nothing to thank me for, honey." I lifted up on my toes to kiss him. "Though if you'd like to show your appreciation later tonight, I wouldn't turn it down."

"You coming on to me?" Reid whispered in my ear.

"Oh yeah."

"You want it fast and rough or soft and sweet?" he asked.

"Surprise me." I kissed him one last time before I turned to leave.

Before I could make it out of the bathroom Reid grabbed my hand and pulled me to a stop.

"I love you, Ava."

"I love you too, Logan Reid."

* * *

"Bedtime, JJ," I yelled from the kitchen as I finished packing JJ's lunch for tomorrow.

JJ and Reid were watching TV in the living room.

Homework and showers done, and I was beat. All I wanted to do was crawl into bed.

"Five more minutes?" JJ called back.

"Nope, you already had five more minutes, ten minutes ago. Up to bed," I shouted back.

"Fine." I waited for JJ to yell back that he wanted me to read with him but the request never came. As a matter of fact, the TV had been turned off and the living room was empty.

When we officially moved in, Reid had all the furniture that was in this house, when it was used as a rental, taken out and donated. We bought all new stuff for the living room and bedrooms. I looked at my beautiful new chocolate brown over-stuffed couch with Tiffany blue throw pillows and contemplated plopping down and falling asleep down here. I was too tired to even make it upstairs. As tempting as the thought was, Reid was somewhere upstairs waiting for me, and that sounded way better than my beautiful new chocolate overstuffed couch that was totally comfy and easy to sleep on.

I checked the doors and turned on the alarm, flipping lights off as I made my way to the stairs. Whoever thought up two-story houses did not run their own business where they were on their feet all day. I hated stairs. I thought this with every step I took. My feet were killing me today. I wondered if I would hate them so much if I sold the café and found a nice desk job somewhere. I could sit all day, eat a proper lunch while sitting down at a desk, and maybe not hate stairs so much.

I walked to JJ's room to give him a kiss goodnight and stopped short. Reid's tall frame was squished into the twin sized bed, JJ tucked into his side, Reid holding a book reading to JJ. Watching the two of them was out of this world beautiful, and at the same time, a stab to the belly. Reading to JJ was my thing.

"Hi mom," JJ said when he noticed me.

"Hey, bud. Whatcha guys reading?" I asked.

"Dad found one of his old books, Chronicles of Narnia, and he said we could read it. It's super long so he said only one chapter a night."

Dad. Sigh.

"That's great. Which one did you start with?"

"The Magician's Nephew. It's awesome," JJ answered.

I walked the rest of the way into the room, closing JJ's curtains before I stopped at his bed and kissed his forehead.

"Sweet dreams, bud. See you in the morning."

"Okay, mom. I love you."

"Love you too, JJ."

I was almost to the door when Reid's words stopped me. "Hey, Ava?"

"Yeah." I turned around.

"I'll be another 20 minutes. You should take a bath and relax," Reid weirdly said.

A bath? What do I stink? "I already had a shower," I reminded him.

"I know, but a bath will be nice and relaxing. Restful even. You should definitely go rest." He winked and went back to reading.

He was obviously trying to talk in some sort of code, but my tired mind couldn't begin to comprehend what he was trying to suggest.

The moment I walked into our bedroom and shut the door I started to peel off my clothes. The bed was calling my name. I contemplated not even brushing my teeth but thought better of it. That was just gross.

When I walked into the master bathroom I fully understood why Reid had suggested a bath. He had lit candles all over the bathroom. There was water already in the tub with a thick layer of bubbles foaming at the top, and the scent of my favorite gardenia bath oil filled the room. Suddenly the bed wasn't so appealing.

I loved this man.

33

WE ALL FALL DOWN

Reid

"Goodnight, little man."

"Night, Dad," JJ replied.

That would never get old, hearing JJ call me dad. When he was first talking about wanting me to be his dad, I was beyond happy. But, I never actually thought about what it would feel like to have him call me dad. In some twisted way, I was happy he had started calling me dad now. Before Melody found out who I was and started calling me dad. It felt right, that the first person to ever use that name was JJ. Melody might be my blood, but JJ was my heart.

I was scared to death to actually meet Melody. She was my daughter but there was no connection there. I felt like an ass even saying that. Shouldn't a parent feel some sort of instant connection or bond with their own child? Sure, I felt an instant protectiveness come over me when I found out, but other than that nothing. And that scared the shit out of me. I hoped like hell that changed as we got to know her.

I still hadn't called Damion or Mac. I needed their help in figuring out what Valerie had been up to the last five years and where Ivory and Kevin fit in. I had a bad feeling. Not about Ivory, I knew he would never harm Valerie, and especially not a child. I simply wondered how long he had been in my daughter's life.

Kevin, now, he worried me. Valerie had said that Kevin hadn't hurt them, but the marks on his face gave me pause. I had no idea where Valerie worked, who took care of Melody, if Valerie had any family. Holy shit, there was so much I didn't know it was over-whelming.

"Hey, Dad." JJ pulled me from my thoughts.

"Right here, bud."

"You sure my sister will like me?" he asked.

"Absolutely. She will love you. You know, every little girl needs a big brother."

"Why is that? Mama doesn't have a big brother."

"She doesn't and she totally missed out. Every little girl should have a big brother to watch out for her and protect her."

"Do you think I'll be good at protecting her?"

"Yep. You'll be great at it. You are a good kid, JJ.

You are growing into a strong and respectable young man. I am very proud of you."

"Can I ask you one more thing?" JJ looked like he had something heavy on his mind.

"Anything."

"Do you think that my dad Jacob would be proud of me too?"

"First, he is just dad, not your dad Jacob. You always call him just dad. Hearing you call him dad will never hurt my feelings, you understand that?" JJ nodded his head in understanding. "Good. I respect and honor his place in your life; he is a part of you. He always will be. And you know what, son? I love that part of you. He gave you some of your best qualities. He gave you his strong sense of right and wrong, and his bravery and selflessness. He gave you all the tools you need to grow up to be a good strong man. So, I would say, yes, JJ, he is proud of you."

"You give me good stuff too," JJ told me.

"Pleased that you think so, buddy. I know you miss your dad; your mom misses him, too. And that's okay, because I will never try and take his place. I can't. But what I can try and do is be the man that you both love and respect. Be the man that helps ease that pain for you both. And I promise you JJ, I will always do my best to be a good dad to you."

"You are a good dad. Melody is lucky."

"Why's that?"

"Because she has the best dad in the world, and she doesn't even know it. And she'll have Mama too. And no offense to Melody's mom. But I have the best mom that ever lived."

"You are not wrong, son. Hands down you have the best mom in the history of moms. And you know what makes you such a great kid? That at ten years old you recognize the fact that your mom is great." I placed a kiss on the top of JJ's head. "You need to get to sleep. If you have a hard time waking up in the morning your mom is gonna kick my as.... butt."

"Okay. I'll wake up on time."

You'd think after that conversation with JJ I would feel better about my ability to be a good dad to Melody, but it only made me feel worse. I was fucking scared I would let JJ down, and Melody too. I wish that this was something I could talk to Ava about, but I was too Goddamn embarrassed to admit out loud that I didn't feel anything for my own child. Shit, that made me a royal asshole.

I went in search of Ava, hoping she'd enjoyed her bath. The last week, albeit uneventful by way of kidnappings and death, was still stressful for her. She visited Suzie at the hospital almost every day and was back at the café trying to relieve some of the pressure off Laura.

True to Ava's word, she baked her ass off and I took her to the clubhouse so she could deliver four dozen dark chocolate raspberry cupcakes. It was hysterical to watch my prim and proper woman bouncing around a one-percenter biker clubhouse like it was a PTA meeting. She strutted her ass around, passing out cupcakes, hugging Damion, Blaze, and Trig. If memory serves me, she even kissed Blaze on his bearded cheek and thanked him. My poor brother stood there helpless as Ava announced in a room full of members that Damion got cupcakes for life since he saved her. Damion looked like he was ready to throw her ass out. However, when no one was watching, his lips tipped up and a ghost of a smile appeared. It was only for a second, but it was there.

Ava was also going above and beyond with April. They spoke every day. Ava even went with April for her ultrasound. She had been strong for April but came home and cried her eyes out in bed that night. All I could do was wrap her up and give her whatever strength I could.

Next week was going to be another big hit for my family. We had Rick's memorial service. And it was the anniversary of Jacob's murder. Mac was already becoming edgy and short in preparation for his and Ava's visit to the gravesite. Ava told me she was prepared to talk to Mac and work things out. She didn't elaborate and that was okay. I'd watch and wait, and wade in if necessary. Hopefully, she could sort this shit out, because it was killing both of them.

I found my woman still in the bath, head back on some plastic bath pillow, her eyes closed. Damn, she was stunning. All the bubbles had dissolved leaving a clear view of her gorgeous body. I don't know what I did to deserve all of this beauty in my life, and I wasn't going to question it. I knew better than to look a gift horse in the mouth. I was simply going to take it and cherish every last second.

As much as I could stand and stare at my woman soaking in a tub naked all night, I had plans for her. Plans which required a bed and me having access to her pussy.

"You relaxed, sweetheart?" I asked.

"Mmmm."

I guess that was a yes. I grabbed a towel and stood next to the tub.

"Time to get out."

"Five more minutes," she replied. And she wondered where JJ got that from.

"Nope. I have plans for you."

"Alright." She opened her eyes and stared up at me with so much love it took my breath away.

Yeah, there was nothing in this lifetime I could've done to begin to deserve all that love being directed at me. There was nothing I could ever give her that would come close to the gifts she had given me.

She took my outstretched hand and stood up. Uncaring that water was dripping all over the tile floor, she waited for me to hand her the towel while I took in every inch of her.

Without a word, I dried Ava off. Starting at her feet, I worked my way up her sexy toned legs, her soft belly, her fantastic tits, slender neck, and shoulders. I motioned for her to turn around and she gave me her back. All that flawless skin begging for my lips to skim down her spine. Two indentations graced the small of her back, right above her firm ass. She had a great ass, full and tight, more than enough for me to hold on to when she was riding me.

After I toweled her off I walked her to the bed and she got on. Laid out before me was a visual feast. My eyes roamed her body as I contemplated where I was going to start. I glanced at her sensitive belly button remembering how crazy she gets when I kiss her there. And further up to her full tits. The last time I started there she orgasmed before I could even touch her pussy. Then I found it, my starting point for this evening.

I peeled my clothes off and watched her eyes go wide as she appreciated my naked body. I worked hard to keep in shape. It pleased me to no end that she couldn't keep her eyes and hands off me. I climbed on the bed, Ava's legs spreading, making room for me to nestle in between them. I honed in on the beautiful slope of her neck and placed a small kiss on her collarbone. Starting on one side, I trailed kisses over the hollow of her throat to the other side.

Her head tilted back at the same time she tipped her hips up. I took my time and savored every kiss, each touch of my lips to her skin. My girl was getting soft and sweet tonight. I was going to draw this out as long as I could.

Her impatience grew and her sounds became needier and needier. She was grinding into me, trying to use my cock to bring herself off. So fucking hot my woman trying to masturbate herself against my cock.

"You ready, sweet girl?" I finally broke the silence.

"More than," she moaned.

With my cock at her slick opening, I took her mouth in a bruising kiss, giving her no time to adjust as I pushed myself into her heat.

"Ava," I breathed once I was fully inside.

With her legs wrapped around my hips, she lifted herself trying to get me to move.

"Slow, sweetheart. Tonight, I want to give you slow."

I watched her face as I slowly moved in and out of

her. Her beautiful whiskey eyes glassed over, her pouty lips making a silent O.

"So pretty, Ava. You are so damn beautiful."

"I love you, Reid," she whispered.

Her words were almost my undoing. I couldn't get enough. When she told me she loved me, I felt it. I knew she meant those words deep in her soul.

Ava was tightening around me, making it hard for me to keep a steady rhythm. The sensation of her pussy squeezing my cock was sensational. Best fucking feeling in the world.

As much as I didn't want this to end, the tingling in my balls had started. If I didn't hurry up and get her off, I would leave her behind. I doubled my efforts, giving her hard-deep thrusts.

"You're close, sweetheart. Let go."

"Baby," she called out, and I went rigid. She never called me baby, ever. She didn't like me calling her baby either.

"What's wrong, Reid?" she asked as my pace faltered.

I didn't answer. I tried to push the word from my brain and keep going. I was too close. She had to catch up.

I pushed in deep and she let out a scream.

"Come on, Ava, I'm there. I wanna feel you come

around my cock, take me with you sweetheart. Come for me."

She started to come, the pulsations in her pussy detonated my orgasm. There was no stopping it, no time to let her enjoy hers before mine took over.

"I love you, I love you, I love you," Ava chanted as we both came together.

Pure bliss.

I gave her my weight for a minute while I kissed her, making sure she understood how much I loved her back.

I rolled to the side, taking her with me, tucking her in close. Ava threw her arm over my gut and gently rubbed the side of my stomach with her thumb. She did this every night. Tucked in close and rubbed my side. I fucking loved it. Loved her close, loved her touching me, loved falling asleep knowing she would be in the same place the next morning when we woke up.

Yeah, Zane Lewis was right. I was a pussy whipped, ex-man card holder. And I was more than good with that.

"I love you, beautiful girl."

She didn't answer for a minute, and just when I was going to see if she was awake, she asked, "Every-thing okay? Umm, I mean, you looked freaked out for a minute. Did I do something wrong?"

"God, no. You did nothing wrong. Honestly, I was a little taken aback when you called me 'baby,' that's all. I called you baby one time at the safe house, and you made it pretty clear you didn't like that word."

She blew out a breath and pulled away from me. I was getting ready to grab her and pull her back when she sat astride me. I cracked a smile. My woman was quick to learn when we were having a serious talk I wanted her touching me. I never wanted any distance between us.

"I'm sorry about that. I should've explained it better then, and maybe I should've talked to you about it again before I just blurted it out." I put both my hands on her thighs and gently grazed her skin with my fingertips. "When you called me, 'Ava baby' the first time, it felt like a betrayal. Jacob called me that. I hadn't heard that name in so long that when you said it I freaked out." Ava stopped for a minute and placed her hands on my stomach, tracing the muscles there. "Since then, I realized it's not a betrayal. That Jacob would want me happy, and cared for. JJ too. I also realized that Jacob would be happy it's you. Now, the whole freak out over you calling me 'Ava baby' seems so silly. I'm sorry, Reid. It doesn't bother me anymore. You fixed it, you fixed me."

I didn't know what to say to that. I did, however, know that it felt good. We sat there in silence. Looking at one another, each of us gently stroking the other. Her naked on top of me, my hands itching to grab and massage her bare tits, suck and bite her nipples as she bounced on top of me. Suddenly a memory hit me from Doc Chesterfield's office. This was exactly what I had seen in my mind's eye that morning. Even though I had come only moments before, my cock started to lengthen and harden under her pussy.

"Already?" she asked in shock.

I had really good recovery time with Ava, but this time it was damn impressive.

"Oh yeah. I've changed my mind. I want soft and sweet, *and* hard and rough."

A wicked smile played across her lip. "Is that right?" she teased.

Gone was my shy Ava. She was absolutely wild in bed, loved to talk dirty to me, and loved it, even more, when I talked to her.

"That's right, Ava. So, are you gonna ride my cock or should I bend you over?"

"Can I have both?" she asked.

"Greedy," I said as she took ahold of my cock giving me a firm tug.

"You love it when I'm greedy. You love when I can't get enough of your cock." Her sultry voice hit my ears ratcheting up my excitement.

She positioned my cock at her pussy and slammed

down on me, placing her hand on my chest to help her keep her balance as she pushed herself up and down.

"Lean forward. I want your tits in my mouth. Don't fuck around, Ava, if you wanna come this way you better take it fast."

The moment I took her nipple in my mouth her moan filled the room, and she rocked harder and faster on my cock. My eyes rolled back as the intensity grew and she started to orgasm.

"More," she whined.

I sucked harder on her nipple and flexed my ass pushing deeper.

"So fucking good, sweetheart." I moved to her other nipple and gave that one a sharp bite before I licked away the sting.

"Oh God, Reid."

When she started to slow her pace, I reached around grabbing her ass and helped her grind into me harder.

"I'm coming," she gasped.

Yeah, she was. I could feel it. I had to do multiplication in my head to stop myself from coming with her. The moment I felt the pulsing stop, I pulled her off me and put her on her knees.

"This is gonna be hard. Push back on the headboard and brace. I'm gonna fuck the hell out of you."

She did as I suggested and braced against the headboard. This was Ava's favorite position, which was perfect because it drove me crazy having a perfect view of her ass. There was something particularly sexy watching her tits bounce and sway every time I pounded into her.

As soon as I pushed my cock in she started rocking back against me. Her beautiful blonde hair cascading down her back, almost reaching those dimples at the small of her back. My hand roamed her back brushing her hair off to one side so I could lick her neck.

"Turn your head, I want your mouth."

She did as I asked and licked my bottom lip before sucking it in her mouth. Fucking hell. She was killing me. For someone who told me she wasn't very sexually experienced, she sure could make me blow my load faster than I wanted to admit.

She stopped sucking on my mouth and groaned. "Harder, Reid, stop playing and fuck me."

I didn't answer her verbally and simply granted her request and pounded into her.

"You like it hard don't you, sweetheart?" She couldn't catch her breath enough to answer me when I pinched her clit. "Yeah, I know you do. You're so fucking wet you're dripping down my balls and your thighs. I'm gonna come now, sweetheart. Where do you want it? Do you want me to come inside of you or on that fine ass of yours?" I asked as I used my free hand to squeeze her ass cheek. "You have a great ass. One day, I'm taking that, too." I had to suck in a breath when I felt her pussy tighten around my cock. "Fuck, you like that idea. Where Ava, tell me where?"

"Inside. Come in me." She answered just in time, heat spread through my body lightning quick, and my orgasm pulsed out of my cock, my body jerking with every rope of come.

"Fuck," I roared.

Her upper body slumped forward as her arms gave out pushing her ass up. I wasn't joking when I told Ava I was going to take her ass one day. She went positively wild when I licked her pussy and played with her ass at the same time. There was no doubt I could work her up to enjoy anal sex.

"So. Damn. Good."

"Yeah, it is," she agreed.

I pulled out and settled us on our sides, me behind her, cuddling her close. I only meant to catch my breath for a moment before I got up to get a washcloth to clean Ava up. I only meant to close my eyes for a moment.

However, that is not what happened. We fell asleep and what happened next would change the course of our lives forever.

The banging on the door and ringing of the doorbell woke me up with a start. I rolled away from Ava, tagged my jeans off the floor, and grabbed my gun from the nightstand. With a quick drop of the magazine, I confirmed I had a full mag before turning to Ava.

"Go get JJ and take him into the master bathroom. Your fingerprint safe is in the very back of the cabinet. The gun is loaded. There is a burner phone in the safe as well. If I am not back up here in five minutes to give you the all clear, you call Mac."

I didn't wait for her to answer. I passed JJ's room, and he was sitting up in his bed rubbing his eyes. "You don't get outta that bed until your mom comes and gets you. Understand?"

"Yes," his answer came quick.

I took the stairs two at a time and came to a skidding stop in front of the door. I checked the peephole, no one. I walked to the front windows, nothing. I checked the side window, nothing. The back was the same. Nothing.

Just when I was ready to go back upstairs, thinking that some dumb neighborhood kids must've been playing ding dong ditch, something in my gut told me to open the door.

I slowly opened the door, my gun already leveled in front of me.

Holy mother fucker.

Melody.

I glanced around the front yard not seeing

anyone, and I shoved my gun in the back of my jeans before I lowered myself to a knee. This was not the best place to do this, but I didn't want to scare her any more than she already was by yanking her into the house.

I could see tears escaping from under the blindfold she was wearing. She had on her pajamas and no shoes.

"Melody. Honey, my name is Logan, I'm going to take off your blindfold okay?" I asked.

She continued to tremble as she nodded her head.

"Okay honey, here we go." I slowly pulled the folded bandanna from her head, meeting her green eyes. "Do you remember me? I saw you and your mom at Ivory's place?"

Again, she nodded her head yes but didn't speak.

"Good. Where is your mom?"

Big tears welled in her eyes and rolled down her cheeks. My gut twisted seeing the tears in her eyes. I would've done anything, given anything, to take the sadness away. I wanted to wrap her up in my arms and protect her from whatever was hurting her.

Melody shrugged her shoulders.

"Alright, we're gonna go in the house and talk," I told her.

I stood up and stepped to the side. It was killing me not to just pick up Melody and run into the house, but she looked like she was ready to shatter at any moment.

She didn't move. She just stood there staring into the house.

Fuck it.

"Honey, I'm gonna pick you up and take you in the house. It's not safe out here."

Before she could answer, I scooped her up, her little arms wrapped around my neck, nearly choking me she was holding on so tight. Something stirred in my gut, the second my daughter was in my arms, I never wanted to let her go.

"I'm scared," she cried.

"I know, baby. Let's get inside. We'll figure this all out."

I slammed the door and locked it. I ran up the stairs to the master bathroom and yelled through the door, "Ava, it's all clear. You both can come out."

Ava threw the door open, JJ tucked behind her back. The fear in her eyes was quickly replaced with shock, then confusion. "Is that...."

"Yes. Can you please grab me a tee and my cell, sweetheart? JJ, son, let's all go downstairs. You can lie on the couch and go back to sleep if you want. I know it's early, but I want you in eyesight."

"Okay," they said in unison.

I turned to leave and felt something slide down my back. I glanced down to see JJ picking up a piece of paper. I was halfway down the stairs when I heard JJ.

"Dad."

"Yeah?"

"Dad."

"Right here, son."

"Dad!" JJ shouted.

I stopped to see JJ at the top of the stairs, the piece of paper shaking in his outstretched hand.

"JJ, son, come down the stairs. Everything is fine. Promise we are safe."

JJ walked down the stairs with the paper out in front of him. He looked as if the paper was getting ready to jump out and bite him. He came to a stop in front of me and nearly threw the paper at me. I awkwardly grabbed it before it fell to the floor again.

I unfolded the paper –

HERE THIS BELONGS TO YOU.
WE ALL FALL DOWN

"Mother fucker," I growled.

Melody jumped in my arms and tightened her grip around my neck, and JJ winced at my outburst.

"Sorry, buddy." I gave Melody a squeeze and whispered, "Sorry, everything will be fine. You're safe here."

"What's wrong?" Ava asked as she came rushing down the stairs, my tee and phone in her hand.

Fuck. I was quickly running through everything I had to do in my head, trying to prioritize what I needed to do first.

"Sweetheart, please try Valerie's phone," I asked

"What's that?" She pointed to the note and reached for it.

I debated not showing her but JJ had already seen it. Reluctantly I handed the note over and watched her eyes scan the words written in red block letters. Her hand came up and covered her mouth, and her eyes flew back to mine, pleading for answers I didn't have.

"Ava, I need you to please try and call Valerie, yeah?"

"Yeah, okay," Ava answered.

"I'm scared," Melody screeched in my ear.

Something in me snapped, hearing my daughter say she was scared for the second time in the span of a few minutes. I was helpless to help my own daughter.

"I know, baby. We're gonna sit down on the couch and talk a minute. Bud come with us okay?"

"Yeah, Dad."

He followed us to the couch and sat down next to me.

"Melody, can you look at me?" I waited and she lifted her head off my shoulder. "Hi there, pretty girl. This is JJ, my son," I told Melody.

JJ smiled at her and raised his hand to wave. "Hi, Melody."

She remained quiet.

"Are you hurt anywhere?" I asked, wondering to myself why the fuck I hadn't thought to ask her that before now.

She shook her head.

"Good. Do you know where your mom is?"

She shook her head. Fuck.

"Do you know how you got here? Who dropped you off?"

She shook her head. Fuck. Fuck. Fuck. I wasn't going to get any answers from a scared little girl.

"No answer," Ava announced.

34

AMAZING GRACE

Ava

Reid looked positively devastated, he was holding on by a thread. It must be killing him not to be able to spring into action, but with Melody wrapped around him like a baby monkey clinging to its mother, it was impossible for him to do anything but hold his daughter. JJ was plastered to Reid's side, very obviously scared and confused.

"I left her a message to call us and gave her my cell number and the house number as well," I rushed out. "Should I call Mac?"

"Yes," he clipped.

I scrolled through Reid's contacts and found Mac's number and pushed send.

He answered on the second ring, "Reid?"

"No, Mac, it's Ava. We have a problem. Can you come over?" I asked.

"Fuck, I'm on a call out. Whatcha got over there? You guys safe?"

"Umm, Reid's here, we're safe. But..."

"Spit it out, woman. I am standing over a dead body with some nasty shit coming outta her belly that I cannot even begin to fathom what the fuck this shit is."

"Crap, sorry. That's gross. Don't tell me stuff like that." Mac let out an impatient growl, and I hurried into the kitchen so Melody wouldn't hear what I needed to say. "Long story short, Reid found out yesterday that he has a five-year-old daughter with a woman named Valerie. Yesterday when Reid and Valerie spoke, Valerie said she was leaving town but would stay a few days so she and Reid could talk. A few minutes ago, there was banging on the door, and the little girl was left on the porch with a note. The note said, *here this belongs to you.* And at the bottom it said, *we all fall down.* Melody, Reid's daughter, is scared shitless. Reid is freaked the fuck out, Mac. And Valerie is not answering her phone. I called her three times."

"Come again," he said.

"Which part? Reid has a daughter?" I repeated.

"No, you called her three times?"

"Yes, three times, back to back. No answer."

"Motherfucker. You got your cell handy?" he asked.

Why the hell did that even matter?

"Yes," I answered.

"Good. Hang up. I'll call you on your cell."

Before I could protest why we were switching phones, and how that was going to help find Valerie, Mac had hung up on me.

My cell began to ring in my hand and I answered, "Great, now that we've played round robin with the phones, can you please tell me what I need to do to help Reid. He is freaking out, Mac." I hissed.

"Call her again," Mac insisted.

"Call who?"

"Valerie. Call her again, from Reid's phone. Don't hang up with me."

I quickly unlocked Reid's phone and went to his call log and swiped Valerie's number again.

"Done," I announced.

There were a few seconds of silence then an explosion of cursing. At least I thought they were curse words, some I think Mac had just made up on the fly.

Oh, no. Oh, please sweet baby Jesus. I prayed that I was not understanding what just happened.

"Did it ring on your end?" I whispered.

I didn't need to explain my question any further, Mac would understand.

"Yeah, honey it did." Mac's voice was full of compassion. "But, we don't know for sure that the phone belongs to the victim," he said, trying to placate me

"Brown hair, slim, mid-twenties, pretty girl?" I asked.

"Honey, without getting into details with you, none of what you just said would help me identify her at the moment. Except for the hair color."

"Oh, no. Mac, what do I do?"

"You don't do or say anything. Tell Reid that I am handling it, and I will be there as soon as I can. Do not tell him I am on a call out. Do not tell him anything. I will call Austin and Dustin and tell them to get over to your house. I'll need them to help me lock Reid down when I tell him."

"Okay. Please hurry Mac. I'm scared." I lowered my voice to a whisper, "If that is Valerie, that means the killer had Reid's daughter, and he knows where we live."

"Yep, and that is gonna fuck with Reid's head more than anything. That is why I'm gonna need help. This kid really Reid's?"

"Yes. She looks just like him," I answered.

"Then Reid is gonna go ballistic when he finds out that the person that killed his kid's mom had a hold of his kid too."

Holy shit. Reid was going to tear down this city.

"Hurry," I begged.

"Gotta go. Ava, you have to be strong for your man right now. Find whatever it is you need to be the strong one in that house. Your family needs you."

"I'm not strong, Mac. Not like this."

"Ava," Mac snapped. "Wake the fuck up and pull your head out of the sand. You are the strongest woman I know. You got this. No doubt."

Ouch. Mac had no finesse when he was trying to give someone a compliment or encouragement.

"I'm good, Mac. But hurry the fuck up," I snapped and disconnected the call.

Ass.

I needed a second to form a plan of action. I busied myself making a pot of coffee. If my house was getting ready to be infiltrated by a battalion of badasses, they would need coffee. I looked through the pantry and was relieved I had splurged and bought a box of donuts at the grocery store. They could have those, and the leftover cinnamon rolls I baked yesterday.

I check the time on the microwave, 5:55 am. How long did the killer have Melody? Shit, we left the tattoo shop in the late afternoon and it was now morning. Who knows when he took Valerie and Melody. This was going to kill Reid.

I walked back into the living room trying to think

of a way to coax Melody out of Reid's arms. As soon as the guys ascended on the house, Reid would have to jump into the fray.

"Mac's on his way over. He said not to worry about calling Austin and Dustin. He'd call them for me and have them come by too." I smiled as I sat next to JJ. "Hey, bud, do me a favor and run upstairs and get Melody one of the new dolls you picked out for her. And remember the blanket that you had when you were a baby? The soft brown one? Please bring that too."

JJ looked at Reid, when Reid nodded his head, JJ shot up and raced up the stairs.

"Hi, Melody," I brushed the hair off her cheek so I could see her face. Her head was back on Reid's shoulder, her head tilted in my direction, her beautiful eyes, Reid's eyes, staring at me. "My name is Ava."

She didn't speak, just continued to stare.

"How would you like to sit with me and JJ and watch some cartoons?"

Still nothing. Damn.

JJ came bouncing back in the room. He plopped back down in between me and Reid, essentially cutting off any further conversation with Melody.

"Mel?" JJ called out. "Do you want to use my blanket? It's my favorite. I've had it since I was a baby.

Mom said she bought it for me before I was born. It's really soft."

Melody looked at JJ for a minute before she reached out and took the blanket cuddling it close to her face.

"Oh, and yesterday, Mom and Dad took me to the mall, so we could get you a doll. It's pretty." JJ held up the doll for Melody to see. "I know it's not an American Girl doll. But don't worry, Mom and Dad said that we could go to the store and you could pick one out. But it was too far away yesterday."

I really don't think Melody cared much about a doll right now, but bless JJ's heart for trying to talk to her.

"I like dolls," Melody whispered.

"I knew it. I told Mom and Dad that you would like it. Do you want to watch some cartoons with me? We have all the Disney channels." JJ reached his hand out to Melody.

Then the miracle of all miracles happened. Melody reached her little hand out to JJ and slowly lifted her head off Reid's shoulder looking at him, "You won't leave us, right?" she asked. Her voice still barely above a whisper.

"No, baby."

"Okay." She turned back to JJ. "Can we watch Mickey Mouse Clubhouse? That's my favorite."

"Sure. We can watch whatever you want. Right, Dad?"

"Right," Reid assured them.

Reid carefully deposited Melody on the couch next to JJ and grabbed the remote. He turned the TV on, but before he could change the channel, a breaking news alert came across the screen. Lit up in red at the bottom of the screen were the words: News Alert!

"We begin this morning with breaking news. We'll get to your morning traffic and weather in just a moment. But first, we have breaking news on the urgent manhunt currently underway for the serial killer, Simple Simon. Yesterday, authorities confirmed several bodies have now been connected, with another possible victim just found early this morning. Let's go to Paul Wesley on the scene where he's waiting with the latest."

Reid's body went rigid. And short of tackling Reid and grabbing the remote, I couldn't think of a reason to get him to change the channel fast enough. Shit, he couldn't watch this. This was really bad.

"Thanks, Gloria," Paul said. "Paul Wesley live on the scene of what appears to be another gruesome murder of the serial killer, Simple Simon."

The camera angle widened to show the yellow crime scene tape blocking off a dark alley behind the newscaster. Fire and rescue trucks surrounded the area, red and blue lights flashed on the screen.

"The police on scene have yet to answer any questions regarding the victim's cause of death, or if Simple Simon has left his calling card. We have received confirmation Simple Simon is indeed placing food items into the wounds of his victims. Police have not released what those food items are as of yet. News 9 will remain on the scene and bring you the latest when it becomes available...Simple Simon met a pie man," Paul paused, a snarky smile crossing his face. "Is this an odd coincidence or a twisted take on a beloved toddler's tale? Back to you, Gloria."

"Thank you, Paul. Now, for an update on the Swift Fleet employee who was struck by a car after receiving the call from the killer who dubbed himself, Simple Simon. The dispatcher, who told detectives the caller whistled the children's nursery rhyme Ring around the Rosy before laughing and confessing to having killed multiple people. Has been released from the hospital. She is expected to make a full recovery."

Oh no. Oh, Fuck. Whistling? How many times had I heard that tune whistled in the café? My eyes shot to Reid. His face was a mask of concentration, his features hard, and I swear I could see the wheels in his head turning. This was not good. Not even a little bit.

"The police chief is urging the public to be vigilant

about personal safety. A toll-free hotline has been set up. If you have any information regarding the investigation please call,

1-888-99-simon. Stay safe Bay area. And we'll be back after these messages."

I didn't know what to say to Reid. But I better figure it out fast because he looked as if he was ready to blow, and that could not happen in front of the kids, most especially Melody.

"JJ, honey, you turn on Mickey Mouse for Melody." I took the remote out of Reid's hands. Actually, it was more like I pried the remote out of his hands just in time. His grip was so tight the remote was getting ready to be a useless pile of broken plastic. "Melody, I need your da... er... Logan's help for just one second in the kitchen okay? We'll be right there." I pointed in the direction of the kitchen. "I am going to bring back some donuts and chocolate milk for both of you. Okay, sweetheart?"

She didn't answer me, but nodded her head. I watched as JJ reached over and grabbed her hand, holding it. "Everything is okay. You don't have to be scared anymore. My dad will take care of everything. If he promises we are safe, then we are. He never breaks a promise. He is the best, dad. You'll see."

Right then and there I vowed never to bitch again when Mac bought JJ new toys, skateboards, games, whatever. After this, JJ deserved them all. I couldn't have been prouder of my son. Damn, I love this kid.

"Come on, Reid. I need help." I pulled him into the kitchen.

He didn't speak, didn't blink. What he did do however was grind his teeth and growl a whole lot. Freaking A. The guys better get here quick. He was damn near broken. I didn't know what to do to fix it. Then a lightbulb went off, I had a genius plan.

"The garage," I said.

"What?" he growled.

Oh boy.

"You. In the garage, now."

"What the hell, Ava. Why?"

"You look like you are ready to explode. Go in the garage, and use your bag. Get some of this out. You can't do anything until Mac gets here. We don't have any information. You go out in the garage and blow off some steam, before you blow in here and scare the shit out of the kids. I got this, Reid. Oh, and please take the gun out of the back of your jeans and put it on top of the fridge."

"I can't..."

"Yes. You can. And you will. I'll push you out there myself, Logan Reid. Go."

He grumbled all the way to the door, stomping like a two-year-old. Sheesh. I quickly got the donuts, the milk, and a cup of coffee arranged on a tray and went back to the living room.

JJ and Melody were both watching TV, holding hands. Melody had JJ's blanket tucked around her and the baby doll on her lap.

I set the tray down on the coffee table, and sat on the other side of Melody with my coffee. The funny thing was, as we sat in silence watching Micky Mouse clubhouse, I could almost pretend this was a normal Saturday morning. Lazing on the couch drinking coffee with the kids. Only it wasn't Saturday, and it wasn't normal, and this poor little girl was going to get her heart ripped out of her chest.

I had to hold back the sobs as I thought back to when JJ was about her age and he had his life ripped out from beneath him. At least he had me. He had another parent he knew, one he was bonded to, someone he could fall into every night and find comfort in. This poor little girl didn't have that.

"My mom told me that Logan is my daddy," she said. Her sweet little voice was so soft, I had to turn down the volume to hear her when she continued, "Does that mean that now that I have a daddy, my mommy doesn't want me anymore?"

"No, baby, that is not what that means at all. Your mommy loves you so much," I assured her.

"I heard my mommy crying."

No. No, please God. I wasn't sure what I needed to do. She had to tell us what happened, and I didn't want to stop that, but I didn't want JJ to hear this. It wasn't so long ago he heard me crying too when I was taken. He got me back, I feared that the call out Mac was on, was indeed Valerie.

"She was crying. She was yelling at someone to leave me alone. She was hugging me so tight it hurt my back. She told me she loved me forever and always. And she was crying some more."

I heard the door to the garage open and didn't think it was such a good idea for Reid to come back in and hear this. But there was no stopping him before Melody continued.

"I didn't want her to go. I couldn't see anything because my eyes were covered. I tried to hold on to her, but she let me go and cried some more. I was so scared I didn't go after her."

"Where were you, sweetie?" I asked.

"In a car. We were driving for a long time. Mommy kept crying and hugging me. Telling me she loved me. I couldn't see anything. We stopped and mommy got out. I couldn't hear mommy after that."

I looked up, and Reid was in the doorway leaning against the frame, his arms crossed in front of him, looking like he was plotting murder. And I had no doubt, the plan would be carried out, when he found out who had taken his daughter.

"Were you alone with your mommy?"

"No, someone was with us. He didn't talk, he just kept whistling, *Ring around the Rosy.* When mommy got out of the car the whistling stopped for a few minutes, and he started to talk."

"What did he say to you?"

"He held my hand real tight, but it didn't hurt like when mommy was doing it. He told me his name was Jacob, and I didn't need to be scared anymore because my daddy would find me. But I was still scared so he sang to me, until the whistling started again."

"What did he sing to you," JJ asked.

"I don't know the name. I think it was about a girl named Grace. It started out saying she was amazing."

Three loud intakes of air was all you could hear. It was quite possible Reid, JJ, and I had sucked all the oxygen out of the room, because I thought I was going to pass out.

Amazing Grace.

Jacob's favorite song, the only song he ever sang to JJ, the song that played at his funeral.

Jacob.

35

LOGAN SMITH

Reid.

Someone was going to bleed for this. Just thinking about my daughter in the car with a killer made me crazy. The only small sliver of relief I felt was knowing that Jacob was in the car with her. I didn't know what to make of that. Honestly, I had never believed in that kinda stuff. As a matter of fact, I would've laughed my ass off if someone had told me that their woman's dead husband kept talking to them. It was absolutely outrageous, yet it was happening. Around every turn, Jacob was there. And I was pleased as hell my daughter had felt a moment of safety and peace while she was with that bastard.

As soon as I started looking for my keys so I could go out and start hunting, there was a knock at the door.

Melody jumped into Ava's lap and buried her face in her neck.

Yeah, someone was fucking dead. My family had been through too much over the last few weeks. Now, I find out I have a daughter and she is traumatized.

I knew, I fucking knew, that Valerie was dead. There was not a chance in hell she would leave Melody here and run. There were too many coincidences here, and I had been in the business of investigating crimes for too long to believe in coincidences anyway.

That fucking smug news reporter thought he was being cute by making a snide reference to Simple Simon meeting a pie man. Yeah, I knew the nursery rhyme. Bastard thought he was being clever. He seems to have forgotten that the victims of these murders were human beings. I'd love to find Paul Wesley and smack the shit out of him too. Why did the news media insist on giving details to the public that should never be released? Some sick fuck out there might try and copy these murders for some sort of notoriety. Idiots.

I opened the door to find Mac, Dustin, and Austin all standing on my porch. Oh good, Mac brought reinforcements. He'd need them if he thought for a second that he was going to lock me down.

"Mac," I greeted and stepped out of the way for them to enter. "Austin. Dustin."

Mac and Dustin came in, Austin remained on the porch. "April's in the car. No way in hell I was leaving her alone at the house."

"Bring her in," Ava said from across the room.

Without a word, Austin strolled down the walk to the driveway. He looked like hell. I wondered if he had gotten any sleep lately. Jesus Christ, the shit just kept on coming.

Austin returned with April in tow. "Morning, Reid. Sorry to intrude. I'm still scared to be by myself. I can wait in the car though if you want."

"Sweetheart, you could never intrude. Come in, please." It took every bit of my energy to summon up what I hoped to be a reassuring smile.

"Thanks," she murmured and walked in.

I watched as my three closest friends took in the scene playing out in my living room.

One brave but scared little boy, one extremely frightened little girl, who clung to my equally if not braver woman, were all curled up on the couch together. Melody looked as if she was trying to crawl inside of Ava to hide. JJ had a look on his face that could only be described as a badass in training. He looked mad as hell, that his mom and new sister were upset.

I then watched as my three friends' expressions changed from watchful to murderous.

April bee lined it for the couch and took a seat next to JJ.

"Garage," Mac grunted.

I glanced at Ava and she nodded her head. She was already rocking and talking softly to Melody.

"I see you've been in here already," Austin observed as I walked into the garage behind them.

I might've gone a little crazy on the bag. I was honestly surprised my knuckles weren't broken. The bag that was once hanging from the rafters was now on its side on the cement floor.

"I'm only gonna ask you this once." Mac started. "You sure she's yours?"

"Positive," I answered.

I noticed Dustin and Austin moving into position each one covering an exit. Stupid idiots, if I wanted out of this garage, not a man in this room could stop me. Austin would give me a run for my money. But, how I was feeling, he wouldn't be able to take me. Mac, always so dramatic.

"She's dead." Mac always straight to the point.

"I know," I admitted.

"You know?" Mac questioned.

"Man, I am not dumb, nor am I wet behind the fucking ears. I think I've been around the block more than enough to know how this played out."

"How do you think this played out?" Mac asked.

"Mac, my patience is as thin as it's ever been. I need my friend right now. Not Detective Mackenzie." I stopped to gather my thoughts. "Where were you when Ava called?"

"A call out," he answered.

"Right. What'd he leave behind this time?" I questioned.

Both Austin and Dustin remained quiet, both still guarding the doors.

"Man, this is not..."

"Answer me," I demanded.

"Not sure. The M.E. that came out had suggested eggs, but you know we won't know until Sally takes a look."

"Come on man, I know you've put it all together. You don't need me spelling this shit out for you. Cloves, milk, eggs... I know you have at least one more body you haven't released yet. Word is he left behind cinnamon sticks there. I saw that jacked news report. Simple Simon. Whistling. Ring around the mother fucking Rosy."

"Listen, Reid, there are things that even you don't know," Mac argued.

"The fucking whistling. Melody heard it too. The person who brought her here was whistling. The sick bastard had my daughter."

"I get that, but man, you do not know all the details," he tried again.

"Details? What more do I need? There is one fucking person that I know who whistles that fucking song over and over again. That's all I need, Mac. And mark this friend. I am going to kill him."

"Cool your jets, Reid. I'm telling you, let me handle this. Your family needs you here with them right now, not off searching the city. You go off half-cocked, not only will you fuck my investigation, you could make a mistake and wind up in more trouble than I can get you out of."

"You're really telling me to cool my jets? My kid's mother was murdered this morning, and he had... my... daughter. You get that? Think on that a minute. If a killer had his hands on your kid even for one second, would you be able to, cool your jets?" I spit out.

"Reid. I need you to dig really fucking deep here, and trust me. Have I ever asked you to stand down? Ever? But I am telling you, you need to stand down, and trust me. I swear to Christ that if your suspicions are right, I will turn my back and let you and your crew do your thing." He held up his hand to stop me from speaking. "Trust me to handle this. Let's just be one hundred percent."

Fuck. Mac was right. He had never asked me to stand down. He was also right, that while I had been dealing with all things Ava, I hadn't been following the case as closely as I had been before. Shit, I hadn't even touched base with Sally. Did I trust Mac? With my life.

"I'll give you a week, Mac. That's all I can promise. If you don't have answers in a week, I'm hunting."

"That's all I need. In the meantime, it looks like you have your hands full. Congrats by the way. Looks like I have a new niece to meet." Mac smiled.

Jesus, niece, I hadn't even called Damion yet to tell him the news.

"Yeah, we're gonna hold off on that. She is scared shitless at the moment. Apparently, Valerie did talk to her about me before she died. Told her I was her dad, but I don't know exactly what was said."

"Goddamn. The whole situation is whacked. Happy that she is safe and sound. There is no doubt you and Ava will make this right for her."

"Not sure how you make something like this right. The kid just lost her mom," I replied.

This was so screwed up, there was so much that was fucked, it was hard to decide where to start.

"Really? You of all people should know how to make this better for that little girl. I have watched you over the years do just that with both JJ and Ava."

"No, Ava did that for JJ," I argued.

"Bullshit. You think for one second that it was all

Ava, you are fucking blind. I'll agree that she started the healing process for JJ. Lucky for you she is one hell of a mom, and I guarantee that bleeds over to Melody. But, Reid, the rest was you. You gave JJ the strength and confidence to heal. Showed him the love of a father. You know those two are in there right now wrapping your daughter in their love. Melody will get through this. You all will."

I thought about what Mac said. He was right, Ava was one hell of a mother. JJ was the best kid I knew. Between the two of them, they would help Melody get through this. What I didn't agree with was what he said about me. JJ getting through the loss of Jacob was all Ava. I was the wildcard in this scenario.

"Before I head out I wanted you to know I have two units assigned to you. One is on the house, the other is personal protection," Mac went on to explain.

"Christ. How bad was it?" Mac didn't need any further words; he knew what I was asking.

"The same as the others. He is escalating. Gaining confidence. There were no hesitation marks. It was clean and precise. What are we doing with her body when Sally is done? Does she have any family?"

"Man, I'm ashamed to say, I have no idea. Can't tell you anything about her. I met Valerie on her twenty-first birthday. We had one night together and I never saw her again."

"And you're sure she's yours? No disrespect, but damn man, one night..." Mac let his words hang.

"I know she had her face buried in Ava when you came in, but you take one look at that little girl, look at her eyes, there is no doubt she is mine. Man, she looks just like me. And I'll be honest, at this point with Valerie gone, even if that little girl wasn't mine, she'd be staying."

"Alright. I have to get back to the station. Austin, Dustin, thanks."

Mac gave a chin lift and made his exit through the side door.

Austin and Dustin both stood staring at me like they both expected me to freak out.

"I'm cool," I said.

"No, you're not, but that was a nice try," Austin said.

"That obvious?" I asked.

"Not only do I know you, but even if I didn't, the vein in the side of your neck looks like it is ready to explode. What's the plan?"

There is was, Austin had my back no matter what. "For now? Keep my daughter, JJ, and Ava safe. Figure out how to fix a broken five-year-old girl. And learn how to be a dad to a kid I've never met."

"Easy, just be you." Dustin spoke for the first time. "I'll run Valerie when we get back in the house and let you know about next of kin. Also, Royston looked into your Lake Street house security system hack. He emailed you a report. I didn't want to say anything in front of Mac, but Carl didn't hack into your system. He had the codes. I know for a fact the only person outside of the three of us who had those codes was Mac."

"You're not suggesting Mac had something to do with Carl, are you?"

Dustin was good at his job, and had great instincts, but he was way off base if he thought for one second Mac would betray me, or Ava.

"Hell no. He also had a spare key to Ava's house and her security code. I think that Carl broke into wherever Mac kept those and took them from him."

Shit.

"No one mentions this to Mac. If Carl did steal the codes and Ava's keys from him, he will go ballistic."

"What are you doing about Simple Simon?" Austin asked.

"Not a damn thing for the moment. I'm gonna give Mac his time. I'll put a call in to Damion and brief him on the situation. Other than that, I'll stand down and give Mac the space he asked for. But if that mother fucker shows up at Ava's café, I'll save the taxpayers of San Fran the cost of a trial, we'll move straight to the sixty-cent execution, and the whistling freak will get one to the forehead. Which will throw a monkey wrench in my friendship with his brother, Ivory. Which is gonna totally suck, because Ivory is the best artist in the Bay area."

"Goddamn mess. Did you see that shit on the news the last two days? Fucking vultures circling for the story," Austin spit out.

"Sure did. Hey, how's April feeling?" I asked Austin.

"Good. No more morning sickness. She is sleeping a little more."

"That's good. She needs her sleep. Speaking of... let's get inside; I want to see if maybe Ava can get Melody and JJ to lie down for a while."

"One more thing before we go in. I called and changed Rick's headstone to include, *father*. It will now say: Friend, Brother, and Father."

"Yeah, that was a good idea. April will appreciate that."

As soon as we opened the door to the house, the smell of bacon filled the air. My stomach grumbled in response, reminding me it was now breakfast time. I hoped that Ava wasn't planning on sending JJ to school today. There was no way he was going to be out of my sight. Hell, at this point I needed to talk to Ava about just homeschooling the kids so neither of them ever had to leave the house. I didn't want her leaving either.

I could lock all three away and keep the crazies of the world away from my family.

The guys followed me into the kitchen. The sight in front of us had all of us stopping short. Ava, April, and Melody were all giggling. JJ looked like he didn't know if he was going to laugh or if he was mad. Melody was stirring something white in a bowl, and whatever it was had splattered all over JJ's face.

"I'm sooooo sorry, Jake. I didn't mean to fling it on you. April said to stir it fast. I was stirring as fast as I could," Melody laughed. She didn't look like she was sorry. She looked like she wanted to do it again.

Ava glanced over at us and smiled so bright, it took my breath away. There she was, already working her magic.

"Jake," I mouthed to Ava. She just smiled and shrugged her shoulders.

JJ grabbed the towel that April was handing him, and he wiped his face.

"That's okay," JJ replied.

Poor Melody didn't see it coming. JJ dipped his finger in the bowl scooping a nice big dollop of batter. Before anyone of us could warn Melody, he smeared it across her face.

Ava's eyes widened in shock, and April laughed. I held my breath waiting for Melody's response.

"I'm gonna get you back for that. That was a purpose, not an accident," Melody pouted.

"I'm sorry Mel, I was only kidding around with you," JJ quickly explained as his smile faded, remorse clearly written on his face.

"Burn. Gotch you so bad, Jakey," Melody laughed.

I heard the deep rumble of laughter coming from behind me, and the high-pitched giggles of the women. JJ's wide eyes met mine, and his lips twitched with a smile.

"Come here, son." I called out.

JJ walked to me, I tagged him around the back of his neck and pulled him in close.

"Proud of you, boy. So damn proud. Thank you," I whispered in his ear.

"She's my sister."

He had no idea what that meant to me. JJ being the kind of boy he was had opened his family and his heart to a broken little girl that he'd only just met. Hell, he'd done it before he ever met her.

I released JJ and he walked back to the gaggle of giggling women. Ava went back to cooking, and April was cleaning the mess off the floor. Melody sat perched on the counter looking very pleased with herself, until she noticed Dustin and Austin. Slowly her expression changed, and she looked a little unsure.

"Melody, honey, this is Austin," I said. "And this is

Dustin." I pointed to each man as I made the introduction. "They are both very good friends of mine. Is it okay if they stay and have breakfast with us?"

I don't know what compelled me to ask, but when Ava looked at me and smiled, I figured I'd done the right thing.

"They... they are good guys?" she tried to whisper to JJ, however it was loud enough for the rest of the room to hear.

"Oh yeah. The best guys. They work with Dad, protecting people. You don't need to be afraid of them. Dad would never let someone come over unless he trusted them with his life. Because me, you, and Mom are his life. So, if they are here we can trust them."

I heard Ava suck in a breath and she quickly wiped her eyes.

"Okay," Melody answered.

"Thank you." I smiled at Melody. "Ava, sweetheart, you need any help in here?"

"Nope. Why don't you men go do man stuff and I'll holler when breakfast is ready," Ava suggested.

God, I loved this woman.

"Okay."

Dustin and Austin started for the living room, and JJ high-tailed it out of the kitchen.

"Hey, where are you going, Jakey?" Melody called out.

"To do man stuff with Dad," he yelled back.

That was met with another round of laughter.

BREAKFAST WENT WELL. Ava and April, with the help of Melody, made quite the spread. Dustin looked into Valerie's next of kin and found out that both her parents died in a car accident years ago, and she had no brothers or sisters. She was all alone. When Dustin dug into her personal life, I was a little pissed. Okay, more like really fucking pissed she had dated a known gang member. There was nothing I could do now, but it really bothered me. Up until yesterday, she had worked at Red's bar. I knew Red, the owner, he was a decent guy. Fair with his employees. The crowd could be rough, but Red was protective of his people. Valerie hadn't been working there very long or I would've run into her sooner.

I debated whether or not I should call Ivory and ask him for more information about their relationship but thought better of it. While Mac was running his investigation I really needed to stay away from Ivory, and his tattoo shop. I didn't want to say or do something I'd regret later.

Dustin also found Melody's birth certificate, further confirming what I already knew, Melody was mine. The father listed on the birth certificate was Logan Smith. That twisted my gut thinking about Valerie walking around San Francisco pregnant with my child with no help. The fact that she didn't know my last name and used 'Smith' left me with a bad taste.

Now I just had to find a way to tell a five-year-old that she would never see her mommy again.

36

HEAVEN

Ava

I tried to keep the kids and April occupied while Reid and the guys worked. We had turned the downstairs bedroom into his office. It was comical to see three hulk sized men stuck in a small room. I suggested they worked in the kitchen but Reid had said no. They needed privacy and there was no way he was leaving the house to go into his actual office. So, they were crammed into the small room doing whatever it is they do.

I was getting worried about Reid. When Melody first showed up, and all through breakfast, he had a fire in his eyes that was murderous. Now the look was one of sorrow and guilt. I don't know what information they had found or why there was a change but I would prefer the look of rage over defeat.

The kids had helped clean up the kitchen and were now in the living room scanning the channels for something to watch, leaving April and I alone in the kitchen. It was so nice to see the woman smile and laugh through breakfast. There were a few times I could see a small glimpse of who April was before she lost Rick. One moment her smile was real and full of life, then I could see the exact moment she remembered that Rick was gone. The smile remained, only the shine left her eyes. I remember those days all too well, I had a brief moment when I forgot that my life wasn't shattered. When I forgot that I wasn't a widow, and I was happy for a split second.

Melody giggling at something. Hearing her laugh hurt my heart. She was as sweet as she could be. So polite and funny. When she asked JJ what 'JJ' stood for, she declared she liked the name Jake better. I waited for JJ to protest at the nickname, but he didn't. He just smiled and let her call him whatever she wanted.

"Where does the mixer go?" April asked.

"You can leave it on the counter. Depending on how the kids are feeling we might bake cookies later," I answered her.

Growing up, my parents were always standoffish. I was lonely most of the time. It seemed the only time either of them spoke to me was to reprimand me or criticize something I had done. The only good memory I had of my childhood was baking with my mother. I guess it stuck because when times are stressful or something is bothering JJ we baked.

"I'm beat. Who knew growing a human would be so tiring?" April sighed.

I couldn't help but to laugh at her comment.

"The first part, you are always tired. The middle gets easier and you have more energy. By the end, you feel like someone has kicked you in your vagina. I swore the week leading up to JJ's delivery, every time I stood up, I thought he was gonna fall out. That was wishful thinking, because after twelve hours of labor I was begging for a C-Section."

April laughed and thought I was joking. I wasn't. I could still vividly remember JJ's delivery. Twelve hours of pain, wondering why I had been so dumb to turn down the epidural when I first arrived. Still to this day I find it amazing how quickly I forgot all about the ring of fire that was my vagina, the moment JJ was placed on my chest.

"I see an epidural in my future. I have seen videos of natural childbirth. That is not for me. I am not one of those strong women who can push past that kinda pain."

"Smart. Now, go sit down. I'll be right in," I told April.

I made another pot of coffee for the guys, and

wiped down the counter. I was just about to go into the living room when I heard April yelling my name.

I quickly rounded the corner to the living room, my eyes falling on the TV chills running down my spine.

"... another breaking news story. This time we are in front of the Motor Quill tattoo parlor," the newscaster Paul Wesley announced.

The shot widened and yellow police tape surrounded the front of Ivory's tattoo shop. The front window was smashed in. Holy shit. Reid needed to see this. I turned to run and get him and smacked right into a hard wall of vibrating man.

"Sorry, I didn't know you were there," I apologized.

Reid remained silent, his eyes glued to the TV.

"A source has told News 9 that an employee of Motor Quill was detained and questioned in connection to the Simple Simon murders but was released without charges. We have yet to find out if the break-in was an act of vandalism or if the owner of Motor Quill, James Wilis, was the intended target. An unidentified source has told News 9 that the words 'we all fall down' were found painted on the wall..." Before Paul Wesley could finish his report a very angry Ivory came stomping out of the tattoo shop.

"Mr. Wilis, could we please have a word with you? Was anything taken? Do you think Simple Simon is after you? Will you go into hiding?" Paul yelled out trying to get Ivory's attention.

What an idiot. Ivory glared in his direction and started towards the newscaster.

"Leave," Ivory yelled to Paul Wesley. "All of you, leave now. Get off my property."

Ivory stayed on his side of the yellow tape. A huge man with a beard came out of the shop and stopped at Ivory's side as a barrage of questions were peppered at Ivory.

"Is it true that your brother was questioned by the police?" Paul asked.

"How long have you known that your brother was a deranged murderer?" a woman's voice yelled.

"GET THE FUCK GONE," the bearded man yelled.

That was going to cost the news channel a mint. Being that it was a live shot there was no chance to bleep out the F-bomb. Good slimy bastards, I hope they had to pay out the ass for that.

"Well, that is quite the scene in front of Motor Quill tattoo parlor. We apologize for the use of profanity. Unfortunately..."

"Turn it off," Reid said interrupting the rest of what Gloria Styles was saying.

JJ quickly changed the channel, his eyes wide as he stared at Reid.

"Sorry, Little Man. I didn't mean to snap at you. No more news. If you are flipping through the channels and you see a news broadcast on, don't stop," Reid said.

"Okay, Dad. Sorry, I was trying to find…"

"I know you were, son. It's okay. You're not in trouble. Just no more stopping," Reid interjected.

Melody had JJ's brown blanket again, pulled up tight under her chin. Reid's eyes cut to Melody and his face softened. "You okay, Melody?"

"No," she answered.

In three long strides, he was in front of the couch, and he was crouched down in front of her. "You are safe here. No one is gonna hurt you. I promise."

"I want my mommy," Melody cried.

"I know, baby, come here."

Reid scooped her up and she immediately wrapped her arms and legs around him.

"April, you ready to go?" Austin asked.

April looked at me with sad eyes and got up. "Yeah, ready when you are," she answered.

She whispered something in JJ's ear that had him nodding his head before she walked over to me. "If you need anything you call me. I know you all think I am on the verge of breaking. But I am stronger than you all think. You are my best friend in the whole world.

Promise you will call me if you need me," April spoke softly.

"Of course, I will. And no one thinks you're weak. We all know how strong you are."

April nodded and kissed my cheek. "Bye, Ava."

Reid walked the guys and April to the door with Melody still wrapped around him. He looked so natural with her in his arms. It made me wonder what he would look like with a tiny newborn in his strong arms. After Jacob died and I suffered a miscarriage, I never thought I would consider having any more children. Now I wondered if that was a possibility. If Reid wanted to have more, or if I could even have another one.

After my Ectopic pregnancy and removal of my damaged fallopian tube, the doctor told me there was only a forty-five percent chance I could get pregnant again. At the time that number didn't mean anything to me. Now, the thought of not being able to have a child with Reid made me sad.

Reid came over to the couch and sat down next to JJ.

"Melody, there is something that I have to tell you," Reid started.

Oh no. No, no, no, he was going to tell her. I looked at JJ and he was already crying. He knew what was coming too. He had overheard enough of the conversations to understand something bad had happened.

"Baby, I need you to hold on to me real tight, okay? Did your mommy ever tell you about heaven?" Reid asked. Melody nodded her head. "Good. Do you remember what she told you?"

"Mommy said that grandma and grandpa were in heaven with God, that's why I never got to see them. She said that they were happy in heaven, that it was much prettier than San Francisco where we lived. That grandma and grandpa got to be happy forever now that they were with angels and God. That I couldn't ever see them but they could see me," Melody explained.

Reid didn't speak for several minutes. No one did. As a matter of fact, I don't think any of us took a breath. I looked at JJ and hoped having him involved in this conversation was the right thing.

"Melody, your mommy is in heaven now with your grandma and grandpa," Reid whispered.

"Why? Why did mommy want to go to heaven and leave me here? Was she not happy in San Francisco?"

Oh. My. God.

"No, baby, your mommy loved you very much and never wanted to leave you."

"My daddy is in heaven, too," JJ said.

"He is?" Melody asked.

"My dad, Jacob, was a police officer and a bad guy killed him."

"So, he's in heaven with my grandma and grandpa and mommy?"

Reid and I watched as JJ took over the very hard conversation telling Melody her mom died. It was simply amazing watching my son.

"Yes. Mama says that when good people die they go to heaven. I know that my dad can still see me, and he watches out for me, my mom too."

"If my mommy is in heaven with your dad, does that mean she died, too?"

"Yes, baby, she did," Reid took back over the conversation.

"Will I get to stay here with you, or will Mandy take me?" Melody asked.

"Who is Mandy?" Reid questioned.

"Mandy lived with us. She would watch me while mommy worked. Mommy called her a roommate," Melody clarified.

"You will live here with us from now on. But we can go back to your old house and bring all of your stuff here." Reid brushed Melody's hair back and gently rubbed her back.

"Okay." Melody closed her eyes, her head still resting on Reid's shoulder.

I was a little concerned that Melody hadn't cried

but then I remembered when I told JJ about Jacob's death it took him a full day to process what death was and that he wasn't going to ever see his dad again. As hard as I tried to explain it, at five, it is difficult for a child to process.

We all sat in silence. Reid continued to rock Melody and rub her back, until she fell asleep.

"I'm gonna put her in bed. She needs to get some rest," Reid said before he stood with Melody in his arms.

I waited until Reid was up the stairs before I turned to JJ. "I'm proud of you. What you did, talking to Melody about your dad. That was brave and very kind." I pulled JJ closer to me and he settled in my embrace.

"I'm sad her mom died."

"I know you are. We all are. Thank God Reid found her when he did or she would have no one."

The thought of that broke my heart. What if I hadn't got the tattoo? What if Valerie hadn't come into the shop when we were there? What if she had lied and said no, Melody, wasn't his? All the what ifs were swirling in my head.

"I think Daddy did it."

"Did what?" I asked.

"I think that Daddy made sure that Reid found her. Daddy was the one in the car with Melody. I know he was. She said Jacob was in the car and was singing the song that I remember him singing to me. I know it was my dad. He is a hero."

Damn, but, I loved this boy. As crazy as it sounded, and I wouldn't have believed it if I hadn't lived it, but I thought JJ was right. Jacob was watching out for us.

"I agree with you, son. Your dad was watching out for Melody and brought her to us when she needed us. No doubt in my mind," Reid's voice cracked. "What you did, the strength and compassion you just showed, never been prouder of you."

JJ tucked his head trying to hide his tears.

Reid, however, did not. There standing in the living room, my big strong man allowed his tears to roll down his face. I had never loved him more than I did in that moment.

***

Jacob "Jakey" Jr. - Upstairs in Melody's bedroom

Mom and Dad think I'm in my room playing. I'm not. I'm sitting on the floor of my sister's room watching her while she takes a nap. Dad said that girls needed big brothers to watch over them and protect them.

I'm her big brother now. So, I need to sit here and watch over her.

"Jakey?" Melody whispers.

"Right here," I answer.

"I'm scared." Now she's crying. I don't know if I should get Mom and Dad. "Can you come sit with me?"

I stand up and sit on the edge of her bed still not sure what to do.

"Jakey, I miss my mommy. I want to go home."

"I know you miss her. I miss my dad too."

"Will your mommy be my new mommy now?" Melody is crying harder now.

"Yes, my mommy will be your mommy. But only if you want her to be."

"Are you my brother now?"

"Yes, I am your big brother."

"Will you stay with me?"

"Always."

"Promise you won't leave me?"

"I promise."

Melody's eyes close and I sit on the edge of her bed staring at the wall. I wish I brought a book or something. I can't leave to go get one now. I promised her I would stay, and you can't break a promise.

GOOD-BYE MY LOVE

Reid

I'd really like to say the last few days have gotten easier but they haven't. They've fucking sucked. Every time Melody cried over Valerie my gut twisted and I wanted to kill someone. The only silver lining was that she had taken to JJ, and the two of them were inseparable.

Something big that had changed in the last few days was Ava had decided to sell the Café. I tried to talk her out of it, she loved her restaurant, but she was adamant. Michael and Suzie actually asked if they could purchase it. It was shocking that Suzie would want to step foot back in the café after what had happened there. Without even discussing money or details, Ava had said yes.

I overheard Ava and Suzie talking while we were

visiting her in the hospital. Ava told her with the sale of her old house and the café she could afford to stay home and be a full-time mom for at least a year if not more.

Of course, an argument ensued when I told Ava she didn't need to worry about money, since she wouldn't be paying any bills anyway. And as long as she wanted to stay home, she would. The discussion got heated when I laid it out for her—that I was the man and I was going to take care of my wife and family. It ended when she called me a caveman and stomped away.

Mac called the day after Melody showed up, spoke two words, and hung up.

It's done.

That was all I got from him. Before I could question him further he disconnected. The moratorium on watching the news had not lifted. I didn't want Ava or the kids to watch any of that shit. The fucking jack ass Paul Wesley's smug ass needed to be throat punched. The last newscast I saw, he was yelling out the most jacked up questions to Ivory.

Mac was not in a good place with the anniversary of Jacob's murder right around the corner. Ava and JJ were both slowly pulling into themselves. That had to change. Mac was not returning calls. It was beginning to piss me off. If I wasn't so wrapped up with Melody I would track his ass down and demand that he talk to me.

It was after dinner and JJ was upstairs getting ready for bed. Ava was cleaning up dinner dishes. I had just walked into my home office to shut down for the night when Melody walked to the door and stopped.

"You wanna come in?" I asked.

"Would it be okay if JJ stayed in my room again?" she asked shyly, not moving from the doorway.

This was also something that happened. Melody wouldn't sleep by herself. Not that Ava and I expected her to. The first night she was here, we all piled into our king-sized bed and slept together. Even if Melody hadn't been afraid, I would've pulled them all in there. I wanted my family close. Everyone in one room where I could watch over all of them.

The next night, Melody asked JJ to come in her room and sleep. JJ being JJ jumped at the chance to be her big brother.

"If it's alright with JJ. You know, if you want, you can stay with me and Ava, too. Wherever you want."

"Mommy, I mean, Ava said you and JJ were reading a bedtime book. Can I hear it too?"

"Of course, you can. We are reading a Narnia book," I told her.

It fucking broke my heart that my own daughter

was standing ten feet from me asking if it was okay if she listened to a bedtime story. I had to remind myself that it had only been a few days since I found her, a few days since her mom died. It would take time before she felt comfortable.

"Mommy told me that you were my dad before she went to heaven. She said that she was so happy that you found us. That she always wished I would get to meet you."

Holy shit. I knew that Valerie told her I was her dad, but I didn't think the details of that conversation were very important in light of everything else that was happening.

"I am very happy I found you, too. The minute I saw you walk into Ivory's I knew that you were my daughter."

"You did?" She smiled. "How did you know that?"

"It was your beautiful green eyes."

"How did my eyes tell you I was your daughter? Are you playing a funny with me?"

She was so damn cute. I wished I could scoop her up and hug her. But she wasn't ready for that.

"No, I'm not playing a funny with you, silly. Come here and look at my eyes." I motioned for her to come closer. She did and stood a few feet from me. "You may have to get closer to see, but look at the color of my eyes and tell me what you see."

Melody took another timid step closer and stared into my eyes. I swear to God, it freaked me out that her eye color was exactly like mine. The more I studied her face, the more features I found that resembled mine. I couldn't wait for Damion to meet his niece. He was up to his ass in club shit and stressed out. But he promised to make it over here to meet her as soon as he finished up this next run.

"Hey. You look like me," Melody said enthusiastically.

"Nope, you look like me." I smiled back.

As worried as I was when I first met Melody about not feeling an instant connection with her, I was happy I felt one now. It's funny how that worked. How one minute this little girl could be a perfect stranger, and the next I would give my life if that meant she would be happy. Every time a smile hit her face, I swear warmth spread through me reminding me that life was good. Thankfully her smiles were coming more and more.

"Am I allowed to call you daddy?" she blurted out.

"Of course, you are." I had to swallow a few times before I could continue. I'm not gonna lie... I was more than a little choked up. "I would love it if you called me daddy. But only if you want to, okay?"

"I want to."

I looked up and found Ava standing in the

doorway watching us with a huge smile on her face. She was so beautiful.

"Hey, Melly you wanna come upstairs with me and get some jammies on so you can watch a little TV with JJ and your daddy before bed?"

Hearing Ava call me daddy to Melody was a thing of beauty. I knew my woman was happy with the latest progress. Her family was healing.

"Yes. And Logan... I mean, Daddy said I could listen to the bedtime story, too. I have to ask Jakey if it's okay with him." Melody was bouncing up and down.

"Run upstairs, baby, I'll be right behind you."

"Mom... I mean Ava, can you braid my hair pretty again before bed."

Melody slipped all the time calling Ava, 'mommy,' but always corrected herself. Each time Melody did it, Ava winced. I wondered if she didn't want Melody calling her mommy.

"Sure will. I'll braid it while we are watching a show."

"Okay."

Melody ran out of the room, and Ava continued to stare at me from the doorway.

"See, there was nothing to worry about," Ava said.

"What?" I didn't quite understand what she was talking about.

"You and Melody. She just needs some time to

adjust. It will take time, but she will slowly come around."

"How did you know?" I had never told Ava about my doubts or insecurities.

"I know you, Logan Reid. I know you worry about everything. It was written all over your face from the moment you told me about her." She walked further into the room coming to a stop in front of me. "I know you're worried about your relationship with her. I know this because you're a good man and a good dad. Tonight was a huge step. I'm thrilled she is starting to feel more comfortable around us. I thought it would take months before she called you daddy. She is one amazing little girl. I love her dearly."

Goddamn, my woman was perceptive and fucking amazing.

"Does it bother you when she slips and calls you mom?"

"Yes and no. Yes, because it reminds me that Valerie is gone. And my heart breaks all over again. I hate that she is hurting. I hate that I cannot take that for her just like I couldn't take it for JJ. No, because one day I hope that she will come to love me like a mother figure. I could never replace Valerie, but it would be an honor to have her love me enough to want to call me mom. It could take years, and something I would never force. Just because she doesn't call me mom doesn't make me love her any less. But, honestly, I would love to be her mom," Ava admitted.

"You amaze me, Ava. Your kindness and love knows no bounds. I am so fucking lucky to have you."

Before she could protest, I pulled her into me and brushed my lips against hers. What was meant to be a tender kiss to convey how much I loved her quickly turned into something else entirely. The moment I felt her soft tongue lick my bottom lip, my cock twitched, a painful reminder I hadn't had her in days. I deepened the kiss, and she moaned in my mouth. Just as I was considering locking the door and bending her over my desk we were interrupted.

"Jakey!" was yelled from upstairs.

Ava giggled into my mouth, and I could feel her smile against my lips. I didn't see what was funny, my cock didn't either. It throbbed in my jeans, begging for me to ignore the yelling from upstairs.

"Duty calls, handsome." She slid her hand down my chest, down my stomach, and grabbed my cock through my jeans. "We'll take care of this after the kids go down."

I watched my woman strut her fine ass out of my office, forcing myself to stay put and not go after her. Yeah, we'd take care of it tonight, alright.

THE FOG WAS STARTING to roll in as the warm air from the central valley mixed with the cooler air near the ocean. It was a beautiful phenomenon, and fitting for today's mood.

I clocked April and Austin the moment we pulled into the cemetery. She was standing in front of the freshly dug grave in a knee-length black dress that showed off what Ava called her baby bump. Whatever the fuck that was. It looked to me like someone had taken a basketball, cut it in half and placed it over her stomach. She was so slender that her belly was extremely noticeable. And this new bump seemed to pop out overnight.

We left both of the kids with Mac. It took a little convincing for Melody to warm up to him, but JJ saved the day with stories of how great his uncle was, and how he was her uncle now too. I knew all that spoiling Mac did would come in handy one day. Mac showed up with an American Girl doll. This one had red hair, fair skin, and freckles.

Melody was so excited that she ran to her room to get the American Girl doll we had gotten her so the dolls could play dress up together. Score for Mac. Ava walked to him, wrapped her arms around him and thanked him for being such a good uncle. I'd say that was improvement.

Mac was torn about coming to Rick's memorial or

staying behind to watch the kids. I felt like shit having to ask him, but there was no one else. He was the only one we felt comfortable asking. When I conveyed that to him, he said that Rick would understand and he'd pay his respects later.

I hoped after Ava and Mac worked through what was going on between them, Mac could finally put the unwarranted guilt behind him and finally move on. I'd watched my friend fuck mindless twits for the last six years. Falling into whatever warm body he could, to take his mind off of the constant pain. It was time for him to move on.

"It's just gonna be us, right?" Ava asked as I parked the Camaro.

"Yes, April decided she only wanted us here today," I answered.

Ava pulled a small powder blue jewelry box out of her purse and checked her phone again. In the fifteen-minute drive here she must've checked that phone twenty times. Before we left, I found her crying in the bathroom. I thought with today being what it was, it was bringing up bad memories for her. I was a little surprised, but I shouldn't've been, when she told me she was worried about leaving Melody. That she was worried she'd get scared, or upset and she wouldn't be there. After a little reassuring, she dried her eyes and finished getting ready. Only further reminding me how good my life was.

I rounded the hood and opened Ava's door. The moment she was free of the door I grabbed her hand. I needed it. I needed to feel her warmth. She had a way about her that soothed all the jagged edges, made the swift points not so painful.

When we closed in on Austin and April, Ava let go of my hand and wrapped April up in a hug. Both women stood crying. Both sharing something that no woman should have to. Both burying good men way too early. Both men only living half a life. A life that promised them good things. I could only hope that April found it again one day. A man that would be deserving of a good woman. And I could think that standing at Rick's gravesite because I knew that is what he would want for April. He would want her to move on with her life and find happiness.

"I have something for you," Ava said as she wiped her eyes. "Something for you, and something for the baby."

"You didn't..."

"I know I didn't," Ava cut in. "It's just something small."

Ava held out the jewelry box to April. She didn't immediately reach out for it. Instead, she just stared.

No one said a word or rushed her. Austin stood behind her, ever the watchful guard.

When April finally took the box from Ava, her hand fell to her side and she grabbed my hand. April slowly opened the box and when she did, tears streamed down her cheeks when she saw the two pendants Ava had made.

"Thank you," April spoke softly, "I don't know what to say. They are perfect. Now I will always have a part of him."

After Sally had released Rick's body he had been cremated. Ava had two custom pendants made that would each hold some of Rick's ashes.

Ava didn't reply. She couldn't. Her face was buried in my chest, tears soaking through my suit jacket.

Austin stood beside April as the Pastor spoke about Rick. A steely look that was so full of grief he couldn't have masked it if he tried. I had to find a way to get him to open up. He needed some fucking sleep, and to unload. Dustin stood on the other side of me. He had always been more open and forthcoming than Austin. Dustin had unloaded on me. In my garage hitting my heavyweight bag with a bottle of whiskey. He drank and beat the shit outta my bag until he crumpled to the floor knuckles bloody and unleashed his grief.

It guts a man, to watch another man break down in front of him. After witnessing Dustin, I had more respect for him as a brother than I ever had. That took more trust than most are willing to give to a friend. Him allowing me to see him vulnerable, and low. It was a Goddamn honor, is what it was. One I will always be thankful he gave me.

After the Pastor was done speaking, April took the shovel being offered to her and walked towards the fresh pile of dirt. She slowly pulled up a shovel full of the loose soil and stared at the hole. Austin started to walk around the grave to where she was standing but she shook her head. It visibly pained Austin not to go to her side.

"I promise to take care of this life we created. I vow to keep your memory alive, every day for the rest of my life. I pledge that from this day on I will allow a small amount of joy into my life every day, because I know you loved me so much that you would be mad if I gave up. I believe that even in death our love is strong and real and everlasting. I never got to call you my husband. And that is okay, because while I had you, I had the honor of calling you my very best friend. Good-bye, my love." April gently turned the shovel allowing the dirt to spill off and fall into the grave.

She brought her head up and pinned each of us with a stare. "Rick would..." She blew out a breath and tried again. "Rick would be so thankful, and proud of each and every one of you. Each of you have shown me more support than I could've ever hoped for. Dustin, Austin, Reid, the three of you were his best friends. He loved each of you, thought of you all as his brothers. Even though I might be shocked at the kindness and support you all have shown me. I know he is in heaven looking down smiling, in the knowledge that each of you are exactly what he knew you to be, the best men he knew. Men he looked up to, men he aspired to be."

April stopped and pulled three envelopes out of her purse.

"I have an envelope for each of you. I know each of you will open them at different times, maybe not even open them for months. And that's okay. I know what they say. When you are ready, you can read his words to you all. In the meantime, while I can feel Rick's presence around me, I'm going to tell you what they say."

Ava squeezed my hand tight, and I wondered if April had shared the contents of the letters.

"When we found out I was pregnant, Rick being Rick went into over-protective hyperdrive. Sorry babe, but you did." April laughed and looked up towards the clouds. We all chuckled along with her. That sounded like Rick. "So anyway. He had to update his will of course, set up a college fund, research all sorts of stuff on drinking water and lead paint. I won't bore you with all the details. But one other thing he did was sit down and write each of you a letter. In the letter, he has requested each of you to be the baby's Godfather. He has a reason for wanting each of you to stand up for his child. Those reasons are yours alone and you will find them in the letter. Now I tried to dissuade him, with three over-protective hyper-vigilant badasses as Godfathers, I feared if this baby is a girl she will not only never get a prom date, but never get a first kiss."

"Goddamn right she won't," I chuckled.

"Not a boy good enough for her," Dustin added.

I waited for Austin to weigh in, but it never came. He was stone-faced.

"So, it would be an honor if all three of you would stand up for this baby and help me teach it all the things he or she will need to know about life. If you could all help me teach this baby about Rick and who he was and what he stood for, I would be grateful. I'm going to need it. And Ava, I was hoping that you would be the baby's Godmother. You, friend, are a force of hope and love and embody everything a mother should be."

Ava tried to answer through her tears, her head nodding. "There would be no greater honor than being the baby's Godmother."

"Great. Now that all of that is settled and out of the way. I'll give you all whatever time you would like with Rick before we head off to Red's to toast one hell of a guy."

I was in shock. Total and utter shock of April. I don't know where she found the strength to get through all of what she just said. But, she impressed the hell outta me. Damn but Rick was a lucky man to have had her standing beside him. I understood now, when he told me he was stronger with her by his side, that she made him a better person. At the time I thought he was blowing smoke up my ass and was turning soft. Now... now, I got it. All of it. Even if I didn't have that same great love with Ava now. Seeing April up there pushing through her sadness, I would've understood. She was remarkable.

April handed us our letters, and each of us said good-bye to our friend, our brother. And we did go to Red's and celebrate one hella good man.

By the time we left the bar, Ava was on pins and needles to get home. She wanted to see the kids. But there was something different about her. I couldn't put my finger on it, but it was like a fire had been lit in her belly. Her eyes were bright, her smiles came quick, and she somehow looked lighter. Like a cloud had been lifted.

Whatever it was, it was pure beauty. And mine. All mine.

I was one lucky bastard.

38

──────

FULL CIRCLE

Ava

Today was the day.

It was the one day of the year that I hated. I dreaded it with every cell in my body. Only today, when I woke up wrapped up in Reid's shield, I didn't hate it quite as bad. Sure, today still hurt. Sure, today held sadness and the memory of loss. But today, on this anniversary of Jacob's murder, the day also held hope.

Hope for the future.

Today was the day I was going to make things right. I was finally strong enough to do what I should have done a long time ago.

I knew that Reid was worried about me. I had been secretive and needed to pull into my head to work out the rest of my feelings. When he asked what he needed to do to help me, I didn't shut him out, I gave him honesty. I just needed his quiet strength and his promise he wouldn't give up on us. That was all I needed to pull through today.

Today was a new beginning.

"Jake. Melody. Do you want to come down here and put the frosting on the cake?" I yelled up the stairs.

Two resounding yeses came floating down. Two sets of feet ran to the top of the stairs.

"Whoa, slow down there, speed demons. A trip to the ER is not on today's agenda." That sounded hauntingly familiar.

Melody and Jake made their way into the kitchen. The cake had cooled and was ready for frosting. We only had about fifteen minutes until Reid and Mac got back. If I wanted this cake frosted before we left, we had to hurry.

"Alright we don't have much time," I said to the kids.

"Can I help? I've never put frosting on," Melody asked.

I glanced at JJ waiting for him to answer. This was a special tradition for him. I had baked cupcakes for Melody to frost in the off-chance JJ didn't want to share.

"Of course, you can. You frost that side, and I'll frost this one." JJ pointed to the cake.

I watched as the kids each frosted their side and

smiled when Melody tried to get her side to look as perfect as her brother's. I listened as they prattled on about licking the leftover chocolate frosting off the spatulas. Their sweet voices filled my heart.

Today was a good day.

Melody was resilient and making huge improvements every day. She had stopped asking JJ to sleep on her bedroom floor now that she had a bed full of stuffed animals to sleep with her. Her hugs and kisses came fast and frequent now. She was healing. And it was beautiful.

By the time the kids were done licking the bowl and spatulas clean, they had chocolate all over their faces and hands.

"Go wash your faces. We're gonna leave in a minute."

"Okay," Melody said and jumped off her stool running towards the stairs.

JJ hung back a minute, a worried look on his face.

"What's going on, little man? You alright? I know today is tough," I asked.

"I was just going to ask you the same thing. Are you okay, Mama?"

"Yes. My sweet boy. I am okay. Today will always be a sad day for us. But today, we are going to do things a little different."

"I'm okay too. I'm happy. Well, I mean, I'm sad

today is the anniversary of when Dad died. But I am happy, too. Is that okay? Would Dad be mad at me?"

"My beautiful, thoughtful son, your dad would never want you to be sad. Not one single minute. He would want you smiling and happy. Today we are not going to be sad. We've had five years of sad. Today, we celebrate your dad. No tears. No pain. Only joy and happiness. Today, we remember a good man, a good husband, and good father..." I looked up to see Mac and Reid in the doorway to the kitchen. "... and a good friend."

JJ looked over his shoulder at Mac and Reid "Hey Uncle Mac, hi Dad. I have to go wash my face."

Without waiting for them to reply, he was out of the kitchen heading for the stairs.

"I see the kids decorated the cake," Reid commented on the mounds of chocolate frosting.

Mac chuckled sticking his finger in the leftover bowl of frosting, coming up with a huge glob. After he licked his finger clean he threw a wink my way as he exited the kitchen. "Damn that's good woman. You almost ready?" he asked.

"I am," I replied.

"Yeah, you finally are."

THIS TIME, when we pulled up to the cemetery, there were no blue and red flashing lights. There were no first responders lining the street. When we piled out of the car, this time there were no bagpipes to greet us. I was not in some dowdy black dress fit for a grieving widow.

Today was about celebration.

This time, I arrived at the cemetery with hope in my heart. I had finally found peace. We walked to Jacob's final resting place and came to a stop. JJ was holding a dozen white lilies. Every year on our wedding anniversary Jacob would bring me white lilies. Now, we brought them to him every year. JJ knelt down and placed the flowers in front of Jacob's marker.

"Hi Dad," he whispered.

Mac, Reid, and Melody were all standing a few feet behind us. Mac was standing in the same place he stood each time we came. Ever faithful in his duties to watch over JJ and I.

"Hi, Jacob." I sucked in a breath and prepared for what I had to say. I had practiced it in my mind a thousand times. "I owe you an apology." I looked over at JJ. He was so handsome, and so brave. God, I loved that boy so much. "I know that I have disappointed you, I have disappointed myself. I have been so lost in my head, lost in my grief, lost in my anger, and most of all my guilt that I have shut everyone out except JJ. I even pushed Mac away. But, of course, you know that. I did this all wrong. He promised you he would watch over us and I made him break that promise. I didn't let him fulfill the vow he made to you. Well, not to the fullest extent I know he wanted to. And for that, I am truly sorry. I also pushed away our child, the one I lost. I refused to acknowledge that loss. We created that child out of love. I realized that by doing what I was doing, I was denying that the baby ever existed. I am sorry for that too."

I turned to look at Mac. "I am so sorry, Mac. I know I don't deserve it but I hope you can forgive me. I want you to know, that even as I was pushing you away, I knew that you wouldn't let me. I knew that you would always be there to care for us. I know that makes what I did even more wrong. But that is the truth. Thank you, Mac, for everything."

"Nothing to apologize for, Ava. I'm just pleased as fu... just pleased that you and JJ are happy again. That is all I ever wanted for the both of you." Mac's voice was full of emotion.

"I need to thank you, Jacob. I know that when Carl took me, you kept our son safe. I know you spoke to him the same way you spoke to me. Hearing your voice again was a Godsend. I miss your voice. I miss your laughter. I just miss you. I also want to thank you for Melody. For bringing her to us. For sitting with her and singing to her. For giving her strength when she needed it. I want you to know that not a day goes by we don't think about you. Thank you for bringing us Reid. I know that was you, too. I know you are watching out for us. He loves us, the same way you loved us. We love him too. He protects us and watches out for us. He is helping those seeds you planted grow. Him and Mac both. He's a good dad. I love you, Jacob, always."

I stepped back and found myself in Reid's strong arms. Careful not to crush the bouquet of wildflowers I was holding, he hugged me. "I love you, Ava," he whispered.

JJ was smiling looking at his dad's marker. I looked at the marker next to his that was covered with a black cloth and prayed I had done the right thing. The plot next to Jacob used to be mine. We had bought two burial plots together.

I pulled out of Reid's arms and looked at Mac. He nodded his head, encouraging me to continue.

"Melly, baby, can you come sit over here with me?" I asked.

She let go of her dad's hand and sat where I was pointing. JJ had come over and sat next to me too.

"Do you understand what this place is?" I asked.

"Yes, it is where dead people are buried," she answered.

"You're right. And you see that stone there," I

pointed to Jacob's marker. She nodded her head and I continued. "That has Jake's dad's name on it. It marks where he is buried so we can visit him." I pulled the black cloth of the stone marker. "Do you know what this says?"

Melody leaned over and studied the freshly cut stone. "Valerie Fairman. That's mommy's name."

"Yes. That's your mommy's name. This is where your mommy is buried. Right next to Jake's dad. Now, anytime you want, we can come and you can sit and talk with mommy, and we can bring her flowers. For today, I brought these for you to give to your mommy." I handed Melody the flowers. "Next time we come you can pick out your mommy's favorite flower."

"What do I do?" she asked.

I stood up and left Jake and Melody sitting next to Jacob and Valerie.

"Anything you want, Melly. Just set the flowers down. You can talk out loud or in your head. Whatever you want. Sometimes, I talk out loud. But today, when I talked to my dad, I wanted to tell him a secret, so I just thought it in my head."

"What was your secret?" she asked.

"It won't be a secret if I tell you."

"Please. Pretty please. You're my brother, you have to tell."

Oh boy, that girl was good. Almost as good as JJ

when he wanted something. I see bad things in our future with these two swindlers.

"I told my dad, that I was happy that Mama had Reid. That she wasn't sad any more. And I told him that Reid tells me cool stories about him. Ummm, oh and I thanked him for bringing my sister home and for protecting you until dad could."

Wow.

"Hi, mommy. I miss you." Melody started to cry. "Sometimes I am still scared, but my big brother sneaks in my room and sleeps on the floor. Daddy is nice, and he tells me every night when he reads us our bedtime story that he loves me. Like that? Am I doing it right?" she asked JJ.

"Yep." He smiled, obviously thrilled that Melody was telling Valerie about him.

"Okay, good. I'm back Mommy, Ava lets me help her cook and she brushes my hair pretty. Wait, Ava is JJ's mommy. When I asked JJ if Ava was my new mommy he said that it was up to me. I'm not sure yet. Is that okay with you? Oh and, Uncle Mac is super cool. Jakey was right. He tells us funny stories. And there is a swear jar just for him, because he says those naughty words. JJ says he is gonna buy a car from the F-bombs. That's cool, right? Maybe Uncle Mac will give me F-bombs, too."

I felt Reid shaking beside me, trying not to out and

out laugh. His lips at my ear again before he spoke softly, "There are no words for this. What you've done today. What you just gave Melody. I don't know how you pulled this off but thank you."

"Mac helped. And there are no thanks necessary. I love you, and I love her. She needed a place to visit her mom."

"... that's all for now. But Ava said she'll bring me back here, and I can tell you more. I love you, Mommy. I wish I could see you." Melody whispered the last part.

Both kids walked over to us, and I suggested we walk to the nearby fountain to give the guys a minute.

The kids talked and I allowed my thoughts to wander. I saw Mac bend down and touch Jacob's head headstone and walk back toward the car. Reid took longer, first in front of Jacob, then in front of Valerie. He looked in our direction and his smile was so big and wide it took my breath away. I didn't need to see them to know his dimples were out, and the smile lines were around his eyes.

When we got back to the Rover the kids piled in and I called over to Mac before he could get in his car.

"Hey Mac? You got a few more minutes?"

He didn't reply. He just shut his car door and made his way over to me.

"You got this, sweetheart. I'll wait with the kids."

Reid kissed my forehead and I grabbed the sunflowers out of the back of the truck.

"I'm sorry." I didn't know how to start this conversation. "I think I've blamed you all these years. I don't know. Maybe because it was you that told me, that I illogically blamed you for telling me. Like, if you had never told me, then it wouldn't be real. I don't know, I was all kinds of screwed up."

"I know you did."

"You knew?"

"Of course, I did. And, honestly, I knew you needed someone to blame. And I was okay being that person for you. If it made it just a little easier for you to be mad at me, I was willing to take it. But, I was on the verge of helping you pull your head outta your ass when Reid finally got his outta his ass and decided to claim you. I figured Reid could sort you out."

"Do you really think that Jacob would be happy that I have moved on?"

"Yes."

"Just yes, huh?" I laughed.

"What do you want me to say? Jacob loved you so much. He would never want you and JJ to be sad for the rest of your lives. And before you ask, yes, he'd be pleased it was Reid. They didn't know each other well. But, Jacob respected him, and thought he was solid. More than that, I know that Jacob trusted Reid."

We came to a stop in front of a place I hated to go. Every year I fought with Mac about coming here. Yet, this year he walked straight to his car after we visited Jacob.

"Why didn't you suggest that we come here?" I asked.

"Because, you didn't need me to."

"What if I decided not to come? What would you have done?"

"Nothing. Me bringing you here wasn't about you coming here to stare at a piece of stone. It was about forcing you to acknowledge that you losing the baby wasn't your fault."

"I know that I couldn't control the ectopic pregnancy. And I know I didn't do anything wrong. Thank you. Thank you for not giving up on me. I was a bitch; you didn't deserve what I gave you."

"It's all good."

I leaned down and placed the sunflowers on the marker. I placed my fingers over my lips kissing them before placing them on the marker that Mac had made.

It simply read, *Kelley*.

WE WALKED BACK into the house and I looked around.

Today was a good day.

I looked at our comfy chocolate brown overstuffed couches that my family sat on nightly to watch TV together. My eyes scanned the living room where my family laughed enjoying each other's company. I noticed Melody's crayons and coloring books on the coffee table and JJ's tablet next to them. There were little girl shoes mixed with not so little boy shoes thrown near the shoe basket never having actually made it in. Reid's boots sat next to them neatly lined up.

My eyes hit the shelves and I looked at the framed pictures. Jacob and JJ together. Valerie and Melody at her last birthday. Pictures of Mac and Reid, Jacob, me and Mac. Me with JJ. Even one of Damion and Reid when they were teenagers. All that was missing was a family picture of all of us.

One day that would be added to the shelf as well. We would have a lifetime to fill the walls with pictures and fill the house with memories.

"Who's ready for cake?" I called out.

Four 'mes' called back and we all went into the kitchen. I handed JJ the candles and he added the thirty-eight candles.

He still had one candle in his hand. "Here, Melly, you can add the luck."

JJ handed her the candle. "Where should I put it?" she asked.

"Wherever you want," JJ told her.

Melody took a moment and studied the cake. "Here," she said and pushed the candle in.

"It looks perfect. You all ready?" I asked as I lit the candles.

I felt Reid's arm go around my middle pulling me into him, his lips pressed against the top of my head.

"I love you," he said into my hair.

"I love you back."

When the first line of 'happy birthday' hit my ears, warmth hit my belly and left a trail of happiness as it filled my heart. JJ was belting out the song loudly, Melody trying to keep up. Mac was staring at the cake with a broad smile, lighting up his whole face. Reid? Well, Reid was holding me tightly wrapping that shield around me. Only now I didn't need that shield. I was free of guilt and at peace.

Unbroken.

The song came to an end, and JJ prepared to blow the candles out just like he had done for his father every year in his absence. Only this year, JJ didn't have a chance to blow out the candles. A soft gust of wind floated through the room, and all thirty-nine candles danced in the breeze before they extinguished. *Jacob.*

Of course, the window was cracked open, and it

was a windy day. But, I choose to believe that Jacob was in the kitchen with us that day. That he was celebrating his birthday with us. That he was finally at peace with the knowledge his family was finally happy.

We sat and ate Jacob's birthday cake, laughing at Mac as he told the most outrageous stories about the shenanigans he and Jacob got into while they were still beat cops.

Today was a good day.

The best day.

My home was full of laughter, love, and more joy than one person could handle.

Yeah, we were gonna have a great life.

Thank you for purchasing Unbroken. I hope you enjoyed Ava and Reid's story.

I have written a bonus scene from Mac's point of view. You can download the content directly from my website for free. (No sign up required) The scene takes place during Chapter Twelve and what happens when Reid leaves Mac alone to deal with Jimmy Kelley.

www.rileyedwardsromance.com/unbroken-bonus

Mac and Laura's story is now available, grab your copy of TRUST now.

ALSO BY RILEY EDWARDS

Riley Edwards

www.RileyEdwardsRomance.com

Romantic Suspense

Red Team

Nightstalker

Protecting Olivia - Susan Stoker Universe

Redeeming Violet - Susan Stoker Universe

Recovering Ivy - Susan Stoker Universe

Rescuing Erin - Susan Stoker Universe

Romancing Rayne - Susan Stoker Universe

The Gold Team

Brooks - Susan Stoker Universe

The 707 Freedom Series

Free

Freeing Jasper

Finally Free

Freedom

The Next Generation (707 spinoff)

Saving Meadow

Chasing Honor

Finding Mercy

Claiming Tuesday

The Collective

Unbroken 1 & 2 – Season One

Trust – Season Two

Romantic Suspense

Red Team

Nightstalker

Protecting Olivia - Susan Stoker Universe

Redeeming Violet - Susan Stoker Universe

Recovering Ivy - Susan Stoker Universe

Rescuing Erin - Susan Stoker Universe

Romancing Rayne - Susan Stoker FanFic

The Gold Team

Brooks - Susan Stoker Universe

The 707 Freedom Series

Free

Freeing Jasper

Finally Free

Freedom

The Next Generation (707 spinoff)

Saving Meadow

Chasing Honor

Finding Mercy

Claiming Tuesday

The Collective

Unbroken

Trust

ACKNOWLEDGMENTS

First and foremost, I need to thank my fellow Collective authors—Chris Genovese, Ellie Masters, Erin Trejo, Elias Raven, and Carver Pike. I cannot begin to express how honored I am to collaborate with such a great group of authors. I've had so much fun plotting and planning this series with them. They all have taught me so much, and I could not be more grateful.

Chris Genovese, my brother, thank you for always being my sounding board. You are by and far the most creative person I know. Your imagination knows no bounds. It is a beautiful thing to watch your brain work.

Ellie Masters, as always, you pushed me to finish this book. Our word sprints and you reveling when you beat me always pushed me to do better. You have been instrumental in my progression as a writer. Knowing that you will be reading my words and critiquing them is both terrifying and yet comforting. You make me a better writer. Thank you for everything.

Erin Trejo, I was a huge fan of your work long before I ever wrote a single word on a page. You are a mentor, a great friend, and a talented author. It has been so much fun working with you.

Elias Raven, you friend, are a force of nature. You are the tornado that blows through, and all you can do is pray your grip is strong enough to hold on. I have said it a thousand times before, but it bears repeating, you are an outstanding writer. You cross genres, eras, and writing styles with ease. I am so thankful to have had a chance to work with you.

Carver Pike, I can only thank you for the many sleepless nights. 'Who knew scary could be so sexy?'

The Collective is so blessed to have a huge support team behind us! Thank you to all the BETA readers and reviewers that gave us feedback. It undoubtedly made this series better. We cannot thank you enough for your time, hard work, and dedication to this project.

The Collective PA and Overlord Michelle Thomas, thank you doesn't begin to cover what we all owe you. You have five authors to keep straight, five authors to wrangle, five authors to promote. It is a wonder how you pull it all off. Thank you.

Thank you to all of my readers! You are, as always,

the reason I do this. The reason I stay up until the wee hours of the morning. The reason I agonize over each and every word I type. The reason I pull my hair out during editing. The reason I love what I do. The reason I get to be who I've always wanted to be. XOXO—Riley

ABOUT THE AUTHOR

Riley Edwards is a bestselling multi-genre author, wife, and military mom. Riley was born and raised in Los Angeles but now resides on the east coast with her fantastic husband and children.

Riley writes heart-stopping romance with sexy alpha heroes and even stronger heroines. Riley's favorite genres to write are romantic suspense and military romance.

Don't forget to sign up for Riley's newsletter and never miss another release, sale, or exclusive bonus material. https://www.subscribepage.com/RRsignup

Facebook Fan Group

www.rileyedwardsromance.com

facebook.com/Novelist.Riley.Edwards

twitter.com/rileyedwardsrom

instagram.com/rileyedwardsromance

bookbub.com/authors/riley-edwards

amazon.com/author/rileyedwards

Made in the USA
Columbia, SC
03 January 2024

29837469R00274